# The Velvet Rose

# The Velvet Rose

## SUSAN HOLMES McKAGAN

A RARE BIRD BOOK | RARE BIRD BOOKS
LOS ANGELES, CALIF.

This is a Genuine Rare Bird Book

A Rare Bird Book | Rare Bird Books
453 South Spring Street, Suite 302
Los Angeles, CA 90013
rarebirdbooks.com

FIRST HARDCOVER EDITION

For more information, address:
A Rare Bird Book | Rare Bird Books Subsidiary Rights Department
453 South Spring Street, Suite 302
Los Angeles, CA 90013

Set in Minion

Printed in the United States

10 9 8 7 6 5 4 3 2 1

Publisher's Cataloging-in-Publication Data
Names: McKagan, Susan Holmes, author.
Title: The Velvet Rose / Susan Holmes McKagan.
Description: First Hardcover Edition | A Genuine Rare Bird Book |
New York, NY; Los Angeles, CA: 2019.
Identifiers: ISBN 9781947856240
Subjects: LCSH Fashion models—Fiction. | Rock musicians—Fiction. |
Men-women relationships—Fiction. BISAC FICTION / General.
Classification: LCC PS3613.C5432 V4 2019 | DDC 813.6—dc23

*For Duff and our children, Grace and Mae,*
*words cannot express my thankfulness for your love,*
*light, and blessings every single day.*

# *ROSEBUD*

## 1991

I WORKED IT OUT slowly, as if trying to understand another language. Everything fell away, as if the world had been severed beneath me, and the gaping absence would swallow me whole. My body was thrown sideways and wrenched hard by the seat belt around my waist. Gurgles and crackling noises seemed to emanate from my blood, bones, and fillings. My body tossed and thrashed around the inside of my car. In slow motion, I surfed a wave of broken glass.

I was somehow sprawled into the passenger bucket seat, my body twisted. The hush that had descended was as loud as the crash had been, as if everything outside my vehicle had crumbled into dust and I was supremely alone. The smell of burnt rubber and smoke turned the luminous evening violet and dark. Heart beating out of my chest, I thrummed with adrenaline. Glittery shards shimmered in the fading sunshine like sequins. I was afraid. Afraid to move, afraid to sit up, afraid to discern exactly how bad the damage was—to Goldie, and to me. The driver side tilted disastrously at a shocking slant on the sidewalk. My day had been redone as a work of abstract expressionism, all sharp edges and harsh lines.

"Scarlett! Scarlett," Imani screamed, her face rushing into focus through my window. Finally, something familiar had cut through my day's odd, nearly deadly detour. Thank God it was my best friend—with her unmistakable, intense dark eyes, and makeup-free, cocoa-colored face beneath her shaggy black hair with its somewhat grown-in shaved sides—and she was attempting to help me.

She yanked at the driver's door, but it wouldn't budge. The whole side of the car had been crumpled beyond function. Her movements increasingly frantic, she ran to the other side. Ripping open the passenger door, she reached for my hand.

Gentle as a mother, she wrangled loose my seatbelt, and ever so slowly, seemed to aid me in sitting up. The pain was everywhere—in my neck and shoulders, even in my skin. The shock receded as reality sunk in, and I started to cry.

"Are you hurt?" she asked in her familiar and most-comforting, laid-back Southern California tone.

"I…I've been better," I managed to get out, brushing splinters of glass from my lap.

"Please don't joke," she said. "I was terrified. I honestly thought you were killed. A huge Dodge pickup truck came out of nowhere and pummeled your car."

"Did you see the accident?" I asked. "Was I the only one hit?"

"Yes, luckily no one was behind you. It could have been an awful pile up."

"Goldie," I said through tears. "Please don't let anything happen to Goldie."

"I just want to make sure you're all right," Imani said. "As for the car, I'm afraid the worst has already happened."

Sirens blared in the distance, swelling in volume as they drew nearer.

I leaned on Imani as she helped me onto the street, but my legs were feathers beneath me. I couldn't feel them until my knees dropped to the sidewalk.

What followed was a dreamy blur as the paramedics rushed in, shined a light into my eyes to check for concussion while a cop directed traffic around the accident scene that obstructed one lane, and tow trucks growled up and carted off the rest of the wreckage. Grimacing, I watched as they took Goldie from me. My grandma had loved that car. I had loved my Gran. Now my only remaining connection to her was gone. That loss hurt more than the crash itself.

As dire as the accident had been, the other driver and I had both been fortunate enough to live. And now it was all over. I had waved my right to go to the hospital. It would have only made my mom worry, and we couldn't afford any more bills. Shaky and confused, I sat on the sidewalk, surveying the bleak reality of my future. My life had been hard half an hour ago. Now I couldn't think about it. Perhaps a cup of hot, black coffee among friends would provide an antidote.

The sympathetic crowd parted when I floundered my way into the coffee shop, subtly making way for me to sit down in an empty chair. Imani went to the counter to order my coffee for me, knowing exactly how I preferred it. As the triumphant opening of Faith No More's "Epic" reverberated from the speakers overhead, everyone seemed to jump back into their own reality. The song had been on heavy rotation for months, and it ran through their veins by now. I inhaled the scent of fresh brewed coffee, hugging myself to keep it together, and tried to ease back into this normal Friday in May.

The beguiling barista, Ed, adorned with a nose ring and a wave of dyed blue-black hair falling across his eyes, approached me with the two coffees with cream Imani had ordered.

"I literally just heard the crash you were in outside," he said, with a considerate smile. "You all right?"

"Sure, nothing like a major accident to get the blood pumping," I joked, aiming for lightness even through the sharp pangs of sadness. *I can't afford a new car. I can't afford an old car. I can't afford anything, really. What if I not only have to skip the move to Paris, but college altogether?*

With a flourish, he placed a sloshing cup of joe on the table in front of me, ducking his head, so his hair further eclipsed his face.

I peeked into my wallet and found a single twenty that had to last me until payday, *next* Friday. Coffee was suddenly an extravagance. I forced a weak smile, barely looking up from my wallet.

"This one's on me." He winked sheepishly, indicating the clay pannikin mug he'd presented. "We're hiring, by the way, and if you work here, you can drink all the free coffee you want, so that might help."

"Thank you so much," I said. "Too bad I already have a job."

"Oh right, you work over at the blah."

"I do, but on further reflection…do you have an application?" I said, a plan forming. "I'm F-O-R-E-V-E-R saving to do a semester abroad—or if nothing else, for a semester at USD. And, well, apparently, to buy a new used ride. So, you know, it's become abundantly clear that two jobs would pretty much be better than one."

"Yeah, grab an app before you leave," he said. "I'll put in a good word for you."

I raised my cup to him in an appreciative toast, and then sipped gratefully as he returned to his barista duties.

Still shaky and sore but cheered by this small kindness in an otherwise rotten day, I took my beverage outside to the front porch. There were perks to being a regular here. And it wasn't just about the complimentary coffee, either. I felt connected, knowing everyone was just like me, into good music, great banter, and the classics. We shared a deep and abiding connection, and working here wouldn't really be work at all. Plus, I was in dire straits. Hmm…maybe I'd get some sort of an insurance settlement, but not for ages. I'd never be able to replace Goldie.

Encircling my shoulders with one arm, Imani fished into her army surplus backpack for a clove cigarette and held it out to me. "You deserve a pick-me-up," she said.

We settled into our usual spots at the high counter along the railing. I leaned forward to get a light from Imani. My neck twinged, and I winced. The speaker trumpeted the triumphant sounds of "We Are the Champions" in homage to Freddie Mercury.

"Are you sure you don't want to go home?" she asked.

I shook my head, fighting back another onslaught of tears. The enormity of what had just happened was beginning to sink in. "It seems, no matter how hard I work, I never get ahead," I said, pausing to take a drag. "Hell—or even catch up."

"I can absolutely relate," Imani said. "I have a couple hundred bucks in savings you can have."

"Thanks, but you're supposed to use that money to buy your books for next semester. Did you look at my notes on your essay?"

"Yes, professor," Imani teased, playing with her coffee stirrer.

"This is serious." I took the stirrer from her. "College is kind of, sadly, our only way out."

"That's easy for you to say," Imani complained. "You earned all those summer school credits, and now you're a nineteen-year-old college junior. You're practically done with school. Plus, you get to jet off to Paris."

"If I can save enough. And, besides," I said defensively, "I want to visit Europe to study design, not just for the croissants."

"Okay, okay," Imani said. "You don't have to sell me. Just your mom. But by that logic, don't you think I could learn more by moving to LA and joining a band?"

I sighed. "Probably." The truth was I didn't know why I was fighting so hard to finish college. It wasn't exactly a requirement for what I wanted to do, which was more along the lines of the art world—being creative and doing the things I loved: painting, writing, or maybe even designing. But taking a big risk and starting out on my own with zero safety net wasn't exactly in my comfort zone.

"I'll be lucky to finish my freshman year of college," Imani mumbled.

"Which is why I'm helping you with your essay." I shook my thoughts away. The reality was there only seemed to be one way out of Southern California, and this was it. "We're a team. If we don't create a strategy, we'll be earning minimum wage for eternity. That's terrifying. I mean, I haven't drawn, painted, or sketched in weeks. When I get home from a double-shift, I'm asleep, literally, with my Doc Martens on."

"I hear you. I'm the one trying to sleep on the couch in your room while you snore," Imani said. "But I got what you were saying about my essay. Be more *me*."

"Exactly. The whole point is they want to hear who you are."

"Can't you just write it for me?"

"Um…now that's pushing it too far…" I said, then seeing the look of worry on my best friend's face, I changed course. "But we'll make sure it's perfect."

"Thanks, Scarlett," Imani said. "All right, now I've gotta get to work."

I looked down at my watch, a bolt of pain shooting through my neck as I moved. I wished I could hide out from reality all day at the ol' Pannikin Coffee & Tea, a place that seemed to draw the patronage of every twenty-something within driving (or walking) distance. Inclusivity was key here: people showed up to organize marches against the Gulf War or made plans to figure out how to secure tix to Lollapalooza or sometimes just to flirt with the nerdy, Brit rocker boys or Bohemian babes who were always hanging around. I could try sweet-talking the day manager into hiring me and letting me start work immediately. But I was already buzzing on coffee, and I really couldn't afford a refill, just to hang out a little longer. On top of everything else, I'd have to bus it home eventually and tell my hard-working mom about the crash.

A loud hissing sound jolted me with the realization that the bus barreling down the street was drawing near. I stood as hurriedly as I could on my unsteady legs, still too banged up to run, and I winced with every step down to the bus stop, making it just in time. Normally, I would have heard a mouthful from my mom about being late, but I knew she'd just be glad I hadn't been seriously hurt in the crash.

*** 

I PAUSED AT THE front path to my house and looked longingly at the dwelling next door, a 1920s Spanish cottage with fragrant fuchsia and crimson buds gracing a trellis on the front exterior. Our neighbor, Aurora, was a onetime scream queen who'd starred in all sorts of B movies and then moved to San Diego with her realtor husband (her fourth—husband, not realtor) once she grew too old to land parts. And she was my sweet pal (and tightest friend after Imani). I was in the habit of checking in on her, and because her eyesight was poor, even reading to her sometimes.

I rang the bell and waited the long moments I knew it would take for her to creak her way to the front entrance and welcome me into her home.

Aurora swung her door open, paused for a moment, then held her hands out to me.

"Hello, darling Scarlett."

"How'd you know it was me?" I asked, beaming a shy happy smile at being instantly recognized by one of my all-time favorite people.

"I can tell by your perfume. Anais Anais is a classic. Most young women wear those trashy drugstore scents, but you have the discernment, my beautiful flower, to care about quality. Maybe that's why you seem like such an old soul in comparison to others your age."

"It cost me practically a whole month's wages to buy it," I said, beaming. "Even though no one notices but you. How do you feel today?"

"I feel old. But it's better than the alternative," Aurora said.

"You don't look old," I said through my laughter. "You look beautiful."

Everything in Aurora's immediate orbit had to be one of her favorite colors—pink, hot pink, and red. She wore a blush pink silk nightgown adorned with leopard-print trim at the neckline, looking as if she were hosting a lover, rather than recuperating. Her lips and nails were decked out with perfect ruby red, which I had seen her apply with ease on past visits, even though she couldn't see well enough to truly assess her appearance in a mirror.

"I was supposed to be home hours ago, but I had the worst day," I said.

"Come in, child," she said. "I'm sure your mother will forgive you—I'll tell her that I shanghaied you for a rendezvous and to help me for awhile."

The day's horror melted away as I stepped into her living room. The glamour shots of Aurora in mirrored silver and gold frames; beautiful, handmade velvet floor pillows; and vases of sweetheart roses everywhere gave the place the feel of a stage actress's dressing room. As I recounted the accident to Aurora, she listened with rapt attention.

"It's as if your Gran was up there, protecting you," she said. "If you'd been in one of those tin cans they pass off as an automobile these days, you'd be singing with the angels right now. I know it's sad. But you must be grateful."

"You always know just what to say," I said. "I'll stay a few minutes longer before my mom figures out I'm here. What are we reading today?"

"*The Day of the Locust* by Nathaniel West," she said. "You're a gem."

"Never heard of it," I admitted, knowing better than to try to fool Aurora.

"They ought to teach it in school," Aurora said, reaching for a book on her side table. "It's about the ins and outs of Hollywood, which means, *really*, it's about life. I had a small part in the film adaptation. I even stole a kiss from my costar, Donald Sutherland."

"You stole a kiss from everyone."

"Not true. Some stole kisses from me. Soon, you'll know the difference. What do you think your Prince Charming will look like?" I'd gotten used to questions like this from Aurora. It was nice to sit in a stylish, cozy—albeit vermillion—room and let my inner dreamer out for a gambol.

"Once I make it as an artist, I want to share my life with someone of equal stature, someone who's on the same wavelength, I mean," I said, picking at my fingernail polish as I considered her question. "I think I'll marry…a brilliant artiste. Or a rock 'n' roller, and he'll write songs around the house, sometimes even just for me, and play them on his beautiful, black, seventies Stratocaster guitar. While I admire him from our hippy chic love nest's living room, in my bare feet, watching old movies and eating popcorn." I felt my cheeks growing a little hot, describing such a crazy, specific fantasy.

"Popcorn," Aurora said, nodding. "So shall it be."

If only it were as easy as Aurora made it sound. Deep down, I feared I had at least a million steps between now and the shiny future Aurora saw for me. But I wanted to believe she was right, so I hoped she was in possession of a crystal ball she'd yet to reveal to me.

***

MEANWHILE, ACROSS THE COUNTRY, Johnny, singer of The Westies, was "backstage" in the tent that doubled as a green room, touching up his black eyeliner (it was the nineties after all, the decade of guyliner, before that term was even coined). He was primping in advance of his band's performance at Rentiesville, Oklahoma's *Dusk Til Dawn Blues Festival*, the biggest gig he could have landed near his hometown of Tulsa.

Slinking onto the stage, owning the crowd's attention from the first moment they laid eyes on him, Johnny was a sexy incarnation of the blues, dressed all in black, accented with his scuffed Addison motorcycle boots, a bandana worn round his neck, and snaking coils of vintage silver chains. He was fighting to prove to his Pentecostal working class folks that his rock 'n' roll aspirations did matter, and that his songs would be blaring from every car radio someday soon. As the sun set behind the stage, and the lemony-sweet smell of magnolia kissed the sultry air, the stars shone like diamonds in the midnight blue, velvet sky. Johnny's ever-enthralling spirit and soulful vocals turned this grim life and its poverty and strife into inspiring, lyrical poetry.

The crowd swelled, drawn by the music and Johnny's powerful charisma. He didn't just belt out the blues, he embodied them. Raised on the legendary gospel and country artists, he created a sound that was both of the heartland and full of a new, progressive energy that had never been heard before. His piercing blue eyes connected with everyone in the audience as he cradled his mic stand, leaning over the crowd, delivering the music down to them. He hadn't seen a razor in three days, but who cared with a jaw that defined, and a bod as naturally toned and tight as a marble statue of a Greek god?

Their set building momentum, the band kicked it into high gear. Johnny was joined at the center of the stage by his rhythm guitarist/ stepbrother, Devon, whom he'd known since the cradle, and his bassist/best friend, Jet, the band's ripped, athletic member, who could drink him under the table while somehow still being the group's Zen center. Drunk Devon thankfully sagged away from the mic, his sloppy, off-key backing vocals carried away by the night air. Johnny and Jet harmonized, working the audience's ardor into a frenzy, their spirits lifted by the palpable excitement of the moment and the stadium-sized success they felt poised to make their own. It was all happening for them. Johnny rocked back on his heels as he wailed, singing it all out as only he could.

Devon, so buoyed by bourbon that his band mates had already turned off his amp, was, as usual, carried away by the audience's pulsing energy, like catching the Holy Spirit. He pulled himself onto the scaffolding crowning the stage.

And he climbed.

And he climbed.

And he climbed.

The audience cheered, inflaming his fearlessness, until he reached such a great height that to lose his grip would have been fatal. A few of the more faint-hearted members of the crowd had to look away, which only encouraged his inner daredevil. He grinned like a wild banshee, with his dusty black Army boots dangling a good ten feet above the ground, swinging over the audience.

What he couldn't see from his vantage point was that Leila Lynn, the girl he'd dogged and deserted, had craftily maneuvered her way up to the front row. Climbing on top of her roommate's shoulders, she stretched herself up toward Devon. He fluttered his legs to evade her reach, almost losing his grip on the slick metal scaffolding, but she was on a mission and wouldn't be dissuaded. Grabbing hold of his stylishly skinny, Trash and Vaudeville denim trousers round the ankles, she yanked them down, revealing his Spider-Man underwear. (Yes, you read that correctly…his seventies Spider-Man Underoos. Like most rockers of his kind, he apparently owned nothing manufactured after 1977.)

Loud, sudden laughter emerged, the crowd pointing up at his flailing, emaciated, porcelain-white legs. Devon let go of his grip with one hand, trying to pull up his pants, but it was too risky. He dangled in the breeze, all of his secrets revealed for the world to see. So much for being cool and mysterious. But Johnny was a born star. He made a sweeping gesture with his arm, as if he were a circus ringmaster presenting this latest attraction for his devoted audience. Under the enchantment of his special magic, the snafu became the greatest stage prank of all time. Johnny moaned into his microphone, as the band brought its set to a fiery conclusion. The crowd roared as one, anointing the band with its adoration, ending their set in triumph.

*\*\*\**

"I HAVE MEASURED OUT my life with coffee spoons!" I recited my favorite poem with mock gravitas as I gratefully took my first sip from the biggest cup of coffee available at the mall's food court. I had surveyed all the purveyors. This was the most caffeine I could mainline in one go. *I wonder if T. S. Eliot ever worked a double shift, because that stanza definitely exudes the kind of exhaustion I'm feeling right now.*

I'd arrived at Polo Ralph Lauren at seven this morning to stock new inventory before the store opened. That meant I'd already been at the mall for twelve hours, and I had another three to endure before closing. Not to mention the time it would take me to count out my till, and to do my closing paperwork, before I caught the bus home. My skin felt plastic from the hours under fluorescent lights amid piped-in Top 40 hits. It's not like Depeche Mode is the *only* possible soundtrack for shopping, even though the citizens of San Diego seemed to think so. Okay, deservedly so, they'd sold out three nights at the SD Sports Arena the previous summer, but did they have to be on constant repeat at the mall? I myself was more into the local underground bands like Mojo Nixon and The Beat Farmers, or righteous, riffy rockers like Sabbath and Metallica. But, sadly, I didn't get to DJ at work.

While waiting in line for a slice of Square Pan Pizza, I surreptitiously checked my compact and adjusted the strip of black velvet I'd fashioned into a headband to hold back my hair. I also automatically checked the gap between my front teeth. After years of being called "Bucky," or "The Beav," in school I'd begged my mom for braces, but there just wasn't the money to spare. At least I'd finally broken the habit of always smiling with my lips closed—which, quite frankly, could look creepy after the tenth time.

As my order was called, I closed my compact and straightened my skirt. I'd won the jackpot at the Del Mar location of the Goodwill. I could not believe my eyes when I'd uncovered the crème de la crème of ultimate thrift store finds: an authentic, vintage Chanel suit in canary yellow bouclé wool. The fitted silhouette seemed to accentuate my waist, smartly proportioning my extra weight into an attractive hourglass. And because its beautiful bright hue was in the primary color palette, making it so on-trend, I knew I'd put together a perfect, of-the-moment ensemble. Especially when I'd accessorized it with a geometrically inscribed black choker and gold hoop earrings from the store. Too bad I was only at the mall. I sighed as my delusions of grandeur were crushed by reality, when a slouchy, grimacing mall rat spun abruptly, and nearly smeared his drippy Swenson's chocolate ice cream cone on me.

I found a table with a view looking down over the mall's pièce de résistance—the indoor rink, where skaters circled the ice even while the Southern California sun blazed outside. I pulled on my headphones to immerse myself in my own mini Stone Temple Pilots oasis, while luxuriating in my final fifteen-minute break of the day.

*Nice rotation and landing*, I thought, as a female skater smoothly executed an unbelievable double axel on the ice below.

"*Scusi, bellisima*, can I ask you question?" a man said bluntly, stopping directly in front of me.

Realizing he was addressing me, I pulled off my headphones.

"Yes?" I said, not wanting to be rude but not exactly wanting to encourage him either. He had black hair, slicked back with what looked like pomade, and the kind of five o'clock shadow that resembled a costume. He was wearing oxblood red loafers with no socks.

"Buonasera," he said, his Italian accent sing-songy and exotic. "My name is Franco. And you are, *mi bella amore*?"

"Scarlett," I said, flattening my voice to discourage further conversation. My workday was grueling enough without dodging advances from a middle-aged Romeo.

An old black camera hung from his arm, with L-E-I-C-A etched in silver font across the front. As he talked, waving his hands expressively, he snapped a pic. "You are a model, no?" he asked.

"Yeah, right, and you're the Pope," I couldn't resist saying.

"How tall are you?" he asked, scanning me from my feet to my hair. His eyes lingered on my shoulders, face, arms, and legs with an intensity that made me fidget.

"One point seventy-eight," I finally said with a little smirk. I was at least somewhat knowledgeable of my overseas measurements from studying, like a textbook, the British *Vogues* my cool flight attendant aunt had brought home for me over the years. This was also how I had best honed my fashion-forward sensibility.

"Ahh…very clever," he said, gazing deeply at me until I had to look away. "Your eyes are most alluring, il mia gattino."

I didn't know whether to laugh or yell for mall security.

"Yeah, the better to see you with," I finally joked, borrowing from "Little Red Riding Hood" in an attempt to diffuse what I thought might be his advances.

"*Alzarsi in piedi*," he commanded, immune to my sarcasm.

"Excuse me?" I said, already embarrassed at the scene he was making. "I don't understand."

"Si," he said. "Stand up. *Per favore*."

Something in his voice compelled me to do as he said, even though he was beyond strange—a forward little man who'd stalked me in front of the local Hot Dog on a Stick franchise. In spite of everything, he had panache and presence.

He ran his eyes slowly over every inch of me until I was blushing.

"Hmmmm…" he murmured. "Now if you could turn."

Again, I couldn't help but do as I was told.

"Yes, you have the makings of a model," he said.

"Who are you?" I asked, unable to contain my curiosity any longer, even if, as I feared, encouraging him turned out to be an incredibly stupid move.

"I am Franco Giovani," he said. "I am in the states to shoot a cover story for *Sassy* magazine, tomorrow, right here, at how you say…'The Jewel', La Jolla?"

Yeah, right…whatever…Luigi Ratatouille…that's a pickup line no one's ever heard…

"…Oh…wow," I finally said, wanting to believe him enough not to be rude.

"And you, bellissima, should call me if you are ever in New York," he said, pulling out an embossed, dark crimson Cartier holder, from which he removed an elegant, cream-colored business card, handing it to me, and then flouncing off.

*What just happened?* I thought. *Am I on* Candid Camera?

Checking my watch, I realized I was late returning from break. *Shoot.* I tossed my half-eaten pizza into a trash bin and hurried as fast as I could back to the store. I was still bruised and fragile from my recent accident, even if the injuries weren't visible, much as my potential advocate, Franco, hadn't been able to see the deep internal pain of all the dreams I'd had to put off for far too long. I knew he probably wasn't legit, and yet, I couldn't help but be hopeful, or at least intrigued.

*Could he possibly be right about me? Could he really be a photographer for Sassy? Or was he just a lowlife, entry-level, wannabe fashion photog, on the lurch for his new "model," à la "victim," posing as this big-time fashionista?*

No one had ever singled me out for anything before. Except for teasing and ridicule. It felt exciting and scary all at once. As I reached the store and pushed through the racks of clothes to clock in, I caught sight of myself in a mirror. I knew I was tall and, well, curvy, (okay, the kids at school called me lardo, but Aurora always said I was a voluptuous bombshell who reminded her of a doppelgänger for Sophia

Loren.) Either way, I knew I was not cut from the same cloth as the white bread "cookie cutter" girls I'd grown up with, being taught to admire their aesthetic in all areas of my generation's pop culture. But maybe I was actually more than that, too.

✳✳✳

BACK HOME, MY MOM was grading papers at the little table in our miniscule breakfast nook. She was gorgeous, as always—a real natural beauty. But she looked exhausted. I couldn't remember a time when she didn't.

"Hi, honey," Mom said, glancing up with a smile. "How was work?"

"Interesting," I said, trying to keep it cool, while noshing on some grapes that were out on the countertop. "Mom, it's probably nothing. But…this Italian guy started talking to me. He had the *best* accent. He's a photographer who's in town for a cover shoot in La Jolla for *Sassy* magazine. He asked if I was a model!"

"Well, we all know you're very beautiful, Scarlett," Mom said cautiously, taking off her readers and gazing directly into my eyes.

"He wants me to call him if I'm ever in New York."

"Now, Scarlett, I know you're nineteen now and therefore an adult. But I can only hope I've raised you to have better judgment than—"

"No, Mom, it's not like *that*," I said, sitting down across from her and leaning in to make my point. "He wants to take photos of me. He really thinks I could model."

"Well, maybe, if you have enough free time, between your courses and your job," Mom said.

"If he's right, and I could make a career of it, I wouldn't necessarily need to finish college."

"And then, what would you do after that?" she asked.

"I don't know. Travel. Make art."

"But remember our discussion about your getting your MBA? And *then* you can do whatever you like. Maybe you could learn to run your own modeling or advertising agency. Heck, you could be the CEO of an international business. Now that would be glamorous."

"You're absolutely right," I said, not keen to discuss my rapidly fraying future with one whose dreams for me were so far from my own. "Which is why modeling would be a great way to break into the industry." I pushed back from the table abruptly, my chair creaking on the worn linoleum. "*And* it's not your decision."

I didn't want to admit how much I needed this crazy opportunity to be real. Even with all the double shifts I'd taken on lately, I hadn't even come close to saving enough to pay for my regular curriculum at USD, let alone amassing enough to bolt off to Paris. After how hard I'd worked, the thought of having to take a semester off to push myself to full-time at the store, while maintaining my new part-time job at Pannikin Coffee & Tea, was soul crushing. It was time to make a new plan. And if no one else would assist me, I'd have to help myself.

✳✳✳

As JOHNNY COOLED OFF outside the "backstage" area after the band's set, Devon stumbled up, so drunk he'd either forgotten the embarrassing retribution he'd just received onstage, or he couldn't be bothered to care. Jet grabbed Devon's T-shirt to keep him from careening into the festival attendees, who were downing an infusion of BBQ and beer between acts. Johnny caught the eye of a cute young woman in a cut-in-all-the-right-places blue and white gingham dress. When he winked at her, she dissolved into a fit of laughter with her girlfriends.

"Come on, man, I've got a powerful thirst," Devon slurred.

"We gotta talk," Johnny said. "What was that onstage?! Are you in a competition with Blackbeard, the pirate? You sure as hell didn't come here tonight to play your damn heart out like the rest of us. This was a BIG show. You blew it."

"You're such a buzz kill. I need a beer. If we're gonna talk, let's talk about that."

Johnny and Jet exchanged a look. Jet shrugged. Clearly there was no reasoning with Devon when he was in this state. They pushed their way into the crowd and toward the Coors tent. Johnny grinned as people who'd just seen their set said, "You killed it," and gave him high fives. No way. He was getting rockignized.

Hey, it might have only been in his home state, but he'd take it.

Emerging out of the sea of local blues fans, Shiv stood grinning at Johnny and his band mates. Johnny instantly rockignized *him* as a founding member of the *major* rock act, Blood Line. He wore what looked like late sixties Steve McQueen Gucci shades, black leather pants, and the best punk rock haircut since fucking Sid Vicious. Needless to say, he clearly wasn't from around these parts.

"Bloody 'ell, Mate…that was feckin' BRILLIANT!" Shiv crowed.

Johnny felt about as high as a giraffe's nuts—even if he couldn't make heads or tails of what he'd said, Shiv was still a rock god.

"It's a compliment, aye," Shiv said.

"Uff da!" Johnny said.

"Huh?" Shiv asked, equally stumped by Johnny's rural colloquialism.

"It's a good thing," Johnny said. "Come on, bud, we're gonna get some beer."

The two cracked up, embracing each other, instant brothers in arms, sensing that beneath their regional dialects, they shared a matching snarky, dark, dry sense of humor. They fell into step together and weaved through the crowd.

"So, how did *you* end up in Oklahoma?" Johnny asked.

"Playing the Reunion Arena in Dallas, and on our off day, I insisted on making a pilgrimage to Tulsa, the home of my all-time favorite legend, the mad hatter of blues, Leon Russell…and when I saw there was a festival nearby, I decided to pop over…I didn't realize it wasn't *really* close till I arrived. But I'm chuffed I saw you."

"I dig," Johnny affirmed. "I can show you where his old studio was sometime, if you like."

As they pulled up to the bar, Shiv reached for his wallet.

"Let me," Johnny said. "They gave us drink tickets."

As he proudly pulled the paper tickets out of his pocket, he looked at Shiv sideways, suddenly wondering if maybe they weren't as cool as they'd seemed when the festival's organizers had handed them to him earlier.

"Thanks, mate," Shiv said, punching Johnny's shoulder lightly. "We don't get drink tickets anymore…we, um, get the whole bar."

Johnny could tell Shiv wasn't being mean. He was just teasing him like an older brother would, and he joined in with Shiv's infectious, braying laughter.

"Sounds pretty rough," Johnny said. "How do you deal?"

"You'll get there," Shiv said. "I'd say maybe sooner than you think."

Johnny handed around the shots of Jack he'd ordered for all. Devon sucked his down and tapped his empty glass on the bar for the bartender to refill. Johnny shook his head at Devon's usual lack of social graces, lifted his glass, and toasted with Shiv and Jet. They tossed back their drinks. Johnny handed out a round of beers.

"Lad, if you're ever in New York City, you should look me up," Shiv said.

Johnny, used to being the coolest dude in every room, looked at Shiv shyly, measuring how serious he was. When Shiv threw his arm around him and clinked bottles, Johnny realized he was starting to make a new solid mate and unfurled his wolfish grin. Of course, he was *dying* to leave for New York City *immediately*. And hang with Shiv there, navigating The Westies to the next level, with shows at CBGB, The Limelight, Roseland Ballroom, and all the cool clubs he'd only ever read about. But Johnny was so nervous and excited to have had such a cool, worldly guy befriend him *and* like his music, he was struggling for composure. He ordered another round of shots. That seemed to help. Then, Shiv ordered them a round, and that helped even more.

Flash forward to two hours later, when they had downed so many shots of Jack and a plethora of Coors, they were laughing and ribbing each other as if they were lifelong friends. Shiv was an old pro, though, knowing how to hold his drink and composure well. He never lost sight of where he needed to be, no matter how many rounds he'd had.

"Bollocks," he said, looking at his watch. "I've got to go. I seriously can't miss that call sheet time. It's ironclad. Management, you know…"

As Shiv was well aware, their tour bus driver, Tank, was about to finish his mandatory eight-hour sleep shift, and Shiv had to get back.

"Wait," Johnny said, flailing like he'd just fallen down the rabbit hole and was about to get kicked out of Wonderland. "How are you getting back to Dallas?"

"Car service," Shiv said. "Got the number for the gent who drove me here."

"No way, mate," Johnny said, having already picked up some of Shiv's slang. "Hitch a ride with us to Dallas."

"You're too kind," Shiv said. "I couldn't possibly let you go to the trouble."

"It's nothing…as the crow flies it's only three hours and sixteen minutes away," Jet said.

"Bloody 'ell, you actually look fit to drive," Shiv said, appraising Jet.

"Yep, well, that's what I do," Jet said, beaming. No one was immune to Shiv. "I'm pretty much a professional drinker. It's only taken me about three years, and a major financial investment. Ya know…it's a full-time job."

In a blaze, they loaded their gear out from the VIP area into their sprinter van, got paid, and tore off into the night. Devon passed out on the bass case in back. Johnny and Shiv sat on the ripped vinyl van seat together, bonding, and joining in on their favorite Stooges song, "Search and Destroy."

"I'm a streetwalking cheetah with a heart full of napalm," they sang in unison.

"Cheers! I mean, when you're talking about the best of the best…" Shiv said.

"…Of the best of the best…" Johnny said.

"…Iggy is…" Shiv said.

"…The BEST FRONTMAN EVER!" they both said at the exact same moment.

"Well, it's more like a two-way tie, with Mick," Johnny said, thinking out loud.

"A three-way tie, with Mick and Joe Strummer," Shiv said. "The best of the best of the best."

They grinned at each other, happily wailing along until the last note rang out.

"Aye…play me something you lot have recorded," Shiv said.

"Um…let's see…" Johnny said, once again overjoyed and terrified at once.

"Come on, mate," Shiv said. "You already know I dig your band."

Johnny sheepishly agreed. He made eye contact with Jet in the rear view mirror and nodded his head. Jet punched a tape into the deck and the first song purred to life. Johnny's vocals were as silty as the Mississippi river after a flood, full of pathos, and the raw power of his rock 'n' roll dreams. His lyrics slinked over the bluesy rock guitar licks, throbbing bass lines, and steady backbeat.

"Bloody 'ell, that's brilliant," Shiv said. "I'm completely gobsmacked!"

"Yeah?" Johnny asked, too thrilled to say more. "Cool."

Shiv reached behind him and grabbed a loose acoustic guitar from the loft, where Devon slumbered amidst the gear, and started jamming along. Johnny was in rock 'n' roll heaven.

*Jesus, this stuff only happens in the movies, right?* Johnny thought, hoping if he was indeed dreaming, he'd never wake up.

***

HIS SYNCHRONOUS ENCOUNTER WITH Shiv was just the dose of encouragement Johnny needed to propel himself headlong into his dreams. Within the year, he and The Westies moved to NYC and landed their inaugural gig at the Continental Club. It wasn't quite Irving Plaza, or even CBGB, but it was pretty cool. And on someone's utmost dream come true night, one might even see a "flesh and blood" bona fide rock god stroll in, like Joey Ramone. Just as miraculous, Shiv had talked to Blood Line's high-powered manager, Deirdre Mulvey, who lived on Diet Coke and drama and claimed to have no time for anything. He'd somehow gotten her to agree to check out The Westies' first NYC appearance.

Johnny hardly had time to appreciate his new friend's generosity. Or the good fortune he was experiencing. He was having a harrowing night. It was only minutes before their set time, and Devon was nowhere to be found. He had been on a booze bender since they'd gotten to town. Johnny had, perhaps naïvely, hoped Devon would rise to the occasion and get it together now that they were making their sortie on the majors.

Johnny pounded on the men's room door. After banging and banging, with no response from within, he finally summoned Jet, who threw himself at the wood again and again. Finally, Jet gave up, gripping his shoulder as he walked away. The door opened a crack from within. Johnny cursed as the stench of old piss hit him. And there was Devon, sitting on the floor, rambling incoherently to himself, clearly in no state to play. Being that his old man had passed away from a heroin addiction after the Vietnam War, Devon never would have touched the hard stuff. Johnny knew that and was glad for it. And he knew Devon would eventually be okay. But he was still short a guitar player.

"Fuck this," Johnny said, pushing his way out of the bathroom.

"Want me to get him some coffee?" Jet asked, holding his aching arm.

"I want you to get him a clue," Johnny said. "I'm so over this. How's your shoulder? Are you going to be able to play?"

"I'll be okay," Jet said. "I always am."

Johnny gave his bassist a high five, gratefully acknowledging that Jet spoke the truth. Then, he rushed up to the bar, where Shiv was nursing his Johnnie Walker.

"Please, man, you've got to sit in with us," Johnny said.

"What's up?"

"Devon. He's passed out in the bathroom."

"Devon is pissed in the pisser?" Shiv said. "I don't know, mate. We haven't rehearsed. I'm sorry. I don't want to *not* do your band its justice and play your songs wrong."

Deplorable Deirdre stalked into the bar—never a smile, always a scowl—air kissed Shiv, and glared at Johnny. "This better be good."

*Oh shit. How is the band going to turn this around?* Johnny wondered.

"We'll do our best, madam," he nodded his head, an alluring sparkle in his eye. He was always on his best manners. And he could turn it on when he needed to, like any front man worth a damn, whether he was an emerging rock hero or not.

Jet had set up Devon's gear along with his own while Johnny and Shiv ran through the songs at lightning speed in the gritty, closet-like space, a.k.a. backstage. They threw in a few covers by their absolute favorites, The Stones, The Clash, and, of course, The Stooges, cobbling together a set list that would just fill out the forty minutes they'd been allotted. Johnny beamed at Shiv, amazed at how good he really was. Having carried Devon for so many years out of family loyalty, Johnny was stunned by how thrilling, and fun, it could all be without Devon's dead weight. This might actually be the best thing that had ever happened to the band, if they could just get through tonight.

They took the stage in front of the iconic black and white sign bearing the venue's name, Johnny and Shiv grinning like Mick and Keith at the height of their powers. But they were still running late, and Johnny was still rattled. He downed a shot of Jack and said a little prayer. Shiv winked at him, Jet nodded, and Johnny felt as ready as he'd ever be. Shiv unleashed the opening riff to their set opener and the crowd turned toward the stage. Deirdre didn't look up from her Diet Coke or Rolex. Twisted with nerves, Johnny approached his mic.

✳✳✳

I COULDN'T SLEEP. My clock read 4:00 a.m. Faint snores wafted over to me from the couch, where Imani slumbered in her sleeping bag. As much as I longed to launch myself into the grand adventure that awaited me beyond my hometown, this was all I'd ever known. Surveying my most beloved childhood stuffed animals, which continued to adorn the top of my bookshelf, I felt a pang.

I tiptoed around my room, dressing and making up my face carefully in the low light. Once outfitted for the stealth mission at hand, I crept out of my house and tiptoed next door to Aurora's cottage. I rang the bell tentatively. It wasn't quite dawn yet, but I was sure this constituted an emergency. My whole existence was at stake.

Aurora answered the door in a magenta satin ball-gown-like-robe, adorned with a bubblegum pink sheer scarf tied over the rollers in her hair. Her face looked soft and almost girlish without its usual makeup mask.

"Scarlett, darling, come in," she said. "I do hope you're not in any trouble."

"I'm sorry to bother you so late," I said, fidgeting with the strap of my bag.

"Don't be silly," Aurora said. "I live for such moments. I'll make tea."

We were soon settled together on her granny-style brocade love seat, while Aurora poured Earl Gray into bone china teacups festooned with delicate roses. I'd told her all about how I didn't want to disappoint my mom. But, somehow, I knew this could be an opportunity that proved to have happened for a reason. This was going to be my escape. I longed for Aurora to tell me I wasn't crazy for wanting to take such a risk.

"Well, my dear, it's quite clear to me that there's only one path before you," Aurora said. "This is your destiny. It has come for you. And you must welcome it."

"He did say he's shooting *today*, right here at La Jolla Cove," I said. "And I read somewhere the best light's at dawn."

"The time is nearly upon us then," Aurora said. "The sun is almost up. Go there this morning. Everything else will happen as it should."

My heart galloped in my chest at the thought of being so forward.

"Drink your tea, child," Aurora said.

A buttery sugar cookie melted on my tongue. I felt sleepy from the late hour yet energized by the tea and the thrill of my burgeoning plan. Before I knew it, Aurora warned me the sun would be up soon, and I should be on my way.

She kissed me goodbye on both of my cheeks, and the back of my throat choked with swallowed tears. She was my fairy godmother and my own spiritual orb, all in one. Something about this goodbye felt profound.

***

I HID BEHIND A palm tree and watched Franco position the model, tilting her face, the honeyed light making her look beautiful and fresh. A team of frenzied assistants scampered around him, responding to his every whim, moving photo reflectors, and checking all the details of the myriad stacks of equipment, even bringing over an Evian bottle— with the straw bent just so, for him to take a sip.

Although I'd never witnessed a professional photo shoot before, or any kind of photo shoot, for that matter, everything before me made a perfect kind of sense. I could clearly comprehend Franco's instructions, how they accentuated the model's best features, and could anticipate her every move in response. And the fashion? Oh my God—it was reminiscent of peeking into one of the fables I'd loved as a child and seeing a magical kingdom before me. Even as the minutes ticked by, and finally a few hours had passed, I never grew bored or restless. I was exactly where I wanted to be.

After what felt like no time at all, Franco kissed his model on both cheeks and waved over his assistants with instructions about packing up and organizing the endless film canisters. He had a small fashion army at his beck and call. There was not only a makeup artist, a makeup artist assistant, a hairstylist, and a hair assistant, but also what seemed to be two stylists and an editor from the magazine.

Finally, having dispatched his orders, Franco was the last on set. Unable to resist snapping a few final pics of the view, Franco then walked out to his rental convertible, only to find a surprise waiting for him.

In the passenger seat sat a young specimen, shaking like a leaf.

I flashed him my most winning smile and said, "Take me with you."

# ROCK 'N' DOLL

## 1995

NOTHING WAS WHAT IT seemed, and no one desired it to be. Adventuring from the street into the club gave the sensation of stepping into a music video that had been art directed to the hilt. Skateboarders executed ollies around them, adding to the bedlam of maximum velocity and volume. Voracious wind machines distorted Hawke's raggedy black hair into a rat's nest as he tried, and failed, to act casual. Johnny laughed, dug his elbow into his guitarist's ribs, his own inky black pompadour indifferent to the elements. The thundering dance beat kicked them in the heart with its insistent, percussive power. Lights splashed sweet tart hues across their skin—baby blue stars and pale yellow circles distorted their faces and the visages of those around them. The insatiable club goers—all bare, sweaty flesh—compressed tighter than a midtown subway car at rush hour. Outlandish figures emerged from the flashing lights, then faded back into the darkness.

Johnny and his cohorts liked to start their night here at The Tunnel, a NYC nightspot known for its uncensored vibe, eclectic music, and melting-pot scene. The cavernous main room offered a packed, sunken dance floor and several airborne cages in which sexy go-go boys and girls in short-shorts gyrated above the manic crowd below. They usually did a few laps through the club—with their birds, a.k.a. babes—winnowing their way through the Lava Lounge, designed by "It" artist Kenny Scharf, the S&M lounge, and then, past the infamous unisex bathrooms, and into the hip-hop portion of the club, nodding hello to some of the well-known regulars: Ice Cube, Billy Idol, and Marky Mark.

The night was young. They had only consumed a few celebratory shots of Jack so far, but as they settled into The Tunnel's rock 'n' roll area, it was possible to get high on the room alone, with its joyous inclusiveness and high-octane, anything-goes vibe—it was freedom personified. They felt right at home.

And tonight Johnny was flying. He had experienced the culmination of his childhood dreams, the decade of hard work, in which he had literally played guitar until his fingers bled, and his courageous decision to leave home and strike out for the city. It had all finally paid off, and—drumroll, please—he had just signed a motherfucking record contract with MCA Records! Johnny had secreted the fat sheath of papers inside the pocket of his black leather motorcycle jacket, superstitious that if the lawyers whisked his copies of the documents back to their office, the spell would be broken and the deal undone.

Johnny smiled as if disbelieving his good fortune. Somehow, he was beside his right-hand man, and his band's new lead guitarist, Shiv Bloody Babcock, who had played with them ever since the Continental Club. Shiv knew everyone worth knowing, everywhere worth going. As soon as they'd entered the fray in the rock 'n' roll room, one of the impish, S&M inspired cocktail waitresses materialized at their side with a tray of the club's top shelf whiskey and beers. Johnny nodded his head in gratitude.

"Thanks," Johnny yelled, trying to be heard over the roar of music.

"What, mate?" Shiv shouted back.

As Johnny reached for a drink, Hawke swooped in and grabbed one in each hand, downing them in quick succession before peering through the bottoms of the empty glasses and dropping them onto the tray. Bone, their drummer extraordinaire, laughed uproariously, always getting caught up in Hawke's constant attempts at comic relief. Jet raised his glass in a toast to Johnny, downed the liquid in one go, and then, seemed to make the glass vanish into thin air with a subtle magic trick.

"Whatever," Johnny said to Hawke, reaching for a drink and saluting Shiv.

Shiv raised his eyebrows in a sign of annoyed solidarity regarding Hawke.

"Making music with yer mates is, well...brilliant," Shiv said. "Doing business with 'em can be bollocks."

"Tell me about it," Johnny said.

Deirdre swanned over from a nearby banquet where she'd been air kissing a table of radio DJs as if she were the queen of rock 'n' roll. Since that historic night at the Continental Club, Deirdre had carefully cultivated every moment in their career.

"Champagne," she barked, clapping her hands as if the waitress were a goddamn desperate dog.

Shiv slid a neatly folded fifty into the tip cup balanced on the waitress's tray. "Don't mind her, she was raised in the dragon's lair," he said, taking advantage of a lull in the music.

"Lucky for you, too," Deirdre said. "Dragons eat snakes and everything else that dares to cross their path. That's why your deal with MCA was so primo."

"At least a snake bite we can survive," Hawke said. "By the time the greedy dragons divvy up the kill, there's nothing left for anybody else."

"If you don't write the songs, you don't cash the checks," Deirdre said.

"It's hard to write when your singer just *has* to call all the shots," Hawke said.

"I've said you're welcome to write with me any time," Johnny said.

"Whatever," Hawke said. He'd caught the eye of an otherworldly Amazon in a patent leather bikini top and cool, low slung, plaid men's pants. He trailed her into the throng, promptly vanishing as the music detonated at ultimate intensity into the latest extended NIN dance remix.

"You know that old joke...what's the difference between God and a guitarist?" Shiv bellowed.

"God doesn't think he's a guitarist, but a guitarist thinks he's God," Johnny bawled back. "They're all conceited pains in the ass—except for you, of course."

"They're all a dime a dozen," Shiv joked into Johnny's ear. "Except for me."

The two laughed and drank deep. The beer was cold and refreshing in the hot, narrow room. Johnny's euphoria once again ascended. The lights exploded aggressively, with bright beams sweeping up and down from the ceiling to the dance floor, as if a rock 'n' roll spacecraft was hovering above them.

In the wake of the visual sunburst, Johnny blinked his eyes. There at the forefront of the crowd, resembling a woman adorning the prow of a ship, was the most radiant girl Johnny had ever seen. Wavy dark golden hair fell over her broad shoulders and curvaceous figure, and her beautiful big green eyes expressed multitudes. And then she smiled.

Magnetized toward his dream woman, Johnny did something he hadn't had to do since gaining a certain amount of local notoriety in his hometown and then quickly becoming a club darling in his new city: he made the first move. Never breaking eye contact, he bridged the space between them and came to rest right before her.

"Hi," he said, the room far too loud for him to express much more.

"Hi," she replied, revealing the most beguiling, downright sexy space between her top teeth as she smiled.

"Me, Johnny," he joked, palm against his dark as night V-neck T-shirt.

"Ah—me, Scarlett," she said.

A volatile disturbance commenced over Scarlett's right shoulder, as an older, squatty, muscle-bound man with a ratty goatee and frosted tips to his dark mane had insinuated himself between Scarlett and a younger, more petite, yet stronger-looking girl. Sporting a buzz cut, a cropped and torn tank top, and army surplus pants, she was so androgynous she could have passed for a boy. From across the room, Johnny hadn't guessed that she was with Scarlett. The man was grinding himself on the more diminutive woman in a most unpleasant, belligerent manner. She raised both hands in front of her chest, pushing the man back a full step.

Mr. Aggressive assessed the onlookers around him to determine how many people had seen him get put down by this girl, and how big his retaliation needed to be in order to save face. He took two powerful steps forward into her space, again closing in on her, and began grinding his crotch against her.

But before he had a chance to unleash his full assault on her, Scarlett intervened.

Towering over him in her mega five-inch heels, she scowled down on him, withering him with her scorn. Scarlett lifted her vodka tonic and held it aloft for a wonderful, anticipatory moment before arching her wrist and pouring the drink down onto the cad's awful head. He spluttered and puffed his chest, pit bull style, but the damage to his image was done. As the club goers in their vicinity couldn't help but laugh at his distress, the angry little man spun and sulked off.

If Johnny had been curious about Scarlett before, he was now officially smitten.

"Nicely played," he said. "But you're in need of a drink."

"What?" she said.

Utilizing this excuse to lean in toward her and say more, he found himself enveloped in the spicy bouquet of her perfume. A beefy bouncer hustled over to them followed by Scarlett's peroxided nemesis, who was dramatically dabbing his cocktail-dampened face with a small paper napkin. The two men looked like Tweedledee and Tweedledummer, not the hint of a brain between them.

"He started it," Scarlett said, pointing at her adversary.

The bouncer shook his head and jabbed his finger toward the door.

Scarlett turned back to Johnny and unfurled a sweet farewell wave.

"But…wait…your drink…your number…" Johnny sputtered.

The house lights dimmed for an instant, and when they flared up again, Scarlett was gone.

"Tough break," Shiv said, coming up beside Johnny.

It would be an untruth to imply that when Scarlett disappeared, like a rock 'n' doll Cinderella, the entire night was ruined. Johnny had, after all, experienced the culmination of his wildest, most heartfelt dreams. He had signed a *major* label record deal. He was hanging out with his musical idol, now his best mate, band mate. Johnny proceeded to imbibe many a shot and a few less than street-legal substances, throwing himself into the night's celebratory mayhem. But, always, in the recesses of his mind was a memory of Scarlett's tendrils of flaxen hair, and her warm intelligent eyes.

***

As the sun bloomed over the Manhattan skyline, Johnny and his band mates hurtled onto the sleepy streets, still adrenalized from the night's triumphant celebration. Even before the day's heat and humidity kicked into full gear, the asphalt was ripe with urine, garbage, and exhaust—the particular mélange of a hardworking, hard-partying city that didn't have time to stop and worry about niceties the way the suburbs did. Even the air here was abrasive, in your face—just like the taxi drivers, pedestrians, and the resident rodents.

Johnny was too revved up to sleep just yet, and besides, cabs cost money. The group straggled toward their shared Lower East Side walk-up, their motorcycle boots clomping on the empty sidewalks. Hawke, inserting himself into the already picturesque scene, merrily dropped his trousers and began pissing into the gutter.

Shiv laughed. "That's horrible."

Encouraged by their protests of disgust, Hawke spun around in their direction, still pissing, and nearly teetered backward into an oncoming bus, Johnny jumping forward to rescue him just in time. Hawke laughed derisively as he wetted Johnny's boots. But Johnny was indifferent to his friend's coarse christening and his laughter. Right at eye level, meeting Johnny's gaze with that particular blend of acumen and wit, were green eyes he already knew so well—eyes he hadn't stopped evoking all night. As the bus charged away down the street, he absorbed all he could: Scarlett, amid a constellation of models in a Marc Jacobs 1995 Spring/Summer ad campaign, an urban fantasy on the side of the city vehicle that had nearly pulverized Hawke.

An auspicious omen, if ever he'd seen one.

What was not positive, though, was Johnny's sudden realization that the street numbers were going *up* not *down*. Johnny tried to focus long enough to identify their locale. Was that Rockefeller Center on the horizon? But the Rockettes high kicked in midtown, and they were supposed to be downtown-bound. Behind him, the guys had thrown their arms around each other and were belting out an impromptu rendition of the Rolling Stones' mournful country ballad "Dead Flowers."

"My brothers," he said. "It appears we've ventured in the wrong direction."

As he addressed them the motley crew stumbled into a circle around him.

"Maybe that's because we've got no proper captain steering the ship," Hawke said with a sneer.

"Didn't see you catching onto the fact that we'd strolled twenty blocks in the wrong direction, boy genius," Shiv retorted.

Johnny rocked back and howled, greeting the promise of the new day. The few yuppies already beginning their frantic morning dash to their office coffins gave him and his leather clad band mates a wide berth. Jonny didn't care that Hawke was a dick. Or that his legs were like lead weights in his heavy boots. He was full of hope, and he wanted to vault to the top of the nearest skyscraper and kiss the firmament. More than any other urge in the universe, he wanted to sing.

"We've got the studio booked all week," he said. "Let's go there right now."

"Nobody ever turns up until at least noon," Shiv laughed.

"Well, let's shake them out of bed," Johnny said.

"I'm down," Jet said.

"Good man," Johnny said, giving him a friendly slap on his back.

Hawke spit and turned away, lighting a cigarette. What else was new?

✳✳✳

THE BAND'S ADRENALINE CARRIED them through the day and into the night. They were, after all, recording their major label debut at Jimi Hendrix's legendary Electric Lady Studios on West 8th Street in Greenwich Village. And they had their fair share of musician's little helper—a.k.a. yayo, a.k.a. cocaine—to convey them out of any temporary valleys into which they may have slumped. Over the next week, Johnny was whipped by a tsunami of artistic eddies. Mornings faded into endless nights and into fresh new days. He traipsed cheerfully through the blur of hours, pursuing the transcendent music echoing within his head, shaking it out into the world around him, with help from his closest allies—his band.

Nothing could dampen Johnny's joy. Not when midway through the third night of recording he reached across the body of his acoustic guitar between takes and took a swig of his drink, only to taste the gritty hint of ash. Before he had time to investigate, he observed Hawke, doubled over his six string, laughing in glee. That fucker. But it didn't matter. Hawke could literally put ash in his brew and devour the last of the Shanghai Noodles when they ordered in from their fave Chinese food place, Rong Phuc, which always made them laugh uproariously, and be a complete idiot in pretty much every conceivable way and even in some ways unimaginable to anyone but Hawke. It didn't matter. The sounds in Johnny's head were articulating themselves through his voice and his fingertips, and his brothers were courting the muse right alongside him. Prolific riffs progressed into some pretty brilliant songs, and those songs into a sweet and utterly soulful album.

Johnny sat at one of the studio's two grand pianos. Transported as he was by the whimsy of his songwriting, he was startled back into his surroundings by a familiar, harsh female voice.

"I only drink Diet," Deirdre hissed. "With thin slices of lemon, please. On the *side*."

"If it ain't the deplorable Dragon Woman herself," Shiv joked.

"Oh, bollocks," Johnny said, having picked up a bit of Shiv's Cockney slang. "Is today Wednesday?"

"'Tis," Jet said.

"Nah, it's Monday," Hawke said, forever offering the contrary opinion.

"Seriously, man, you're going to fight me about the goddamn day of the week?" Johnny asked, spinning off the piano bench.

Deirdre swooped in, sporting the same shiny black mini dress with the gargantuan, baby pink bows Courtney Love had worn earlier that year to the VH1 Fashion and Music Awards. Which is to say their manager seemed committed to the fallacy that money and access were tantamount to style and taste.

"Kids…kids, c'mon, can we please stop with the shenanigans?" she said, briskly bringing her hands together.

At the same instant, out of her sight line, Shiv mimicked her trademark schoolmarm clap, which they all knew and loathed so well.

The guys did their best to keep from laughing in her face. Deirdre might have been a nightmare, but she was undeniably in charge. A no-nonsense power broker they needed in their corner. No, she was not to be fucked with.

"Why don't you help me help you out, lads, and come talk to the MCA folks?" she said.

Much like errant schoolboys, the five musicians shuffled into the lounge area that held the studio's intricate mixing board. A trio of middle-aged men in carefully constructed business casual attire perched on the edge of a gray tufted leather sofa.

"It's the moment of truth," Deirdre said. "Where we show our patrons exactly what you've been spending their money on. Now… shall we begin with the hit single…or the other hit singles…?"

Everyone in the studio got a chuckle out of this solid, and hopefully true, opening statement. If nothing else, bulldog Deirdre knew how to command and unite a room full of suits.

"Sure," Johnny said, offering the three men a jaunty salute.

He didn't want to concern himself with what they—or anyone— thought of his music, and most particularly how the commercial, HIG (huge industry giant) aspect collided with the blood, sweat, and tears of his poetic craft. But the knots in his stomach and the sand in his mouth were giving away his secret: he did care, very much.

He nodded to their engineer/producer, Stu, for him to play the track. As the sick bass line steamrolled out of the speakers, Johnny bowed his head, feeling every note, every hesitation, every breath between every lyric, in his bones. He dared a look at the three label reps. All of them had their eyes trained on what seemed like outer space, shipwrecked on their own solo islands. It wasn't until the song ended that he realized he'd been holding his breath.

"Not for radio," the head MCA guy said.

"But…" Johnny began to say.

"Not for *pop* radio," Deirdre echoed, as if she'd invented the idea herself.

"Well, you know, writing for the radio isn't really my modus operandi," Johnny said. "I write for the people…real people…who want to hear and feel *real* music."

"None of the other members of the MCA family have seemed to have such a resistance to writing for radio—not Tom Petty, not Mary J. Blige," the main label stooge said.

"And these lads certainly have radio hits in them," said the band's A&R rep, Duncan, trying to smooth over the widening rift.

"Agreed," Deirdre jumped in. "While I second your disappointment, I can assure you these were just rough demos. I've only been witnessing how tirelessly hard at work the band has been on even more epic tracks."

"Yeah, what she said," Johnny said, hating this moment with every molecule.

"You mean all those wonderful, perfect, radio-ready tunes you have standing by, just hidden under your hat?" Hawke laughed.

"Yeah, those," Johnny said.

"Now that's music to my ears," Deirdre said, deaf to Johnny's ironic tone, as she was so intent on getting her way, always, even if it didn't line up with reality. "Now let's go enjoy our dinner, and shall we let these songbirds get back to work?"

"Thanks for stopping by," Johnny said.

"Cheers," Shiv riffed, already handing Johnny the bottle of Jack as the suits left.

An hour later, Johnny was back at the piano, clowning through a rendition of "Jealous Guy," joint burning in his ashtray. It had never occurred to him that he might not have what it took. The only thing keeping his father's voice out of his head—the one that told him he was a worthless you-know-what and a useless good for nothing—was the ocean of booze and the Nor'easter of weed. Shiv came and crouched next to him on the bench, facing the other way, adding his own bits of texture and harmony. At least one miracle had emerged from of all of this, Johnny figured.

Time, which had already become unmoored, drifted even further away. Smoke clogged the air like morning fog. Johnny's mouth was sweet from the whiskey, sour from the lack of sleep. His nose burned from the coke, and he wanted simultaneously to run the length of Manhattan and sleep for a million years.

The engineer had long ago turned off the tape and gone home, certain that he wasn't going to miss any moments of accidental genius until the band members had gotten a good night's sleep and a gallon of strong coffee into their systems, in that order. A flurry of activity in the sound room tugged at the edge of Johnny's perception.

"Time to rise and shine," he slurred, earning laughs.

A good-looking teenage boy in a backward baseball hat peered into the room.

"Got a special delivery for Johnny Bird," he said.

"I hope—" Hawke said, clearing his throat, "it's an attitude adjustment."

The kid shrugged. "Need a person in charge to sign," he said.

Johnny stood, realizing only then just how unsteady on his feet he was, and toe heeled it across the room, shaking off Hawke's eyeball daggers as he swayed. Johnny managed to grip the pen in his fist and make a squiggly mark on the extended clip board. Now that he'd gone through all that trouble to cross the room, he followed the kid out into the lounge, feeling lightheaded at the infusion of fresh air. The messenger dropped a colossal photo album on the coffee table and left.

Johnny fell back onto the couch, feeling like he was aloft for an infinity longer than the three feet between him and the couch. When he touched down, his eyes fluttered closed for a brief sweet instant. Shaking off his drowsiness he leaned forward, lighting a smoke from the pack that seemed to always adorn his surroundings.

"No sleep for the wicked," he laughed to himself, flipping open the book.

Staring back from the first page was a familiar pair of luminous emerald eyes in a face he'd memorized, crowned by waves of honeyed hair. Scarlett.

*It's meant to be*, Johnny thought. He'd been in his own creative cocoon for so many days and nights, he could only assume everything that happened was within his direct control, that his every whim had been guiding the hand of fate. *But what is this book?* Marking the page containing Scarlett's modeling info from her agency, so he wouldn't *again* lose her to the great maw of the city, he flipped to the front of the book. Someone's secretary had scrawled a note on MCA Records letterhead to scout a dozen girls to audition for their first video.

"Why would they shoot a video for a song we haven't written yet?" he wondered aloud.

*Oh fuck, I'd better write a song worthy of this video, worthy of this girl's heart.*

As if Johnny really were the boss of the world, the engineer returned at just that moment, carrying a takeout tray of "the world's finest," a.k.a. NYC deli cups inscribed with "Cawfee."

"Thanks, mate," Johnny said, taking a container of brew. "I'll be ready in five."

Hawke strutted in and sat down next to Johnny, snaking a cig out of the pack.

"Ooh, yum, the agency sent over a takeout menu," Hawke said. "Let's see what looks delectable today."

Johnny rolled his eyes. If anyone could discern his soul mate by her physical assets alone, it was Hawke, who was rifling through the pages with confidence.

"I'll take these three," Hawke said, having turned down the corners of the pages featuring the photos of the girls he fancied.

Johnny didn't want to care who Hawke had picked, but he couldn't help but take the bait; a gorgeous gazelle-thin goddess with skin the color of mocha, an equally statuesque Brazilian beauty with cheekbones that could cut glass, and Scarlett.

*No way, nope, absolutely not.*

"Don't you recognize her?" Johnny asked, indicating Scarlett.

"Yeah, from my wet dreams?" Hawke said. "Yeah, sure, what?"

"If I catch you dreaming about her, I'll…give you a righteous Oklahoma spanking, that's what!" Johnny said, stopping short when he registered that Hawke was laughing in his face. "I met her the other night, and I was going to ask her out, so…"

"So let me get this straight, the mighty and powerful Oz, the *leader* of our band, was *going* to ask her out, so now she's off limits?"

"The video audition is later this week," Johnny said, trying to deflect conflict.

"Oh goody, be sure you order these two other girls for me, too."

"They're not Chinese takeaway."

"Sure, Romeo, whatever you say," Hawke said. "Isn't it time you went in there and wrote us a hit?"

✳✳✳

THE BLARING RUCKUS WAS crushing out all other thoughts beyond my desire to flee. Blinking emergency lights infused the hallway with an unearthly quality. The narrow space teemed with two-dozen exotic beauties, all poised in their folding chairs, giving each other side eye, keyed up on jealous, competitive energy.

Hair slicked back, lips stained red as rubies, miniskirt dyed dark as night—check!—these were the directions for rock couture we'd received in advance of this MTV audition. The costume was an homage to the immortal Robert Palmer video for "Addicted to Love." And the harmonized, sexy/sophisticated/androgynous vibe in the corridor had embedded the song in my head: "You can't be saved / oblivion is all you crave / if there's some left for you / you don't mind if you do…might as well face it, you're addicted to love…"

Such moments seemed to take place in a sort of void. At auditions I often felt like just another model, though deep down my passion was to be an artist, an inimitable being who dreamt and created inspired visions.

The young female assistant who had checked us all in rushed from the studio and endeavored to shout over the racket. I could see her mouth moving, but I couldn't catch the words. Just then, torrents of water from the overhead sprinklers baptized everyone. Coiffures were ruined, eyeliner streaked and splattered like a Jackson Pollock. A woman with the delicate refined beauty and nervous watchfulness of an Italian Greyhound actually began to cry. Not me. Once I'd used my designer bag to protect my sketchpad and modeling book, I laughed, all of my nerves transmuting into giddy merriment. This was the kind of unpredictable, uncontrollable moment I actually thought kicked ass—way more than the bated breath casting call monotony of most auditions. Life was grand.

Finally, realizing the futility of her attempts to be understood during the high decibel distraction and aquatic deluge, the assistant waved her hands aloft, indicating we were to follow her. We awkwardly snaked down the wide industrial stairs and spilled outside onto Christopher Street in Tribeca. A tall Asian stunner with bleached blonde hair and two nose rings held up a Chanel compact mirror for a curvy brunette with alabaster skin and full sleeves of tattoos doing her best to salvage her makeup. They seemed to know each other from past auditions, or because they frequented the same psychic, or both. I took a moment to make sure neither of my books had been damaged.

The gaggle of women around me suddenly stopped complaining about their impromptu shower and came to attention as if responding to a nonverbal command. I turned to see two men, dressed all in black, remarkably dry compared to the sodden lovelies, ambling out of the space. On the left was a face I'd visualized at least a million times in the past month, although I'd despaired of seeing him again: *Johnny!*

His colossal sunglasses made it difficult to interpret his expression, but then he abruptly froze, his head inclined in my direction. His companion, who also sported monster shades against the late afternoon glare, hustled over to me.

"Hawke," he said, grasping my hand, bowing over it with a dramatic flourish.

*Oh, brother. We've got a live one.*

"Scarlett," I said. "Is there some kind of emergency inside? Are we getting punked?"

"Feels like it, doesn't it?" Johnny said, chiming into our conversation with a proprietary air. "This genius lit up under the smoke detector and tripped the alarm."

"It's not that dramatic…as if I'd ignited an M-80 firecracker," Hawke protested. "It was just a ciggy, not my beloved ten-ounce bong or something fun like that."

The irritated expression on Johnny's face made me feel guilty about laughing, but I couldn't help myself.

"Hey, Hawke, could you go anywhere but here?" Johnny said. "Pretty please?"

"I'll give you pretty please," Hawke grumbled.

Moving toward me, Hawke resumed his overtly gallant demeanor. "Sorry about the downpour," he said. "This one thinks he's the king of the free world. If you get sick of listening to him run his motor mouth, find me inside."

With a mock salute, he sauntered off and began chatting up the nearest cluster of milling models, trying to interest them in a bit of a "runway tryout" right there on the sidewalk.

"Doesn't look as if Naomi has to worry about the competition from this one," Johnny joked, indicating Hawke's lame attempt at striking a pose.

"What *was* that?" I said, attempting to signal I'd been immune to Hawke's charms.

"My guitarist, Hawke," Johnny said. "He's got a problem with authority. Or maybe just a problem with me."

"You guys definitely emanate a sibling rivalry vibe."

"I possibly let it slip to him that I was looking forward to seeing you again today, and of course, that meant he had to try to sweep you off of your feet," Johnny said. "When we met at The Tunnel, you disappeared before I had the chance to…anything…"

"It's hard to make an elegant exit while incurring a lifetime ban," I said. "When my agent sent me to audition today, I had no idea it was for your band."

"We were actually celebrating our deal with MCA the night I met you," Johnny said. "I was about to invite you to join me for a celebratory drink when you vanished."

He was showing off a smidgen, but I admired his poise and the fact he had something to boast about. Since moving to New York four years ago, I'd met a showy parade of sycophants and wannabes.

Johnny indicated the leather-bound notebook in my hand. "What's this?"

"There's so much clockwatching at auditions, I always carry my sketchbook."

"Can I see?"

My stomach tensed as I handed it over. I was intimidated enough by the prospect of having him examine my rough drawings. Even more alarming: *what if he flipped back a few pages and saw my attempted renderings of his face, recreated from my vague memories of the night we'd first encountered each other?*

As if he'd been able to read my thoughts, he turned to a depiction of him.

"I beg your pardon, but my nose isn't *that* big," he said.

I moved my gaze back and forth between the page and his face, without meeting his eyes.

"No, it's not," I said, laughing through my nerves. "It was dark in the club."

"You're good, though." He flipped through the pages, actually seeming to examine each and every image, as if genuinely intrigued.

"Thanks," I said. "This 'in front of the camera stuff' isn't a forever job. Maybe I'll be an artist someday."

"You're an artist now."

I levitated above the cracked, filthy sidewalk. I could hardly remember my purpose for being there.

By the time we were herded back inside for the auditions to begin in earnest, Johnny and I had disclosed a shared passion for sushi, opera, Twizzlers (but only the original flavor), old school punk rock, gritty NY actors (Pacino, De Niro), the lovely Kate Bush, Sly and the

Family Stone, and Jeff Buckley, as well as rambling through Chinatown at all hours of the day and night, and Darjeeling tea. I suspected Johnny might have been making that last one up, but I couldn't help but be charmed he was trying so hard.

The next thing I knew it was my turn to strut my stuff. I found myself crammed into a tiny—a.k.a. NYC—studio, facing off against a camera; Johnny; Hawke; a sour-faced woman with big, mousy brown hair, who apparently was their manager, Deirdre; and a crew of men involved with the video's production. Florescent lights buzzed above us. Pacing in front of the table was a refined, chiseled looking Swedish man, donning the kind of glasses that look like modern art. He was the director, Sven, and theoretically, the one I had to persuade. Seeking to gain the upper hand, he couldn't resist taking a little dig at Johnny and Hawke for elbowing in on his creative process.

"Aht most music video auditions, ze band is nowhere to be found," he said. "They are off making ze music. But beauties are a mahgnet for—and sordidly so, it would seem—these ones here."

*Is Johnny blushing?* That should have relaxed me, but his embarrassment didn't preclude me from my own anxiety, which was bordering on a panic attack. Talk about awkward. We hadn't yet been on a first date, which would have been stressful enough; here I was *trying out* for the guy I thought I might like.

I pretended I had some idea what I was doing. Attempting to get in the mood, I did my best to ignore the way my damp hair clung to my head when the wind machines switched on, gusting over me. And then, a slithering guitar part filled up the room, and above it, the raw velvet of a voice that sounded like it was confessing a secret. I felt the vocals and the piano melody inside of me, could sense myself expressing all of the music's longing and power with my body. When the song ended the room suddenly grew silent and I was hurled back into reality. It took me a moment to exit the spell.

"Brilliant!" the director enthused. "You are ze music."

"Thank you," I said, shyly daring a look at Johnny, who was grinning right back.

"This is your car—ze one you will be presented on in ze video," the director said, pointing at the table in front of my artistic jury. "Jump up here and give us some love."

"Pardon me?" I said. Nobody had informed me about this part.

"Okay now...your breasts," he said. "Maybe show us some cleavage, love."

"Show me yours," I said.

Hawke, rife with glee, burst into a standing O, accompanied by a contagious golfer's clap that soon had the whole room emulating his actions. But the director, far from amused, was already calling in the next model.

"You Ahmericans are all Puritans," he said. "When I was growing up in Stockholm, my nanny, she never wear a top. I love it. This video meant to be free...rock 'n' roll."

"I'm afraid...I'm afraid...you've got the wrong girl," I said.

"I'm afraid we do," he echoed, obviously in a huff. "Where is the next lass? My time is limited here."

I didn't have to be told twice to leave. Doing my best to maintain my dignity, I crossed the room toward the door with my back stiff, head erect, gaze straight ahead.

"Come back and see us any time," Hawke said, grinning.

I was too embarrassed to reply or stop and talk to Johnny. I focused on getting out of the room. From the corner of my eye, I saw Johnny stand, as if he were going to follow me out, but the director was already talking with the dark haired bombshell I'd noticed earlier, the song was playing again from the top, and my chance was over. I consoled myself during the walk of shame past the other girls still waiting for their turns.

*I want to make it on my own as a model and artist. Not some dumbed-down video vixen.* These thoughts reverberated at maximum volume in my brain.

After the strut and fluff of an audition I always loved to get back home and wash off my makeup and remove whatever exoskeleton I'd been instructed to wear. I luxuriated in my happy place, lavender rose tea steeping in the real china teapot I'd treated myself to on a shoot in London; pastels and heavy linen sketch paper spread out on the table in front of me; Imani in the background, singing along to Nina Simone, L7, or whatever music inspired her at the moment.

Today, that sanctuary was even more essential to me than it had ever been before, since I'd decamped to New York City and embarked on my modeling adventure four years earlier. *Johnny. Johnny. Johnny.* He was all I could think about. The becoming furrow that creased his brow when he listened; our brief but inspiring conversation about the power of dreams and the joy of sushi; my fear that I'd been lucky enough to be reunited with him once, and it certainly wasn't going to happen again in this lifetime. But, tormented as I was, I knew I'd been right.

Imani, however, was a young romantic and unable to accept my actions.

"Why didn't you at least give him your number?"

"I was borderline humiliated," I said. "Besides, he didn't even bother to ask for it."

"I know..." She crossed into my eyesight, gripping the lapels of her bathrobe. "You could have snuck back onto the video set from the bathroom and then made a grand entrance and flashed him, revealing your number, written on your chest in red lipstick."

Imani demonstrated what she had in mind, ripping open her robe with a dramatic flourish, revealing a gently worn Joan Jett T-shirt beneath.

"The whole point was to *not* show him my girls." But I couldn't help but get carried away by her fit of hysterics. Leave it to her to find the humor in the whole ridiculousness.

Imani headed for the CD player. "Is it Schoenberg time?"

"Does it make you crazy that I can only draw to one composer?"

"No, I like to see you inspired. It's not like you're having a polka period or something."

I was well into one of my new charcoal drawings, happily smudged up to my elbows, when the phone rang. It was Sabina from my agent's office, calling with news so electrifying that I threw on my motorcycle boots and hopped onto the subway immediately, with only half an hour to spare before she closed up the office for the day. When I appeared at her front reception desk, it was just as she had reported over the phone: a beautiful art deco vase of vivid wildflowers, attached to which was an envelope containing a gold vintage YSL necklace. But the best part was the handwritten card.

Sorry about the audition. Please let me make it up to you with dinner. Call me. Call me. Any time. —Johnny

Roses. Yves. Blondie.

Here was a man who knew the path to my heart; not only had he sent me flowers, but he'd also woven lyrics by one of my favorite bands into his love note.

Normally Sabina intimidated me, what with her perfectly poreless skin and cybernetic ability to remain cool and collected, even with six telephone lines discharging and the room arctic with impatient ice queens. But I was too excited to be nervous around her.

"Oh Sabina, isn't it romantic?" I glowed. "What should I say when I call?"

"Merci," she said, a hint of a smile creeping onto her normally placid face.

"Yes, of course, thank you is the best place to start! Oh, I'm so anxious. Can I please use your phone? I know this might sound strange, but I'd feel better if you're here with me."

By the time I dialed, Sabina was crouched beside me in anticipation, our cheeks flushed like schoolgirls.

✴✴✴

I'D NEVER BEEN TO Harlem before—not that I was about to admit it—and I hadn't counted on just how long it would take me to reach the restaurant on the subway. Applying much the same concentration required on the runway, I navigated my Robert Clergerie gray suede boots through the rutted sidewalk, mortified to find myself nearly an hour late for my date. When I rounded the corner, Johnny was huddled against the late winter chill, gazing the other way up the street, which allowed me to slow my pace to a saunter.

"Apologies," I said as he suavely leaned in and kissed my cheek.

"Time is relative," Johnny said.

Just then, Hawke popped outside with a tumbler of ice and whiskey and placed it in Johnny's hand.

*Could this guy so much as breathe without his entourage?*

"Oh," I said, trying to hide my distress at finding myself on a double date.

"The ever-radiant Scarlett," Hawke slurred, already soused.

"When the gang found out I invited you to Parkers, everyone just had to join the fun," Johnny said. "Oh, and they all want to meet you, of course."

"Of course," Deirdre sneered, as she snaked her head into our conversation.

My chagrin at being chaperoned by the entire band—and management—was quickly dispelled by the group's kinetic verve. The restaurant's owner, Jerome, and his wife, Loretta, joined us at a large overflowing table. I wanted to inhale every fragrance, sample every flavor, and get in on every inside joke. This was living!

"You still working for the man?" Jerome teased Johnny.

"Rock 'n' roll is the antithesis of the man," Johnny said, taking the bait even though he clearly should have known better by now.

"Anyone who tries to put a contract on your music, that's the man," Jerome said. "You ever want to really sing, you come up here. I've heard you school us in the doctrine of Aretha. Few men got the soul to sing the female blues. That's deep."

Johnny ducked his head, the charming blush I'd come to expect spreading across his cheeks. I caught him looking over at me to see if I'd noticed.

"Unfuckingbelievable…I got to sing on the stage where all the greats played. Billie, Dizzy, Charlie," Johnny demurred. "I think their spirits were speaking through me."

"You got that thing, that's for sure," Jerome said.

I'd stuck to sparkling water all night, wanting to keep my wits about me. But Deirdre now appeared at arm's length, holding a glowing pink blended drink.

"We're celebrating," she said as she set it down. "I got you a treat."

"Thank you," I said, unable to resist the influence of Deirdre's gravitational pull, as I expanded with relief that maybe she didn't hate me after all. "What is it?"

"It's like a daiquiri," she said. "Just fruit…mostly."

"Lovely, thanks," I said, taking a big sip, getting caught up in the night's wonder.

To the left of disparaging Deirdre was her husband, Clint, who she treated like an incompetent employee. On her other side was Shiv, and his absolutely fabulous haute hippie wife, Persephone, who glinted like a 1947 Collector's Tiffany lamp, her platinum hair and fire engine lips topping an elaborate, intricately colored plaid Christian Lacroix ensemble.

Before I'd sipped more than half my drink, Deirdre materialized beside me with another. When Johnny went to feed me a little piece of chocolate in a gold wrapper, I broke myself off a piece.

"Magic mushrooms," he said, after I'd already swallowed and it was too late to tell him I'd never before indulged. I certainly wasn't going to embarrass myself by asking him what to expect. My cheeks flushed. The room's colors swam, or maybe that was just my paranoia about the alternate reality I was about to enter.

"I'm all for the latest and greatest," Shiv said. "And my dear one does appear as fresh as the day we met, so her interventions must be working. But next thing I know, she wants me to get fucking stung by bees. How can that be healthy?"

"Bee venom, darling," she said. "I promise you it will soon be all the rage."

After a completely innocent blink of my eyes, the mural's jazz musicians, seated with their brass instruments extended, were suddenly in motion. The thrust and jive of their gestures corresponded with the music in the room. The seat beneath me felt as if it were breathing. I was gratefully certain that Johnny had read my mind when he laced his fingers through mine: I had a life raft. Still my head was so heavy, my neck so flimsy, I could barely hold it aloft.

"You all right, doll?" Persephone asked me, her long, giraffe-like lashes looming surreally into focus, as if she were a character in a Fellini film.

"Air, I need air," I pleaded.

"I sympathize," Johnny said. "When this lot gets going, it's enough to squeeze the breath from you. Let me take you outside."

"Once you've collected yourself, we're off to the Roseland to see Slayer," Persephone said, standing on the banquet to demonstrate her headbanging technique.

"I don't know if Scarlett has much concert going energy in her tonight," Deirdre said.

I apologized to the group. "This is absolutely not my usual modus operandi."

"I'll call you a car," Clint said, his voice kind, as he nodded to the waiter to guide him to where he could use the restaurant's house phone as Johnny steered me toward the door.

The late-night February air slapped me awake, and I breathed deeply, grasping for my composure. I turned to Johnny, an apology on my lips. Before I could speak, his mouth met mine. Ah, the sweetness of a perfect first kiss.

A black town car pulled up. Desperate to exit before I embarrassed myself further, I quickly opened the door and slid inside, my body humming with pleasure.

As Johnny settled back into the booth, his own system agog with the recent kiss he'd relished, the restaurant house phone was brought over to their table. Clint took the call and then reported what he'd just heard to the group.

"It's the town car company, calling to apologize for the fact that their driver isn't here yet," he said, a troubled look on his face. "Apparently, the rear tire went flat—he's got it repaired now, and he'll be here any minute. But where's Scarlett?"

They all turned toward the front entrance at once, but the street wasn't visible from where they were seated. Johnny darted outside, whipping around in both directions. The gust of wind that welcomed him was blowing up and down an empty street. Scarlett was gone.

# FRIENDS, FORTUNE, + FRACAS

I AWOKE UNDERWATER. CHURNING waves choked my mouth and pounded my head, rhythmically, with force. Sunlight cut through the surf, teased my eyes open. I wasn't submerged after all. I was asleep in the loft of my small one-bedroom. I sat up carefully in the truncated space. My tongue was fuzzy and thick, my head full of sand.

"Immi," I called out uncertainly, using my pet name for Imani.

There was no answer. If Imani was already at her lunch shift as a waitress, I must have slept *late*. Distorted fragments from the previous night arose in my mind: Johnny's handsome lean face and tentative smile. Hawke's braying laugh. Persephone's sparkly magic. The earthy taste of collard greens. The sultry howl of jazz saxophone. The bliss of discovering the person you fancy has feelings for you in return.

I touched my lips uncertainly.

*Did Johnny really kiss me goodnight?* He did, and it had been lovely. But the moments after that were blurry.

*How did I get home?* Shaking off my fog, I deduced the noise from my dream was the same sound I'd been hearing in real life, an insistent knock at my door. So this was a hangover. I wasn't in the habit of drinking much, and if the corollary was this nauseous, out-of-body experience, I didn't think I'd take it up as a regular pastime.

I opened the door a crack and peered over the security chain, confused by the mirage on the other side: Johnny. I opened the door wide to welcome him.

"Jesus, you had us so worried," Johnny said, almost entirely out of breath. "We literally thought you were kidnapped! We called nine-one-one, called your agent. I would never have forgiven myself if you were hurt."

I rubbed the sleep out of my eyes and wondered at this improbable scene unfolding in the dim light of my building's stairwell.

"Scarlett, I'm trying to confess to liking you!" he said, laughing at my confused expression as he pulled me into the biggest hug.

I was enveloped in the aroma of his well-worn seventies leather motorcycle jacket, his citrusy smoothed hair, and the sensual, natural smell of vetiver oil layered with just the right amount of sweat. His grip was strong and self-assured, and I fit perfectly into the space between his arms.

I was so purely happy that I overcame my discomfort at greeting Mr. Romeo with my morning breath/bad hair day combo, and I started laughing, too. "What are you doing here?"

"Being a first-class detective if I might say so myself," he said. "You've no idea how hard it is to find a beautiful girl who vanishes in the middle of a Harlem night."

"But how did you do it, Johnny...?" I asked. "My agent would never give out my info."

"You're in the book," he said, proudly. "Under your given surname."

*Oh no...how did he know my real last name was Xanthopoulous?*

"I told you *that*?"

He smiled at that. "Loads happened last night," he said. "Including the unveiling of the true identity of up-and-coming international fashion model, Scarlett X."

"Good thing you're a handsome lad, and not a stalker." Now that the manic euphoria of our reunion had ebbed, we both hesitated. I dared a self-conscious look at my apartment from the corner of my eye—art supplies over every surface, along with an avalanche of clothes I'd tried on and discarded the night before—and then decided to just go for it anyway. "Would you like to come in?"

We stood close together in my small rental, smiling bashfully, both seemingly ultra-aware of ourselves, without alcohol, or music, or band mates to obscure our insecurities.

"Have you ever had cinnamon pull apart bread?" I asked, breaking the spell. "It's a recipe my grandma used to make for me, and it's like a warm, sugary heaven."

"That sounds nice."

"She was the best," I said. "I used to drive her sparkly gold, '68 El Camino, until, well, someone crashed into me and totaled it. But that was a different life. You're going to love this dish—trust me."

His face took on its now-familiar bashful glow. "I do," he said.

For once the apartment's diminutive size was a plus. I nearly swooned as Johnny serenaded me with ballads by Johnny Thunders and Robert Johnson. I tried to hold it together well enough to brew coffee in my little stovetop espresso maker and prepare our repast. As he played, Johnny asked me questions about the many exotic destinations my modeling career had taken me. I quizzed him back on the Tulsa sound and he was only too happy to deliver a dissertation on the finer points, namely, the distinction between Elvin Bishop and J. J. Cale, as well as the unmitigated genius of Leon Russell, from whom Elton John had learned *everything*.

And so the afternoon passed happily until Imani returned from her shift at the restaurant and ruptured the enchantment in which we had been cocooned. As I made the introductions, I tried to deflect Imani's shocked, tell-me-everything expression. Johnny suddenly bolted onto his feet and handed Imani her guitar.

"Does anyone know…what time it is?" he asked.

"Five," Imani said.

"Oh no," Johnny exclaimed. "I need to get uptown, *now!*"

"You just got here," I couldn't help but say.

"Come with me!" he said. "Everyone will be so glad you're okay."

"Really? Everyone? I feel like they might think…I'm overstepping a little…?"

"You're practically a member of the band," Johnny said.

✱✱✱

HOWEVER, IT QUICKLY BECAME apparent, Johnny's stellar opinion of Scarlett was not shared by all in the band's entourage. They'd already gathered at the Gramercy Park Hotel for the industry showcase Deirdre had put together, featuring important HIGs. The major players included two label reps, an agent from CAA, and a programming director named Gavin from the biggest radio station on the eastern seaboard—who had insisted the event occur at this exclusive property, owned by his brother. The session had been planned for weeks, and Johnny worked his musicians hard, running them through rehearsal after rehearsal of the new material. He remained rattled by how much push back the suits had given him and the band when he'd tried to select the single of his choice during their meeting at the studio. Not to mention the overboard label loyalty Deirdre had displayed during that "dust up." And so, Johnny had furiously written and rewritten the set list during his cab ride uptown with Scarlett (even though they really only had six viable, recently penned songs at the moment). His anxiety did not in any way diminish when they walked into the lounge and Deirdre glared at them.

"Don't Yoko our meeting, you…*model*," she sneered, somehow making the word "model" derogatory.

Scarlett faltered backward as if she'd been struck, her shoulders slouched and her eyes watery. Johnny searched for the perfect means of comforting her without alienating Deirdre, who had thoroughly convinced him that she was the key to his stratospheric rock stardom, and that without her, he and his fellow Westies would be pumping gas back in Tulsa. Before he could devise a solution, Jet strolled by, balancing several guitar cases on Hawke's wheeled amp, which he was pushing in front of him as the band grumpily loaded its gear through the side door and onto the stage.

Onstage, Bone set up and tuned his drum kit.

"Why isn't Hawke loading in his own stuff?" Johnny asked, instantly anxious, as he enquired after their always maddening guitarist, whose drugging had recently worsened, and was nowhere in sight. Johnny realized, instead of romancing Scarlett, he should have insisted on escorting Hawke to the gig.

"He's a no-show," Shiv said. "I might kill 'em if he has the bollocks to turn up."

"Maybe he's late," Jet offered. "He's not great with time management."

Shiv sighed. "Now there's a euphemism for what's ailing Hawke."

"If he's not here by sound check, we'll let Deirdre know," Johnny said.

Shiv shrugged and made his way for the rest of the gear. "Aye, you alert the Dragon Woman, not me."

Johnny helped the others get primed. Every time he caught sight of the slightest motion out of the corner of his eye, he felt the lift of hope, as he convinced himself it was Hawke, rushing in with an apology—or at least just hurrying in.

Finally, there was no avoiding it any longer. He needed to tell Deirdre.

"Miss D, could we have a word with you please?" Johnny said into the mic, his voice echoing out into the empty bar.

Deidre approached the nervous huddle, not taking her eyes off her embossed crocodile agenda organizer, crossing items off her to-do list. Clint, as always, was a step behind her, as if her shadow. She peered up anxiously, urging them to get on with it already.

"Hawke isn't here," Johnny said.

"Where the F is he?" she hissed.

"We're not sure of his location. No one has seen him since practice last night. There's no answer at his apartment."

"Who's his, oh hell, what's the word—his GOM?" Deidre fumed. "You know...his girlfriend of the month, his latest little tart? C'mon—"

"Violet?" Johnny asked uncertainly.

"Gina?" Shiv offered up, with no greater certitude.

A petite stunner in platform boots and blood-toned lipstick stepped forward timidly from where she'd been smoking at one of the tables in the front row.

"Gianna," she said, introducing herself without much more conviction than the guys had expressed when trying to remember her name.

"Right," Deirdre said. "Where is Hawke?"

"He left my apartment a few hours ago?" Gianna said, not so much as a statement and even less so as a question. "And he said to meet him here?"

"Well, spit it out, where did he get off to?" Deirdre snapped.

Gianna crossed her slender arms across her chest and bit her lip.

"It's okay," Johnny said, gently. "We know what he went to do. You're not revealing any secrets. We really need to know where he is. We need him to play."

"He only let me go with him once," she said. "And he made me wait in the cab. It was on Avenue B. No...C...?"

"You have forty-five minutes until HIGs arrive. Find him," Deirdre said, turning her wrath on Gianna. "Or else I will personally make sure your mommy and daddy know you were once again playing hooky and weren't in school today."

✳✳✳

Which is how Johnny discovered himself, less than an hour before one of the most crucial gigs of his life, stalking the blocks north of Houston with a small group. They paused outside each derelict tenement and half-fixed up squat while Gianna struggled to remember if it was *the* rundown structure she had once seen Hawke enter in order to score drugs. Even though the winter evening was windy and cold, they'd abandoned their taxi blocks ago, needing to be on the street for her to assess each edifice sufficiently. They struggled to concentrate on the landscape of empty, narrow, trash-clogged lots, constantly glancing down to avoid squishy piles of rotten garbage and the twitchy rats such refuse attracted.

Johnny tugged at Scarlett's arm, just barely registering the glint of a discarded needle before her foot could land. When her eyes met his, they were wide with fear.

*A quest through the city's worst neighborhood, in search of the dealer who's supplying our errant guitarist is DEFINITELY not on the list of most romantic second dates.* Johnny squeezed Scarlett's hand and pulled her closer.

"Did you know, number four St. Mark's Place, which we just passed, and which now houses Trash & Vaudeville, was once the residence of James Fenimore Cooper?" she offered up. "You might remember him as the author of *The Last of the Mohicans.* The location was also once occupied by Alexander Hamilton."

"Fascinating, luv," Shiv said.

Johnny smiled at Scarlett. He was digging her intellectually precocious means of lightening the drama. Maybe she wasn't going to give up on him after all.

"Gianna, can you remember anything about the street on which Hawke frequents his supplier?" Shiv asked.

"I'm sorry," Gianna said, her voice wobbly, as if she might cry.

"No one's mad at you," Johnny said. "It's just that the clock is ticking, and it would be helpful to narrow our search even the tiniest bit."

"There was graffiti on the outside," she said.

"Could you be more specific, please? That doesn't really narrow it down," Johnny said, gesturing at the facades along this block, all of them choked with tags and other assorted adornments.

"It said 'Rest in Peace,'" she continued, twirling the Greek evil eye charm on her necklace. "I remember because I worried it was a bad omen—I'm—I'm superstitious like that. I pointed it out to Hawke when he got back in the cab. But he thought it was funny because right below, it said 'Bimbo.'"

No one laughed.

"I guess you had to be there," Gianna said.

"Unbelievable," Scarlett chimed in.

"What's that, babe?" Johnny asked.

"I was sent on a go-see a few months ago," she said. "It was on Bowery and Second, but I got turned around coming off the subway. I ended up lost on Avenue B, and I saw that inscription. I figured Bimbo was a nickname, and I wondered who it was. I'd made up this whole story in mind, about how he was an artist, and…"

Scarlett's voice trailed off, as she realized everyone in the group was staring.

"That's just a few blocks south of here, then," Johnny said. "You're a lifesaver."

Johnny and Scarlett exchanged an affectionate glance as they passed a building so dilapidated it resembled a pile of bricks more than anything else. On the sidewalk and ebbing into the street was a swarm of two-dozen parked motorcycles—chrome shining in the faint light. A crew of muscly bikers hulked nearby, bare arms and chests beneath their dark denim and Harley leather vests, impervious to the frosty air. Their breath was visible as they smoked on the cracked steps, passing a bottle back and forth. Someone told a joke, laughter erupted, and a fierce biker with face tattoos stepped back, running directly into the path of the little band of explorers.

"Fuck off," the Hell's Angel spit as he collided with Johnny.

Johnny hesitated.

"You have to play guitar in twenty minutes," Shiv whispered close to his ear. "No punching."

The throng of bikers moved down the stairs toward them, en masse.

"What we've got here, fellows, is a classic misunderstanding," Johnny said.

"We understand you perfectly," the head biker huffed, cracking his massive ass knuckles. "Now apologize." *Ggggrrrr.* A heavyset man behind the leader actually growled like a pissed off pit bull poised to take care of its prey.

"We were simply passing through…" Johnny began to explain.

In a blur of flapping leather and flying flesh, the bikers started swinging. With his years playing in dive bars, Johnny had evaded his fair share of beat downs, and his response was a perfectly choreographed step backward. Which left another face in the direct path of the blow that had been meant for him—Scarlett's. The smacking sound of fist hitting bone made Johnny physically ill as the punch threw Scarlett back and into his arms. At least he'd managed to keep her from falling all the way down and hitting her head on the filthy cracked pavement.

"All right, that's gone far enough," Shiv said, his voice steely. He was normally as mild mannered as a pup, but it seemed clear that at this moment it would be a mistake to underestimate him.

Just then, wouldn't you know it, a compact black man in a red beret—one of the neighborhood's anti-crime volunteers, the Guardian Angels—rolled up on the scene.

"Since 1979, we've been fightin' the crime," he play-rapped. "I'm just here tonight to help y'all out."

As tough as the bikers appeared to be, they seemed genuinely shocked to have hit a young woman, inadvertent though it had been. And they had an unspoken agreement not to tussle with the blessed NYC Guardian Angels, unless, well, it absolutely couldn't be helped. The bikers dispersed as quickly as their cigarette smoke, disappearing into their headquarters, slamming a mammoth metal door closed behind them with a whump, and sliding a thick bar across it from the inside.

"Thank you for your gallantry," Shiv said to their Good Samaritan rescuer, shaking the man's hand before he vanished off into the night to assist others.

"Oh, Scarlett, please forgive me," Johnny said. "That wasn't supposed to happen. Obviously."

Scarlett had turned away from him and was shaking fiercely, her hand covering the place where she'd been hit, the iris of her good eye pinned with shock.

"Let me see, honey," Johnny said.

"No, I don't want to know how bad it is," she said. "I have a booking for tomorrow. My agent is going to murder me."

"We'll ice it as soon as we get back to the Gramercy," Johnny said.

She nodded, but her expression was vague, as if she hadn't heard him.

"And we'll get you a nice spot of brandy," Shiv said. "That'll calm your nerves."

The group had finally washed up at the steps of an imposing building next to a brightly colored font that, lo and behold, read: "Rest in Peace," and below it: "Bimbo." They lingered as if outside the most exclusive club in the city.

"Shiv, you stay outside with the ladies," Johnny said. "We have exactly ten minutes to grab Hawke, somehow convince a taxi to stop for us on this godforsaken no-man's-land of a street, and haul ass twenty blocks to our gig."

Johnny kissed Scarlett's cheek and dashed inside before he had time to worry too much about what he might discover across the threshold. The hallway was pitch black, and he had the unpleasant sensation of wading through mysterious detritus. Finally, he thought to flick his lighter, and in the faint illumination, he saw that the structure's insulation had been pulled out of the walls and cluttered the floor. He kicked his way through the mess and up the first flight of stairs. Although there was barely any internal framing left, all of the doors they encountered were closed. It was like some kind of a terrible, surreal haunted house. Behind each one, Johnny was able, with the help of his lighter, to just barely make out a few slumped figures that were as waxy and unmoving as cadavers. Finally, in the third room, his dim light illuminated a distant mess of inky hair that crowned Hawke's head. He strode into the room, picked up his guitarist, and draped his inert form over his shoulder.

"Hey, man, come back, that dirt bag owes me forty bucks," a faint voice cried out in protest as Johnny dragged Hawke away, his boots scuffing the floor behind him.

Johnny's blood was spiked with adrenaline, and his breath was coming in uneven gusts, when they emerged onto the street and he saw that, for once in this bloody brutal day, a miracle had been visited upon them. Scarlett was standing on the sidewalk, her sweet face turned imploringly toward a taxicab that was drawing to a stop right before them. And Johnny found himself, along with their entire group, clambering into the back and front seats with their errant guitarist, safe and sound.

Well, not to overstate the phenomenon. As soon as they'd settled in, Hawke nodded out again. Johnny was forced to quickly deduce that— even after their Herculean efforts, the best option was for Gianna to take Hawke home and get him into bed. They were going to have to salvage their show for the HIGs without him.

*** 

DEIRDRE WAS SO AGGRAVATED when they finally hustled back into the hotel's lounge that her face resembled a Halloween mask of a witch.

"You're ten minutes late," she said. "And where in God's name is Hawke?"

Johnny blew past her, not stopping until he'd managed to convince the stuffy bartender to give him a clean bar towel full of ice. He delivered first aid for Scarlett's black eye with as much gallantry as possible under the circumstances. And then, in a single fleet motion, he spun around and joined the uneasy gathering of HIG's, who had circled the table of hors d'oeuvres, each holding a drink in his hand. Deirdre gave Johnny a warning look to not let the band's drama leak out, and then started on introductions.

"Ah, look, the slackers have arrived," quipped a well-coifed man with a maroon checkerboard tie that was the exact same color as his pressed dress shirt.

"This is my brother, Ethan, the hotelier, who was benevolent enough to host our festivities at this venue," said Gavin, the head honcho from the radio station. "I'm looking forward to hearing some of those quality '*Top 40 hits.*'"

"Then you came to the right place," the band's A&R rep quickly replied.

"Thanks so much for being here today," Johnny said, working the room as if it were a stage. "I think you'll agree we've blended elements of our streetwise, working-class licks with some glorious rhythm guitar, and precocious melodic grooves, eh."

"Can I get you a drink, or perhaps some foie gras, or hors d'oeuvres, while we settle in?" Deirdre said, indicating the ample buffet she'd requested the hotel provide.

Johnny glanced over his shoulder in search of Scarlett as he was swept away toward the stage with the rest of his band. She had tucked herself into a safe corner with a Cherry Coke, and her improvised ice pack, and she declined to make eye contact with him. His heart cracked with shame. *What if she'd really been hurt? Why was he such a moron?*

He'd have to do something truly remarkable to make restitution. But first, total sonic domination of the powers that be.

The band quickly tuned, warmed up, and was primed for show time. There was just one hitch. A *major* glitch. Even after their harrowing adventure, an orphaned guitar loomed in its stand on the right hand side of the stage in the hotel's lounge. Deirdre joined them for a preperformance huddle.

"We found Hawke, but he was in no condition to play," Johnny explained.

"We'll deal with him later," she said. "Johnny, pick a track you can rework into a stripped-down version. No matter what, don't let them know anything is amiss. If they smell weakness, they'll drop you in a heartbeat."

Johnny gave her a grateful nod as the others fell into place, no instructions necessary to implement their plan. Now they just had to hope their delivery was seamless, too. As if they were one mind, the band simplified their in-the-works album's likeliest candidate, "Late Night in the City." For a moment, the room's energy teetered uncertainly, and then, one by one, the HIG's nodded their heads along vigorously. Yet another disaster averted…just barely.

The band finished their second song and as Johnny steadied his nerves with a quick shot of Jack from their communal bottle, he noticed an animated conversation in the lounge. His heart stuttered. Deirdre crossed the room back to the front of the stage, and he leaned down to hear her instructions.

"These gents have a dinner meeting in fifteen," she said. "They want to hear the single. Now."

Johnny surveyed the others. Jet, their mostly silent yet dependable pinch hitter, flashed Johnny a kamikaze smile and laid down the pogoing bass line that led into their first single, "Easy Come, Easy Go."

Grinning like a lottery winner, Johnny winked at Jet, and then, he opened his throat and sang, as Shiv delivered his guitar part with dynamism, and Bone drummed his heart out. Truth be told, it wasn't their usual genius, stellar performance, but it was raw and real and did the trick. After they were done, they were summoned to meet the others at the bar for a pronouncement. Johnny felt nervous at what it might be, but at least the label reps had remained unaware of the evening's many mishaps.

"Not too shabby," said the big chief. "Now you just gotta crank it up to eleven. I'll have Deirdre deliver the vital news to you. We'll see you on the other side."

That figured. Just when Johnny dared experience relief that *maybe* they'd barely pulled it off, and feel proud of the songs he'd written with The Westies, the universe was doing the equivalent of scratching the needle across the record.

"What's that all about?" he asked Deirdre as the HIG's moved away in one big herd. "They hate the single, right?"

"The label has offered us a very exciting opportunity," Deirdre said. "Actually, it seems…they'd like you to mix the album in Los Angeles. So you can be closer to…um…headquarters…to benefit from their input, and then launch the debut from there. I've spoken with our booking agent and they've got a few stellar UK shows in the works for you, and then we'll all fly directly from England to LA."

"I think we're close enough to the mother ship and its participation where we are right now, thank you very much," Johnny said, then quickly corrected course, as he realized he should at least play nice with the label. "I mean, but that could be cool."

"LA, baby, here we come," Shiv said. "Think of the brilliant ballads we could write in the City of Angels…à la Jim Morrison and Robby Krieger, or Lindsey Buckingham and Stevie Nicks. We will explore Laurel Canyon and immerse ourselves on the Sunset Strip as a real band of bards."

"Does sound pretty sweet," Jet said.

"Aye, it's paradise," Shiv continued. "Persephone and I always shack up at the Chateau Marmont when we visit. You'll looooove it, J-Bird."

Johnny had been so caught up in the whirlwind of the band's unfolding drama, he'd completely lost track of Scarlett. He looked up to see her, clearly bored, but still breath-shatteringly beautiful, huddled alone at the room's end. When he went over to check on her, she offered him an empathetic, heartfelt smile.

"I'm sorry that took so long," he said. "But it meant a lot to me that you were here, and you heard our songs."

"They're perfect," she said. "And now…I should really go."

"No, no, no, let me take you to dinner," he said. "It's the least I can do."

Immediately, Deirdre inserted herself into their shared moment.

"We have a very important band meeting tonight," she said. "No GOM's allowed."

"Like Gianna?" Scarlett queried. "What does 'GOM' even mean?"

"Girlfriend of the Month," Deirdre sneered.

Scarlett started, "Oh, I'm not his—"

"There's nothing momentary about Scarlett," Johnny cut in. But there was no point in trying to do battle with their manager, especially with so much on the line. Reluctantly, he escorted Scarlett to the front door and put her in a cab. Meanwhile, he made a mental note to send her a cheeky poem (naughty yet romantic, and totally from the heart). Plus, the perfect token of his affection to show his gratitude—and that he was supremely cognizant of her cool support and interest. Now, if he could only deduce what that one-in-a-million gift might be.

He crossed back through the lobby of the Gramercy Park Hotel. It was an undeniably gorgeous locale, but one where he and his band mates had been talked down to by the kind of clueless Upper East Side snobs who thought first, and possibly only, about their bank balances. Johnny surveyed the ceiling and was visited by a stroke of inspiration. He just had to implement a way to pull it off. And that's how, forty-five minutes later, he and Shiv were once again in the lobby, outfitted in the tan, pressed uniforms of the hotel's maintenance crew, wielding a pilfered ladder. All of which they'd temporarily borrowed from a few sympathetic hotel employees in exchange for several primo joints and the opportunity to aid in the progression of a grand romance.

Shiv and Johnny chortled like schoolboys, as Shiv held the ladder's legs, while Johnny ascended to the room's pièce de résistance—a gorgeous, shimmering, 1920s chandelier adorned with a half-ton of high-grade fixtures and decorative brass accents, the sparkle of which had reminded him of the particular twinkle in Scarlett's eyes. Whistling while pretending to repair the light fixture, Johnny extricated a gorgeous, icicle-shaped crystal teardrop and slid it into his pocket, as Shiv kept watch down below. Around them, employees and guests flitted to and fro without taking any notice of their prank.

And then, at the edge of his hearing, Johnny became aware of an angry fracas.

"Excuse me...Excuse me...You...I know *you*...and you're no hotel employee," a man shouted.

"Incoming," Shiv warned, but he stayed put, not the kind of man who would leave his friend behind in order to save his own skin.

Johnny inspected the room from his elevated perch and saw the hotel's owner bearing down on them from the registration area. In a New York second, he was down the ladder and out the front door with Shiv close behind him, both stripping their costumes as they ran. And so they found themselves falling out into the street, howling and laughing conspiratorially, dressed in nothing but the white Hanes ribbed tank tops and boxer shorts they'd been wearing under their disguises. They managed to hustle across the busy intersection and reach safety on the other side just before the light changed. A massive wave of traffic bore down the street, dividing their pursuers from them.

They didn't stop running until a few blocks later, when they finally paused to catch their breath and light a celebratory smoke, which Shiv had hidden in his boot. Johnny took the cig Shiv extended to him. He was infinitely grateful that, a few months back, when the leader of Shiv's more established, successful band had joined an obscure goat cult, leaving Shiv out of a regular gig, Johnny had convinced him to throw in his lot with The Westies. Good thing, too, as they were clearly on their way up—as long as they managed to stay out of jail long enough to ascend to the shimmering heights of fame.

# HEART OF GLASS

I GLARED AT THE tall ladder that loomed above me, separated me from my heart's desire.

Johnny's face peered down over the edge of his loft, smiling with reassurance.

"Don't worry," he said, offering me his strong hand, adorned with a black phoenix rising tat on the triangle of flesh between his thumb and index finger, which I guessed was emblematic of his proud eastern Shawnee Tribe heritage. "Honestly, I climb it every night, even when I'm completely hammered. And I've never fallen. I mean, well…there was that one time…but that's because Hawke had it out for me."

"Don't go telling tales of out of school," Hawke growled from the leather couch behind me, where he was idly plucking on his Gibson Les Paul six string and swigging an ice-cold bottle of beer.

Johnny glared at his errant guitar player.

"I thought you were going out to the bar with the guys," Johnny said.

"Cool it," Hawke said. "Jet's doing his Protocol 50 doorway-pull-ups thing. Then we'll bail."

*No one tells you that dating a musician really means dating his whole band, I guess.*

The guys rented one whole floor of an old, rundown prewar building on the Lower East Side. Their "living area" was cavernous and dim, with a makeshift skate ramp with a drum kit set up at its center and a worn mandala psychedelic medallion tapestry tacked to one side, forming an improvised room. A faded stack of orange traffic cones had washed up in the corner, next to what looked like an orphaned old school Marilyn Monroe blowup doll with a forties vibe. Let's just say empty green Rolling Rock beer bottles lurked beneath the furniture as prevalent as dust bunnies.

I steeled my nerves and clutched the sides of the stepladder Johnny and his friends had lifted from a nearby construction sight and set up below Johnny's loft. At the pinnacle, a foot-wide gap loomed between the top and the platform where Johnny lay on his stomach, providing me with a steadying arm as I climbed. I awkwardly scrambled up next to him, my fear of dropping to the cement below mixing with the thrill of being near him.

When I'd relaxed enough to actually take in my surroundings, I was pleasantly surprised to find that Johnny's little section of their shared quarters was orderly, well-styled, and cozy. His bed was neatly made up, and an impressively cool, old-fashioned, hand-sewn quilt made entirely of silk ties, was folded at its foot. He'd displayed a few white candles at various staggered heights, nestled in recycled liquor bottles and brass filigree candleholders on an upended wine box. Next to them was an open bottle of Châteauneuf-du-Pape and two glasses. Well-thumbed coverless hardbound books lined one wall next to a stack of equally well-loved records. A seventies portable turntable played Sly and the Family Stone's "Thank You." Although the high, narrow perch was chilly this winter evening, I could have happily stayed there with Johnny forever, while the city rushed and pushed outside. But I was still burning with shame at the memory of how low Deirdre had made me feel, and how inadequately Johnny had defended me. My heart wanted to gallop toward the object of my affection, but my mind sang out, "R-E-S-P-E-C-T."

Johnny fussed around nervously, turning the volume of the music up and then down and then up again, and pouring us each a glass of red wine. He handed me one of his thrift store goblets, as well as a small bundle wrapped in a page torn from the *Village Voice*, folded over precisely, and somehow fashioned together with guitar string and two safety pins.

"Cool—what's this?" I asked, genuinely surprised, as I turned the package over in my hands.

"I felt bad about the last time we were together…Deirdre and some of those wretched yuppie souls were such a nightmare…and there was that one crazy cat from the Angels…and well…I'm sorry. So I got you this."

I bowed my head, letting the waves of my hair blanket my face while I composed myself. Resisting his charm was going to be harder than I'd anticipated, especially because I wanted nothing more than to be one of those fools who rushed in. Slowly, I began to unwrap the crisp paper. Johnny's well-worn black bandana, which he often tied around his neck, revealed itself. A faint whiff of his Vetiver cologne wafted up from the fabric. On the inside, within a solid gold wrapper from a fancy pack of smokes, in fine black Sharpie ink, was written:

"Truth revealed is transparent, my dear,

My love shines brighter than crystal is clear."

Swoon. This guy is an old school romantic.

Tucked inside the note was a small idyllic dose of magic—a beautifully etched, icicle-shaped crystal that caught the flickering candle flames and seemed to light up from within, strung on one of Johnny's own silver chains, which I'd never seen him without—until now.

"It looks beautiful on you," he said, as he gazed deep into my eyes while sliding it over my head. "Do you like it? Shiv helped me to kind of, um, borrow a ladder. And then, I nicked it off the chandelier in the lobby of the fancy hotel where the label dudes were staying…"

"Thank you," I said. "I love it. Truly."

"Really?" he asked, his cheeks taking on their familiar faint crimson hue. "I finally got something right! I'm so glad, Mitchell."

"Mitchell, who?" I asked, stifling a laugh.

"Margaret Mitchell…who wrote *Gone with the Wind*," he said. "…It's stupid…but…you always remind me of Scarlett O'Hara, and so I thought that'd be a suitable nickname for you…hope you don't think it's too familiar…"

"I'll take it over Ruby Tuesday," I joked.

"You hate it," he said, bowing his head.

"I'm just teasing," I said, finally daring more closeness. "It's cute. You're cute."

Johnny and I leaned toward each other, as if pulled together by a magnet, the whole moment coalescing perfectly into a sweet, hot—

Just then, a commotion erupted below. It was hard to make out exactly what was happening, but it sounded like Bone and Jet had come in and sat down on the couch next to Hawke. Bone rat-a-tat-tatted his drumsticks against the road case they'd repurposed into a coffee table, cluttered with drinks and colored glass ashtrays. Could Jet and Hawke really be playing dice right now? It seemed like it, from the rattling sound and the play-by-play provided by Hawke: "They were neck and neck as to who would double six it."

Johnny and I paused, our faces a breath apart. He rolled his eyes dramatically. I laughed, but I wasn't going to let his band ruin yet another potentially perfect moment. I gently bridged the final, miniscule gap between us. Once again, I was swept up in the perfect, firm-yet-soft pressure of his lips.

But the bedlam below us would not stop. I finally gave up and pulled away, laughing despite my annoyance. I took the *Village Voice* wrapping paper from his gift to me and carefully ripped a small rectangle section of it. I then sprinkled some weed from the stash in my coat's inner pocket and rolled us a respectable joint, Johnny grabbing a candle to ignite it.

I inhaled deeply of the soothing herb, then passed it to him.

"Hey, man, don't bogart the spliff," Bone called out below. "We're right here."

"Which is right where I *don't* want you to be," Johnny shouted, crawling back to the lip of the loft, and extracting his wallet in order to rain bills, and a few coins, down onto them. "The first round's on me. Now go, before I stop feeling so generous."

"Sweet," Jet said, the word garbled as he caught some of the falling money in his mouth, and even down his pants.

"Okay, love birds, don't do anything I wouldn't do..." Hawke said, not exactly limiting our options.

Finally, mercifully, they'd shuffled out, and the heavy door slammed behind them. We were actually, completely, unquestionably alone.

Johnny extinguished the joint in the ashtray next to the bed, then boldly stretched out and motioned for me to lie down next to him. I hesitated a moment, but I was beyond caution, and I moved toward him. Smoothly, he slid his arm around my shoulders, leaned close, looked into my eyes with wanting, and proceeded to slowly and sexily kiss me, and this time, full and open. The kissing went on and on, and his hand slid under my blouse, finding the edge of my black lace bra. A wave of heat manifested throughout the synapses of my body. I felt beneath his softly worn Ramones T-shirt to his thin, muscled chest and, together, we slid off his shirt. Nervousness that the band might explode back into the room below at any moment added excitement and urgency as we kissed and caressed each other, meeting at the intersection of tender affection and hot desire. After, we lay close together, his hand gently caressing my ass, our heads angled toward each other on one pillow.

Somewhere, deep in the vast apartment, a phone rang, but Johnny made no move to answer it. "Let whoever it is call back," he said. "...and I'm sure they will. It's been nonstop around here. I wish we didn't have to fly out tomorrow evening."

"So soon?" I asked, trying to keep my voice strong.

"Yeah, we're shooting our video in the a.m., and then we jet off to the UK."

"Oh, so you found another beautiful Betty to star in your cool, if somewhat sexist, video then?"

"It's business, you know...but she seems okay...I guess," he said, turning his face away as he busied himself with selecting a new record. "She's a bit of a guitar prodigy, actually, apparently."

"Ahh," I said, pulling up his quilt to cover myself.

"I wish you would have accepted the job," Johnny backpedaled. "But I get it. Anyhow, we needed to find someone to be in our video. And she just happened to be available—and not bad to look at."

I knew he didn't mean to hurt my feelings—*did he?* But I suddenly found myself back on shaky ground with him, and it didn't feel safe to show my true emotions. The last thing I wanted was to be there when the band returned and find myself enduring more adolescent ribbing from Hawke. This evening was not unfolding as I'd dreamt it would. In fact, this fledgling romance was not developing well at all.

"I should go," I said, sitting up and reaching for my clothes. "I've got an early wake up...a Top Shop billboard for their latest lingerie campaign—I guess it's being shot by this British bloke, Gavin Rossdale," I added, feigning nonchalance at working with such a hot rock star as revenge for Johnny's complimentary words about the video vixen. "Apparently he's some sort of singer who does the occasional photo gig. You know...it's business, babe."

"I've got to get up with the sun, too," he said, dropping the needle on a new record and turning back to me as Etta James began to sing "At Last." "But...do you really have to go so soon? It's my last night in town...I thought..."

"This was extraordinarily sweet," I said, forcing myself to be strong and sliding on my boots. "But I'm still in the dog house with my agent for showing up to my last shoot with a shiner. Better not push my luck."

"Sure, yeah," he said, matching my neutral tone. "Well, I'm sure you'll be super busy with tons of bookings and all that. We'll be gone for, um, around six months, back in...September...I guess."

My heart cracked at the thought.

"Yeah, we've got two weeks in the UK, and then we head straight to LA for the spring and summer—mixing and mastering the new tracks, promo, the album release. I think our next NYC show is around Labor Day or something. You should come."

"Sure, I'll try," I said.

I pulled on my winter coat and scarf as quickly as I could, my head thick with red wine, and pot, and the tears I was trying hard not to shed.

"Right," he said. "Okay, I'll make sure you get into a cab okay."

It was only when I was in the back seat of a taxi, rocketing across town to my apartment that I finally let myself sob. Sometimes the best days were also the worst, and nothing was more confusing than the moments in life that seemed to be both.

And then it got worse.

I staggered up the final steps of the four flights that led to my apartment. The door stood ominously ajar. This wasn't right. I knew Imani had picked up a dinner shift at the diner where she worked and wouldn't be home until midnight. I shivered in the drafty hallway, but I couldn't bring myself to push into my apartment, fearing I might disturb a lurking intruder there. But when fifteen minutes of nerve-wracking silence had passed without any sign of Imani's return or any movement from our living space, I finally summoned my courage and tiptoed inside.

I momentarily thought I'd accidentally walked through the wrong door. Imani and I weren't the world's best housekeepers, but we both liked our space comfortable and relatively neat. And right now, it resembled a post-hurricane beach, strewn with driftwood and seaweed. Everything appeared to have been shaken out of its rightful spot—and anything fragile had been shattered. Flowerpot shards were mixed in with dirt and bedraggled houseplants on top of mangled books and piles of disfigured art supplies. Worst of all, they'd shredded my paintings and sketches and left the tatters fluttering on top of the rest of the mess.

I sank down on the couch and cried out all of my day's disappointments. I wasn't exactly surprised—New York City was rife with property crime, and every day of living here was like playing a game of Russian roulette. Both Imani and I had been incredibly lucky that in the four years we'd called the metropolis home, neither of us had ever been mugged, that our living quarters had not been burglarized. Until now. But this was so much worse then I'd ever dared to fear.

They'd taken our TV and our new Sony stereo. So what? We'd live. And eventually be able to buy new ones. But they'd senselessly destroyed *years* of my artwork, which were irreplaceable. And they'd trodden on my supplies, which I couldn't afford to replace. For the first time since I'd bravely lit out for the Big Apple, I wondered if the city had gotten the best of me, and if maybe—just maybe—I might be better off back home.

***

A NEW DAY DAWNED and The Westies' first ever video shoot was starting off about as well as their industry showcase earlier that week. Hawke had actually deigned to make an appearance this time—nothing like the sobering promise of a spotlight and a beautiful girl to focus his woefully scattered attention. But Hawke was so unsteady on his feet that the director, Sven, had improvised a solution whereby they had him quasi-rest in the prop casket during the majority of the video. All Hawke had to do was to strum a few chords and lie there with his eyes closed, which was about all he could manage. Meanwhile, he would be transported in the imposing hearse on which Bambi, the bombshell video vixen, whom had taken the job in place of Scarlett, was set to dance in a most provocative manner.

"I hope that's not some kind of bad mojo, putting Hawke in a coffin like that," Shiv said as they watched from the sidelines while the director rehearsed the scene.

"Maybe it'll scare him straight," Johnny said.

"Now that's a prayer I could get behind. How's your bird, Scarlett, in the wake of her run in with that biker's restless knuckles?"

"She came over last night, we had some fun, and…um…well, she's very beautifully special, I gave her the crystal we 'borrowed' from the Gramercy Park Hotel the other day," Johnny said.

"Did she dig it, I hope?"

"She did," Johnny said. "But it got, I don't know, weird between us."

"It took me months to convince my lovely Seph I'm not a total waster," Shiv said with a chuckle. "Not entirely sure she's always so convinced, still. Have heart. You're about to be sitting on top of the world. With Scarlett, no less, I'll bet you."

"I don't know," Johnny said, gasping for an extra dose of oxygen.

"She's a *model*," Deirdre interrupted. "She's a headache you absolutely don't need in your life right now." Deirdre's ability to insert herself seamlessly into every conversation, even—and especially—the most private moments, was truly uncanny. "Come on, boys, get your head in the game," she continued. "Nothing matters but what's happening in this room right now. Capiche?"

Johnny's stomach knotted at the thought of how much was riding on this day.

"Now, Johnny, you've really got to sell it," she said. "People need to believe in your words, in your music, in your *passion* for her—"

On cue the eye candy hired to play his love interest in the video emerged from hair and makeup wearing the off-white lace Betsey Johnson minidress they'd decided on and her hair pulled away from her face in a tight ponytail. The dress fit her flawless body so perfectly, and her legs were so insanely long and toned that it was impossible not to imagine her undressed. Even Johnny, who could still feel the soft warmth of Scarlett's kiss, couldn't help but take notice. Deirdre caught this and practically salivated at the implications.

"Now...Johnny, meet Bambi," she said, coaxing the girl over. "I'd like you two to spend a little time together, getting acquainted, before the cameras roll. I've even thought to put some Dom nineties champagne on ice for you over there..."

"Guess I could fancy a spot of champers right now..." Shiv said.

"Not for you," Deidre said. "You and the lads are going to come over here and practice while Johnny gets warmed up."

"Practice what?" Shiv asked. "All we've got to do is play our instruments. If we can't be convincing at that, then maybe we're in the wrong profession?"

"Thank you," Deirdre said in her most saccharin tone.

An hour later, the members of the band—minus Hawke, who was snoozing in the coffin where he'd been placed—were testily running through their single for the fifteenth time. Meanwhile Johnny and Bambi had polished off their second bottle of champagne. Deirdre flitted about, taking Polaroids of the proceedings. They would make for a great means of documentation, for promo press purposes, when the album dropped. A sort of behind-the-scenes with America's soon to be favorite rock idols! Bambi was so easy to talk to—well, she didn't actually say anything herself, just stood there looking stunning and laughing uproariously at Johnny's jokes, as if he were the second coming of John Belushi.

It was a very good day.

When it was time to start the shoot in earnest, Sven had Johnny take the wheel of the hearse while the guys played behind him on a spinning platform. They looked suitably pissed off and rock 'n' roll. (Perhaps Deirdre's method had been on point after all). Bambi was placed on the hood of the car, crawling toward him, coiled sex appeal radiating from every inch of her body, her eyes locking with his through the windshield. It was *hot*. Johnny could feel the molten chemistry between them, no acting required. As the song ended, Johnny peeled his gaze away from Bambi's long enough to seek direction.

"Okay, you ahhct like you slahhm on ze breaks," Sven instructed, demonstrating for Johnny. "Ack, ah, ze horror, ze horror."

The man threw up his arms in front of his face, as if he were Tippi Hedren, getting pecked by the birds.

"Bambi, you get down, zee," Sven said, exhibiting a gesture of surrender with his arms. "And rohll, rohll, rohll," he continued, twisting his body and demonstrating what he had in mind. "We puht down ze stunt pad."

Sven moved in front of the car, gestured for Johnny to get out and follow him.

"And, now, you're dev-ah-staated," he said, in his thick Scandahoovian accent, bending down, seemingly distraught. "You have keelled ze womahn you love. Trahgedy. Heartbreak. You pick her up. Carry her to ze rear of ze car. Now…a mirahcle. She wakes up. You kiss in ze bahck of ze hearse. It is very, how you say…naughty? Very dahngerous. Very dahrk. Extremely hawt. Think *Sleeping Beauty* meets…*Blue Velvet*."

Johnny was fuzzy on how the action he'd just been instructed to take matched up with the lyrics of his song, which were about longing for love in the underbelly of New York City's Lower East Side. But with

Deirdre bringing him icy, medieval-looking flutes of dry champagne—and double vodkas—between takes, and Bambi clinging to him most convincingly when he carried her in his arms, he found himself letting go of everything beyond how good it felt to be in the moment.

By the time Sven had positioned the camera for some close-ups of Johnny and Bambi embracing in the body of the hearse, they *definitely* weren't acting anymore. With a wicked smile the size of the Chrysler Building, Deirdre perused the photos as they developed, then, tucked them away in her oversized indigo alligator bag.

At the end of the long day's (and night's) shoot, Johnny was pretty wasted and somewhat euphoric, suitably punch drunk. He and Bambi were etched tightly together on a chocolate colored leather couch against the far wall of the cavernous studio. Deirdre slithered up, made some innocuous small talk about the frigid weather, took a couple of quick Polaroids of the band, the set, and Johnny and Bambi, semi-passed out on the couch, before Johnny could react. Then she cleared her throat with menace.

"Bambi, my beauty, your services are no longer needed here," she said. "You may go."

Bambi obediently separated herself from Johnny's lap with the same easy elegance she'd exuded all day. She dashed out the door, but not before she'd mouthed the words, "Call me."

Johnny's head was spinning. Something nagged at the back of his consciousness, like the name of an old school friend that had been erased by the flip of calendar pages. He couldn't quite pull the thought into focus. The next thing he knew, he found himself in the back of a limo with only Deirdre and Clint, on his way to the international terminal at JFK airport.

"Where are the lads?" he asked.

"In a cab," Deirdre said. "Clint, darling, give Johnny the items I rallied you to purchase for him."

Wordlessly, Clint handed Johnny a Woolworth's shopping bag. It was surprisingly heavy. Johnny peered inside, confused.

"Why aren't the others with us?" he asked. "And what's all this?"

There were four liters of Evian water, and a big bottle of Excedrin.

"Drink *all* the water, and take two of these," Deirdre said. "You won't have a champagne hangover. We have some business to attend to on the flight."

"Wow, you think of everything," he said, impressed despite his unease.

Deirdre reached into her bag and produced the stack of Polaroids. "I really do."

As she placed them into Johnny's hand, he looked back and forth between her and the pics, rifling through them, a bit confused. "Is this album art I need to approve or something?"

"Not exactly," she said.

Johnny flipped through the images, a sickening sensation enveloping him as the thought that had nipped at the rear of his mind bloomed into clarity: *Scarlett. He had betrayed Scarlett, which was hideous enough, and now Deirdre had proof of his disloyalty, which was...*

Her face was haggard and ominous in the shadowed car. She held out a plethora of documents to him, which appeared to be a revised version of the contract that governed their working relationship.

"Here's what I need to see manifest," she said. "You're going to suggest to the others, and to the lawyers, that I get an extra point on the record, in exchange for my disposal of these photographs and my promise that they are never seen by the person I am sure you most want to keep them from."

Clint's impassive expression signaled to Johnny that he had seen Deirdre do much worse over the years, and he was a master at neutrality.

"Or else?" Johnny said, soberly.

"It's 1995, Johnny," Deidre said. "These beauties could be on their way to Scarlett in a matter of minutes."

"*Wow*, you really are good at being bad," Johnny said, his heart sinking. "Where do I sign?"

***

FASHION WAS PURE IMAGINATION and pleasure, carefully orchestrated into one extraordinary, luscious facade. But creating the illusion of such rarified magic required a few slight tricks, such as taping my breasts down, stuffing my feet into shoes that were two sizes too small, and maintaining an alluring expression of confident sex appeal, which on this particular day was proving to be a bit beyond me. The tape kept unsticking from my skin, because the furnace was on the fritz and couldn't be turned down, and on top of that, the studio lights were as hot and merciless as ever. My skin was slick with condensation beneath an elaborate, hand-constructed, obsidian-hued Rifat Ozbek coat made of seventy-five pounds of eco-friendly, recycled from found, ostrich feathers.

I was dressed for an eight-page editorial (plus a cover try) that would be for the September issue of *Vogue*. It would hit newsstands just in time for women-in-the-know to flip through the highly anticipated fall fashion guide while sipping sugar free vanilla lattes in Norwegian-style sweaters. This reality felt like the actual fantasy amid the swampy, overheated mess of the current moment. And, somehow, I was being blamed for every little mishap, as if I were the vengeful God who had orchestrated the wire that had shorted out the studio's heating source and the factory that had made the tape that was currently malfunctioning on my person.

"Frederique, would you please, please, please, do something about that tape?" the photographer hissed to one of several editors on set. "Her breasts are uneven, giving the impression that one is some sort of deflated balloon."

"Perhaps if she didn't have quite so much cleavage to tape back," the art director snarked while observing the hapless stylist tugging on my chest, as if it weren't actually attached to my body. "Mon dieu. They need to invent this tape in extra strength."

The industry of dreams had transported me to my new life in New York City, as well as some incredible work trips to Paris, Milan, London, and Tokyo. And it had taught me to observe the world around me through different, more wondrous eyes than the paradigm I'd grown up with in San Diego. On a daily basis, I rubbed auras with true visionaries—magnificent designers, like Anna Sui, Marc Jacobs, and Stephen Sprouse; stellar photographers, including Ellen Von Unwerth, Steven Meisel, Arthur Elgort; iconic fashion editors Grace Coddington, Anna Dello Ruso, and Andre Leon Talley; as well as legendary models, including the gorgeous Kate Moss and Cindy Crawford. All of these luminaries possessed a uniquely inspired impression of existence and did their utmost to reshape the space around them into an aesthetic rendering of their fancy. It was truly a mesmerizing experience that had grown me as an artist and a woman.

But my self-esteem? That had been shredded even more completely than it was in high school, which I would have thought impossible. Back then I was being teased mercilessly about my bug eyes, the gap in my front teeth, my massive mouth and baby fat curves. After four years as a working model, I now knew what was considered wrong with every single millimeter of my face and body, and while the sophisticated fashionistas used slightly more professional terms than the insult of "heavy" I'd been deluged with as a teenager, their criticisms sometimes weren't any less piercing or hurtful.

For the past few weeks, when I'd faced an especially challenging day at work, I would transport myself in my head to my new euphoric zone—the one where I imagined Johnny playing his '73 Les Paul custom for me on some ethereal, puffy cloud in a grand celestial palace in the sky. But ever since the wobbly nature of our recent goodbye and our uncertain plans for a future reunion, it seemed a dangerous and precarious fantasy.

Finally, Veronique, the petite crimson-haired stylist, had finished fussing over my décolletage. I was again alone in the shot, posed on the edge of an elegant turn of the century settee, sipping on a bone china tea cup, resembling a Victorian madwoman in my extravagant Alexander McQueen Union Jack coat and dark, panda bear, smoky eye makeup.

"Pretend you're with your passionate one, Scarlett—maybe your boyfriend?" the photographer said, his tone intense, as if he were speaking to me alone, although a half dozen curators patrolled the set.

I lifted my chin, tilting my face to find the light. I turned on a secret flame, deep inside of me, one that was both regal and approachable, one that communicated something directly to others about my essence, beyond what I could say with words. In these transcendent moments, I knew exactly why I'd been called to this art form, which was a crucial boost of affirmation. Honestly, the challenges—the pre-dawn call times, twelve-hour work days, and constant, confidence-tarnishing assessments of my appearance—were debilitating my perspective on the whole "modeling" thing in the first place. And so I held onto such energizing connections with true artists, and the personal inspiration with which they infused me.

By the day's end, when the feathered fortress of the last look's jacket was finally lifted from my shoulders, my body felt if it were made entirely of golden air. I was both bone-weary and euphorically energetic at the same time. I knew it would be hours before I'd be able to wind down enough to sleep. Luckily, I was meeting a cadre of my model friends, as well as Sephy and Imani; we were going out into the bright lights of the night to rub shoulders with the fabulous people of the city we so adored.

I had slipped into my new "out-on-the-town" uniform: an ivory YSL silk blouse, paired with a sixties raven leather, silver zip front Courreges skirt and jacket combo I'd extra made my own by intricately hand painting them with dozens of blue images of the Eye of Horus (the ancient Egyptian symbol of protection). The recent break-in at our apartment had forced me to reinvent my artistic vision and how I rendered it in the world around me. Having lost nearly all of my "real" art supplies, I'd turned to the one possession I had in abundance— vintage clothes—and started improvising all new designs, mixing my passion for eccentric adornment and the potent symbolism I'd previously employed in my paintings.

I was toning down my makeup slightly in my compact mirror, when I heard a ruckus from the street below—a horn honking, a woman's voice shouting. The accent was unmistakable.

"Scarlett, luv, come out and play," the voice called. "Bubbly awaits you!"

Out on the sidewalk, Persephone resembled a dazzling, exotic bird—with a rich, emerald green, velvet hat complete with a jaunty veil positioned on her platinum hair, and a fitted, sexy-but-elegant green tailored Gaultier jacket that glowed against her porcelain skin. Even though mid-nineties street fashion had gone oversized and sporty, with its voluminous overalls, streety snowboarder sweaters, and flannel PJ sets as daywear, Persephone always exuded decadent grace, as if she were dressed to attend the (rock) opera.

*How can it be that this mesmerizing creature has chosen me as her dear friend?*

She swept me into her waiting tricked out Town Car and poured me a glass of Cristal as we pulled into early evening uptown traffic.

"How was your day, darling? Spectacular, I trust. I confess I always become melancholic when my dear heart, Shiv, first departs for tour. It's as if he's been shipped off to war, I suppose. Although, of course, I know exactly when I'll see him again—next week, when I fly to celebrate Karl and Yves at Paris fashion week, and then catch up with him in lovely London. We really must give you the grand tour."

My eyes welled, and I focused on my delicate glass flute with superhuman attention.

"Oh, I'm sorry, luvvy," she clucked. "I've gone and turned on the water works. I'm a right moron, aren't I? Now tell me, did you and Johnny not part on the sweetest of terms? Has he not been sending you any bouquets, or buzzing your ear with sweet phone calls?"

I shook my head viciously, unable to put my intense disappointment and longing into words.

"You know what I always say, then? Fuck 'em!" she said, chuckling merrily. "We're going to paint the town bloody fucking fuchsia tonight, and before you know it, you're going to find yourself fully imbued with your former vivacity and sense of delight. I promise you!" She somehow managed to get all of this out while lighting a smoke.

Ninety minutes—and two additional bottles of champagne later—Persephone was executing her trademark move, dancing on the banquet at the sedate steak house where we were dining with my model chums, Zola and Mariel. Mari was being romanced by the restaurant's proprietor—who also owned a high-end department store chain, a well-known Las Vegas casino, *and* a major league basketball team—and he had reserved the primo table in his luxe dining room for his belle and her entourage. As opposed to being scandalized when our fashion friends drank too much and carried on, he loved it, though his staff was a little more reserved in its enthusiasm. Such outbursts meant that his was the kind of hip establishment that just might earn the finest, most delicious stamp of approval the city had to offer—an item in the *NY Post*'s juicy gossip column, "Page Six." As far as I could tell, we were well on the way to such a distinction on this particular evening.

Mari had invented her own signature cocktail that called for the rarest, most expensive elderflower liqueur, as well as a live orchid to adorn each glass. After a few rounds, Persephone's hair was alight with gorgeous blooms she'd pilfered from the table in order to adorn herself. Amid such revelry, Imani had arrived from her second job as a barista, in her tomboy uniform of men's flannel shirt and baggy olive green Army surplus pants. While the others were mostly ignoring the artfully rendered appetizers that had been sent to the table by the head chef, Imani was working her way through a hearty helping of gnocchi with truffles. She might have been a vigilant vegan, but she was not above taking advantage of a free meal at a fine establishment when the opportunity presented itself.

Zola nibbled a shrimp cocktail while absorbing Mari's riveting tale about a camel tour she'd taken through the desert beyond Marrakech, where she'd traveled the previous week for a shoot. "I was raised riding horses in Santa Barbara," Mari enthused, "and you'd think that camels would be even easier to travel on, with their hump to balance you, and yet they're the bumpiest, grumpiest form of transport you can imagine. But, my oh my, once you're miles from the city, beneath those rapturous desert stars, with all of that luminous sand around you, any thought beyond pure wonder disappears."

"That reminds me of swimming out deep into the waves, at sunset, where I grew up in San Diego," I said, my voice exuding the blissful serenity I could still recall so well. "You float on your back, extend your arms out, almost like a peaceful, floating wooden cross, and look up at the great beyond. Everything as far as you can see is complete velvety ocean and lovely lapis sky. You can't feel where the water stops and your skin begins, as if you're floating in heaven."

My ruminations were brought to a dramatic halt as Persephone nearly tumbled off the bench where she was dancing, balanced on her chic golden metallic Marc Jacobs boots. I pulled her down to safety beside me, suddenly finding myself enveloped by a mist of her divine lotus and sandalwood infused scent, Issey Miyake L'eau d'Issey.

"Sephy, honey, you truly are *the* liveliest life of the party, ever!" I said.

"*Absolument*," Mari gushed. "Garret is going to lose his mind at how beyond fabulous you're making his establishment. I only fear it will provoke him to go out on the town with us tonight. He surely won't be able to stand to miss out on the fun."

"The piper must be paid, dahlink," Persephone said. "I was kept aloft thanks to several sugar daddies before I met my main attraction, Shiv. Anyone who tries to claim it's not a legitimate job is deluded. It's the hardest work there is, constantly taking care of the sweet old geezer and setting yourself aside infinitely the whole time. I remember having this vulgar so-and-so encounter me in my mink, and say, 'Oh, you're wearing a real fur coat…do you know how many animals had to die to make it?' To which I replied, 'Do you know how many animals I've had to sleep with to get this coat?' Now…just for the record I only wear vintage fur, as unfortunately it's already been made, and made a long time ago, and so I see it as a matter of recycling. I would never wear fur manufactured today. And earn it I had. It was always, 'Sephy, go to the drug store again. Pick up my meds. Sephy, handle my kids. Can you massage my wrinkled and crinkled feet?' And, yes, you must laugh, laugh, laugh, even harder, although you've heard my old and tired jokes fifteen times already."

"Thank you, my dear Persephone, for understanding so completely—and you haven't even seen him on the dance floor yet," Mari laughed as she signaled to the waiter for another round of drinks.

"The capitalist machine makes for prostitution in every form," Imani groused, looking up from the strong black aromatic coffee she preferred.

"I suppose it is fair to look at all employment as a type of soul sale," Persephone ruminated, never one to be put off by any idea, even an incendiary one.

"Art isn't prostitution," I said, thinking of the happy hours I'd spent painting the clothes I was wearing, and the feeling of quiet centeredness it gave me.

"Galleries make prostitutes of artists," Imani said. "Once you get representation for your art, all bets are off."

"There's no need to be so grim about money, darling," Persephone said. "I have the most wonderful method for manifesting abundance. I'm thinking of calling it 'The Secret'...or maybe 'Purposeful Destiny by Persephone.'"

"Definitely 'The Secret,'" I enthused. "That title absolutely has a mysterious and alluring power to it. And it sounds fun! Let me try! What do I have to do?"

"Simply picture the objects of your desire—professional, romantic, even the most divinely crafted pair of boots..." Sephy said. "In the most precise detail possible—feel the quality of the leather embracing your feet—know what it is to have made this particular moment come to pass with your every molecule...and it shall."

Slowly focusing in, I tuned out the piano music now reaching a crescendo in the background, as well as the pleasant buzz of conversation and clacking cutlery in the dining room. I concentrated my inner vision and breath with the utmost clarity. There I was, wearing one of my original, hand painted, ethereal creations, at the packed reception for my first solo show at The Tony Shafrazi Gallery on Wooster Street, a dapper Johnny beside me in loving, devoted solidarity...and I wished...and I focused...and I wanted...until I could smell the oil paint and the red wine at the art opening, as if I were really there. But then, my reverie was interrupted by the timbre of a man's voice, trumpeting over my left shoulder. "Look at these lovelies."

"Byron, darling," Sephy gushed to the man who had materialized beside our table. "I haven't seen you since Ibiza, when was that, in ninety-one? How is Philippe? How are the schnauzers? How are you, dear one?"

"Persephone, you are simply as transfixing as ever," he replied, double air kissing her. "All is well in the empire. I have launched another design atelier—this one in Milan—and I must confess to having been drawn over not by your radiance alone, but by this stupendously inspiring ensemble being modeled by your companion here."

I suddenly realized they were *all* staring at me.

"Isn't it divine?" Sephy enthused. "I've been simply begging her to embellish such a chic suit for me. Stand up, Scarlett, and let him see you in all your glory, luv."

Moving slowly, as if through a dream, I pushed my way out of the chaise and pulled myself up to my full height, conscious of every note I'd ever heard during my many modeling jobs, attempting to radiate an understated coolness like no other.

"And you designed, sewed, and painted this yourself, my dear?" he asked me.

"Yes," I said. "I've always painted on canvas, and just recently, circumstances forced me to graduate to a moving canvas: denim, silk, leather—handbags, coats, shoes, and well, this suit, which I found at my fave thrift palace, Cheap Jack's, on Broadway at Fourteenth. I guess my medium is whatever wonder the city deposits at my feet."

"Ahhh, truly remarkable, my dear," he said, pulling a business card from the holder in the inner pocket of what looked to be an Armani suit. "You must be my guest in Paris. I insist. I want to learn more about…how you say…your handiwork," he said, without pronouncing the "w," in his deep French accent. "And discuss, perhaps, a possible capsule collaboration."

"What a genius stroke of luck," Sephy said. "Scarlett is accompanying me to Paris fashion week, and we'll of course visit you and pay our respects."

"I'd be enchanted to host you," Byron said again, kissing our cheeks and departing.

I was floating on angel wings, on a rainbow, on a field of stardust.

"I must say, Sephy, that 'Secret' of yours is a pretty powerful cosmic elixir," I said.

"Isn't it wonderful?" she agreed. "Now let's manifest ourselves some celebratory bubbles. I believe your destiny has just been launched."

The night unfolded in a marvelous, spirited frenzy. The next thing I knew, we'd whirled into a downtown nightclub and were moving as a shimmering collective across the dance floor. As she'd warned us, Mari's sugar daddy, Garrett, had zero dance moves and no rhythm, but he shook it like he owned the place, which he might have. Unlike the tastemakers and sex symbols around him, Garrett was undeniably a member of what we liked to call the "blue blazer club," one of those men who had never, ever gotten laid in high school, and who had subsequently channeled all of his repressed desire into earning and acquiring so that decades later he could date women who were younger than his daughter—dewy beauties more rarified and costly than any antique Rolex.

I spotted a familiar figure across the room, and my skin went damp with unease. The others danced on around me, unawares. They were swept up in their transcendent next level merging of music and substances, surrounded by the fervent mania of a few hundred reverent souls working it out under the disco lights.

Lurking amid the crowd at the edge of the dance floor was absolutely the last person in the entire world I'd expected to see in this locale: the handle-bar-mustachioed biker who had inadvertently used my face as a punching bag during my prowl of the Lower East Side with The Westies. Instinctively, I flinched, instantly equating his figure with violence and pain. My ever-loyal sidekick, Imani, was quickly aware of what was happening and had drawn close, ready to fight for me if need be. The tension all around me was palpable. Fearful as I was, I decided I must act. I was determined to extract an admission of guilt from him. With Imani close at my side, I was dimly aware of the crowd parting around me, my adrenaline spiking as I came up beside him and delivered a forceful tap on his shoulder. He turned around to face me, clearly perplexed, as he tried to make out who I was and what I wanted from him.

"Look, Lady," he said, instantly on the offensive.

My heart fluttered outside my body—*what had I ever done to him?*

"You, sir, owe me an apology," I said, indicating my lingering black eye. "Look at this. You hit me last week, and while it may have been an accident, that did not exactly diminish my pain...or my bruising."

"Oh, it's you," he said, his whole demeanor changing. As I listened to the rest of his words, I slowly comprehended that his voice happened to be of a particularly deep and terrifying resonance, and that he could have been reciting "Mary Had a Little Lamb," and it would have resembled a scene from *The Silence of the Lambs*. "I recognized you right away because you have such a kind face," he continued. "I am really sorry for the knuckle sandwich I served you up last week."

"Apology accepted, thank you," I said, positioning my hand for us to shake on it—*mano a mano*, tattoo to tattoo. "But...you hang here?"

"My type of party lands me just about everywhere in this town," he said. "Let me make it up to you and buy you a shot of Goldschläger."

The next thing I knew, I was enjoying a master class in the dangers of stereotypes and how "every single individual truly is a beautiful snowflake," as my new friend, G, explained to me. And not long after that, I was somehow on the back of G's motorcycle, Sephy in the sidecar laughing like fireworks exploding as we revved through the late-night streets of Manhattan. She later told us G was a hoot, and the G actually stood for G-String...and he was one of the few, little-known, openly gay Hell's Angels who'd begun to find acceptance within certain corners of the group. As the wind tangoed across the bare skin of my face, a feeling of infinite beauty and possibility rose within me.

\*\*\*

MEANWHILE, A MOOD OF happy hysteria also infused Johnny and The Westies as they settled into their first-class seats for their long flight to London.

"Can you believe we're leaving the country for the first time?" Hawke enthused over a complimentary whiskey on the rocks, for once excited enough about something that he'd actually snapped out of his usual, jaded, sarcastic persona.

"I know," Johnny said. "I'm going to be sure to send my mama a postcard of her favorite place, Buckingham Palace. She'll never believe it."

"What a flippin' Mama's Boy," Hawke sneered, his familiar personality returning.

There it was, the guitarist they all knew and tolerated, having offered up exactly fifteen seconds of good will toward his fellow man. Hawke never stopped feeling benevolent toward the ladies he encountered, however. He now turned his attention to a well-heeled, buxom woman across the aisle from him, who'd taken her seat with a loose shimmy of her hips that suggested she'd already imbibed a few martinis in the airport lounge. She wore a silky satin blouse and forties-style suede purple pumps, even though they were departing on a red eye, and many others in the cabin around them were dressed much more casually and comfortably.

Deirdre pulled out the stack of photos from her bag and began innocently rifling through them, as if they were nothing more scintillating than a *People* magazine she'd picked up at the airport newsstand. A wave of nausea overtook Johnny, and it wasn't from any in-air turbulence. He squeezed his eyes shut and did his own version of praying only to be brought back to his surroundings as Hawke threw himself down into the seat in front of him. Meanwhile, across the aisle, the sophisticated beauty he'd befriended was also refastening her seatbelt.

"Mile high club, eh?" Shiv laughed, leaning over the seat toward Hawke.

"You don't even know the half of it," Hawke said through a leer.

A few minutes later, the woman gestured to Hawke and he waggled his eyebrows at her suggestively. They both stood and disappeared into the loo simultaneously, before the flight attendant was able to dash over and stop them.

"That bastard," Johnny said. "I really have to piss."

"Don't tell him that," Shiv said. "He'll stay in there till your bladder bursts."

When Hawke and his newest lady friend returned from their impromptu engagement, Johnny pouted his way to the bathroom. By the time he got back to his seat, the mood had shifted and taken on a surreal quality. The woman, who before now had been tipsy but composed, was sobbing into her second empty tall glass of Merlot. A concerned stewardess leaned down to her level, attempting to comfort her.

"Maybe it's the alcohol," the stewardess said. "I know sometimes it gives me the blues, alcohol being a depressant and all. Let me get you a nice glass of cold water. Or should I see if there's a doctor on this flight for you, miss?"

"I'm sure it was this lout's fault," Johnny said, indicating Hawke. "What did you do to her? Tell us, so we can help the poor girl."

The woman in question seemed to be far away from the melee she had inspired.

Johnny and Shiv exchanged a perplexed look and couldn't help but chuckle.

As if suddenly coming into focus, the woman peered up at the flight attendant.

"Who me?" she said. "I'm fine. Better than. Sorry to have troubled you."

The stewardess appeared less than convinced but she nodded and moved away to check on the others in the first-class section.

Before long, Hawke and the girl were once again exchanging loaded glances, and they found themselves waiting in the bathroom line, next to each other, magnetically rubbing shoulders, and they popped into the bathroom, *together*. Next thing anyone knew, a distinct rhythmic thumping could be heard from the direction of the lavatory. Finally, their cheeks flushed red with embarrassment, the two stewardesses began banging on the door with an unrelenting force.

"Excuse me," they called. "You must exit the bathroom immediately. Or we'll be forced to call in the federal marshal to escort you off the plane."

After what seemed like forever, the door flew open and Hawke tumbled out as if he'd just stepped off the wildest roller coaster at fucking Six Flags. Behind him, the woman he'd befriended was looking less and less glamorous and more and more mad hatter. "Have you taken anything?" the stewardess demanded. "Please tell me. If you don't comply and seriously start to behave, we'll have to ground the plane immediately."

"Don't worry your pretty heads," Hawke said. "We just took a bit of Ecstasy is all. It's her first time, so it's really knocked her for a loop."

By this point, Deirdre loomed over the cabin, intent on smoothing over the "misunderstanding," as she called it. But with the rest of the flight crew, and a slew of passengers, griping, and the stewardess having been worked beyond her last remaining nerves, they claimed there was nothing anymore they could do. They were making an emergency landing in Nova Scotia, and Hawke would be removed.

# A ROSE BY ANY OTHER NAME

As I settled into bed I experienced an unnerving sensation—a creepy, tingling sensation along the back of my neck, suggesting I was being observed.

*OH MY GOD!!!*

There was, in fact, a face staring back at me through my window. I screamed Bloody Mary with raw, piercing alarm. Fearless Imani instantly appeared in my room, gripping the '81 Ozzie Smith baseball bat she kept hidden under her bed. The lifelong tomboy and self-described daddy's girl had been gifted the sports souvenir by her father, as both were huge Padres fans.

By this point, I'd had the opportunity to identify my terrifying lurker. And I didn't know whether to slap her to Sunday or to kiss her to the moon and back. Sephy's platinum hair blew in the midnight breeze, as she nonchalantly balanced on the fire escape outside my window, excitedly waving a sheaf of pages. When she registered that she'd quite clearly captured my attention, she cheerfully banged on the glass and began talking at an excited clip, although I couldn't understand what she was saying through the pane. Just then, the wind kicked up, and one of the pieces of paper blew out of her hand. She teetered precariously off the edge in an attempt to retrieve it from the vortex of swirling air. I raced over to grant her entrance before she took an inadvertent tumble.

"Are you out of your mind, Persephone?" I shouted, pulling her to safety on the floor beside me. "We're one…two…three…four…five stories up. How the hell did you even access the bottom of the fire escape to reach my room?"

"Jeremy, my driver boosted me up," she chirped, kissing Imani and myself on both cheeks in her customary greeting, as if it weren't the middle of the night, and she hadn't just climbed into our apartment from a ladder in the sky in five-inch Versace stiletto mules.

"The hell—? Why didn't you just ring the bell?" I asked through groggy, slaphappy laughter, my fear having left me awash in nerved up adrenaline.

"Well, tis the middle of the night, dahlink," she cooed. "I do possess proper manners. I thought I'd just have a looksee if you were slumbering. And happily, you're awake!"

"Yah—you're lucky we realized it was you," Imani said. "I nearly hit a homerun with your head."

"Never mind that," Sephy said, merrily ensconcing herself against the pillows, and popping open her giant lip-shaped purse. Throwing back her head, she targeted each eye with a drop of Visene. With her left hand, like a sharpshooter in a slick Western film, she pulled a bottle of Cristal from her other bag, a fire engine red 40cm Birkin. She patted the mattress on either side of her for Imani and I to join her impromptu bed-in.

"Listen, loves, I've made the most asinine error, and it's caused you and me needless distress," Sephy explained. "I had to remedy it immediately. You see…I began receiving faxes from London earlier this week, and I was absolutely reveling in my sweet Shiv's newfound flair for poetry. I mean, listen to this, 'Distance only brings me nearer, to the absence that makes my heart grow clearer…' How lovely is that? And then, just now, when I received the latest communiqué, I realized they'd been from your Johnny all this bloody time. Shiv is such a dear heart. You must remember how I've told you, repeatedly, what a hopeless romantic he is. He must have given Johnny the number for our fax line, so he could write to *you*, Scarlett, my luv."

"I don't understand…" I said, almost not daring to believe. "They're for me?"

"Oui, ma chérie," Sephy said, piling the stack of well-read pages onto my lap and handing me the champagne bottle for a celebratory libation. "Only…I was fawning over them, thinking they were *pour moi*. As soon as this last one barreled through the damn fax line, I figured out my error and dashed over, sweetie."

I had already tuned Sephy out as I incredulously examined the treasure that had materialized in my lap. *Johnny does miss me! He is thinking of me!* My heart leapt as I digested the words of his final fax: "As the ocean wide. / The days so long. / To have your body next to mine / Is my favorite song."

I looked up to discover Sephy and Imani studying me closely.

"He's presented me with the gift of a plane ticket…" I said.

"First class?" Sephy asked.

"The offer is written as a love poem," I laughed. "It doesn't include a seat number, Seph."

"All I'm saying is you can tell a great deal about a lad from if, and when, he reaches for his wallet," Sephy retorted. "They're not as sentimental as we does are."

"I appreciate the gesture, I do," I said. "It's just, we parted on such strained terms. I just really want to demonstrate my independence… and I do have a job in Paris soon."

"Mmmm…yes, of course, pet," Sephy said. "And you and I will kill it at PFW—the best model/businesswomen that side of the Atlantic. And then you can simply hop to London with me."

***

A FEW DOZEN MODELS were clustered together in a buzz of pre-show activity that resembled the heart of a beehive, as we all received last minute adjustments to our fabulous fantasy-like hair and makeup. My hair was teased into a bouncy sixties-style bouffant, my lashes extended long, and my lips made up into a classic light-colored pout. We were about to walk in the iconic 1995 Chanel F/W show, and then decamp to a lavish gala hosted by *French Vogue*. I was doing my best to catch glimpses of the gorgeous Danish girl next door, crème de la crème super model, Helena Christensen, without giving away my inquisitiveness. My attention was tugged from Helena by girl talk unfolding behind me, rising up from the chatter in at least three languages.

"No one knows them *yet*, but The Westies are the next big thing," said a girl with a thick Russian accent. "Johnny is natural star. We are acting our love story."

"*C'est complètement*, no?" responded another model whose accent was French.

I craned my head to hear better, amid the ambient conversation and the booming, hooky, house soundtrack pumping through the grand white tent, where the show would soon happen. An impeccably coiffed hair person utilizing a scorching curling iron millimeters from the bare skin of my neck resisted just as forcefully as I tugged. I found myself frozen in place.

"...Our chemistry was obvious, everyone said so, the director, the band manager," the Russian model continued, blithely gushing about Johnny.

A sour, sick feeling knotted in the pit of my stomach. My forced immobility and my resulting inability to set the other model straight as to the truth of the situation was revving my adrenaline higher and higher. *Seriously, you ONLY got that job because I literally turned it down. If anyone has chemistry with Johnny, it's me. I'm the one he faxed heartfelt handwritten notes to from London. Not you, you Russian pierogi pig. If I were able to move, I'd teach you a few verses straight outta "Stand By Your Man."*

"Mademoiselles...girls..." barked the right-hand man who was overseeing the show. "Five-minute warning. You should be in your first look and lining up, *now*."

Reluctantly, the stylist liberated my hair. Whipping around, I tried to identify the source of the voice I'd just overheard, waxing romantic about Johnny. But half of the girls resembled Russian goddesses, and everyone had been scared into silence by the knowledge that we'd be under the lights, and the appraising eyes of the world's fashion elite in mere seconds. Still fuming, I took my space in line, suspiciously eying those around me. My look was quickly refined by a pack of roving hands, and then, I was gently pushed toward the stage entrance. I stalked the runway as if it were a battleground.

"Fierce," a voice from the shadows intoned as I blew down the runway. Apparently vengeful wrath was a good look on a fashion model.

The rest of the show passed in a blur of frantic fussing backstage, alternated with the Zen trance I fell into when it was finally my opportunity to walk—for those moments, time seemed to stand still, and all that mattered in life was making these beautiful clothes come to life and the graceful swagger of my footfalls. Before I knew it, I was standing backstage, surrounded by the pack of models. All of us were giddy with our recent accomplishment of having garnered a "standing O," for the King of prêt-à-porter himself, Mr. Karl Lagerfeld. Again, just behind me, I heard La Russe.

"I have flight to London early in the tomorrow," she said.

This time, when I turned, she was *right* there. I actually recognized her from the casting call. She'd been one of the girls Hawke had chatted up so relentlessly, and I'd instantly felt intimidated by her endless legs and poreless skin.

"Excuse me…sorry…excuse me, but I'd like you to apologize, please," I declared, trying to be confidently severe.

"I don't apologize," she said. "I do not know you from the hole in the ground."

"Well you seem to know my boyfriend, Johnny, from The Westies," I said.

"You make the mistake," she said. "Johnny did not mention girlfriend when he kiss me."

Fueled by adrenaline and the fear of losing the love I was sure was mine, I pulled back my arm and slapped her hard across the cheek.

The group let out a collective gasp and instinctively closed in tighter, as if drawn by the promise of blood. The cocky Russian teetered on her heels but quickly recovered and lunged forward at me, grasping for my long hair. I managed to dodge her reach and she came away with only a snippet of the extension they had clipped in for me for the show. It unclasped from my head easily, allowing me to evade her grasp and sneak in a slap to her other cheek. She was left indignantly waving the golden hair in the air, like a shrunken scalp. Just as I had risen up to my full size, prepared to pin her to the wall and force an apology out of her, Sephy exploded into the center of the assemblage.

"Scarlett—oh, Scarles, are you all right, dahlink!" she called. "My dear friend Grace is on her way back here. I'm sure I could introduce you two, and it wouldn't do you justice, to have her first impression of you be while you're scrapping, uh?!"

"Thanks, Sephy," I panted, trying to calm down enough to catch my breath. I wheeled around on the Russian hooker one last time. She flinched a little and then tried to cover quickly, mugging as if she weren't afraid of me at all.

"If you so much as think about Johnny again, I'll find you, and it won't be pretty," I hissed. Then I used all of my inner strength to present a calm mask as I turned around with a broad smile. I was poised to enjoy the wonderful opportunity of meeting the genius, Grace Coddington herself, and also thank the designer, too.

✳✳✳

MEANWHILE, ACROSS THE CHANNEL, The Westies were embarked upon an extended, and extremely spirited, meet and greet with the locals. Although Mariah Carey was still topping the charts that winter, the spring would see a rise in Brit Pop's favor, with Blur and Oasis dueling it out on the radio throughout the summer, and English ears were thirsting for the soulful rock 'n' roll The Westies were pumping out.

They'd been given a London gig opening for labelmates, Blink-182. This show at the 2,300-capacity London Forum, an "intimate" performance for the headliners, happened to be the biggest crowd The Westies had ever faced. (Not that Johnny or his band mates would have admitted to the night's novelty, especially as they watched the veteran act's set from the wings. They got to play a series of smaller venues throughout England—Liverpool, Manchester, Brighton—for which they were the headliners, with baby rock band Useless ID opening for *them*. Now that was a feeling Johnny and the lads could see themselves getting used to—and fast.

Their label had sprung for tour support, and that meant the members of The Westies were traveling on an actual tour bus, and staying in genuine hotels. (This was a major step up for them. It used to be dubbed the "Five Stinky Guys in a Van Tour," where after a gig, they'd literally drive all night in their 1981 Sprinter van. And then, they'd park behind the next evening's venue, trying to catch a little shut-eye with only their mirrored Ray Ban's blocking out the daylight.)

Traveling with another band was a good time—collectively, they were like a big, roving band of brothers. Too much so, perhaps. Within the first twenty-four hours it was impossible for any of them to eat or drink anything without first tentatively checking the item for signs it had been tampered with—from beers surreptitiously dosed with vinegar from a nearby pub, to burgers secretly laced with incendiary Satan's Blood Chile Extract hot sauce, things were just getting started. Jet was particularly adept at pulling off such pranks, as he had the most impressive poker face. And pity the fool who fell asleep—or passed out, as it were—before the others, as he might end up with his boot laces tied together, coupled with an intricate black marker clown drawing all over his face. Or as time would soon reveal, much worse.

When the band played Manchester, the locals took a shine to them and bought them pint after pint of lager in the bar after their show. By the time they staggered back to their hotel, they could barely stand, but that didn't stop them from pulling the booze off the bus and bringing it up to their room so they could drink into the wee hours of the night. When they finally consumed all there was to be had, and were at the point of seeing double—well, triple—Johnny looked up from the sing-a-long he'd been having with his mates. The ID's lead singer, Fisticuff, had taken the liberty of passing out in Johnny's bed. Exhausted, indignant, Johnny turned back to the others to point out this major party foul.

"Would you look at this one, smellin' of piss and vomit, hogging up my rightful rest zone?" he said. "We share our stage, our booze, and yet, this lout has the audacity to take even more—my fuckin' bed."

"Uncouth young bastard he is," Shiv laughed.

"I've got just the thing," Hawke said, flashing his crocodile smile, as he tore off a large piece of their gear's silver duct tape. As Fisticuff snored, completely oblivious, his mouth open wide enough to catch flies, Hawke and Johnny passed the spool back and forth. First, they wound it around Fisticuff's ankles and then around his entire body, zigzagging the tape spool with his arms against his sides and covered him all the way to the top of his head, leaving just enough space to breathe. By this point, they were laughing uproariously, but he was so blacked out wasted, he didn't stir at all. When he was stiff as a board, they carried him to the hotel elevator, where they placed him inside, and then pressed "L" for lobby.

Johnny was still chuckling over this escapade when he finally drifted to sleep in his, mercifully empty, twin bed. But by the time he woke up late the next morning, hungover and parched with thirst, he was instantly fearful as to what the other band's retaliation might be.

The bands rolled back into London for the final show of their UK tour. It was a relief for Johnny when he and Shiv snuck away for a few hours to take the Underground to Buckingham Palace. During their jaunt, he was, mercifully, able to momentarily lower his guard. Johnny posed outside the regal iron gate, trying for a look of cool nonchalance. He got Shiv to take his picture with the disposable camera he'd bought at a tourist stand, along with the postcard intended for his mom. He couldn't believe he'd really made it, all the way to the home of Her Majesty The Queen. His music had been the magic carpet that had carried him across the sea to another country. And here he was, at a grand manor his mother had always loved, even though she'd only admired it on TV. Like Sinn-Fein leader, Gerry Adams, whom had recently visited the White House after helping to broker an agreement for peace between Northern Ireland and England, in an event that was covered feverishly in the British press just then. The unlikely could occur. One man could embody the hopes of so many by pursuing his dreams. And this moment was just the beginning, he was sure of it. He was going to bring the whole world to its knees.

For Hawke, of course, the most exciting part of any enterprise was the pursuit of the fairer sex. He couldn't have cared less about sightseeing, or sampling regional cuisines. But he could not seem to leave any port without having made at least one new very close and personal friend. The moment they arrived in London town, he was immediately on the prowl. Shiv had arranged for a night out at his local pub, in the neighborhood where he'd last lived in London, with some of his old mates. Once assembled, the group made merry with copious whiskey shots and pints of Guinness. Hawke took one look at their waitress for the evening, a petite Gypsy beauty with caramel skin and jet-black hair, as she crested through the thick scrum of cigarette smoke like a mermaid materializing from the fog.

"What's your name, love?" Hawke asked as she set down their next round.

"Blondie," she said, sizing him up.

"But your hair is as dark as they come," he quipped.

"You're mighty observant," she retorted. "What do you go by, then?"

"Hawke," he said.

"But you're more of a sparrow then a bird of prey, ain't ya?"

Hawke couldn't quite cover his irritation at being teased, especially as the other guys were roaring with laughter around him. And yet he was obviously smitten, too. And he knew better than to let his friends get wind of the fact that, for once, he actually fancied one of the birds he was trying to bed. So he kept his flirtations on the down low. But every time Blondie returned to their table with a round—which was often—he managed to hand her a neatly stacked row of empty glasses from their table, as a means of displaying his chivalry.

Although he'd never know how he finally won her over, here's how it happened: when she went back to the bar to retrieve their umpteenth round of drinks, the bartender pulled her aside.

"Oy, whose that slag?" he asked, nodding at Hawke. "He seems annoying."

"Aye, he is," she replied.

"Well, go figure, all those guys in bands are the same."

"What band then?"

"You know they sing that dreadful song, 'Easy Come, Easy Go,'" he said.

The track in question had enjoyed advance airplay in recent weeks on the local rock station. And being a bit of a super groupie herself, Hawke's pedigree was enough to seal the deal. He used a petite note, slid onto her drink tray, to surreptitiously set up a rendezvous with her. And so, when Blondie's shift was over, she met him around the back of the club, where the empty bottles were put out at night's end. From there, he snuck her onto their tour bus so he wouldn't have to risk encountering any of his band mates at their hotel.

They quickly hid away in his bunk with the curtain shut. No one would ever have been the wiser that they were in there—well, except for the sounds of animated snogging. But for now the bus was empty, save for them. They were so swept away by lust that it wasn't until a brief break in the action, while Hawke struggled to peel off his skintight black stretch jeans, that Blondie finally broke the mood.

"Bloody 'ell! What's that horrible stench, then?" she cried out in horror.

Now that his face wasn't buried in her tea rose and talcum powder dusted décolletage, Hawke too noticed a F-O-U-L scent emanating from somewhere beneath them. He shifted nervously in the narrow space, trying hard not to gag. As if his movement had stirred up the aroma, it only intensified. Horrified and increasingly claustrophobic, all the sex appeal and glamor irreparably dissipated, Blondie leaned back, kicking her leg out and up.

"Jesus Christ," she called out. "I can't pull my foot loose."

Her stiletto was jammed in the bus ceiling.

"Here, luv, let me get it for you," Hawke said, but when he grappled with her boot, he too found he was powerless to budge it. Just then his hand slid beneath the pillow, and he yanked it back in horror.

"There's fucking brains under there," he called out.

"I wish you had brains," Blondie said. "I wouldn't be held hostage in this disgusting place!"

Hawke tugged at the pillow, revealing a mess of squished, moldy tomatoes. "Those bastards in Useless ID! I'll skin 'em alive."

Realizing the source of his current discomfort, and its impact on a date that had previously been a smashing success, Hawke punched the bunk in a fit of pique.

"Will you calm down?" Blondie yelped. "My leg is attached to that ceiling. Be careful, aye? And how the fuck are you going to get us out of here?"

"The driver is at a hotel for the night," Hawke said. "That was the whole reason I brought you out to the bus—for a little romantic privacy."

"Well, I think we can safely say *that* plan's been ruined. Don't you have a cell phone?"

"Not for the UK," he said. "We're only here for a few weeks."

"You'd better figure something out—and fast. My whole right side is all pins and needles, and my foot is trapped in my shoe."

After Hawke had pounded on the inside wall of the bus for thirty minutes, he finally drew the attention of a passerby, who called the police. The next thing Hawke and Blondie knew, the Bobbies from the nearest station had used a battering ram to open the front door. Guns drawn, they swarmed aboard, seeking the person in distress.

Hawke winced. "Ugh, that's coming out of my paycheck."

"So is the lifetime of complimentary tickets and backstage passes you're giving me and my friends to make up for this."

Hawke pretended to grumble, but secretly he was thrilled that Blondie would agree to see him again after everything he'd just put her through. Now, he had to think up the perfect revenge strategy for the guys in Useless ID—he was determined it would be utterly revolting… and beyond embarrassing…in even greater measures.

As the Bobbies were trying to figure out how they'd somehow gotten drawn into this shag session gone awry, Bone bounded onto the bus, blowing merrily on a dayglo green plastic whistle that hung around his neck. He wore a blissed-out expression on his face.

"Hawke, my brother," he shouted merrily, upon seeing his guitarist. "I love you."

"What's all this, then?" Hawke asked. "Are you just getting back now?"

"Yeah, man, I went to the most epic party, and we danced till dawn…and then some. I've got glitter in my bloodstream, and it feels like pure sunshine."

"You've officially lost your fucking mind."

"What's that now, lad?" a gruff older police officer asked Bone, shining his flashlight in his eyes. "Have you taken something then?"

"Love, my brother," Bone said. "I'm high on love."

"Ugh, I'd say our work here is done," the cop griped as they filed off the bus.

"What's that smell?" Bone beamed. "Everything is so incredibly… wonderful!"

✳✳✳

I DIDN'T WANT TO jinx myself. And yet, as I opened the door to my London hotel room, I couldn't help but envision some rose petals scattered on the bed, coupled with another heartfelt note. They would, of course, have been sent to my suite in advance of our reunion by my poetic, rock 'n' roll dream man. Why else had he insisted on knowing my room number, when we'd exchanged a fevered flurry of faxes the previous day, making plans for my imminent arrival?

When I crossed the threshold and found only dust specks in the rays of afternoon sunshine insinuating themselves through the half-open curtains, the bloom on my heart wilted. I wistfully checked the red message light on the phone by my bed, but it was woefully un-illuminated. Throwing myself down on the plush duvet, I had the front desk connect me to Sephy's room.

"'Allo, my pet," Sephy answered. "How is Johnny looking then? Handsome as ever?"

"I wouldn't know," I said. "He's nowhere to be found. Want to meet in the hotel bar for a pick-me-up?"

"Apologies, luv, but Shiv has just come round, and well, I can't possibly leave his side until we've become properly reacquainted. I hope you'll understand. We'll all go out on the town tonight and celebrate our reunification with caviar and champers."

"Of course you're with Shiv!" I cried. "I'm so sorry to have bothered you."

"Nonsense, dear heart. Let's meet in the lobby in…give us…four hours. Ta ta."

Just as Sephy was about to hang up, I caught the sound of Shiv growling like a bear somewhere just beyond the phone receiver, which unleashed Sephy's ecstatic wind chime laugh. I tried to be happy for my friend, but it was hard not to be commandeered by the dark ghouls of jealousy. Sleep eluded me, although I was exhausted and stretched out on the bed. I'd been so excited all day about reuniting with Johnny after our three weeks apart. And I was running full throttle on adrenaline in spite of the jet lag I still hadn't shaken since earlier in the week. The clock read 4:00 p.m. Or…10:00 a.m. back home in NYC. In an instant, with vast relief, I was certain of the best possible remedy. Calling down to the front desk for assistance, I actuated my plan.

A half hour later, my mood somewhat improved, I applied my favorite Chanel Ve Vernis nail varnish, in my preferred color, VAMP, matching it to my "Scarlett Empress" Nars lipstick, as an amulet against sadness and defeat, and then amped it up another notch by grabbing my small sketchpad and charcoal pencils. I was soon happily tucked into a corner table in the famed RNR Columbia Hotel bar. Sipping a Pimm's cup, I drew a clandestine portrait of a gobby dignified older gentleman, the rendering of whose elaborate whiskers was requiring great focus.

Glancing up at my subject, I caught sight of a shock of frizzy hair as it appeared around the corner of the bar. My system spiked with anxiety. I realized just how little I had considered my plan for a blissful reunion with Johnny in merry ol' England. Because, of course, wherever Johnny was, his band was, and wherever his band was, the dragon lady was. And here she was now: *Deirdre.*

"Scarlett, my dear." Deirdre sounded legitimately pleased to see me, which instantly aroused my suspicions.

"…Hi…Deirdre." I desperately wanted to know where Johnny was, but in equal measure, I did not want to let on to Deirdre that I didn't already possess this information.

"Let me treat you to a drink," I said, deciding to try the diplomatic approach.

"I couldn't think of allowing you to buy me an overpriced five star hotel drink on your short lived, albeit impressive, fashion model salary," Deirdre said. "I mean, with *your abundant* curves," she continued, as she eyed me up and down, sizing me up. "The ascendency of the waif look must be costing you considerable work. I will buy my own tipple, thanks."

I pasted a fake smile on my face and left it there. Deirdre rummaged in her bag for what seemed like an eternity before dropping the leather tote on the table and heading off to the bar with her wallet in hand. All the riff raff inside her overly packed purse began to spill out, and I hurriedly began scooping up items before they could fall onto the floor—her real fur lined gloves, one of the old-fashioned room keys for our hotel, and a stack of Polaroids that began to cascade onto the table and scramble out in a broad arc. *Holy hell!* The last thing I wanted was for Deirdre to accuse me of snooping. I glanced up at the bar, where Deirdre was delivering a dissertation on the proper way to prepare a martini. I quickly gathered up all of Deirdre's belongings and began to shove them back into the bag when I registered what the pictures actually were: *Johnny* and *another woman*, in fact, the very woman I'd recently come to blows with in Paris. *Kissing!!!*

I didn't want to look, but I couldn't tear my gaze away. In a kind of a trance, I spread the photos out in front of me and connected the dots. It wasn't until Deirdre spoke, close to my ear, that I was able to peel my eyes away.

"Aren't those delicious photos of the lads' recent video shoot?" Deirdre clucked, proving once again with her lack of self-control that she wasn't a particularly good blackmailer, but damn, the woman could meddle with a fucking vengeance.

"You, Deirdre, are one cold hearted B-I-T-C-H," I said in the coolest tone I could muster. "Now if you will excuse me, I have somewhere else to be."

With that, I drained the last sip of my cocktail, set the glass down firmly on the table, and walked out of the bar with as much dignity as possible.

***

AFTER MORE THAN FOUR hours of tossing and turning in my vast hotel bed, I gave up and pulled a lounge chair up to one of the windows. I'd feigned a headache to avoid partaking in Sephy's night of revelry—I simply couldn't fake a good mood for that long. And now, overthinking, insomniac, and bored, I didn't know what to do with myself. My junior suite overlooked a little park. And while there was nothing in particular to observe in the middle of the night, at least I felt like I was doing *something*, instead of just not sleeping. As I peered into the tranquil square, I weighed my options, contemplating whether I should even bother to see Johnny before I left London. As if I had conjured him, I heard a familiar voice, right outside my door.

"Scarlett, luv...open up," he said. "It's imperative I speak with you...post haste."

This was a world away from the joyous, romantic reunion I had imagined on my flight over from Paris. I was tired and sad. I pushed myself out of my chair and across the room, my heart heavy, my steps slow.

Be strong.

"What!" I barked, opening the door just a sliver.

"Scarlett, you're actually here!" Johnny crowed. "How...wonderful!"

"It's the middle of the night, Johnny."

"I know, but I couldn't wait to see you," he said. "I had to come right away."

"If that were true, you would have met me at the airport, *twelve hours ago*, when my flight landed. Or *ten hours ago*, when I was trapped in the bar, *alone,* with Deirdre and she showed me some most illuminating photos."

"I can explain. I can. Just let me in. Please."

"There's nothing to say," I said. "You didn't even remember I was arriving today. You clearly couldn't care less. And you've played me—played me for a fool."

"You don't get it," Johnny said. "Deirdre insisted Hawke and I go on a pub crawl this afternoon, in the company of a few of London's finest radio DJ's. You know, a kind of a roving meet and greet, if you will. We couldn't ditch out on them, or else our singles might never receive airtime. And as for the video model, we were just acting. And it had to be…you know… realistic."

"Oh, thank you for the edification," I said. "Now I understand where you were, physically, but not the source of your sudden indifference emotionally."

"Scarlett, don't be cross," he said. "You must let me make it up to you. We're going into the studio tomorrow…with Jimmy Page guesting on guitars—can you believe that, Jimmy Fucking Page from Led Fucking Zeppelin, literally playing with my band! And, of course, we have a dinner with our UK label, but maybe we could squeeze you in at the table for that, and either way, we should definitely rendezvous back at the hotel tomorrow night…oh…let's see…I should be done by no later than eleven p.m."

I began to shut him out. In a drunken fit of bravado, Johnny stuck his hand into the crack where the door's swinging guard had fallen into the space I'd gapped open. He gripped the wooden trim, refusing to let go, preventing me from closing it.

"Scarlett," he pleaded. "Don't do this to me—to us. You're playing with my heart. Pretty much shattering it on the ground, bashing it irrevocably."

"You've done this to yourself, Johnny," I said. "Now move your hand."

"Not until you agree to really listen to me."

"As you like," I said. In one fell swoop, I closed the door, except for the crack where Johnny's fingers remained. Barring his entry with my body, I latched the security lock. That way Johnny couldn't get in, but

I didn't have to injure him. With a flourish, I produced my earplugs from the pocket of my satin robe and slid them into place. Then I turned and went back to bed, switching out my bedside light and feigning slumber, even as Johnny tried to wear me down, piteously calling my name, again and again and again and again. Of course I wasn't really asleep, but I wasn't going to give him even a modicum of my attention after how egregiously he'd behaved. Finally, after having to steel myself against endless pleading from my heartsick former beau, someone in one of the other rooms must have complained about the racket. I could hear hotel security come and take Johnny away. In the end, it was a relief. I had remained resilient, and Johnny couldn't hurt me anymore.

✳✳✳

I WAS SO BONE-TIRED, I felt as if I were floating in a murky, underwater realm, but I forced myself to rally, applying extra care to my hair and makeup. I was determined to at least create the illusion of rest and ease, even if both were the exact opposite of my reality. Thankfully, reflected beside me in the expansive hotel mirror was Imani. My bestie had heeded my SOS when I'd called her the previous day with my tale of heartache and woe, and agreed to let me fly her directly to London. It was so generous of her to offer to come, and so the least I could do was to pony up the cash. Imani augmented her now-impressive full-on Mohawk with a purple and silver safety pin and winked at me as our eyes met in the glass.

"How do you like my new piece?" I asked nervously, smoothing the fabric. I had made the thrift store score of an emerald green seventies Halston slinky jumpsuit, resembling the one modeled back in the day by Farrah Fawcett. Then, utilizing metallic gold paint, I had rendered the silky fabric on one side of the lower hip into a narrow, exotic landscape of peacock plumes. Finally, I had capped the entire ensemble with a forties hat with delicate feathers, echoing the color palette and aesthetic. If my designs were my metaphorical armor, I had never needed them more than I did in this moment. Once I'd attended to my own look, I added the pièce de résistance of her street and edgy, cool getup, tying a vintage black-and-blue Hermes scarf (I couldn't help but upgrade her from her usual uniform of a four dollar black bandana, while still maintaining her typical streety, edgy cool).

The dynamic duo was complete.

"You look mah-val-ous," Imani vamped. I had been rattled by the previous forty-eight hours, but I knew Imani would never be anything but completely candid with me. And, this time, I had to agree with my friend.

We were in fine spirits as we stepped out of the hotel's front door and asked the doorman to hail us one of London's finest taxicabs.

"Excuse me, sir, please wait back here while I procure a ride for you," the hotel employee said, as Imani prepared to step into the street.

Her posture visibly stiffening, Imani turned and looked the man dead in the face. He became visibly flustered at her confrontational air but did not back down.

"I didn't mean to be rude, *sir*," he said. "It's just that I didn't want you to run the risk of stepping into oncoming traffic is all—"

"Do I look like a *sir* to you, *sir*?" said Imani. "Never mind. Don't answer that. Apparently I do. I suppose as far as you're concerned, all women must wear proper princess attire and stay on the inside of the curb while their brave protectors shield them by walking nearer the street."

I knew better than to interrupt Imani when she was provoked, especially on this topic, which was a particular sore spot for her. I simply ducked into the taxicab as it docked at the curb, letting Imani have her full, impassioned say. When we were both tucked into the backseat, I squeezed my friend's hand.

"I'm sorry that happened," I said.

"Honestly, you have no idea. As if it isn't bad enough, having my best friend be a freaking high fashion super model—I mean you're synonymous with the very ideal of female beauty. Plus, just because I personally would prefer not to look like a pretty little baby doll, I am constantly forced to defend my right to just be…myself."

"I get why you would assume I can't relate," I said, carefully. "But, actually, I get told all the time why I'm not a proper, quote unquote, girl, especially now that this size zero waif thing is all the rage. It hurts to be dismissed like that. And now I'm the one being scrupulously judged and told why and what's wrong with me, and every square inch of me. Imagine all that fun you're missing. And I'm out of work, more and more—"

"I know you're attempting to be kind, Scarlett," Imani said. "But I get mistaken for a boy *every day*. And sometimes I think it would be easier to be one. So please don't pretend you can relate just to placate me."

"I'm sorry, but you have to try not to let it get to you, Immi," I said. "I mean what are you always telling me?"

"Don't listen to anyone but yourself," Imani said, finding a smile. "Oh, and me."

By the time our cab pulled up at Madame JoJo's, the legendary Soho burlesque club, we were both feeling gregarious. Our moods were only improved by the nightclub's decor, which was tarted up with an air of intimate glamour, thanks to red and golden accents with a baroque vibe. The air smelled of lush jasmine, smoky velvet, somehow mixed with melted wax. The twenty-foot-ceiling room was dim, mysterious, and a little dangerous, with a wink-and-a-nod to clandestine hedonism that made New York City's clubs feel like kindergarten.

We sipped blackberry Patron margaritas and allowed ourselves to be completely swept up in the room's aura of wit and naughtiness. Onstage a woman blessed with a Botticelli figure, and va-va-va-voom hips, teased the crowd with delicious poise and skill, her petal soft skin adored by the spotlight's caress. From the tips of her long, satin gloves—one cream, one gold glitter—which she removed with precision and verve. To the plunging arcs of her black-as-night bustier, which she stripped down to reveal perky pasties—one red heart, and one black diamond—she frothed the crowd up into a frenzy, bumping and grinding her way to her saucy finale. As the night progressed, Imani and I amused ourselves by dancing on one of the raised balconies at the room's edge, and cheering on the performers with fervent appreciation. It wasn't long before our sincere merriment and inimitable costumes drew the attention of a roving pack of the room's most fabulous denizens, including several disgraced lords, half a soccer team, and Alexander McQueen—the latter being absolutely smitten with my outfit. He thrilled us by removing a silver metallic marker from his pocket, and adding a drawing of a fox skull on each of my shoulder blades, in order to further embellish my ensemble. I was for sure never taking this off.

All of the fuss and fervor was enough to finally turn my thoughts—and Imani's, too—away from the dark brooding subjects that had occupied us earlier. Our hearts were aglow with the astonishing glory of the many-splendored experiences possible under the sun—or the chandeliers, on this particular night.

As we left the club for a neighboring after party, we were awash in joyous ease. It seemed perfectly natural for our new buddy, famous (not to mention handsome) footballer, David Beckham, to give me a high five, as if we'd won the world's cup, just as we burst out of the club. My face was alive with humor and surprise. Imani was held aloft on the shoulders of one of his teammates, just a step behind me. Right beyond the door, the throng of simmering paparazzi outside couldn't get enough of what they were seeing and snapped photograph after photograph. So ecstatically original were our looks, so fawning and prestigious were our accompanying companions, so electric was my smile, that I apparently made quite the impression on these photographers.

"David, aye, who are these lovelies you've got with you tonight?" one photographer called out as we got tangled in the crowd and paused on the sidewalk.

"That's right, luv, give us a smile for everyone at home," another called out. "Who are you wearing, then? You look pretty as a beautiful peacock, you do."

Having modeled for as long as I had, I knew how to work a camera, even amid chaotic conditions after a long night of revelry. Even though we were simply en route to a party, it certainly didn't bruise my ego to be photographed in the company of one of Europe's top footballers, and to have special notice taken of my original design. What had started as the worst day, had bloomed into the best night.

Still, I was shocked, the next morning, to see my face gracing the cover of all of the city's Red Tops, a.k.a. celebrity mags, with the headline: "THE VELVET ROSE."

And so a new persona—and a fresh adventure—was born.

# MEMORIES FROM THE VIPER ROOM

I F JOHNNY HAD, PERCHANCE, glanced up from the Jack Daniel's he was imbibing at the bar in the first-class lounge at Heathrow, he would have assumed he was in a dream. For there was Scarlett, gliding to her departure gate, looking every millimeter the Velvet Rose. Her travel ensemble included a dusty mauve velvet jacket, hand painted with lush, overexcited blooms—a hot house of wine-colored roses, dahlias, and lilies—and her biggest, boxiest Chanel sunnies. She herself was far too occupied turning heads and smiling beneath the baptism of paparazzi photographers' flashbulbs to take any notice of Johnny. Nor, honestly, did she pay much attention to ever-loyal Imani, who was, as usual, by her side. It was simply too transcendent, not only to be noticed, as such, but to be noticed for her own original designs.

"Scarlett, look this way!" one of the photographers yelled.

"Blow us a kiss, Rosie!" another called, using the newly popularized twist on her tabloid nickname.

"What are you wearing, Scarlett? Is that jacket one of yours?"

The thrill was incomparable, and all consuming, to say the least.

For his part, Johnny didn't raise his head. He was feeling hungover and full of dark shadows, in the way months of hard living can do, creating a crossroads where you either have to keep going—harder—or stop overindulging altogether. And he was only getting started, poised as he was to light up the tequila sunrise skies of Los Angeles with his star quality. From there, all the world would be his stage. He ignited a Gauloises cigarette off the one he'd just finished, nodding his head to the barkeep for another round of libations.

✳✳✳

TWENTY-FOUR HOURS LATER, JOHNNY yelped as he dodged a torch-like projectile. He'd just managed to whip his head around in time to avoid being scorched. As the firework fizzled out in the silky water of the pool, inches from where his body floated on an inflatable raft, he laughed like a sugar-addled kid. He quickly retaliated with the rocket protruding from the empty beer bottle he was holding. Barely managing the necessary eye-hand-coordination, he ignited the incendiary device. Johnny then aimed toward Hawke, firing seconds before it would have exploded in his hand. These two rivals were enmeshed in a hotly-contested battle to see who could hit the other with the most *flaming* bottle rockets. It was a nihilistic activity they'd drunkenly dreamed up within their first six hours in LA. Johnny's fiery launch fell short and hit the pool with a disappointing sizzle. Hawke paddled closer to Johnny, before his opponent could make sense of this direct offensive strategy, and managed to score a hit to Johnny's bare chest.

"Ow, fuck," yelped Johnny, as the firecracker ricocheted off him and crashed into the water.

"Match point," Hawke crowed triumphantly.

"What kind of psychopath does that to his mate, anyhow?" Johnny tried to hide his disappointment at having allowed his adversary to best him, even in this inessential way. "We're in LaLa Land, brother. Weren't you the one who regaled us with wondrous tales of the gossamer sun-dappled adventures we'd have in California? We're finally here, living a few palm-lined blocks above *the* ground zero for rock 'n' roll: the Sunset Strip. And mere miles from the storied eucalyptus-scented hills and dales of Laurel Canyon. And you're gonna put your energy into this kind of nastiness?"

"All right, then, Mr. Daydream Believer, light some Nag Champa, eat some fuckin sprouts, and go get your tarot cards read or some shit."

"Ay, that's enough, lads," Shiv said, mildly, from the side of the pool, where he was carefully positioned so as to be lounging in the *full* shade of an umbrella, his white skin pale as bone except where it was crisscrossed with elaborate tattoos. The sun had set, the lights were flickering on, and still he feared UV rays, like a rock 'n' roll vampire. "We've been here six bloody hours. Save some bile for tomorrow."

Johnny tipped himself into the pool water and drifted beneath the external fray for as long as his breath held out. He was taking in how the lights of the house their label had rented for them twinkled dreamily, far above the illuminated depths in which he swam. Now *this* was the life. Next to him, underwater, Jet's submerged face appeared for an instant. Grinning, he completed his twentieth lap of the evening, swift as a coursing river.

Johnny propelled himself in one long glide just beneath Hawke's raft, ambushing him from below. He tipped Hawke over into the pool with a great crescendo of crashing and splashing, and when his air reserves were depleted, he pushed up to the surface. Gasping and laughing, Johnny barely managed to evade Hawke's retaliatory stranglehold.

"What the hell?" Hawke said.

"If I were you, I'd be more worried about the damage I did to your hair," Johnny teased back.

✳✳✳

By the time they piled into their limo a few hours later, their luscious manes had dried into perfect messy tangles. They would have preferred to travel by motorcycle, or muscle car, but their label had sent this black stretch number for their dinner with the HIGs, so they figured that was another matter altogether. From the moment the door slammed shut behind them, even Hawke couldn't hide his wonder at the magical kingdom in which they now resided. He poured liquor from a large decanter, into the heavy leaded glass tumblers, merrily sloshing some over the side of Bone's as the driver rounded a corner.

"Well, looky here, my brothers…libations…" Bone said, licking his fingers, then swigging from his glass.

Shiv sniffed his drink with curiosity. "I'd wager it's a single malt, from the Highlands, aged in oak. He took a sip. "Mmm—lovely."

"Okay, boys," Deirdre cautioned as Hawke topped them off again. "The night is young, and they do serve alcohol at the restaurant. Let's pace ourselves, shall we?"

"Blasphemy!" Hawke said. "This is rock 'n' roll, not the Vienna Boys Choir. I'm tellin' ya, if we mind our P's and Q's, the label will be *disappointed*. They want fire and brimstone. They want hits. They want headlines. And we're gonna make 'em cry their balls off!"

"That's quite enough of that nonsense," Deirdre said. "Now, listen. You may think you've entered a period of fun and games financed by your devoted record label, but I can assure you, they will make you pay them back for every sip of that liquor you're so gleefully downing and every square of toilet paper you use while visiting their penthouse office. So look sharp and try not to muck it up too badly tonight."

Johnny's gut twisted. The intense misery of his heartache was compounded by the sheer terror of facing the men financing the realization of his lifelong aspirations. He'd felt like such a stupid country hick when the HIGs he'd encountered in New York had talked down to him as they did. The stakes were only getting higher. He finished the contents of his glass in one go and held his empty out to Hawke, hoping liquid courage was indeed a real thing.

Perhaps the label executives should have known better than to take a group of overgrown adolescents for a culinary experience any fancier than Shakey's Pizza. In retrospect, it's easy to see how things ended up where they did, but as the night's most dramatic events were unfolding, they were difficult to fathom.

When their car first pulled up at the valet for the swanky Beverly Hills eatery, Matsuhisa, the lads were not impressed.

"Mitsubishi?" Bone said. "What kind of restaurant is that?"

"It's sushi," Deirdre said.

"I'm not eating any rank raw fish," Hawke huffed as they made their way outside.

The group paused on the sidewalk to make room for a large entourage leaving the restaurant, with none other than Bobby De Niro leading the pack. No matter how chill the guys tried to act, they couldn't help but gape and elbow each other. Their first day in LA, and they'd already spotted their first certifiable movie star.

"He's one of the owners," Deirdre whispered as they finally entered.

"Sushi?" Hawke said. "I can't get enough of the stuff myself."

Their enthusiasm for the night, the restaurant, and its top-shelf sake had soon reached a fever pitch. As when Bone managed to pilfer the chef's white toque from where he stood, slicing tuna, on the other side of the sushi bar. With his prize in place atop his head, Bone merrily mamboed around the restaurant with double chopsticks extended in each of his hands, pretending he was Godzilla.

Meanwhile, Hawke was instructing the other members of his band in the fine art of Sake bombs, which found them screaming in unison, "Sa-ke Bo-mb!!!" each time they dramatically fizzed up their beer by dropping in yet another shot. And their label reps, and other assorted record industry execs, were huddled at the table's far end with Deirdre, trying to go over the facts and figures related to the band's upcoming debut. About the only time the suits had the guys' full attention was when their A&R guy presented them with their official band Amex platinum card, which as they'd requested had been printed with their publishing name: Dick Tater. As far as the band members were concerned, they'd made it! As far as the label reps were concerned, they'd better sell some records *soon* or the jig (and gig) would be up!

***

AFTER DINNER, THEY HAD the driver park around the corner from Sunset Boulevard and wait for them there. The Westies were not about to be seen in this ridiculous prom mobile pulling up to the Viper Room, which had been the hottest rock 'n' roll hangout in town since Johnny Depp had opened it in '93. Good thing, too, as there was a cluster of rockers and their sex kittens outside on the sidewalk, smoking and posturing. You bet our lads swaggered into the venue, in search of more drinks and thrills, and maybe even a little recognition of their ascending star.

For once, the others (even Hawke) fell into line behind their ostensible leader. And Johnny had the distinct pleasure of approaching the bar, wielding the band's personal Amex card in his '78 motorcycle jacket pocket, as if it were the key that could open the door to rock 'n' roll paradise.

But then, Johnny momentarily fell out of time and place. He found himself face-to-face with the familiar impressive black Mohawk, earnest dark eyes, and makeup-free, cocoa-colored, perfect-cheekboned face of Imani, the best friend of his one and only true love.

"Imani!" Johnny said, attempting to wrestle against the chaos of booze within his system and appear sober, or at least coherent. "Is Scarlett here?"

"Hey, J-bird," Imani said. "Believe it or not, Scarlett doesn't come to work with me during my bar back shifts. We are two independent organisms capable of being apart for whole minutes at a time."

"So she's not here…?" Johnny asked, unable to understand her sarcasm in his inebriated state, with the din of the hard rock band banging out its noisy and raucous set.

"No," Imani said. "And it's a good thing, too. You don't deserve to even lay eyes on her, let alone talk to her, not after the way you treated her."

Even this brief exchange was too much conversation for the rest of the band, which had been left, parched and bereft of liquid refreshments, this whole time.

"Hey, hey, hey, any babe's gotta understand, the band comes first—*always*," Hawke said, bellying up to the bar.

"Oh, please, it's not like you guys are curing cancer," Imani said. "I think Scarlett will survive without you. Now, what are you Neanderthals drinking?"

Bone, who'd crowded in on the other side of Johnny, couldn't help but laugh at Imani's attack on Hawke. "Cool Mohawk," he said. "I used to have one. I put it up with Elmer's glue, and one night all this beer got spilt on it while I was playing a show, and…"

"Your head got glued to your pillow?" Imani said.

Bone gasped. "How did you guess?"

"I used to use Elmer's, too, but then I got a comb stuck in my hair, like legit," Imani laughed. "I had to cut it out with scissors."

The two grinned at each other for a long moment, until Imani did something completely uncharacteristic for her—nervously lowered her eyes. And then, of course, Hawke swooped in, always ruining anything even mildly intimate or pleasant.

"All right, touchy feely time is over," he said. "This is what we need: whiskey. From that end of the bar…" He stretched his arm out to the left. "…to this end of the bar." He extended his other arm to the right in an equally grandiose gesture.

"You want me to pour whiskey down the length of bar?" Imani asked, puzzled.

"Nah, he wants to order twenty shots of whiskey, lined up all along the bar," a male voice said behind her.

Suddenly, standing next to her, was none other than Adam Duritz, lead singer of the Counting Crows, who'd had a huge hit in '93 with their debut single, "Mr. Jones."

"All bands do it when they first sign to a major," Adam clarified, as he began lining up empty shot glasses as Hawke had instructed. "It's kind of a rite of passage."

"Is everything all right back there, mate?" Shiv asked. "I don't mean to be too forward, but…"

"Why the fuck are you tending bar?" Hawke asked. "You're a huge fucking rock star."

"Being a rock dude is hard work," Adam said, *still* lining up empty glasses. "Tending bar is easy. My friends all play here, or work here, and I know exactly what's expected of me."

"But the whole point of being a rock star is *not* having a job," Johnny said, starting to worry there was, maybe, more to the fantasy than he'd previously realized.

"Plus, your record label will never let you get out alive," Adam continued. "Even Bono didn't make his first hundred grand until U2's third album. I'm warning you, your label will charge you for the holes in the center of your CD's!"

"What the fuck?!" Bone exclaimed, pulling himself away from the increasingly flirtatious conversation he'd been having with Imani, long enough to interject. "How can they get away with that bullshit?"

"Aye, he's joking," Shiv said.

"Half joking," Adam said. "Now, do you want regular or flaming shots?"

"Do you even have to ask?" Hawke said.

Adam filled the glasses with 151.

"Would you like to do the honors?" he asked Johnny. "You are the front man, right? So if it all goes up in smoke, you'll be the one on this side of the bar in a few months."

Johnny nodded his head, feeling the solemnity of the moment, as if he were a knight, being initiated into an ancient tribe of warriors. He brandished his lighter. As he ignited the shots, one by one, he felt like he was figuratively torching all of the doubts and fears their rock star bartender had just stirred up with his downer reality check. And if this symbolic burn didn't work, by the time Johnny had downed his share of the shots, he wouldn't recall his anxieties anyhow. Ah, lovely booze.

By this time, the attention of the entire bar was focused on the lads and their impressive alcohol inferno. When Johnny lit the final glass, the room erupted in a cheer. The Westies all threw their arms in the air triumphantly, like they'd just finished playing a scorching encore. When they finally extinguished the shots and began handing them out to others in the bar, Adam sauntered back up to them.

"That'll be two hundred and thirty-six dollars," he said. "And fifty cents."

Johnny felt a little high from the thrill as he handed over the band's Amex card for the first time.

Adam examined the band name printed on the card and began to laugh.

"Good one," he said. "Ours is Barry Schmelly, Inc."

The two singers high fived over the bar. Later, when he was asked about how it had all gone so wrong, this would be the last memory Johnny could produce.

Even though they'd just given shots to half the room's audience, the lads had to put in a bit of elbow grease themselves to consume all the drinks they'd ordered. And by the time they did so, none of them were feeling any pain—literally. Jet had singed off half an eyebrow while taking his first, still slightly flaming sip. And yet, he couldn't register any sensation other than a mounting buzzed euphoria.

"The night is our oyster," Hawke yelled, triumphantly. "Let's go eat it!"

Johnny patted Bone on the shoulder. "We're moving out."

Bone looked up from the conversation he was having with Imani, who was pretending to wipe down the bar in front of him, so she could linger a little longer.

"I think I'll just chill out here for a while," Bone said.

Imani looked down at her rag while they talked, feigning indifference.

"Really, bro?" Johnny said. "But it's only midnight."

"I'll catch up with you back at the house."

"Okay then," Johnny said. "Imani, hey, when you see Scarlett, tell her...tell her..."

"You're sorry?" Imani said.

"Yeah," Johnny said. "Tell her that."

Johnny stumbled off after the others, leaving Bone waggling his eyebrows at an increasingly intrigued Imani. It's true that his technique lacked finesse. But the object of his attention, Imani, had extremely shaky self-esteem, after her many years of having been mistaken for a boy while living in Scarlett's shadow. So as far as she was concerned, he was basically Romeo incarnate.

"What are you doing on Friday night?" he asked.

"Ah, I don't know, probably reading *The People's History* over a cup of black coffee at Canter's," she replied.

"You can't read books on Friday night," he scoffed. "It's not allowed. You should be my date to our industry showcase, right here at the Viper Room."

She cleaned the bar with even greater intensity, unable to meet his eyes for a long beat while she debated what to do. She'd had boyfriends, sure, but she'd never been on a proper date before. On the other hand, Scarlett had already been dreading the band's Los Angeles debut since they'd landed in LA. Scarlett wanted more than anything to be there, but there was no place else she was less likely to be, unless she received an official apology from Johnny. In person. And that clearly wasn't going to happen anytime soon.

"What's the matter?" Bone asked. "I was just teasing you. Of course you can read if you want to—it just seems kinda isolating to me."

"It's not that," she said. "I'm thinking about Scarlett."

"I like Scarlett plenty," he said. "But just because Johnny loused it up with her, why shouldn't anyone else be allowed to have fun? And besides, what she doesn't know won't hurt her, right? Just tell her you're working."

Being the kind of person who read philosophy, and devoted abundant time and energy to thinking about how she could make the world a better place, Imani wasn't in the habit of lying. But. There were sure to be all sorts of record industry bigwigs there, who any up-and-coming singer songwriter would be lucky to meet. And Scarlett had always told her to do *anything* it took to pursue her dreams. So it was sort of like Scarlett was telling her that she just *had to* go to the show.

"Come on," he coaxed, sensing he'd almost convinced her.

"Yes…" she said. "I'll come to your show."

"Thank God that's decided," Adam said, handing her a plastic bucket. "Now would you please go get some ice for the bar?"

Meanwhile, Bone celebrated this development by downing the three shots in front of him in quick succession and belching with great gusto. That's amore!

And then there were four. As the rest of the lads stumbled out onto Sunset, they plotted their next adventure.

"Aye, let's go to The Rainbow then," Shiv suggested, knowing full well that everyone had partied there, from Led Zeppelin to his good mate Lemmy from Motörhead. And so began what was probably not the first impromptu sing-a-long, right there on the Sunset Strip: "If you like to gamble, I tell you I'm your man."

The Westies were so caught up in the moment, they completely forgot they had a limo waiting for them around the corner. And so, they began to stagger up the street, making their way toward the storied bar on foot. They finally arrived, only to find, parked outside, the oxblood red vintage Rolls Persephone drove when she and Shiv touched down in LA. After a few whiskey Cokes at the bar, Shiv excused himself from the night's increasing decadence in order to pop off with his old lady to the bungalow they kept at the Chateau Marmont.

Which left three.

But, somehow, when Hawke and Jet were roused late the next morning by a ceaselessly ringing telephone, from where they had passed out on opposite ends of the gray living room sectional, they were the only souls in the house. Hawke sat up slowly and chugged a half empty beer he found on the coffee table. Neither made any move to answer the phone, which kept ringing and ringing and ringing and...

"Fuckin' hell, nothing can be that important, Jesus," Hawke griped. Finally, he stood unsteadily and picked up the phone from a nearby end table.

"We don't want any!!" he growled into the receiver.

It was Deirdre calling, and she was screaming at such maximum volume that Hawke actually had to hold the phone away from his ear, in order to make out her words. So that Jet, too, could hear her quite clearly when she yelled:

"Did you use your band Amex last night?"

"Aye, but you said it was all right," Hawke said defensively.

"...to buy a strip club?!"

# ITS SEW EASY

SEPHY CAREENED HER GOTH-HUED Rolls up onto the curb, nearly mowing down the valet in front of the Gagosian Gallery in Beverly Hills. As I stepped from the car, onto the curb, I could all but hear the members of the press exclaiming, "Velvet Rose, look over here!"

"Give us some luv, Lady Scarlett!"

I was poised to dominate the red carpet, having received such thorough preparation for the role of "paparazzi dahlink," during my recent jaunt in London. But, much to my surprise, the only yelling was that of the parking staff, who were shouting in excited Spanish after their near-fatal run in with Sephy's notoriously catastrophic driving. *No matter*, I thought, as I nonchalantly struck a pose on the sidewalk. *Nothing like a dramatic entrance to flame the headlines.* And there it was, the familiar sound of rapid-fire shutters clicking, and the insatiable pop and sizzle of high-wattage flashbulbs. I turned my face into the lights expectantly, a come-hither expression on my face. I masterfully positioned my body, so as to best display the pearly white silk Calvin Klein slip dress I'd hand-painted with tall palm trees and miniature metallic gold Oscar statuettes, in homage to my new habitat. But rather than finding myself face to face with adoring photographers, I was somehow staring at the shapely back of a woman with sexy cascades of blonde hair. She was draped alluringly on the arm of an old-school handsome, dark-haired leading man with a killer smile. Together, they were soaking up the fawning photographers' attention, as if it were their birthright.

"Oh my God, Sephy," I exclaimed, grabbing my friend's hand in excited fascination. "That's Kim Basinger! And Alec Baldwin! Standing right there!"

"Of course, dahlink," she purred. "This is LA, land of celebrities. They actually reside here. It is nothing but movie stars, celebs, and beautiful people in this town."

I was accustomed to the many fabulous, larger-than-life personalities of nineties' high fashion, but certifiable Hollywood legends, who were household names even without their frequent *People* magazine covers and regular *Entertainment Tonight* segments, were a different breed altogether. I couldn't help but be starstruck. And, here I was, about to be photographed right alongside them! I held my pose as casually as possible, until the golden couple had passed. I watched in awe as they deftly navigated the crowded entryway and gawking fans, but the photographers didn't seem to notice me at all.

I knew that we lived in a time of two worlds—"fashion" and "celebrity," both respected and revered in culture, but famous to greatly disparate degrees among the masses—and yet this reminder hit like a bucket of cold water dumped on my expectations for the night. Sure, fashion models were on the covers of all the fashion glossies, but feature film stars were *everywhere*. As their agents were well aware, they didn't need magazine spreads or billboards to tell people to adore them, they were already beloved—for their films, for their fabulous lives, and for their rarified, untouchable status itself, which only made us love and admire them all the more.

As if on cue, the paparazzi now yelled, "Drew! Drew! Gorgeous! Over here, Drew." In response, the pixie-haired cutie offered them her most winsome smile.

"What are you waiting for, sweetie?" Sephy asked, turning back to discern why I wasn't close behind her.

"Oh, somehow I thought…" I mumbled, too embarrassed to admit I'd believed I would be as sought after in Los Angeles as I had so recently been across the pond in the UK.

"Don't fret, *ma petite chérie*," Sephy laughed. "As the great Mr. Warhol so wisely pointed out, everyone gets their fifteen minutes of fame. We're about to get you discovered all over again, luv. Now, let's go inside, meet some locals, and drink a bucket of complimentary champers."

Persephone was soon prancing about the packed gallery in her six-inch crystal Manolo Blahnik heels, alternating sips from flutes of champagne in each hand and stopping every few inches to air kiss and gush over some long lost acquaintance who was apparently her absolute most favorite person in the whole wide world. Although a throng of well-wishers surrounded the man of the hour, gallery-founder Larry Gagoshian, Sephy effortlessly parted the sea of sycophants and eased up to his side, earning a warm greeting. "Persephone, darling, you are the absolute most…" he said.

"Lawrence," Sephy cooed. "You've outdone yourself this time. What a rarified temple to the marvel that is modern art. And while we're on the subject, there is an up-and-coming young artist you must really meet…"

But even Persephone was no match for the centrifugal force of celebrity. Larry made an apologetic gesture in the midst of being pulled away to greet the legendary Jack Nicholson and then, he was gone.

"Never mind, pet," Sephy comforted me. "I'll arrange a lunch at the Ivy, and we'll make sure you're outfitted in your most charming design. He'll go mental."

But her words did little to assuage my disappointment. I'd managed to bank the bulk of my recent modeling income, and let's just say it was more than six figures worth. But now I'd relocated to Los Angeles, which was home to a much more commercial market. And the waify-grunge look was getting the better of my glamor girl notoriety. I had fewer jobs and no idea of how I'd support myself if I wasn't able to turn my art into my new career.

"Chin up," she said. "The only answer is for you to accompany me to the bar at the Chateau Marmont. There's always something on there."

I was afraid we might run into Johnny, if Shiv convened with us and happened to invite his best mate. And my enthusiasm for imbibing Sephy's favorite LA cocktail—the Malice in Hollywood No. 1, invented by notorious forties gossip columnist, Hedda Hopper—had diminished, now that I felt I had so much less to celebrate. I thought my reign as an ascendant, one-of-a-kind painter and designer had been launched, but now it felt as if it was over before it had even really begun.

"I don't mean to be a buzz kill, but I think I'll catch a cab home," I said.

Persephone laughed uproariously. "Aye, you're not in Manhattan anymore," she said. "Taxis are as rare here as non-organic smoothies. I'll give you a lift."

"I'd be lost without you," I said. "Let me just go to the bathroom first."

I was slumped in the hallway outside the restroom, all thought of my personal presentation having left me, along with my enthusiasm for the evening's proceedings. The bathroom door flew open, and I moved to take my turn inside.

"I love your dress," a cool, girlish voice said. "Is that from Maxfield's? I can't think of anywhere else you'd obtain something so elegant and original."

I pulled myself together, embarrassed to be caught sulking like a teenager, and found myself gawking at Drew Barrymore, who was even more adorable close up.

"I actually made it myself," I said shyly, not nearly the vociferous advocate for my own artistry that Sephy was.

"Incredible," Drew said. "I just love butterflies. Did you know that some people believe they symbolize the soul? I've always dreamed of having a dress festooned with them. Do you think you could make one for me?"

"Yes, I'd be honored to make one for you," I agreed. "How divine."

And so it was, I left the first event I'd attended in Los Angeles with the phone number for a certifiable movie star, who also happened to be badass Hollywood royalty.

\*\*\*

I EXAMINED HER DIGITS the next day, as I drove my rental car west, past the Sunset Strip's iconic Tower Records location, with its screaming red and yellow sign. I couldn't help feeling like Cinderella, and I was in need of proof that the previous night's magic had actually occurred.

I checked the slip of paper again beneath the famed striped ceiling, at the legendary Polo Lounge at The Beverly Hills Hotel. On this happy day, I had the distinct pleasure of lunching with my dear friend Aurora. I had dressed especially for the occasion, in my latest piece, which featured the iconography of my astrological sign—Scorpio—painted on a shirtdress of cream-colored raw silk. And yet I felt drab compared to my resplendent dining partner, who boasted a hot pink Oscar de la Renta silk organza gypsy—Hollywood hippie—ensemble with a wide suede belt that kissed her still slender frame. She appeared ready for her close up, indeed. I was too embarrassed to admit how gloomy I'd been the night before. I now felt ridiculous for having expected the royal treatment everywhere I landed, after the special reception I'd received in London. But, of course, Aurora got the truth out of me, not long into our tête-à-tête.

"You must not dwell on the subject of Tinsel Town for one moment more," she reassured me. "For you see, my child, Los Angeles has mono focus and doesn't want it any other way. It is the nineties, darling. The entire place is all about motion pictures. Has been for seventy-five years now. If you're not in the movies, you're nobody."

"Are you saying I should have stayed in New York then, or gone the usual MTA route?" I asked, using the insider slang for model-turned-actress.

"Why no," she said. "Not least of all, because your return to the West Coast means I will see you once a month when I come up to LA for my dermatology appointment, and my shopping excursion to Neiman's and Rodeo Drive. Plus, you'll grow more as an artist if you don't get too much attention too soon—as lovely as your Velvet Rose photos in the international magazines were, and as much as I'm sure you deserve the honor."

"You saw those?"

"But of course," she said. "My housekeeper takes me to the newsstand every Tuesday morning, just as I used to do in the good ol' days when I was seeking the TV and film reviews, my dear. I've acquired every single publication with your picture in it since the day you departed in search of your destiny. No one is more proud of you than I am."

"I fear I've made an awful mess of everything," I said. "In New York, when I had it all, literally—I was in the one-percent club of employment, I had budding love, and a rent-controlled apartment in a doorman building with pretty views and a key to the park. Now, I find myself out here, sort of starting from scratch all over again."

"Welcome to the human experience," Aurora reassured me. "Destiny is capricious. I've gone in and out of vogue at least a half dozen times myself."

"Really? And what do you do when you're on the downside?"

"Get my beauty rest, do good work for others, make shoebox dioramas of my favorite classic movie scenes, water my roses. For I know it's only a matter of time before I'm offered a new role in someone's latest motion picture—or a new husband."

She gave me a mischievous smile and took my teacup in her hand, turning the china this way and that as she peered into its depths.

"Your leaves are showing a reversal of fortune," she said slowly, reading my future in what she saw there. "Fear not, for you are soon to be approached by a suitor...actually, make that two...and find success for a talent you've yet to discover."

"Are you sure that's not your fortune?" I'd already been through so much, and Aurora was better suited to such twists of fate.

"These are your leaves, not mine," Aurora assured me. "And besides, my dear, at my age, I'm happy to assume a supporting role, as your star ascends."

She paused to give a perfunctory glance to her own cup.

"Ah, but not so fast, it does seem I have yet one more husband ahead of me."

I laughed, appreciatively. "At least *one*, I'd say."

"Oh, one more detail of utmost importance," Aurora said. "Call your mother, dear. She worries. And she'd love nothing more than to hear from you."

A pang of regret cut through me. Aurora was absolutely right, as always, on every front. And so, I could only hope she was correct about my future as well.

***

IT HAD BEEN MORE than forty-eight hours since an extremely inebriated Johnny had been separated from the positively pickled Jet and Hawke. They'd accidentally left him behind at The Rainbow the previous Friday night, when they'd gotten a wild hair to hit a strip club, while he'd been using the pissetarium. By the time Johnny returned to their trio of empty glasses, Hawke and Jet had already stumbled off into the night.

And that was the last they'd seen or heard of Johnny.

On this Monday afternoon, when Scarlett headed west to enjoy lunch with Aurora, she'd left Imani bored, restless, and alone in their Hollywood Hills bungalow. Imani's jealousy ignited her gumption enough to actually make use of the digits Bone had left with her on Friday night. And so, having checked that it was, in fact, after noon— the earliest rock 'n' rollers can be expected to be conscious, even on a weekday—Imani called Bone, hoping to maybe make something happen. On the other end, the ringing caused a mad dash for the receiver to see what news it might offer up. Hawke, as usual, was the pushiest and, therefore, the first one to reach the prize.

"Where the hell have you been, Johnny?" he asked, indignant more than worried.

"Excuse me?" Imani said.

"You're not Johnny then," Hawke said. "Just some bird."

"The last time I checked, I wasn't either," Imani said. "Put Bone on, before I teach you some manners, why don't you?"

"Bone, it's your lady friend," Hawke said, handing over the phone.

"Imani?" Bone exclaimed into the receiver.

"Oy, inquire as to whether or not Johnny is with Scarlett then," Shiv said.

"Johnny isn't there, is he?" Bone asked.

"He's got more sense than to show up here," Imani said. "Wait, you guys lost your singer? How does that happen? Twenty shots of flaming 151, I presume?"

"Something like that," Bone said. "Hey, wanna go feed French fries to the seagulls at the Santa Monica pier? Practice is canceled till we find Johnny."

Little did The Westies know that Johnny was actually no more than a mile from their rental house at that exact moment, tucking into a much-needed hot lunch at the Hamburger Hamlet on Sunset Boulevard. He'd wanted to rush straight home and let the lads know he was unharmed, but his companion had insisted they stop for a proper meal before he threw Johnny back into the fray. As Johnny devoured his second bacon double bleu cheeseburger (with extra pickles) he nudged his empty glass with his elbow, indicating for their waitress to bring him another double Jack and Coke.

"He'll take a Coke, hold the whiskey," Clint said, offering up a pleasant smile to the wannabe-starlet who was attending to their dining needs.

"Come on, man, show a little mercy," Johnny protested. "I just spent the weekend in jail."

"For a drunk and disorderly charge, among other offenses," Clint replied. "And you're glad you caught me on the office phone, not Deirdre's cell. Since she never comes into work, you lucked into me as your rescuing angel. She would have let you rot, rather than surrender, even temporarily, a penny in bail money."

"What do you mean Deirdre doesn't go into your place of business?" Johnny asked. "She's always begging off requests we make of her, claiming she's too busy there."

"Deirdre's idea of going to the office is a day at the Four Seasons' spa," Clint laughed. "Never mind that, though. We accomplish what needs to get done, between the two of us. Tell me, what happened, Johnny?"

"I was having a lark," Johnny said.

As the waitress set down Johnny's Coke, he frowned.

"Thanks, honey," he said. "Now, if you could please bring me a double Jack on the side."

"I know you probably think I'm nothing more than Deirdre's chauffeur and errand boy, right?"

"Don't be so hard on yourself," Johnny protested. "You must do *something*...I mean, she's kept you 'round long enough."

"I do just about everything for Deirdre," Clint said. "Including, doing her laundry, and booking her travel. Do you know where she is, as we speak?"

"Four Seasons' spa, according to you," Johnny said.

"Detroit, actually."

"But we're in LA."

"You may be," Clint said. "But the hot new band every label is courting at the moment has a gig tonight in the Motor City. And you can bet Deirdre will sign them before they ink a record deal. And we know she always does."

Johnny hesitated a moment before guzzling half of his second drink of the lunch hour. "But I don't understand."

"Sure, skill helps when you're crafting hits," Clint said. "So does charisma. And, well, let's be honest, a little bit of good old-fashioned luck. But do you know what really goes the furthest?"

"Hooks?"

"Hunger," Clint said. "Who wants it the most? I mean they don't tell that old 'How many musicians does it take to screw in a light bulb?' joke for nothing. Because for every band that hits the big time, there are a dozen that never make it out of the garage, or crash and burn when they do. Don't be that cliché. It takes talent *and* tenacity to keep the train a-rollin'."

"Heavy," Johnny said, pushing his half-finished burger away and finishing his drink.

"Look, Johnny, the label can make your arrest go away," Clint said. "At worst, you'll have to do a few hours of community service. But everything else is up to you."

Johnny nodded his head, a glimmer of reality actually getting through to him.

When Clint dropped him off in front of the house an hour later, Johnny barely paused to explain the series of misadventures that had caused him to 1) Catch a ride to the edge of Barstow. 2) End up at a honky-tonk, just before last call. 3) Get into a bar brawl with a closed-minded cowboy named Hootenanny Hank. 4) Be arrested in a one-streetlight town. 5) Experience all of this on a Friday night, which meant there was no opportunity to get booked and appear before a judge—or to even make use of his one phone call to someone on the outside—until Monday morning. 6) Get let out of the clink, only after the local sheriff came back to work and dealt with the sorry saps and drunks who'd accumulated in the town's single jail cell over the weekend.

For the first time since the early days of rock 'n' roll dreaming back in NYC, Johnny was on a mission. Rather than taking the bait from Hawke and engaging in a battle over who could come up with a better plan to out-swindle the club promoter for more playtime, or even just shotgun the most beers, Johnny went straight to his room and slammed the door behind him.

"Leave him be," Johnny heard Shiv say as he shut out the rest of the world. "He must be knackered. While you lot were messing about, he was in jail."

But Johnny wasn't tired. He was energized. There was something about having Clint tell him the truth—the reality he was most scared of—that was more sobering than a cup of strong black coffee or even a weekend behind bars. Johnny was enjoying their major label experience, sure, but he'd worked his ass off to get here, and he wasn't about to piss it all away for a free ride in a limo, or whatever other shackling perks their label presented to the band. And so, upon realizing how close he was to losing it all, he went straight to the place where he felt the most grounded; a piano bench. As he remarked to himself for the millionth time in the past week just how amazing it was that he actually had a motherfucking piano in his bedroom, his fingers were already right at home, finding the perfect keys.

By the time the sun could be seen setting over the distant lip of the Pacific Ocean from the house's perch in the Hollywood hills, Johnny had worked out the melody and lyrics for his latest opus. Inspired by love and longing and all the best ingredients that went into the purest rock 'n' roll, it was called "The Velvet Rose."

***

INSPIRATION CAN BE FICKLE. I had the entire house to myself, and a whole Friday night ahead of me. A pair of tailored metallic gold velvet trousers was poised for adornment on my draft table. I grasped a black glitter paint pen in my hand, but I fidgeted in my seat, my mind a void. The fragrant spring air wafted in through my open window, carrying the aroma of night blooming jasmine and BBQ smoke, reminders that there was a whole city of people out there easing into their weekend pleasures.

I'd been poised to dive into my latest design for an hour now. All I'd managed to do was fill my iced tea glass three times and fashion my hair into an elaborate fishtail side braid. I was beginning to fear that my muse was where the rest of my Los Angeles consorts seemed to be on this particular evening: at the Viper Room.

I knew I couldn't blame Imani for working her usual bar back shift at the club on the night Johnny happened to be playing. Nor could I resent Sephy for being in attendance to support her love, Shiv, but it was hard not to feel left out and lonely. A month ago, I would have surely been in the front row, singing along to every word, and admiring Johnny's intense, simmering charisma. But, alas, not tonight.

As I gazed out at the sidewalk in front of my house, hoping my creative vision would bloom, a sparkly gold '68 El Camino turned down my street. To my surprise, it stopped at my humble abode. A uniformed driver exited and strode up the path to my front door. I was so stunned by his arrival that, when his knock resounded throughout my house, it took me a moment to go down and answer.

"Yes, may I help you?" I greeted the chauffeur.

"Miss Scarlett," he said. "I've been sent by Clint Bianca, in order to bring you to see The Westies perform at the Viper Room tonight."

"But what do you mean?!" I said. "I'm not dressed…or anything. I'm not even invited."

"Consider yourself invited, ma'am," he said. "I can wait. You're the boss."

When we pulled up to the club, the driver parked, came around to my side of the car, and opened my door for me with a gallant gesture.

I officially felt like a rock 'n' roll princess and was already beginning to warm to Johnny's apology.

I gave my name to the door person and steered my way into the main bar, which was standing room only, packed to the gills with an assortment of the city's most fabulous nightlife personalities, from Steve Jones of The Sex Pistols, to cool cat radio DJ, Rodney Bingenheimer. I craned my neck to find Sephy, so I'd have a companion with whom to form a unified front until my reunion with Johnny. I considered myself lucky to have a friend behind the bar on a night such as this, but when I pushed my way to the area where people were waiting for drinks, I didn't see any sign of Imani working on the other side. As I turned back and wiggled my way through the packed room, I saw her hop down from the side of the stage.

"Impossibly Beautifully Sexy," I called, using my righteous nickname for the radical Imani as I tugged on the back of her vegan leather jacket to catch her attention.

"Scarlett," she said. "What are you doing here?"

"Johnny sent a car for me," I said. "Isn't that romantic?"

"He did?"

"Well, Clint did, but I'm sure Johnny was behind the gesture."

"If you say so," she said. "Hey, I gotta hit the loo."

"I'll go with you," I said. "Then maybe you can get me a drink when you go back behind the bar, pretty please? It's mental in here."

"Oh, ah, I'm not actually working tonight…"

"Really? It's crazy busy. And—what are you doing here then?"

"Oh, you know," she said, moving away from me as she talked. "I figured there might be some record people I could slip a tape to."

"But I thought you told me that you had to work tonight."

"Yeah, well, I don't," she said. "I didn't think it would matter. It's not like you've been around much lately to notice what I'm doing, anyhow."

"You're the one who works nearly every night of the week…" I said. "*You* never have time to hang out…not *me*…"

She looked down quickly, a guilty expression on her face.

Wait, if she wasn't really working tonight, maybe she hadn't been working those other nights, either.

"What's going on, Immi," I asked, letting the excited rock fans jostle us, too upset with my best friend to push back.

"I knew you wouldn't like it."

"Like what?"

"I'm here with Bone," she said.

"What do you mean?" I asked. "As in he gave you a ride?"

"As in I'm his date."

"Oh, but you—"

"Don't date? You're the only one who's pretty enough to get a guy interested in you, right? Just go ahead and say it."

"Of course not! It's just that I wasn't even aware you knew him."

"Yeah, well, I do," she said. "Look, they're gonna start soon. I've got to go."

"Okay," I said. "We can talk about it at home."

She didn't respond, only turned and walked away. My shimmering anticipatory mood had instantly deflated. But before I had time to worry about what it would be like to see Johnny without my best friend to support me, the lights dimmed.

A strobe flashed up from the stage, cutting through the suddenly dense front of house smoke. A giant, shattering riff echoed through the club. The Westies were ready to spank Los Angeles into submission. It was impossible to stay upset, not with the band achieving the taut velocity of a freight train, pummeling out all cares and worries. Or the way a sexy black lock of Johnny's hair kept falling down over one side of his face, shadowing his cheekbone in a most alluring way. I was swept up in the music, singing along, and shaking my fist in the air, in time with the beat.

And then, toward the end of the set, the band paused to gather velocity for their big finish. Cigarettes were lit, drinks were swallowed in one go. Jet grabbed a towel from his amp and wiped his brow. Johnny tuned his guitar, strummed, tuned again, as if the fate of the world depended on the next number's perfect sound.

"This is a new song," he said. "You're the first lucky sods to ever hear it. And I'd like to dedicate it to a very special someone who is—I am longing for her to be—here tonight."

Over Hawke's gentle acoustic guitar, Johnny began to sing:

*"More precious than amber 'n' gold*
*More noble than a lion's repose*
*More lovely than a sunrise to behold*
*She's…the velvet….rose…"*

My love had written me a song! And it was gorgeous and romantic, and full of sweet adoration and tenderness.

When Sephy found me at the end of the band's set and insisted I must come along to the after party, I was blissed out and full of nerved-up anticipation. It seemed like the band would never be done with their official meet-and-greet duties with the HIGs back at the club, in order to be able to come join us at the party. But, finally, there was Johnny, kissing my cheek, ever so gently.

"I'm sorry, Scarlett," he said. "I was a fool. Tell me, did you like your song?"

"Did I ever," I said.

"You're not the only one," he beamed. "The suits loved it. They absolutely insisted it's got to be our album's first single."

*Wow. Just a few days ago, I'd felt like the lowest of the low, and now, here I was, living in a magical dream.*

When I thought the night couldn't possibly improve upon itself, I was approached by the chauffeur who'd driven me to the club in that bomb ass El Camino.

"I'm sorry to keep you out so late," I said. "I can always take a taxi home, if your shift is over for the night."

"Not at all, ma'am," he said, pressing the car keys into my hand. "I was asked to give you these and tell you to enjoy your ride."

"I—wait—what?—I don't understand," I said. "Why can't you drive? Were you drinking or something?"

"It's your car now," he said.

I turned to Johnny, who offered me up a bashful grin. "I'm gonna win you back if it's the last thing I do," he said.

And who was I to argue?

# SLITHER

DOWNTIME IS A MUSICIAN's worst enemy. When blessed with days off, rockers aren't going to research new investment opportunities for their prolific 401K (what's that?!) or take up Pilates. Based on a historical overview of their proclivities, it's probably fair to say they're poised to drink, drug, shag, light things on fire, and stick their fingers in light sockets (mostly metaphorically, albeit, sometimes literally).

And repeat.

The day after their triumphant set at The Viper, The Westies rode their elation into A&M Studio, on their tricked out bikes: a '52 Harley Davidson panhead for Hawke, a '60 Triumph for Jet, and a '67 white shovelhead Harley for Johnny. No one trusted Bone enough to operate a motorcycle safely, God bless him, so he traveled in Jet's sidecar.

They recorded a blistering version of their brand-new single "The Velvet Rose" in just one take. And then, they had a week on their hands until they left for their *first ever North American tour*. Rather than practice on the daily, or make sure they had enough clean socks, they partied.

The debauch went on 'round the clock. Naked beauties frolicked in the hot tub while slugging champagne straight from bottomless magnums of Dom and making it clear they'd do anything for the prize of spending the night with one of The Westies. A near constant stream of the crème de la crème of female guests trailed in and out of Hawke's room, unfazed by being just one of the night's many conquests. An ice fountain served tequila, having mysteriously appeared on the patio one night. A child's birthday party clown, who'd knocked on the wrong door one afternoon and never left, could obviously be found smoking aromatic hydroponic supersonic weed on the upstairs exterior balcony twenty-four-seven. And, always, the greatest, grittiest rock 'n' roll, from The Stones to The New York Dolls, poured out of the speakers at level eleven volume.

Midway through day three of this extended bacchanalia, Shiv and Johnny wandered out back to the pool together. Both were enduring a moment of relative sobriety and actually clear-headed enough to take in the damage. "The Clown," wearing a white men's tank top and his polka dot pants, his face paint smeared, was passed out on a lounge chair. A lingerie-clad prima ballerina did speedy laps in the pool, a wilted feather boa trailing from her neck through the water behind her. A bedlam of empty Coors and vodka bottles, overflowing ashtrays, and discarded items of denim clothing and Harley Davidson-esque apparel poked up from beneath the now-trampled rose bushes and banks of bougainvillea. As Shiv and Johnny digested the carnage, Hawke and Jet joined them.

"Welcome to the zoo," Jet said, standing up a whiskey bottle that had been knocked onto its side and was leaking drops of amber liquid onto the patio.

"Just another day in paradise," Hawke said, overturning the bottle again, just because that's how he operated.

Shiv picked up the disputed bottle and took a healthy glug from the remaining booze, settling the matter once and for all. Holding the fifth in the crook of his elbow, he pulled his sunglasses down from the top of his head, shading his eyes. *Now* he was ready to roll.

"I'm famished," Shiv said, turning back toward the house.

"Let's get tacos," Johnny said, one step behind him. "And…hey, has anyone seen Bone?"

"He was at the studio with us," Jet offered.

"Yeah…three days ago," Johnny said, pausing in his tracks. "Fuck, did we lose him again?"

"I think he said something about going to see a friend in Venice," Hawke said, yawning as he surveyed the current beauties on hand to see if any piqued his interest.

"And you didn't stop him?" Johnny asked.

"He's a grown man, not my teenaged son, Jesus, thank God," Hawke said, wrestling the whiskey bottle away from Shiv and helping himself to a swig.

"You should know by now, the only *friends* Bone has are guys with an eye patch, named Shifty, or those who can be found on the FBI's most wanted posters at the post office—sometimes both. And they *all* sell party favors for a living."

"He went to get a piñata?" Jet asked.

"If only," Johnny said, tapping the front pockets of his jeans, as if checking for his car keys. "Is anyone fit to drive?"

"Didn't that dealer…I mean…um, limo driver, move into the extra bedroom?" Hawke asked.

The boys were soon cruising west toward Venice Beach in the back of the off-duty limousine, whose driver had somehow ended up as part of their entourage. And since they didn't have to do the driving themselves, why not polish off another fifth of Jack Daniel's en route? By the time they decamped near Muscle Beach, they looked more in need of rescuing than the triumphant rescuers they'd intended to be.

Johnny clutched his hand over his eyes, the sunlight too bright, even through his extra-dark shades. Hawke slouched over, trying and failing to light a cigarette in the strong sea breeze. Shiv stood idly, humming to himself, as if not entirely sure of his location in time or space and Jet roused himself to size up the body builders on Muscle Beach. He was soon doing burpees and bicep curls with a zombie-like detachment. The overly suntanned, speedo-clad regulars elbowed each other, marveling at this pale, shaggy haired musician dressed head-to-toe in rock wear—black metal T-shirt, black Levi's, and black boots—who'd suddenly landed in their midst, as out of place as Ziggy Stardust. It must be said, he was pretty impressive, especially given the context.

Perhaps taking in their general aura of party-induced dishevelment, a dreadlocked skater with blurry, faded tattoos sidled up to them.

"What are you looking for?" he whispered. "'Cause I got it."

"Hmmm, that's an intriguing offer," Hawke said. "I could definitely use a—"

"Stay focused," Johnny interrupted. "We're looking for our mate, Bone. He's tall, a drummer. Nose ring. Glazed eye stare. The usual."

"Bone, hmm?" the dealer said. "Is he into uppers or downers?"

"A little of everything," Johnny said. "Make that *a lot* of everything. You seen him?"

"Na, I try not to see anything," the dealer said. "It keeps me out of trouble. You should check with Maurice. He lives on a house boat down on the canals."

"People are allowed to live in house boats on the canals?" Shiv asked. "Now that's suitably baroque. Persephone would absolutely adore such accommodations."

"Wouldn't say the local government *allows* people to live on their boats in the canals," the dealer said. "Maurice just does."

Having picked up a few beers, the lads trailed up and down the slender, whimsical streets of Venice. As the minutes ticked by, with no sign of the mythical houseboat, it became clear Maurice did not want to be found. Finally, on the farthest, narrowest, windiest avenue, behind a walking bridge, they encountered the unlikely form of a lean, low-slung houseboat. As they approached, they saw the windows were draped with batiked tapestries and wallpapered with fliers from old Grateful Dead shows.

"I guess there's nothing doing but to go straight in and see what's up," Shiv said, stepping onto the deck of the boat.

"Let's try to be cool," Johnny said, following close behind him. "We don't know anything about this Maurice fellow."

Just then, Hawke came on board as Johnny reared back to make room for Jet. The slight pitch of the vessel, coupled with the hours—make that days—of heavy drinking were too much for Hawke. He fell backward into the channel with a tremendous splash, and when his head surfaced, he was already yelling: "Stupid motherfucker! Goddamn it! Shit!"

So much for subtle.

The roughly hewn door to the floating domicile burst open and a huge, slobbering, barking Pit Bull burst forth like one of the hounds of hell. Johnny and Shiv huddled together as the mutt growled at them with menace. They bumped into Jet, who was mid-rescue of Hawke, toppling them both over into the suspiciously dark and murky water. By now, Hawke was apoplectic with indignation and rage, especially when Johnny overcame his fear of the fierce guard dog enough to laugh at Hawke's misfortune.

A man who looked like a pirate out of central casting—bandana-clad head, gold hoop earring, and yes, an eye patch—poked out his sleepy, sneering face.

"Good girl, Stinkies!" he called to the dog, who immediately ceased its attack and sat obediently, just in front of him. He turned his attention to the intruders. "You got the message, right? She's a living, breathing NO trespassing sign. So get the hell out!"

"No—no harm intended," Shiv said, gently stepping back and slowly lifting his arms up, indicating that he came in peace. "We've lost our mate, and we heard you're a man with a keen knowledge of what occurs on these streets."

"Sometimes." Maurice twiddled his fingers absently in his right front pocket. "Who's your mate?"

"Our drummer...Bone," Johnny said, turning around from where he was trying to help Jet and Hawke back onto the boat.

"For the love of God, that guy's got an entourage," Maurice said. "Next thing you know, half the Rockettes and Santa Claus will turn up, looking for him. Ah well..." he trailed off, skeptically looking about for anyone else who might be lurking. "You'd better come in," he finally offered.

Hoping for the best but fearing the worst based on past episodes, Johnny ducked his head beneath the low door and followed Maurice into the dim, smoky interior. He tripped against a strange object and stopped abruptly, only to have the others bump into him. As his eyes adjusted to the shadowy gloom, Johnny identified it as the largest hookah he'd ever seen. Next to it was a low, seventies-style, tawny-colored couch, on which Bone slumped, nodding off. And, *oh no*, leaning up against him was a completely-immobile Imani, her eyes fluttering heavily.

"All right, Bone Dog, we're gonna take you home," Johnny said, crossing over to where he could get a grip on Bone to lift him up and carry him out.

"What's your hurry?" Maurice purred, pointing to the hookah that dominated the corner of the room. "The night is in its infancy. Why not indulge in a quick puff?"

Six hours later The Westies had shared their entire life stories with their new best friend, Maurice, while enjoying the languid mystery of an opium high. And, yes, it's true that Johnny had strictly forbidden Imani to take part in anything stronger than one of the beers Maurice offered them, having been suitably alarmed by the fact that Bone had let her smoke heroin. But Johnny also had not succeeded in pulling himself off the couch and seeing that she made it home safely. And by the time he finally did so, at six o'clock in the morning, she had already missed her entire bar back shift at the Viper Room that night, and in doing so, lost her job.

✳✳✳

A NIGHT OUT WITH Sephy meant two ingredients in abundance: champagne and drama. So when she swooped me up on an evening Johnny was in the studio, recording his ode to me, I was not at all startled to find myself quaffing a flute of cold Moët + Chandon '92 Imperial Rose Nectar champagne. Nor, having momentarily lost sight of Sephy, to locate her by the sound of her lurid Cockney accent among a throng of milling art aficionados. We'd only just arrived, and she was already making quite a hullabaloo. I hurried over to investigate, navigating my way, as politely as possible, through a room Sephy had described to me as being "swollen with whales."

Sephy was intent on launching my career as a designer, and had coordinated my social schedule with precision and finesse. Accordingly, we were planning to take advantage of the hottest invite in town—the launch party for the king of celebrity social gatherings, Brent Bolthouse's latest see-and-be-seen club, the Opium Den. But first, we'd begun our evening's adventures at the opening reception for painter David Hockney's new show at the Venice Beach gallery, LA Louver. Sephy had taken the event, quite literally, by storm. When I located her, she'd backed a tall, raven-haired young woman against the wall, dangerously close to one of Hockney's oversized, brightly hued canvases, "Moving Wisp."

"You impudent minx!" Sephy yelled at her foe. "*You* are going to confess your disgusting sins this instant, or I will ruin you, do you hear me?"

"Sephy, Jesus, are you okay?" I asked, placing my hand on my dear friend's arm, and raising my own voice in order to be heard over the melee.

And then, it hit me like a jumbo jet accelerating at top speed into a brick fucking wall. I saw the source of Sephy's outrage: the lady she'd cornered had donned a dress completely identical to the one I'd debuted at last week's Gagosian opening. The resemblance was so spot on.

Oh, wow!! Was my one-of-a-kind frock stolen out of my closet without me realizing it?

"What's going on?" I asked, looking back and forth between them, seeking an answer, wherever I could get it. "That's my dress…isn't it?"

"You'd have every reason to assume so, since it's an *exact* knockoff of your hand-painted, couture dress," Sephy huffed. "I'm interrogating this style poacher as to how she came by it."

"I'd certainly like to know!" I said, unable to contain the emotion in my voice.

The more I looked, the better I was able to discern that this was, indeed, a lesser copy of the design I'd labored over. And the angrier I became on my own behalf.

This woman, who appeared to be forty-something, wore a perfectly constructed façade of dramatic, retro makeup, complete with tons of foundation and a black beauty mark à la Marilyn Monroe. She surveyed us coolly. But her heavy-handed cosmetic war paint couldn't camouflage her guilt, which was obvious from her twitchy body language and shifty, downward glances.

"I have no idea what you're talking about," she said.

"You know exactly," I said, my voice shaking. "I constructed an original dress, which I wore to a Gagoshian opening last week. Since it is from a design I cut, and sewed, and painted *myself*, I can only assume you saw it and decided to knock it off."

"Give me a break—" she said. "Prove it!"

"I will," I said, enjoying a brainstorm. "My good friend, Drew Barrymore, and I were actually photographed on the red carpet that night. All I need to do is request one of the date stamped photos from Getty Images, and I'll have my evidence."

"Don't waste your breath trying to prove anything to this thief," Sephy said. "I know what must be done."

Stepping forward with a wicked jeer, Sephy brandished her empty champagne flute as if it were a weapon. "Take it off."

"Don't...don't...be ridiculous," the woman stuttered. She dodged, quickly, first to the right, and then to the left, trying to break free of Sephy, and as she did so, she shouted out a nasally, "Security! Security!"

"I'm being quite logical, actually," Sephy said. "That dress is the intellectual property of my friend here and therefore belongs to her."

"I'll have you thrown out," the woman whimpered. "You're some old, nobody, poser lady who is clearly insane!"

But when the gallery owners, Peter Goulds and Kimberly Davis approached, trailed by a burly guard in an understated gray suit, they, of course happened to be dear old friends of Sephy's. (Peter had, in fact, gone to school with her brother back in the U.K.) All sympathy was clearly on Sephy's side. After a brief powwow, it was decided that the offending guest would be allowed to change out of the disputed dress in the restroom. She would don a lightweight overcoat she carried with her, rather than make a scene by stripping down, right then and there, as Sephy was still insisting. This was a relatively calm dénouement, especially compared to the public shaming Sephy had envisioned. Still, I was shaking a few moments later, when I found myself in the passenger seat of Sephy's '76 Silver Shadow Rolls with a champagne flute from the opening in one hand and the garment in the other.

"I cannot believe that just happened."

"I can," Sephy said. "You're a true original. It was bound to occur sooner or later. And you know what that means, luv? It means we absolutely must launch your line *immediately*. This is everything. You must get the rightful credit you deserve, dahling, for your talent and hard work."

"But how?"

"Leave everything to me, my pet," she purred.

The next few weeks were the best possible kind of whirlwind. All hours of the day and night, I answered Sephy's calls, in which she asked me cryptic questions about whether I preferred gold leaf or silver chainmail; Kir Royales or French Martinis, and the foxtrot or falconry.

I also became reacquainted with Johnny (and his fraternal band mates, who never left his side) by spending free evenings at their house in the Hollywood Hills. One night when we were leaving The Rainbow in order to keep the party going by the pool at home, Hawke was heard telling the lovely female bassist he'd picked up that evening, "Let's head back to my place. It's so next level, some have been calling our pad, 'The Hunk House.'"

Another local musician, who'd been drinking with us, burst out laughing. "More like 'The Dog House,'" he sneered.

"Ahhh, yeah, that's right, it's just a few blocks west of your crib, 'The Champ Camp,' on 3 Farthing Lane," Johnny retorted, earning shouts and cheers from our rowdy crew as we exited the bar onto Sunset.

But the moniker for their rockers' lair, "The Dog House," stuck, and their party pad was forever known as such.

If I was disappointed to find that Johnny was more into carousing by the pool than nipping off for a romantic rendezvous in his bedroom, he was always unfailingly glad to have me by his side. And when I had to be elsewhere, he always wanted to know when I'd be back. I comforted myself with pep talks about how his major label debut was only two weeks out and he was in need of the reassurance of his fellow Westies, and the relaxation of a few stiff drinks more than ever before. I wanted to be supportive.

I wanted to believe. And so, I did. At least I mostly did, and at least for a time.

Before I knew it, the night of my once-in-a-lifetime design debut had arrived. I was so excited, I finished getting ready a full hour before I was due to climb into the 1939 Packard Stretch Limo Sephy had hired for me, to go pick up Johnny.

I hadn't had any contact with Imani in days, except for the rare occasions, in the middle of the night, when I'd awoken to hear her smoky alto and earnestly strummed acoustic guitar wafting from behind her closed bedroom door. But she was a night owl now, never sleeping at the house, and when I knocked in the morning to say hello she was always gone. Our shared space felt echo-y and empty without her punk records spinning or the smell of her vegan chili spicing up the kitchen. Without her there to talk me down from my nerves, as she'd been doing masterfully for a decade, I paced and fretted. At least Johnny would help, as his sweet handsome face always seemed to put me at ease.

But when I approached "Le Dog House," as my limo waited for us in the driveway, the front door was ajar, and the downstairs rooms were empty. I hastened up to Johnny's bedroom, but he was nowhere to be found. My anxiety spiked as I rushed through one vacant room after another. I found him by the pool, his biker boots instantly recognizable at the end of a chaise lounge. Sneaking up behind his chair, I playfully popped my head around, in order to kiss him on his cheek.

"How silly of me, I thought you'd vanished!"

The only reply I received was a deep, sawing snore.

He was passed out, *cold*.

"Hey, Scarlett," Jet said from his nearby yoga mat. "Hawke dared Johnny to eat the worm in the mezcal, and he had to drink the whole bottle to get to it, so..."

If my face hadn't been so carefully made up, I would have cried. But I bit my lip and held my emotions in check. I knew, even if I could rouse Johnny, I wouldn't be able to get him into any kind of proper condition for an intimate, high fashion event—especially one as crucial as tonight's. "Jet, I'm afraid you're going to have to throw him in the pool," I said.

"Tonight's your launch, isn't it?" Jet said. "I think you're right—it's gonna take some desperate measures to wake him up, but I'm happy to help."

"Once he's conscious, sober him up with hot coffee, and get him over to the Chateau as quickly as possible," I said. "Do all that, and you'll be the guest of honor. I'm certain Sephy has outdone herself yet again, so it's sure to be quite a happening."

"You got it," Jet said. "Now go enjoy your big night!"

Jet's easygoing kindness nearly set off my water works all over again. The fact that Johnny had forgotten about my party stung, of course. Fucking big time. But I shook off my sadness and tried to be happy for all that was going right.

I was rattled, and now, running late. But I forced myself to slow my pace, taking deep, fortifying breaths, as I walked back among the bungalows at the legendary Chateau Marmont. This was, after all, the official launch of my own label, Velvet Rose. I wanted to learn from the reactions of the various stylists, editors, and fashionistas in attendance, and savor the night's hard-won celebration. It helped that lovely Sephy had sprinkled glitter-dusted ruby red and baby pink rose petals along the path, garlanded it with ropes of fragrant jasmine and lilies. I felt as if I was entering a private paradise.

Once inside the bungalow that housed the event, I was not at all surprised to find adorable leopard cubs (rescued from poachers and given a new life as movie extras, who were, of course, accompanied by their trainers and treated ethically), wearing my burgundy berets, each painted with a different, special African symbol of vitality. Waiters passed trays of signature sidecar drinks, each accented with a single hot pink, edible rose petal. Our guests, a who's who of fashion and entertainment elite, were laughing and posing, as they enjoyed the selection of my designs Sephy had put on display, so they could adorn themselves in my vision. Drew Barrymore couldn't have looked more radiant in the softly muted, rainbow-hued, silk butterfly dress I'd made just for her. And next to her, was the always attractive and timeless, Mr. Karl Lagerfeld, outfitted not only in his signature black shades, but also in one of my fitted, elegantly subtle, racehorse-embellished, midnight smoking jackets. This was all pure, wonderful, larger-than-life Sephy, and to be expected.

I was stunned when my presence was detected at the edge of the soiree, and everyone paused to give me a standing ovation. From amid the throngs of fabulous people, and dearest well-wishers from my own life, came a shockingly perfect guest of honor. It was Franco Giovani, the magnificent Italian photographer who had discovered me at the mall, back in 1991. This, I must say, for sure felt like it had been ages ago now.

"Il mia gattino!" he cried happily, upon seeing me. "You have blossomed. You are *il rosa di velluta*. I could not be more proud."

"Franco," I said. "I can't believe you're here."

He kissed both of my cheeks then held me at arm's length to get a proper look at me. Once I had wilted with embarrassment under his appraising gaze. I now stood proudly in the velvet rose couture dress I'd fashioned for the night, having matured into a well-traveled, independent artist, thanks in no small part to his belief in me.

"Your dear Persephone, is good friend," he said. "Her agent fly me to Los Angeles. For me to photograph your beautiful designs. My images will travel out into the world on wings of applause and admiration I have for you. Everyone know now you is…how you say?…Molto fantastico!"

Sephy had made a remarkably demure—for her—entrance into the room. She now stood towering over Franco and me in her six-inch Dolce & Gabbana, burgundy jeweled strappy heels, and Galliano-esque rose-garnished headdress of live, fragrant blooms.

"What a touching scene," she cooed. "Mark my words, Scarlett, this is the moment when it all starts happening for you. Now, if you don't mind, Franco, I must steal Miss Scarlett away. There are many people who are curious to meet her and rep her line."

"*Ovviamente*," he said. "She is *Rocambolesco*!"

Bowing gallantly, he allowed me to be swept up and away by Sephy's centrifugal force. But before I could be introduced to any of the sparkly personalities about whom she was whispering (more like a powerful roar, in her case), I stopped short in the bungalow's front lounge. There was another true friend.

"Scarlett, my dear!" Aurora said, as she laid eyes on me. "Ravishing, you are! Won't you please come over and let me enjoy a glimpse of you in all your splendor?"

Aurora was regally displayed on a sleek midcentury couch, with the French doors open behind her, a faux leopard print throw on her lap, and a bouquet of fuchsia and blush roses in her hand, (given to her by Sephy, I had no doubt). Precisely coiffed in her glam sixties aesthetic, and spackled to the nines, she looked as heavenly as always. However, as I bent down to hug her, I couldn't help noticing how frail and birdlike her frame had become. It had only been a few weeks since our last social call.

"Aurora, I'm so glad you're here!" I said. "This night wouldn't be complete without you. Are you feeling entirely yourself?"

"I know, I hate being trapped here on this infernal couch like some silent film heroine, but I'm afraid I've got a bit of a cough, and it's weakened me."

"I do hope you haven't tired yourself out too much tonight," I fussed.

"Nonsense, nights like this are medicine for me," she said. "Persephone, bless that angel, was kind enough to situate me comfortably. You run off and play. I thought I saw that handsome Leo DiCaprio. I'll be here."

I kissed her soft feathery cheek once again before allowing Sephy to pull me into the midst of the night's spirited festivities. By the time I made it back to the couch, hours later, Aurora's driver had already come and ferried her home.

It was only then that I paused long enough to realize: *I received rave reviews on my original designs from some of the most thrilling innovators in the worlds of art and fashion. I had one of the brassiest, best nights of my entire life. And yet, absent from the evening's celebration was my best friend, and my boyfriend.* For the first time since this odyssey had begun, I found myself shaking off dark thoughts about the gaping maw of rock 'n' roll that seemed to be in danger of swallowing them both. And then, Sephy pulled me back into the company of the few lingering guests, who like me, didn't want to ever exit this magical kingdom she had crafted for us.

I did manage to send Aurora a bouquet of peonies and lilacs (her sentimental faves) with a thank you note, but that was about all the time and mental bandwidth I had to process the launch. In the days that followed, my reality exploded beyond the grasp of anyone's capacity for comprehension, and then some.

Franco had gotten his hands on a Kodak digital camera, created specially the previous year for Associated Press photojournalists. He'd employed it to take some of the photos at the shoot for my Velvet Rose collection. Although I didn't totally understand the technology myself, he assured me it heralded the dawning of a whole new era in photography. And he was right.

My newly hired publicist was working in conjunction with Sephy, who had a formidable knack for creating a certifiable media blitz. They used Franco's gorgeous, carefully curated images for my upcoming 1996 spring/summer look book, and to accompany press releases. And so, they were able to place items on my designs in every women's high fashion magazine, from *WWD*, to *Marie Claire*, to *Vogue*. Franco also took the liberty of emailing digital images, not only to the production place that did art direction for the look book, but also, to Sarah, the head buyer at Barney's, who happened to be his dear, longtime friend. Even before magazine stories ran, I was already due to have a few signature pieces at Barneys, and to design the costumes for an upcoming performance by the Alvin Ailey American Dance Theater.

And with that, for the second time in mere months, the Velvet Rose was launched, proving that old saying about how, sometimes, lightning does strike twice. And now, it was happening in a form that I couldn't have been more proud of—straight from my heart, and catapulting out into the entire world.

***

"Ow!" JOHNNY YELPED, YANKING his hand back from where he was hovering it a few inches above the candle on our table at The Whiskey-a-Go-Go.

"Yeah, it's a flame," I said. "It's hot."

A shadow of irritation crept into my voice, even though I tried to keep my tone positive. Not that Johnny noticed. He was laughing so hard he was snorting, nearly streaming his drink through his nasal passages. Hawke took his turn, holding his bare palm over the candle, to see who could last the longest before giving into the pain, and pulling away. Sometimes The Westies exuded *Peter Pan* meets *The Lost Boys* vibes (while fully twisted on drugs). At the table next to ours, a bevy of bodacious babes in microscopic miniskirts, fishnet tights, and cropped concert Ts, strategically shredded to show off their assets, shot longing glances at the guys. Such displays of fawning devotion from their bolder female fans were par for the course now, wherever we went. Normally, I tried to ignore it. But, tonight I couldn't help but shoot the ladies a glare, telling them with my eyes to stay away from my man.

I was already in a foul mood because Imani hadn't let me help her get ready for her debut performance tonight. And so I was left clutching my drawstring nylon Prada backpack. I'd packed it full of extra makeup and lavender bergamot scented candles to get her in the zone by creating the perfect pre-show, backstage ambiance for her. *What does Bone know about eyeliner...or anything?* I thought. *I can't believe she wanted him back there with her, and not me.*

Just then, the door to the backstage area, which I'd been scrutinizing, began to rattle as if it were locked and someone was trying to get through. Finally, with what appeared to be a tremendous effort, Bone emerged from the other side.

*Man, he must be pretty loaded if he can't figure out how to open a door.*

*Great—I hope he didn't give Imani anything. That's all she needs before her big show.*

Bone ambled across the room as if he'd forgotten where he was headed or why. Catching sight of our motley crew, he veered toward us. When he reached our table, he picked up a pint of beer and drank it down without a word.

"Hey, man, get your own lager," Hawke protested.

"What?" Bone let out a most inelegant belch. "I just did." He suddenly jolted, as if waking up, and surprised me by looking directly at me. "Imani is severely freaking out. She asked if you'd go back there."

"Really?" I said, already standing and rushing toward the backstage area. Rethinking my approach, I detoured to the bar. I ordered a ginger ale, one of the only vices Imani normally allowed herself, being the health-conscious vegan she was. When I found my way to the tiny, cramped "dressing room," and approached Imani, she was seated at a mirror that was more graffiti and band stickers than clear glass. As soon as I laid eyes on her, I was glad I'd brought her a sugary pick me up. Maybe it was because I'd only seen her from afar recently, passing in and out of rooms in our bungalow like a ghost, but her appearance was shocking to me. She'd lost at least fifteen pounds, there were hollowed shadows beneath her beautiful chestnut colored eyes, and something in her bowed shoulders made her look decades older than she was. Her gaze, meeting mine in the mirror, was unfocused and sullen, as if her life force had been trodden down.

"Are you okay, my Immaculata?" I asked, keeping my voice gentle and low.

"Yeah, grand," she said, slurring slightly. "Bone gave me something to relax, a muscle relaxer—get it. Relax. *Relaxer.* And now, everything feels fluffy."

"Oh boy," I said. "Let me get you a coffee."

"Where'd Bone go?" she asked, when I hurried back a moment later and handed her the steaming cup. "He said he'd stay right here, in case I get nervous."

"You sent him to get me, remember?"

"Now why would I do that?" Imani replied. "You'll just get mad at me. You don't like anything I do these days."

"That's not true, Ims," I said. "I just worry."

"See, you think I'm stupid, and I can't make any good choices on my own..." she said, her voice trailing off, then continuing, as if she'd rediscovered the thread. "Not like your romance is killing it. I mean does Johnny even notice you're around?"

"Ouch, tell me what you really think," I said, sitting down in the chair crammed in next to her in the narrow room, cluttered with other performers' gear.

"Two minutes, Imani," the sound person said, popping his head in the door.

"Here, let me help you with that eyeliner," I said.

"See? You think I'm ugly. I knew it."

"Of course not," I said. "You're gorgeous. I just thought it'd be like fierce, mental war paint, that's all. To get you in the mood to take the stage by storm."

"All right," she said, surprising me by capitulating, which was so not her.

As I ran the eyeliner gently over Imani's right eyelid, she seemed to disappear inside herself, almost as if she'd nodded off. *That fucker,* I thought. *If he ruined this for her, I'm going to make him pay.*

The sound guy pushed back into the room. "You're on," he said.

Imani pulled her head back from my grasp and slowly began to stand.

"Wait, Imani," I said, grabbing onto her hand. "I only had time to do one eye. Let me finish. It'll only take a sec."

"Nah, can't be late," she said, stumbling for the door and pushing her way out.

It was only after she left the room that I noticed she'd left her prized 1961 sunburst Melody Maker guitar behind. I hurried after her, cradling her instrument. I rushed to the side of the stage. Imani had zombie-walked out in front of the audience without her guitar. She was standing there, blinded by the lights, a dazed expression on her face.

*Oh no! She's really out of it. What should I do?!*

Trying to act as nonchalant as possible, I strolled out after her. I bowed low to Imani and presented her with her guitar, as if we'd choreographed the move as her dramatic set opener. She swiveled around slowly, considering me. At first, she looked so disoriented and confused, I feared I was going to have to start playing the guitar myself (I knew "House of the Rising Sun," kind of—*almost.*) Finally, she came to and accepted her instrument from me, sliding the strap over her head. And, tentative as a baby bird on its first flight, she lurched into her first song. Maybe her passion for her music, and the mastery she'd achieved after years of practice would see her through—if anyone could pull this off, even in her debilitated state, it was Imani. Or at least I hoped so.

Now that I was out on the stage, I wasn't sure what to do. Thankfully, her first number was one I'd heard her singing around the house for years, and I knew it by heart. Out of the corner of my eye, I saw a tambourine on the drum kit belonging to one of the later bands in the night's lineup. Picking it up, I started adding a gentle shimmer of a beat. When the moment came, I stepped up to the microphone on the side stage and began to sing some of the lyrics to the chorus along with her. We hadn't sound checked. I couldn't hear anything except for Imani's guitar and voice, LOUD, coming out of the monitors on the stage at our feet. Imani has always teased me, lovingly, for being completely tone deaf. But at the song's end, she actually looked over at me with a smile, which melted my heart after our recent tension. So I decided to see her through the entire gig, happily back on best friend duty.

As much as I adore Imani, it was not her best set ever. Her voice was strong and true. Her protest songs were earnestly strummed, and their smart, sassy, humanitarian lyrics about feminism and animal rights came through. Hopefully, I served as moral support, with my tambourine, and the backup singing I added to the few songs I knew. When Imani delivered her final note and let the reverb hang over the stage as we walked off into the wings, I was high on adrenaline. I couldn't help but think maybe my singing had actually been good. I was more than a little excited to hear what Johnny thought, being that he was a blues crooner with pipes of gold.

When we made our way back out into the crowd, while the next act set up their gear onstage, Imani seemed to have sobered up a bit. So I felt safe leaving her for a moment to breathe a sigh of relief and get a celebratory drink at the bar. I detoured to Johnny's table to see if they needed another round (when didn't they?) only to find that Hawke and Jet were alone at the table.

"Don't be embarrassed, girl," Hawke said. "It used to happen to Linda McCartney all the time."

"What?!" I asked, mind racing through awful possibilities (*toilet paper on my shoe, underwear sticking out of my dress, what the hell had happened up there?!*)

"You couldn't tell?" Hawke laughed. "Aw, a rookie."

"What? Tell me!" I nearly screamed.

"They, um…they, well, they turned off your mic," Jet said. "Don't feel bad. It happens."

Hawke leered at me. "And I must say, you looked *fine* up there."

"Thanks but no thanks," I said to Hawke, storming off.

*Where the fuck is Johnny, anyhow?*

As I waited at the bar for my Cosmo, a rowdy group rolled up behind me, nearly knocking me over. I turned around, ready to do some schooling in manners, especially when I saw it was the girls who'd ogled The Westies from a nearby table earlier in the night. But I also came face to face with Johnny and Bone, who were with them, and high in a jittery, disordered way I'd never quite seen before.

"Where were you guys?" I asked, hating the naggy sound of my own voice.

"Bone let me try this cool new drug, Apple Jacks, otherwise known as crack!" Johnny exclaimed. "We smoked it in an alley behind the club. I feel like the king of the world!"

"What did you think of Imani's set?"

"She was cool, she was great," he said. "So poised. What a natural solo artist."

"I can't believe you're going to stand here and lie right to my face," I hissed. "If you'd actually seen her set, you'd know she barely held it together, thanks to whatever this loser gave her," I continued, jabbing my finger at Bone. "And you would have seen that she wasn't solo—I actually sang with her."

Johnny started giggling uncontrollably. "I'm not laughing at you…I just feel so…funny…"

Which set Bone off, and the two were gripping each other, trying to hold each other up. In the midst of this chaos, Imani appeared, tears streaking her face. I'd never seen Imani cry before. "What's wrong, honey?"

"The promoter said I'm not getting paid, because I agreed to play a thirty-minute set, and I only played twenty-five. He said I broke our verbal contract. I don't know what to do. I need that money for rent this month."

She looked beseechingly at Bone, but he was far too out of it to be her knight in scuffed Vans.

The bartender set down my drink.

I nodded toward the idiots next to me. "Put it on their tab." I grabbed my drink, and put my arm around Imani, pulling her toward the back office to get this nightmare put straight. Before I could knock, however, Clint came up behind us.

"Hey, ladies, I couldn't help but overhear your problem when I was at the bar getting Deirdre's Diet Coke," he said, smiling ruefully. "This guy is jerking you around. You could be penalized for running over, but not the other way around."

"I'm going to go back there and give him a piece of my…"

"No offense, Scarlett," Clint said. "But you don't know the lingo. If he's this much of a weasel, he'll try to out maneuver you. Better let me be of some assistance here."

Within five minutes, Clint had talked circles around the shady promoter, even earning Imani a regular opening slot at the club, which was a dream come true for the aspiring songsmith. Imani insisted on buying Clint a drink to say thank you, and he hesitantly accepted a club soda and cran.

Clint blushed into his glass. "No one ever says thank you to me."

"Seriously, that's awful," Imani said. "I honestly can't thank you enough."

"In fact, are you thinking what I'm thinking?" I asked Imani, looking to my best friend for confirmation. "You'd be the perfect manager for Imani. Do you think you'd ever consider it?"

"Yes, oh my God…please," Imani said. "I'll work my ass off, and you won't be sorry, I promise."

"Don't think I can…really…" he said, pausing to consider, as if he were on the verge of changing his mind. "Deirdre's not going to like it." Then, beaming, he reached out to shake Imani's hand. "That's reason enough to do it," he said. "You've got yourself a deal. I'll have our lawyers draw up a standard management contract."

"This calls for a celebration," I cried out. "I'd love to treat you both to a special dinner at my fave spot, the Fenix at The Argyle Hotel."

I knew Johnny had been treating me terribly, but my heart was young and resilient, and I couldn't help but look around the room, hoping our good news would inspire him to join our festivities. But he was nowhere to be found, nor was Bone, or the group of scantily clad groupies. I tried not to think too hard about what that might mean. I could tell Imani was disappointed too, and so I threw myself into our commemoration of her big night with even more verve. It was just us two girls against the world, as it'd always been. (Oh, and Clint!) Maybe that was for the best.

✳✳✳

I held off on answering Johnny's calls for three days. Well, truth be told, it wasn't that hard to resist. The messages he left on our house answering machine were noisy with splashing and crashing, suggesting yet another nonstop party in full swing. And his vague requests that

I should "stop by and hang out by the pool sometime" weren't exactly the romantic enticements I craved.

Plus, I had serious designs to envision and generate! I was more occupied with my own creative endeavors than ever.

And also lonelier.

Imani was still cuddling up with Bone nonstop (at least she let me know what was going on with her again, well, mostly). She'd also, somehow, gotten her job back, managed to cover as many shifts as she could, and still practiced for a few hours a day in the rehearsal space The Westies had set up at their house—they certainly weren't using it. Which meant I had infinite alone time. I loved it when Persephone screeched her Rolls up onto the sidewalk outside my house and "popped in for a tipple," as she called it. But it was nearly impossible to get away without drinking anything less than two bottles of champagne with her, and I needed a clear head. I was actually thinking about adopting a dog to be my new best friend. Maybe that's why I decided to give Johnny one final absolution. I was determined he was going to earn his place in my heart this go around.

The next time Johnny's sexy drawl could be heard on our answering machine, I quickly picked up the receiver.

"Hey, Johnny," I said, trying for a modicum of aloofness.

"...Scarlett?" he stuttered. "Baby, is that really you? I was afraid I'd never talk to you again."

"Lucky for you, I'm a very forgiving woman," I said. "Here's what's happening, Jonathan Leon Jones. You're going to take me on a romantic date. Just the two of us. It could be a picnic in the park, or pizza and candles by your swampy pool. I really don't care. Make it happen. Or we're through."

"Um...okay...sounds great!" he said. "I'll call you with the details... and, sweetheart..."

"Yeah?"

"I miss your beautiful heart—you won't regret this I promise you, Rosie," he concluded, using his newest nickname for me since I'd been dubbed the Velvet Rose.

When I didn't hear from Johnny for three days, I was afraid that maybe I'd been a little too fierce, but I held tough. And, finally, that Friday morning, he called, asking me to be at his house at 6:00 p.m. that evening. He had everything all ready.

I'd been saving an exceptional piece for our next date—a red, raw silk halter dress, illustrated with a Garden of Eden theme. I indulged in a long bubble bath that afternoon, and then I took extra care with my hair and makeup. It was imperative that this date go well. Or else... well, I wasn't ready to contemplate the alternative.

When I showed up at Le Dog House, promptly at 6:00 p.m., I couldn't help but swoon a little at the shiny black 1932 Ford Model V8 parked outside. As I'd learn later in the night, the car had been favored by thirties gangsters, including John Dillinger, Baby Face Nelson, and Bonnie and Clyde, thanks to its powerful, flathead engine and sleek design.

*Wow, Johnny really made an effort to impress*, I thought, flushing with delight.

I continued walking toward the house, in search of my date.

"Hey, Scarlett, get in!" Jet called, popping his head out of the front passenger window.

"Hi, Jet," I said. "Looks fun, but I've got a date with Johnny tonight."

"You sure do, gorgeous!" Johnny materialized from the rear window.

"I thought we were having dinner tonight," I said, my anger rising.

"We sure are, sweet thing. Lobster Tacos in Rosarito! I'm already working on a song about it. Catchy little rhyme there, huh?"

"But we agreed on something, you know, cool and intimate, just the two of us," I said. "I used to go to TJ all the time during my high school days to get drunk. Yes, and it is fun and adventurous, but I also vaguely remember co-eds puking in alleys, and Incredible Hulk piñatas for sale everywhere. Sorry—doesn't connote an especially romantic vibe for me."

"Come on, Scarlett," Johnny called out. "Please. This is different. It'll be fun! This is beautiful Baja, a bit further drive down from there. It is muy romantico."

He placed a long stem red rose in his mouth, a slight impish grin accompanied by playful puppy eyes.

I hesitated on the curb.

As I peered into the luxury ride, Sephy waved back.

The next thing I knew, Shiv, Hawke, and Bone, roared up on their motorcycles, Imani clutching her man from behind. Chattering excitedly and swigging beers, they climbed into a second classic Ford that had been arranged, so our large group could be ferried South of the Border. I had an unsettling presentiment about this development. But everyone else was having an adventure.

What else was I going to do on a Friday night—sit home and knit?

Mistake #1: Getting into a 1932 Ford Model V8 on its way to Mexico with several known delinquents, even if you are in love with one of them (Johnny), and you're also accompanied by your two best friends (Imani and Sephy).

Mistake #2: Inferior, well tequila shots, which are otherwise known as bad headache hangover hell. Always and forever.

Mistake #3: Smoking anything anyone—(especially Bone)—hands you that can't be unequivocally identified as a classic joint and/or cigarette.

Mistake #4: Deciding, in a drunken moment of bravado, to show off to Johnny by eating the worm, which was sold in a novelty shot at the bar.

Mistake #5: See Mistake #2. (Yes, I did it again. And again.)

Mistake #6: Excusing myself to the restroom, around two in the morning.

# ROMEO & SCARLETT

THE NEXT THING I knew, it was two thirty in the morning and I'd spent at least half an hour drunkenly circumnavigating the legendary Pappas & Beer, an enormous beachfront bar in Rosarito, with a spring break vibe. I still hadn't been able to discern any trace of my companions, including Johnny. And, *OH FUCK!!* A vague, tequila-soaked memory surfaced: me teaching runway turns to the local señoritas who had rockognized the dudes and me earlier in the night. Before climbing on a long bar table to fully display my moves, I'd taken off my Levi's jean jacket and handed it to Johnny, who'd slipped it on. He'd apparently left the bar, still wearing it, and that also meant he had my ID and money, as they'd been in the left upper pocket!

This left me stranded in a foreign country on a Friday night, somehow wearing a Pappas & Beer souvenir T-shirt over my dress with no coat and no means of communicating with anyone back home. And zero funds to afford transportation, or even a call on a pay phone. And so, I did what any seasoned world traveler would do. I stood crying outside the bar for a few minutes, throngs of weekend warriors intent on their festivities reveling around me.

I pulled myself together and stopped a relatively non-terrifying-looking grandmotherly type, who was selling long stem roses to turistas from a flat wicker basket. "*Como llegas a Estados Unidos?*" I said, employing my best high school Spanish.

She stared at me a long moment, then turned slowly and pointed up the road, the nearest section of which was teaming with drunk vacationers and enterprising locals, who were trying to sell them snacks, tchotchkes, and more adult distractions. I had no idea if she'd understood me in the slightest or if this was indeed the reverse of the direction we'd traveled hours earlier in the Ford Mafia mobile. I wondered how the others were doing in their luxury ride. But there was no point in wasting any thoughts on them.

I took a deep breath and began striding in the direction she'd indicated. After the first block, I silently expressed gratitude for my many catwalk excursions and the ability they had given me to walk for hours in ridiculous heels while ignoring the pain entirely.

I traveled for what felt like an eternity, through the smell of frying corn tortillas and carnitas, the tequila in my system causing me to weave back and forth across the uneven sidewalk. In the dark corners of the beach, street barkers tried to entice passersby with rooster fights, female companionship, darker things mentioned only in hushed whispers. I did my best to walk the straight and narrow and avoid listing toward the shadows. My heart hammered as I left behind the busy strip of bars and the light that spilled out of them onto the street. There were now only a few tourists sprinkled here and there, and not another gringa in sight. A pack of testosterone-fueled dudes on the lurch paused to assess me, drunkenly lost the thread, and began talking amongst themselves. I drew up near them, trying to appear casual and in control. *Should I—should I ask them to help me?* But before I could fully form the thought, they had passed me by, beelining it for the next bar. Besides, it was difficult to hold much confidence in the rescue skills of these gringos. Most were chugging yards, and/or kneeling on the sidewalk, upchucking the contents of the miles of booze they'd consumed earlier in the evening. A thin, beady-eyed man catcalled me from a darkened doorway. I walked even faster. *Okay, I'm obviously not going to* ask him *for a lift*—I could just imagine riding two hours back home in my miniskirt, with him leering at me the whole time (or worse). I was better off on my own. (I hoped.)

The main drag emptied out into an even bigger thoroughfare, and a large sign read: *Frontera con Nosotros*: eighty kilometers. Tears welled in my eyes, but I was determined not to cry again. I gave myself a pep talk: Sure, that was farther than I could walk in three-inch Bardot-esque, gingham espadrille heels. But it was still my escape route. I was going to make it home safely, even if it took me all night.

I fashioned my oversized T-shirt into a twisted side knot and straightened my skirt. Feeling slightly more organized and ladylike, I took a deep breath. As I said a prayer to the patron saint of drunken hitchhikers, I extended my thumb.

And, just like that…no one stopped.

If I'd been able to observe myself, and the copious streaks of black mascara that obscured my face, or the rat's nest in the back of my hair, I might have understood that I looked like a deranged mental hospital runaway. But I had no mirror, and so I burned with indignation that no one had pulled over to assist me. Exhaustion clouded my thoughts with delirium, slowing them to a crawl. My eyelids hovered at half-mast, tugged down by all the booze in my system. My bladder begged me to empty it. I looked up and down the street, my head wobbling on my neck like a helium balloon, and then once again, right and left. The coast was clear. As quickly as I could manage, I ducked into the bushes to relieve myself. It felt like I peed for an hour, and every noise in the darkness made me flinch, convinced I was about to be discovered. Wrestling my clothes back into place, I returned to my post on the side of the road. I could barely hold my eyes open, and yet, I had to stand there, for as long as it took, hoping for the best.

Bleary and out of it, I blinked frantically to clear the mirage that appeared before me: a vehicle had finally pulled up with a great groaning of breaks, and a dust storm of dirt and street debris. Smelling the acrid exhaust, I rejoiced: it was a real jacked up yellow school bus. Partially painted all the colors of the rainbow, it had huge oversized tires, which had a mint green wheel well that looked scavenged from a junkyard. A small village of teenaged street kids with grubby faces stared out at me from the many grimy windows, giving the whole enterprise the look of a dune buggy orphanage. Descending the steps of the bus, like an angel ministering to wayward souls, came a nun, in a full, floor-length habit.

*Was that a magic worm I ate? Am I fucking hallucinating?*

"*Necesitas ayuda, mi hija?*" the nun asked.

I wasn't sure what she'd just said to me. But I knew "hija" meant "child," and I figured a nun was, by definition, a good person.

"*Si!*" I cried out. "*Si! Por favor. Gracias…muchas gracias!*"

She held out her hand, and I took it, followed her aboard. Piles of hay cluttered the bus. The smell was overwhelming in the stifling heat. The bus staggered into motion, and I collapsed into a ripped pleather seat, landing next to a young woman. A giant green iguana peeked its head over the seatback in front of me, jabbing a forked tongue in my direction. I shied away, crossing my arms in front of my chest, wondering if anyone else had noticed. Only the Blessed Virgin Mary pasted to the bus's ceiling looked back.

My seatmate kept her eyes on the scrub grass and dead trees passing by outside. She was pregnant, visibly so, and on closer inspection, I saw that all of the passengers appeared to be teenage girls in some stage of conception.

I gathered this was some sort of foster child/orphan girl/runaway rescue charity school on wheels. A positive development, I assumed. With the early morning sunrays cascading down on the powerful surf to my left, I could discern that direction was West. So we were headed North. All in all, we *seemed* to be traveling toward Tijuana, which was a fucking miracle.

*Excuse my language, Mother Superior, but it's been quite a night.*

I leaned back in my seat and looked up at the metal roof, where more images of Mother Mary had been taped, along with pictures of Frida Kahlo; Mother Teresa; Mexican President, Mr. Ernesto Zedillo; Latina pop idol, Selena, who had, tragically, been murdered by her fan club president only a few months earlier; and Lucha Reyes, who I recognized from my Spanish 2A class as the first woman to adopt the Ranchera style of singing. All of this was topped off with a variety of bright, shiny, Day of the Dead icons.

The next thing I knew, I found myself suddenly awake on a pillow that was moving—and moaning! As I rubbed my eyes, I comprehended that my seatmate was literally giving birth—at this exact moment!!!

"*SOCORRO!!*" I yelled to the nun at the front of the bus, pointing my finger at the girl next to me. "*El bebe! El bebe!*"

I stood to move out of the way. But as I did, I felt the tinge of warm liquid on my front. I looked down. My "Papas & Beer" shirt was splattered with blood.

The baby's head was crowning.

*Oh my god! What is happening?!*

The nun bustled up and down the aisle in search of what I'd assumed was a first aid kit. Just then, she arrived at the seat. She frantically pulled items from the bus's shoddy stock of supplies, including scissors, rubbing alcohol, a towel, and the pillow she had been resting on. Quickly removing her ring and wristwatch, she doused her hands and the towel with a portion of the rubbing alcohol, so as to prepare for God's miracle.

With a deft hand, as if she'd done this many times before, the woman took her position and began giving instructions.

"*Quiero que se concentre en respirar tranquilamente,*" she said, and then after a pause. "*Empujar! Empujar!*"

Soon, the young woman had delivered her baby. The nun then cleaned and cut the cord, and swaddled the infant, placing it in the new mother's arms. I sat, stunned, smiling vaguely, drinking in the views of the Pacific Ocean through the window, unable to process all that had just happened to me.

We eventually began driving through more populated streets, and I realized with great relief that we were on the edge of Tijuana, moving toward the US border, a mere forty-four-minute drive from my old hometown of San Diego. I don't know how the nun had guessed that this was where I needed to go, but somehow, she had the driver take me as close as possible to the entry point for America and drop me off there.

"*Gracias! Gracias por todo,*" I called out, as I stepped down from the bus, waving goodbye to the nun, and the new mother whose baby had just arrived.

Swaying on my feet, I hoped I could hold it together long enough to explain my misadventures to a border agent and get the help I needed to find my way home—even without any money or my ID. Thankfully, this early in the morning, very little traffic had backed up at the checkpoint. Agents moved among the few vehicles, leading their leashed drug dogs to sniff each one. Men advertised their wares, also walking the lines of cars, selling everything from leather goods and scorpion-studded lollipops, to pretty, sun-colored papier-mâché roses.

Off in the distance, I saw the area where I needed to line up to walk across into the United States. I began to move in that direction, cutting through the lanes of stopped traffic. The long hours of being awake, with no food or water, finally took its toll on me. I dropped to my knees, fainting right there in the hot Mexican street, a cacophony of honking the last thing I heard as I went down.

When I regained consciousness, a border agent had balled up his windbreaker and placed it beneath my head as an impromptu neck cradle. Somewhere beyond my range of vision, a motorcycle revved its motor, and then fell silent. Just then, a man pushed his way through the crowd that circled me and bent down to my level. Hawke wore an expression on his face that I hadn't even known he was capable of: shocked concern.

"Holy fuck, Scarlett," he said, his voice shaky. "The hell happened to you?"

"I went to the bathroom and you guys left without me."

"No, I mean, what *happened* to you? Did you get murdered?"

I looked down at my blood-covered T-shirt. "The miracle of life happened," I said. "Where's everyone else?"

"Freaking out," he said. "I was actually the first one to realize you weren't in the other car with Johnny, Persephone, and Imani, and I… uh…I figured some gringette like you, wandering around alone in a foreign country, might get into some crazy trouble. So I hopped on my bike and came down here. I was on the verge of driving back into Mexico to find you. But then, you, well…caused such a commotion that I was able to literally witness you pass out from the other side of the border."

"Aw, you were concerned for my wellbeing," I teased him, having deciphered the seed of actual human emotion below his carefully curated, gruff indifference.

"Well, I didn't want you to get snuffed," he said, almost sweetly. "Plus, there are advantages to having a gorgeous babe owe you a favor..."

And there he went—ruining the moment, as always. I looked at Hawke warily. He wasn't exactly Romeo. I knew every lowdown, despicable thing he'd done in the past few months, either from witnessing it firsthand or hearing Johnny complain about it. And yet, this was the kindest thing anyone had done for me—by far—in ages, and much nicer than Johnny had been to me for as long.

I climbed onto the back of his bike. And we rode off into the early morning, together.

✳✳✳

THE WESTIES DEBUT ALBUM had been out in the world for all of three days and they were already in danger of breaking up. Or that was the mood of low-grade gloom and doom inside the band.

"I know it's all about you, Johnny, but you could try to show up on time," Hawke sneered, as Johnny sashayed into the band meeting Deirdre had, herself, arrived to twenty minutes late, before ducking out to make a quick phone call.

"You're being a fucking wanker!" Hawke shouted at Johnny's back.

When Johnny returned a few minutes later and found Deirdre and his band mates going through some photos for their cover shoot for *Spin*, he was livid.

"I can't believe you guys started without me," he said. "And don't forget, I get first edit approval."

"What the fuck are you on about?" Hawke asked. "Swallow the Kool-Aid much? Talk about LSD, and what the hell is that on your face?"

"I do *not* have Lead Singer Disease—there's no such thing—and it's a clay mud mask, in order to minimize my pores and maximize collagen circulation and dewiness," Johnny said, without a hint of irony. "And just because I happen to seem like the primary focus of the band, there's no need to be so petty and jealous. It's not like I *want* to do all the interviews. Do you know how much time and work it requires? And honestly, it's just that, for some reason, the press always want to sic their queries on the lead singer of The Westies."

"I, for one, have no idea why," Bone griped. "I'm the one that allows the fucking magic to happen in the first place."

"You all get a goddamn gold star for the day," Shiv joked. "Now can we please get on with whatever we're here to discuss? I've got a date with me lady tonight."

"Me too," Hawke said, grinning like a Cheshire cat.

"What is it now?" Johnny griped. "I've already told you—indulge in all the Playmates you can handle. I couldn't care less. I'm an artist."

"Thanks for your permission, your royal asinine...I mean... highness," Hawke quipped. "I've graduated to a more sophisticated class of woman *myself.*"

"Who cares?" Bone said. "This is a band meeting, not a babe meeting. What did you think about that epic drum solo I laid on the latest roughs? I haven't heard back from you on that yet. We should definitely get it added to the set before tour—"

"Ah, now don't you start, too. What do you think we decided to do about your twenty-fucking-minute drum solo?" Hawke sneered. "We're not the Grateful Dead."

"Listen up, children." Deirdre clapped her hands as she paced in front of where they sat on the couch. "I originally called this meeting to discuss the fundraiser Johnny's requested for the Oklahoma City bombing victims. I respect that it's your home state and a worthy cause, but we're going to have to work a logistical miracle to fit it in among our regular tour dates."

"Be that as it may, I won't take no for an answer," Johnny said.

"Okay, diva, I've already said, *yes*, we're going to make it happen," Deirdre said. "We've got more pressing matters at hand. I've just gotten off the phone with our promoter. We've added a second night in Vegas.

This means we leave tonight, not tomorrow. Bus call is two a.m. We'll get down there in time to do morning radio, a full day of promo, and then the new show, which is—well, tickets are selling."

Bone jabbed his finger at Johnny. "There are a few items we need to discuss before I go anywhere with him."

"Whatever it is, the answer is no," Deirdre said. "A. The promo photo of the band is the one the label chose. B. Your drum solo is not happening. Anything else?"

"My costumes are definitely not going to fit in the space I've been allotted on the bus," Johnny said. "We need to hire a trailer to accommodate them."

"Oh…would you look at the fancy boy now," Hawke jeered. "What a joke."

"No," Deirdre said.

"But I'm really feeling myself coming into my Thin White Duke phase, and I need space so my suits don't get smashed."

"N-O," Deirdre said. "If you're so worried, lay 'em out in your bunk and sleep sitting up in the lounge. Now, enough. You may be the star, but I'm still in charge. Anything else?"

"What's the official management position on birds on the bus?" Shiv asked.

"Not for the first few gigs," Deirdre said. "I want us to garner some unity as a group, if that's even fucking possible, before we add any other personalities into the mix. They can fly in at a later date…now get yourself packed and ready. I'm not your mom. It's not my job to make sure you have enough clean underwear. If anyone misses bus call, we're leaving without you—and don't bother coming back."

Deirdre clapped her hands again, loudly, signaling the end of the meeting. And so it was.

Besides, the moment was at hand for Johnny to wash off his facemask.

\*\*\*

I DEFINITELY DIDN'T FEEL like the glamorous, sophisticated Velvet Rose of legend, as I hid in the miniscule shower stall in the tour bus, clinging to the wall. We ground to an abrupt halt only seconds after we'd finally set off. What I would later learn is that Bone had been inexcusably tardy for bus call. Deirdre had been as good as her word, instructing the driver to depart without him. Rushing up the hill to the house, just as the bus pulled away, Bone had literally stepped in front of the vehicle. He knew it was the only way Deirdre could be persuaded to change her mind about picking up a wayward band member. Thankfully, the bus had superb, albeit squeaky, brakes, and Bone survived to drum another show.

Unfortunately, Bone was having an upper day, and he spent the first hour we were on the road, running up and down the aisle, singing Van Halen's "Hot for Teacher" at top volume while mimicking the band's choreographed dance moves from the video. Finally, from what I was able to overhear through the wall, it sounded like Deirdre had sequestered him in the back bedroom, where he began playing his Quinto Cuban congas.

The past week had been *insane*, by any standards, and this time alone in my secret hideout was the first opportunity I'd had to assess my life. Neither the choices I'd made of late or where they'd landed me inspired much confidence in me. For starters, if I'd known how bumpy the ride would be, literally, I would have opted for something a little more practical than three-inch Manolo Blahnik heels, which I was trying to remove.

The bathroom door slid open, and someone stepped inside to make use of the facilities. I couldn't decipher who it was through the shower's frosted glass door, but something about the way the mystery pisser whistled "The Boys Are Back in Town" suggested it was Jet. Knowing he was generally among the more coherent (and therefore observant) members of the band, I held my breath until he exited.

*How did I let Hawke talk me into this?*

Our secret trysts, which had begun after he rescued me in Mexico, had simply been too sexy and too fun to resist. And, yes, I'm not above admitting it was a bit of a thrill to know I was getting the best possible revenge on the man who had so recently shattered my heart, by taking up with his rival.

Hawke had fallen into the habit of showing up at my house around one in the morning, after the band's promotional responsibilities for the day were done. When there was no one else in the room to impress, he was surprisingly laid back, intelligent, and hilarious. I actually enjoyed spending time with him. Which had made me susceptible to ill-advised suggestions of all sorts. As when he was leaving that morning, and he'd suddenly turned from the front door, a devilish glimmer in his eye.

"Come with me," he said.

"To The Dog House?" I whispered, nervously retying the sash of my kimono. "But Johnny doesn't even know about us. And I need to do some designing today."

"No, I mean come with me on tour. We're covering the whole country. It'll be a crazy, radical adventure," and then, "Fine...come because I'm asking you to."

"I thought you said Deirdre was pretty dead set on everything being 'anti-girl,' at least for the first leg of this tour. Especially after that fiasco with the governor's daughter and the peyote trip. Remember? When she took Wasted Puppy out on that last nightmare on wheels, which became known as the 'Lawsuits and Underage Lovers Tour.'"

He laughed. "What she don't know won't hurt her."

"You're expecting me to hide for three months," I said. "You're mad."

"Just till we get to our first stop in Vegas, sweetie," he said.

"They have an airport in Vegas," I said. "That would be mortifying. I just know Deirdre would love nothing more than to send me packing."

"Trust me." He pulled me close with a throaty growl and started kissing my neck.

"Come on," he said, sliding his hand inside my kimono and up my bare thigh. "I'm asking nice. But I can also ask naughty."

After having been so unceremoniously dropped by Johnny, it did feel exhilarating to be so in demand; to have Hawke even be willing to break the rules for me. And so, I'd been hiding in the shower ever since.

*If this isn't diehard dedication, I don't know what is. Now, what could possibly go wrong?*

I instantly identified Johnny by the intoxicating scent of his Guerlain Vetiver cologne, and the way the molecules in the air seemed to shift when he entered a room.

*Or the way they used to shift, back when I still cared about him. Which I definitely don't anymore.*

I held my breath for as long as it took him to take a piss and wash his hands. He softly hummed the bridge notes to "The Velvet Rose" as he fixed his hair in the mirror. But he didn't seem to be exiting. Finally, when he opened the door, he didn't leave—he extended his head into the hallway and shouted to the others.

"I swear this bus is haunted," he said.

"Aye, I've heard tell of a haunted tour bus," Shiv said. "What'd you see? The apparition of a flaming skull, hovering in the mirror, instead of your own face?"

"It's not that," Johnny said. "It's…I dunno, just a feeling, a spirit… ya know, an energy, white light."

"That's a good energy," Deirdre said. "That's your guardian angel."

"Ah, that's like what my mom used to always tell me, a saying from our Native American elder, Black Elk: 'All over the sky a sacred voice is calling your name,'" Johnny replied thoughtfully, a sweet smile on his face.

My heart leapt at his words, but then I remembered how awful he'd been to me, on multiple occasions—and that I was dating his guitarist now.

The driver hit the brakes. Unprepared as I was for the sudden impact, I fell forward, catching myself against the shower wall with a loud THUMP.

"Oy! Maybe it is haunted," Shiv said. "I heard that. Sounds like a regular poltergeist, it does."

"You really won't let this rest, will ya boys?" Deirdre asked. "Anything else…before we can *finally* truly get our four-plus-hour journey underway?"

"I think Johnny might be right about the haunted loo," Shiv said.

"Oh please, there's nothing in there, I'm telling you," Deirdre said, bulldozing her way through, turning on the lights in the hall and bathroom, tearing open the bunk curtains, and yanking the shower door ajar.

"AAAGGHHH!" she screamed, so shocked to see me that she actually lost her cool for once in her impeccably unflappable life.

"Scarlett!" Johnny said, a warm smile blooming. "So bizarre. I just *knew* you were here."

"The question is *why*?" Deirdre said.

"Hawke?" I said, watching Johnny's face as it crumbled.

"Jesus, it's like a fuckin' clown car in here," Hawke said, popping his head into the overstuffed, miniscule bathroom. "That's right," he continued nonchalantly, while fiddling with a dreadlock in his hair. "I brought Scarlett. She bunks with me now."

"But…" Johnny said, fighting the new reality that was unhappily dawning.

"That's it, band meeting in the front lounge," Deirdre said. "NOW."

Nerved up as I was, I was relieved to escape my claustrophobic hiding spot.

"Not you," Deirdre said. "You see, no matter how many members you date, you're not *in the band*." She added in her most unconvincing and patronizing tone. "But we'll figure out how to get you back safe and sound, sweetie."

Before Deirdre could leave me alone to consider what I'd done—and the probable consequences—a commotion erupted in the aisle of the bus, near the bunks.

"Aw, shit…if you're rustling up stowaways, you might as well count me in too," Persephone hollered merrily, emerging from the bunk where she'd been concealing herself.

As full on chaos erupted throughout the bus, I pushed my way into the hallway with the others.

"Allo, love," Sephy said when she saw me. "Our caper has been foiled. Still, this one will go down in the books. Ha! Anyways, what fun we'll have, touring the highways and bi-ways of 'merica!"

"No," Deirdre said. "Absolutely not."

A pounding began from inside the front lounge's bench seat.

"What now!" Deirdre yelled, clearly on the verge of a breakdown.

"Sounds like the axel to me," Jet said. "Pull over, and I'll fix it in no time."

WHAM! The bench seat's cushion flew off, and out came Imani.

"Um, Imani, I don't think this is an opportune moment," Bone said.

"Well, I'm not going back in there," she said. "It's a fucking coffin."

"You've all gone completely mental," Deirdre said. "Fine, the girls can stay, but only on account of how much time I've already lost dealing with this fiasco. Don't say I didn't warn you. I'm not refereeing any disputes. You're on your own. Clint, please come to the back lounge and we'll go over those numbers for the label."

I couldn't help but feel victorious, as though I'd bested my nemesis, when I watched Deirdre disappear into the rear enclave of the bus. But, then, I surveyed the close quarters, and the complicated web of dangerous liaisons and intense enmity that bound us all together. It was going to be an unforgettable and very complicated, crazy summer.

✳✳✳

In the days he'd first romanced me, Hawke had always ducked out of his band obligations as soon as he possibly could and hurried over to my house. The urgency with which he simply *needed* to see me was a huge attraction after Johnny's indifference, and also, had quieted the doubts in my mind about Hawke's ability to be faithful. Knowing Hawke was devoted to me, I didn't feel the need to keep tabs on him. I didn't want to come across as that kind of jealous girlfriend anyhow—even if sometimes, secretly, I was. And so, immediately after the band's first Vegas show, at "The Joint," in the hotly anticipated Hard Rock Hotel & Casino, I didn't stick around for their meet and greet with local radio DJs, promoters, and area VIPs. Instead, I went with Sephy and Imani to the hotel's upscale steakhouse for a late dinner. We pushed through the throngs of big-haired girls who somehow always managed to get backstage passes. They were camped just beyond the dressing rooms, waving the Sharpies with which they'd entice the band members to sign their naked tits and asses. I'd already seen an overabundance of such fawning at the band's gigs in LA and I wasn't keen to witness anymore. Once the lads had kissed industry ass and signed every bare breast in the venue, they'd locate us, and we'd keep the party going before retiring to our separate rooms.

We were even joined for dinner by the phenomenal new hotelier himself, Peter Morton, who had just opened the Hard Rock Hotel & Casino on the Strip a few months earlier. In a flash, Sephy had me immersed in trying to win her a pink 1970 Corvette Stingray that was the grand prize for a bank of slot machines in our hotel's casino. I lost track of time. It wasn't until Johnny slid into the empty seat next to me that I noticed anything was out of the ordinary.

"Hey," he said. "Look, I don't know how to say this. And maybe I'm just too tired, or too wasted, or too sick of having this thought in my head, but I just wanna say…I'm really sorry. It kills me to think I caused all of this."

I took another pull on the slot. "All of what?"

"Well, you know Hawke isn't the most…focused…guy," he said, seeming to choose his words with extreme care.

I made a show of looking around the room. "Where is he anyhow? Didn't you guys all leave the meet and greet together in order to come join us girls?"

"Scarlett—" Johnny said, pausing dramatically, in a way I didn't care for.

"Johnny—" I said, mimicking his tone in an attempt to lighten the mood.

"He had to restring one of his guitars," Johnny said, not looking me in the eye.

"But doesn't your guitar tech, Seth, do that?"

Before I could interrogate Johnny any further, Hawke swooped in between us—literally—positioning himself so his body blocked my view of Johnny.

"What are you two talking about?" Hawke said. "The painful details of your breakup and how Johnny blew it and was such a wanker you'll never be able to forgive him?"

"Actually, we were talking about *you*," Johnny said.

"I don't like the sound of that," Hawke said, his voice full of menace. "I hope you told Scarlett, *like I told you to*, that I was unavoidably delayed because of that string buzz on my guitar." With that, Hawke grabbed my hand and escorted me out of my seat. "I'm starving to death. Come on, babe, let's go eat. Shall we try that Nobu Sushi place you've been wanting to check out?"

"I ate with Sephy and Imani," I said. "You've been gone for ages."

"Oh, baby, don't go making this bigger than it is. Anyhow, I'm back now." Pausing dramatically, he stuck his finger right in Johnny's face. "You, think before you speak, best keep your mouth shut, if you know what's good for you."

"I'm not thinking about myself right now," Johnny retorted, while giving me a beseeching look that made my heart flutter, until I forced myself to tamp down the emotion. Any care he had for me now was too little, and way too late, as far as I was concerned. Hawke and I turned and walked away, just as Johnny yanked the lever of the slot machine I'd been seated at, and it began to wildly siren and light up.

"Jackpot!" Johnny called out, pointing to the $500 winning amount highlighted on the Wolf Run slot machine. "Scarlett, you won."

"Keep it," I said. "We're retiring to our room. Don't look for us to be down for brekkie like yesterday, either. We seem to have a hard time breaking away from our bed during any time off we can steal."

And with that, I turned away with as much poise as possible and left Johnny, alone, to collect his jackpot and think about what he'd done. Only, when I woke up in the morning, there was no romantic tryst to be had, as Hawke had already gotten up. I tiptoed into the other room, hoping to find him crouched over his guitar, writing a song, or running a bubble bath for us to enjoy together. But the suite was empty, without any sign of his clothes or luggage, and there was no note. The only sign of him was a trail of multi-hued pills leading to the door like breadcrumbs in a fairy tale. I didn't like anything about this scenario. But by the time I'd packed my belongings and made myself up, I'd managed to put on a brave face, knowing I'd see the others at breakfast. In fact, when I arrived at the hotel restaurant, Johnny was the only one who remained at a long table, littered with crumpled napkins and empty Blood Mary glasses.

"I see you *somehow* managed to get dressed this morning after all," he said.

"Yes, well…it must be done," I said, determined that, no matter what, I was *not* going to ask if he'd seen Hawke.

"Hawke is restringing his guitar," Johnny said.

"The one he restrung last night?"

"That's what he instructed me to tell you," Johnny said. "Now, sit down—please join me. How have you been? I saw that *Interview* magazine piece about your clothing line—I remember you talked to that journalist on a day we had a date last month. Nicely done!"

"But that's not on newsstands until next month," I said.

"The same writer was doing a piece for *Interview* on the band, and when I asked him what else he was working on, he mentioned *you.* So I managed to get him to let me see an advance copy," he said. "I was just excited for you."

"How sweet, thank you," I said. "It's going to be major when *all* my press hits—I have so many ideas, illustrations, and designs to get out before then. Sometimes it feels *inconceivable.* But there's nothing else I'd rather do."

"I understand, exactly," Johnny said. "We just dropped our album, and there's already pressure on me to start writing the next one. It's like you have to be on all the time."

"That's precisely how I feel!" I said, wanting nothing more than to sit and catch up, even as I thought better of getting too comfortable with him. "Well, I'm supposed to rendezvous with Sephy to talk to one of her European friends about showcasing my designs in his new, fancy pants Caesar's Palace shop. I'll see you around."

Before I could make my departure, a young bellboy approached us. He was carrying an impressive bouquet of long stem roses, wrapped in brown paper, and tied with a black velvet ribbon. "Excuse me—'scuse me, Miss—Miss Scarlett," he said. "These were delivered to the front desk for you. They're from Mr. Hawke."

"Oh, how sweet and supreme, thanks," I said, taking the flowers. "Hawke is just too much."

"Wow, impressive. Hawke sent you those?"

"You'd be surprised how romantic he can be."

"You have *no idea*."

I handed Johnny the roses, in order to gobble up whatever sweet note Hawke had asked the florist to include. Only, the attached card read: "To the Lovely Mandy. When you do the Can Can, I feel like I can do anything. Thanks for a hot night. Can't wait to do it again. Your Mr. Hawke"

I could feel myself redden with rage and disgrace, but I was determined not to reveal the truth about the flowers' origins. So I assumed the expression I'd dubbed *Xena, Princess Warrior*, during my runway modeling days, for when I really needed to look impenetrable and fierce. And I held onto that mask of confidence for all I was worth, while stuffing the card in my Lady Dior, which was cane work stitched apparently in a nod to the chairs the maestro had used in his haute couture salons, and commonly known as the Princess Bag, because it was favored by Princess Di.

"Is everything okay, Rosie?" Johnny asked.

"Please, don't call me that," I said. "I'm not your Rosie anymore. And, well, I'm fine. Great!"

"Well, then, take care of yourself, *Scarlett*," he said, standing to go. "And I'm always here if you need me."

"C'mon…don't be so serious!" I teased, perfecting his T-shirt by removing some lint from it, all the while disliking his implication that I might require comfort from him sometime soon. "Lighten up. I'll see you at the show tonight."

As soon as Johnny was out of sight, I located the bellboy, Charlie, by the elevator and nearly hurled the flowers at him. I knew it wasn't his fault, but I was too mad to contain my true feelings any longer.

"For your information, you gave these flowers to the wrong girl," I said.

"Oh, uh, but you're, uh, you're…The Velvet Rose…and you're, uh, you're with Hawke…from The Westies…everyone knows that," he stammered. "I saw your photo on Page Six just the other day."

"In that case, I guess I'd better keep them after all," I said, forcing myself to smile at him, so he wouldn't think I was a crazy harridan.

If I felt superbly fucked up that I'd been reduced to absconding with flowers my beau had meant for another woman, I tried at least to be happy that I'd fooled Johnny. Hopefully, I'd maybe even sent him a message that might have somehow shifted his warped paradigm about what it meant to be someone's significant other. Besides, I was sure Hawke had a good explanation. Maybe Mandy was his long-lost cousin. *At least a girl could hope, right?* And roses were beautiful, no matter their source, especially when left as a show of gratitude for the hardworking housekeeping staff, which is what I ultimately did with the flowers.

***

As a kid, Johnny had loved nothing more than to watch old black-and-white Humphrey Bogart movies broadcast late at night. He knew he was destined to be a rock star. If not, he'd have grown up to be a private eye, he figured, able to envision himself devoting long hours to his stakeouts, wearing a dark Army officer's trench coat and Fedora, sipping strong black coffee from a thermos. He hadn't thought about this old dream in years, but he quickly fell back into his aspiring gumshoe role when he misplaced his room key on their third night in Vegas. He was due at the venue for sound check in twenty minutes. First, he needed to don his kohl colored guyliner and stage clothes— the latter of which entailed changing from his one black vintage V neck T to his *other* black vintage V neck T.

He hurried to the front desk, in search of a replacement key card.

"Here you go, Mr. Valentine, your key for room 1224," the clerk said in a hushed tone, using Johnny's tour pseudonym, an homage to his favorite Bogie character.

"I thought I was in 1229," Johnny said.

"Actually, sir, it says right here," the clerk said. "1224."

"Ah, well, it's been a long, lost weekend. Again," Johnny chuckled. "No worries…thanks."

When Johnny exited the elevator on the twelfth floor, he instinctively turned to the right. But when he double-checked the wall sign, he realized he'd gone the wrong way. So he reversed his direction, and was just about to round the corner, when he caught sight of Hawke stepping off the elevator with a busty blond chorus girl. They were headed for the room to which Johnny had just been given the key. Johnny quickly ducked behind the wall, so Hawke wouldn't notice him.

*How could he keep betraying Scarlett like this, again and again?*

Switching into detective mode, Johnny snuck into the elevator. With the assistance of a sizeable bribe to the clerk, Johnny deduced that Hawke had made the impish move of reserving not one, but *two* rooms. One under Hawke's tour pseudonym, Gil T. Azell, and one under what he knew was Johnny's nom de tour—"Rocks" Valentine— so Hawke could conceal his extracurriculars from Scarlett. And should the existence of the second room come out, he'd attempt to pin the blame on Johnny. Not only that, but after much slick negotiating and cold hard cash, Johnny had managed to score a snippet of hotel surveillance tape. It clearly showed Hawke in the hallway, locked in a lusty embrace with this showgirl friend. The obliging security guard had romantic woes of his own (as he confessed to Johnny during their brief but heartfelt conversation). It probably didn't hurt, either, that he was a huge Westies fan. He even copied the footage onto a VHS tape for Johnny, taking a moment to explain this cool, new technology, and helping to advance Johnny's wizardry when it came to his advanced mastery of all things techy. And now, evidence in hand, Johnny was primed to bring Hawke down.

It almost felt fated when Johnny found himself alone with Scarlett, a few minutes later, backstage at The Joint, where the band was to play its final Vegas show that night. The two of them were the first among their group to turn up, and now they stood together awkwardly. She looked gorgeous—giving off bombshell Rita Hayworth vibes, her figure hugged by a slate-colored three-quarter-length bustier, painted up the sides with lightning bolts, her hair pulled back into a youthful, fifties-style high ponytail. He took a deep breath, working up his nerve.

"Scarlett," he said. "There's something I need to…"

Before he could finish his thought, the dressing room was invaded by a crazy, colorful group that included Shiv, Sephy, Bone, Imani, and Jet. And yes, Hawke, who instantly insinuated himself between Johnny and Scarlett, ruining the moment.

By the time the two band mates were sound checking, Johnny was fuming with indignant rage. It didn't help matters that Scarlett wouldn't make eye contact with either of them, as if she were pissed off about something one, or both, of them had done. Johnny hated the idea of Scarlett getting hurt by Hawke's duplicity, but he couldn't stand the thought of her living in ignorance, either. The question was how to best play his hand.

During sound check, Johnny's plan came together. It was taking forever for Hawke to get his levels right—he kept dropping his pick, and he was leaning into his microphone as if he was withstanding a frigging gale. During the extra downtime, Johnny surveyed the massive room, soon to be filled with screaming fans.

Their sound check long over, they were now well into their twelve-song set. This was Johnny's least favorite moment of the night—the seventh song, during which Hawke played his tiresome, over-the-top, grandiloquent guitar solo, preening on the lip of the stage as if he thought he were the second coming of Jeff Beck (okay, well, maybe deep down, Johnny was a wee bit jealous, for he couldn't noodle a guitar like that, even if he tried).

Johnny turned his attention away from Hawke, allowing his plan to unfold in his mind. Under the guise of a tech issue, he approached their sound guy, Dwayne, and nodded; the moment was nigh. As they'd agreed, Dwayne switched the video input channels for the venue's TV screens. Suddenly, the image of a close up of Hawke's tattooed hands, flying over his guitar strings, was replaced by video of Hawke pushing the dancer up against the hotel wall, and kissing her exposed breasts with abandon. As the audience cheered wildly, Hawke grinned with self-satisfied glee, assuming his solo had earned the applause. But the crowd made its loyalty known. At least in Johnny's fantasy.

"Johnny! Johnny! Johnny!" the audience cheered, clapping in time to the beat.

Scarlett was so overcome by emotion, she rushed out from the wings, where she'd been observing the show. Not caring that she was being watched by thousands of the band's fans, she fell into Johnny's arms, knowing exactly what he'd done for her, and feeling herself overwhelmed with gratitude.

"I can't…I don't…I understood he was messed up but not like that. Thank you, Johnny. Thank you."

Meanwhile, Johnny was brought back from his daydream of publicly outing Hawke by a sudden, strange outburst of feedback from Hawke's direction. And then, Hawke's guitar part disappeared altogether. Johnny looked over to where his guitarist stood. Only Hawke was no longer there. He'd disappeared from stage.

# YOU KNOW WHERE YOU ARE?

*"Be considerate of other hotel guests—*
*trash your room by 10:00 p.m."*
—Mick Jagger

Hawke resembled a corpse, his skin waxy, his body disturbingly immobile in the narrow hospital bed. The only clues that he was clinging to life were the subtle whirring of air passing through the oxygen tube that snaked up his nose, coupled with the consistent beeping of his heart monitor.

Johnny halted just inside Hawke's room. He paced in a tight circle, unable to force himself to approach the bed or to fully observe Hawke's condition. Finally, overwhelmed by an outpouring of emotion, Johnny rushed over. "Know what, Hawke? The next time you die, motherfucker, I will personally kill you!"

In the past four years, Johnny had spent thousands of hours in close quarters with Hawke—in their scrappy band vans, and sketchy apartments, and now, in luxury hotel suites, airplane cabins, and tour buses. This was the first time, *ever*, that Johnny had gotten in the last word without some snarky comeback from Hawke.

"Don't you ever fucking cheat on Scarlett again, either. Enough with the—"

As if on cue, Scarlett hurried through the door—an animated blur composed of her elegant, exotic perfume, and the rattling of the vitamin bottles she carried—trailed closely by Persephone, Shiv, and

Deirdre. Johnny appraised Scarlett's expression with concern, fearing she'd heard what he'd just said. But she was clearly too absorbed by her distress at Hawke's diminished state to absorb much else of her surroundings.

Scarlett sank into a chair near Hawke's head, clutching her goody bag of items intended to heal her man, including the small healing crystals and medicinal Chinese herbs she'd learned about while living in New York. Taking his hand in both of hers, she brought it to her lips, before placing it down, gently, on his bedclothes.

Shiv had gone around to the other side of the bed and was peering at Hawke with a pensive expression on his face; Persephone nestled against his chest. Deirdre, meanwhile, was reading Hawke's chart, which hung at the foot of his bed.

"Sheezus…you selfish bastard," Deirdre said to Hawke. "Your toxicology report says you had enough downers in you to tranquilize Godzilla. And now, here we are, stranded in the godforsaken 'glitter gulch,' while you're on the mend, two gigs canceled, booking agents screaming bloody murder, AEG attorneys at the door, hundreds of thousands of dollars at stake."

"Is it really as bad as all that?" Johnny asked, tearing his attention away from Scarlett, whom he longed to comfort, and then, to educate— about the callous Casanova for whom she was currently weeping.

"Yeah, it's as fucking bad as all that," Deirdre said. "I'm sure you know that old saying, 'The show must go on.' Well it should continue, 'or else you'll get your fucking balls sued off.' We're in a waking nightmare right now. And we will continue to be, until Hawke returns to his sickening semblance of a self. And we have no idea when that will be."

As if on cue, Hawke sat straight up in bed, an agitated expression on his face.

"Coke!" he cried out, his voice a hoarse rasp.

"Not on my watch," Deirdre said. "Not after what you've already cost us."

"Oh my God! Babe, you're okay," Scarlett said, crying in earnest now, her relief unleashing a torrent of emotion. "You had us so scared.

But you don't need any more of that garbage in your system. You just need to rest."

"*Scared* is not exactly the word I would have chosen," Deirdre sneered. "It's not like you didn't bring this mishap on yourself."

"Coke," Hawke said, faintly nodding his head toward the window.

The assembled group turned as one and saw the billboard, visible through the half-drawn shade, advertising Coca Cola with an image of a frosty bottle.

"Oh, of course, you're thirsty," Scarlett said, reaching for a plastic pitcher of water on his bedside table and pouring him a glass, then holding it up to his mouth, so he could sip through the straw. "Given the context…"

"What your little groupie stowaway means is…oh, you know what she intended to say," Deirdre hissed, as Scarlett coughed and muttered a string of witty comebacks under her breath. "Now, if you'll excuse me, I'm going to do my job and let the venue in Denver know we'll be there after all."

"But he can't possibly be ready to play by tomorrow," Scarlett protested.

"I've heard quite enough from you," Deirdre said to Scarlett. "He can, and he will. He's a warrior—we all know that. If not, you'll both be left on the side of the road while the tour continues without you. Honestly, what a pity *that* would be."

"Fuckin' hell," Hawke croaked, his voice scratchy from dehydration and the tubes that had been used to pump his stomach and save his life. "Why don't you all piss off and give a man some much needed peace and quiet?"

"Gladly," Deidre said, giving a final side eye, and storming from the room.

"Come on, Mitchell," Johnny said, not thinking as he used his old pet name for Scarlett, which he'd coined, back when they'd been an item. The cute inside joke between them had been a nod to *Gone with the Wind*'s author Margaret Mitchell. Johnny had always teased Scarlett that she reminded him of that book's strong, intelligent female protagonist, who always seemed to get herself into jams, where she couldn't quite express herself around the men she cared about.

Scarlett whipped around to face Johnny, an expression of surprised affection on her face. Their eyes locked, infinite questions and answers passing back and forth between them, a discernible connection noticeable to everyone in the room.

"Hey," Hawke warned Johnny.

The sound of Hawke's monitor sped up, documenting his elevated agitation, as he boiled over with jealousy and rage. It was only then that Scarlett seemed to remember Hawke; the reason they were all gathered together in this hospital room.

"Don't you upset yourself, darling," she said to him gently, resolutely turning her attention away from Johnny and focusing it back on Hawke.

"Maybe you'd better meet us back at the hotel, mate," Shiv gently said to Johnny. "Let's focus on getting Hawke up and about, and getting the band back on the road. All of this drama isn't good for anyone."

Johnny hesitated at the foot of Hawke's bed, willing Scarlett to look at him again, allowing their emotional synchronicity to flourish. But she was resolutely focused on Hawke and Hawke alone, leaning over him, clutching his hand, and whispering soft nothings. And Hawke, well, he'd do anything to best his rival.

"You heard the man," Hawke sneered. "Get out. No one wants you here."

"Fine, you rest up," Johnny said, taking the high road for once. "You always give us a good fright. We need you, you know. We wouldn't be a band without you."

✳✳✳

WHAT A HEARTWARMING SENTIMENT, this idea that The Westies couldn't exist without Hawke, but their dastardly guitarist wasn't one to put much stock in sentiment. In fact, in the days that followed, he seemed hell bent on testing just how far he could push the lads' loyalty. In Denver, Deirdre tried to forbid him from imbibing anything stronger than a Dr. Pepper before taking the stage for the first time post-overdose. Hawke gleefully defied her authority in a most dramatic fashion. During his guitar solos that night, he made a grand performance of kneeling at the foot of the stage and inviting the foxiest ladies in the front row to pour drinks down his gullet while he played. Yes, this spectacle made for an undeniably stellar rock 'n' roll moment, and it also managed to piss off his manager, his girlfriend, and his singer in one go. But by the time the band hit Middle America a few days later, Hawke's booze intake was the least of their worries, as several unpleasant realities were becoming increasingly clear.

For starters, the shows weren't sold out. Not even close. The band's first single, "The Velvet Rose," had been an epic success and so the album had roared out of the gate. Their booking agent had optimistically negotiated them into a series of gigs at small arenas across the country.

But then, the band's second single had failed to get picked up by either mainstream or college radio. For a few weeks, they'd enjoyed the giddy experience of walking into every bar, restaurant, and gas station and hearing Johnny croon his heart out to Scarlett, with the poetic lyrics he had penned just for her. But that joyous sound had soon been replaced by the endless repeat of the season's most popular song: "Waterfalls," by TLC. It was an undeniably catchy tune, but also a painful reminder that while the R&B trio was launching hit after hit from their sophomore album, The Westies were suddenly in danger of being DOA (and not in a way reminiscent of the cool Vancouver punk band of that name). As Shiv so aptly put it, after the band had suffered through the sappy, maudlin videos being played at their hotel bar when they first arrived in Vegas: "I mean, what is this crap? Everything is so mid-tempo, poppy, and *safe*, even my grandma would probably purchase it. Where's the edge?"

And so, going into the band's Chicago show, the last thing Deirdre had time to worry about was Hawke's blood alcohol content. She was in full-on scheming demon mode. As she would be the first to tell you, the band didn't even know how lucky it was to have her plotting in its favor. She even went so far as to print up a fake revised schedule for the day, which she distributed to the band members at their hotel. In doing so, she tricked them into believing they needed to be at the venue two hours earlier than they actually did, in order to get them there promptly.

At 5:00 p.m. sharp, for the first time in anyone's memory, everyone was where they were supposed to be exactly when they were expected to be there. Deirdre paced the dressing room in front of the long table laden with the band's rider like a general preparing her troops for battle.

"All right, kids, reality check number one," Deirdre said, kicking the legs of Bone's chair, so he'd stop nodding off and give her his full attention (or as much as he could rally). "The powers that be at the label are not happy with your record sales, or your ticket sales, or anything. They've decided to ambush us with a visit tonight. Which is going to cause them to find you sad saps playing to a half-empty venue. However, Deirdre the Destroyer has hatched a plan to save your collective asses."

She held out her hand dramatically. As if on cue, Clint joined her, carrying a stack of small paper envelopes. "Persephone, Scarlett, Imani," Deirdre said, indicating that the three women should step forward. "It's long past time for you to earn your room and board."

That's how half an hour later, the three ladies found themselves on the sidewalk outside of Chicago's 9500-capacity UIC pavilion. Each clutched a handful of the envelopes Deirdre had given them, along with a mission. Deirdre had called in a favor with one of Chicago's most popular rock station's DJs and had him announce a contest that morning in order to generate excitement and get extra butts in the seats for tonight's show. Listeners were already swarming around the arena, in search of the hidden tickets that would gain them free access to the show. First, the ladies had to leave them, discreetly, around the venue.

"Watch and learn, mademoiselles," Sephy said, crouching behind a planter, where she tucked an envelope with two complimentary floor seat tickets.

Maybe it was Sephy's head-to-toe Vivienne Westwood ensemble from that year's collection, complete with wide tie, cropped velvet vest, and tall hat—all adorned with brash polka dots. Not to mention the black leather riding crop, which she was striking against the asphalt with delighted zeal. Maybe it was her undeniable *presence*. But Sephy wasn't exactly discreet. She had soon attracted a small circle of people, and an excited teenage boy in a studded biker jacket promptly recovered the tickets he'd just watched her conceal.

Realizing Persephone's approach wasn't providing contestants with much sport, Scarlett ducked away from the crowd. She hurriedly dispersed her tickets around the venue so that those gathered for the challenge could begin to scout them out. Having completed her efforts on the band's behalf, Scarlett returned to Sephy. The two shared a knowing wink. Then, Scarlett looked around for Imani, who was nowhere to be found. Finally, Scarlett was able to locate her, leaning precariously on the edge of a clouded gray glass ashtray outside the venue. Her eyes fluttering, a cigarette burned down in her limp hand. Scarlett hurried over to check on her bestie.

"You okay, Imani?" she asked, gently shaking her shoulder.

"…Don't…wanna…" Imani slurred.

"You don't have to do anything, honey," Scarlett said. "I'm just worried about you, that's all. Do you want me to take you somewhere? Maybe back to the hotel?"

"Allo, you two birds," Sephy said, pausing next to Scarlett. "Looks like this one could use a strong cuppa."

"Yes, a spot of black tea, for starters," Scarlett said, playfully picking up a bit of Sephy's British slang, as she would sometimes do. "How should we manage it?"

"Let's get her inside," Sephy said. "We hid the tickets for the radio contest, as we were asked. Deirdre can't expect us to do more than that."

Forming steady columns on both sides of Imani, they hoisted her up between them. Scarlett took all of Imani's weight onto one hip as Sephy teetered on her eight-inch, mega-platform Vivienne Westwood spiked bondage-style heels. Together, they managed to wrangle opened the door. Staggering, Scarlett struggled under the burden of a carrying a whole human body, and mind you, the nearly unconscious deadweight that it was. Yet she was startled by how light, literally, Imani had become—like a human sized hummingbird. She felt a pang of remorse that she hadn't done more to keep Imani safe and well.

In her studded, inky dark, androgynous combat boots, Imani was a full six-inches shorter than Sephy and Scarlett. Imani's toes dragged beneath her on the waxy floor's surface, all along the bustling walkway that circled the inside circumference of the venue. Finally, they reached the door through which they'd exited the backstage area. As they attempted to pass through, a thick-necked security guard in mirrored Ray Ban's stepped in front of them.

"No passes, no access," he drawled.

"But you saw us exit this very door, not thirty minutes ago," Sephy retorted in her most prim and convincing tone. "If we were anymore with the band, we'd be *in* the bloody band, and we need to get this girl to a quality lie down, post haste."

"No can do, sweetheart," he said.

"I most definitely am not your sweetheart," Sephy said, working herself up into a white-hot rage.

"Even if you were, you couldn't enter this door," he said. "It's called protocol—we got rules. You'd better go. Just keep heading toward that second exit, to your left…go to the will call and see if your names are on the list."

Realizing they were not likely to make any headway with Mr. Rules, they awkwardly turned themselves around and lumbered back through the commotion of T-shirt vendors, beer carts, and early arrivals to the show. Finally, they washed up at the windows marked "Will Call" and "VIP." Only to find themselves waiting behind a dozen people, including a shifty white dude with a serious, prison-style neck tattoo and a janky, eighties pleather jacket.

"What is it about lines that is so bloody dismal?" Sephy mused. "Honestly, it's almost up there with being an orphan in a goddamn Dickens novel, waiting for your portion of porridge, and then you finally reach the front of the godforsaken queue, and you say, 'Please, sir, may I have some more?' And they sneer at you, because they've run out of the cold grub…"

Her voice trailed off as the questionable man in front of them reached the window. She was unable to contain her curiosity about his relationship to The Westies.

"Ellis Dee," he said to the woman behind the counter. "Yah—I'm on the artist list."

"Oh, you think you're right clever, don't ya…ya wank?" Sephy snorted, as the man turned to make way for them, already peeling the sticker off his VIP/All Access pass.

"Sephy…" Scarlett warned.

"Don't you get it, Scarlett?" Sephy said. "Ellis Dee…LSD? ACID?!"

Scarlett attempted to pull Sephy forward with her, as she approached the window. "Scarlett X," she said, offering up her biggest, most alluring smile.

"On the artist list?"

Scarlett nodded adamantly, as if she could make it true.

"I'm sorry, but I don't see your name," the woman said. Her voice was steely, as she prepared herself for a confrontation, like a tow truck driver and motorist battling it out over whether an illegally parked car will get towed or not.

"Let me get a gander at this so-called *list*," Sephy said, ambushing the window to grab the clipboard before the stunned woman could react.

"Candy Liver…Can Deliver…Dylan Weed…Dealin' Weed…who the bloody hell are these people? The fuckin' DOA crew? This list is nothing but drug dealers with a knack for puns."

"Who is on there is not my problem," the woman huffed, arms snaking through the window to snatch the clipboard back from Sephy.

"What I care about is who *isn't* on there—and that's you!" she continued pointing at Sephy. "And you," she said, jabbing her finger in Scarlett's direction. "Now please leave, before I call security and have you escorted out of the building."

"Can you believe the audacity of this one, trying to wind me up?" Sephy said. "What happened to bloody customer service with a smile? At least some of us have proper manners. So I will say, 'Piss off,' and go."

Sephy attempted a dramatic exit, but her share of Imani's weight slowed her down.

"We've got to get Imani somewhere private, so she can rest," Scarlett whispered to Sephy over Imani's lowered head, which bobbed on her neck.

There was no alternative but for Scarlett and Sephy to place Imani on her side on a bench, so they could more quickly fetch one of the crew guys to carry her backstage. As they turned and began to hurry across the increasingly crowded inner entrance area, their progress was slowed by excited Westies' fans who rockignized them from the tabloids, as well as a few of Scarlett's own devotees.

"Miss Velvet Rose, can I get an autograph, please?" asked a young woman who wore her hair in the same high fifties ponytail Scarlett often favored.

The girl's friends, all wearing their finest rock show get-ups—velvet baby doll dresses and somewhat ripped stockings—circled Scarlett and Sephy, excitedly checking out their idols' next-level fashions. Scarlett blushed but was secretly pleased that her own designs got her recognized in her own right, and not just as one of The Westies' girlfriends. She smiled politely but nodded her head, "Ahh."

"I'm so sorry, but we don't have time" Scarlett said. "We're on a very timely, important errand for a friend who's not feeling well. Appreciate you! Enjoy the show!"

Finally, Scarlett and Sephy reached the backstage entrance for a second time. The venue's security guard was clearly perturbed with them already, crossing his arms in a defensive pose. Just then, the door opened from the inside, and Tane, Shiv's brawny bodyguard, materialized over the man's shoulder. He handed them the laminate, which had been clipped to his belt loop. The ladies happily swanned past the snarling guard, who didn't enjoy having his authority questioned, into the UIC pavilion's vast underbelly.

Two minutes later, Tane had fetched Imani and carried her backstage, where Scarlett and Sephy had rendezvoused with the rest of the band. The ladies' gratitude at having been returned to their rightful place, with the band, was short lived, however. Their relief was exchanged, instead, with a feeling that perhaps it would have been better if they had not witnessed the disaster that followed. From their vantage point, it was clear that the massive joint was far from full, even with Deirdre's radio contest and ticket giveaway.

Maybe, the poor turnout was for the best, actually.

Counting off the first song, arms extended dramatically over his head, Bone dropped a stick. The crowd's enormous cheer was cut off abruptly, as the audience watched, in perplexed silence, to see what he would do next. Bone's tech quickly grabbed a backup stick from the stash near his drum kit. Even when Bone recovered and properly kicked off the band's set, the night's show was a comedy of errors. But no one was laughing.

While being supplied with libations by the most buxom female audience members in the front row, Hawke missed several entrances. During his moment in the spotlight, he choked hard on his epic solo. And at one point, he actually started playing the wrong song. He wasn't the only one who disappointed more than he triumphed, either. Jet and Shiv were like two metronomes, swaying back and forth in perfect time on either side of the stage, but everyone else was a mess. Bone's tempo sped up and slowed down without warning and Johnny stood frozen, gripping his microphone stand as if he were counting down the excruciating seconds that remained in their performance.

The band members reveled in their temporary triumph, during their encore, when they launched into their massive hit, "The Velvet Rose," and the audience members sang along to every word, while waving their illuminated cigarette lighters over their heads. But as soon as the song was over, streams of people began to exit their seats, indifferent to what might come next.

When the individual Westies were finally, gratefully, ensconced in the privacy of their dressing room, where they could lick their wounds without any witnesses, Johnny promptly slammed a triple shot of Jack.

He knew what was coming, and he was sure it would be even worse than what he'd just endured. The HIGs from the label would attempt to scare the hell out of them, under the guise of a supportive "pep talk," so the band members would shape up. Or else.

But when the door swung wide, only Deirdre and Clint entered.

"What do the powers that be have in store for us now?" Johnny asked. "An awkward dinner at one of Chicago's finest steak houses? A back-stage meet and greet with abundant portions of cubed cheese and warm beer…ah…and I know, a dry sheet cake from the nearest grocer."

"Your days of being wined and dined at fine steak houses are long gone," Deirdre said. "And so are the label reps. They headed straight for the airport before the encore."

"Oh," Johnny said, too disheartened to come up with a witty comeback…or any comeback at all.

Scarlett looked up from where she sat next to Imani on the couch, trying to encourage her to drink some water, even though Imani detested being fussed over.

"I'm sorry, Johnny," Scarlett said.

"Why are you comforting him?" Hawke slurred. "The way I see it, our high and mighty front man is the one who got us into this mess."

"At least I played the right songs," Johnny said, his voice cracking with anger.

"Boys, no one is in the mood tonight," Deirdre said. "Least of all me."

"But—" Hawke and Johnny protested, both at the same time.

"I'm going back to the hotel to take a Valium and pretend all of this was an extraordinarily bad dream," Deirdre said, turning to leave. "You'd better make sure to be on time for bus call in the morning. And tell *the model* to stay out of it."

Scarlett blushed deeply. She looked to Hawke for a supportive gesture, but as soon as Deirdre left, he'd gone to the door to admit Ellis Dee. The two men were having a hushed conversation in the corner with Bone, of which Scarlett could overhear more than enough.

"What kind of drugs are you into?" Ellis asked.

"Eh—what kind do you have?" Bone replied.

Scarlett tried not to think about the likelihood that some of these drugs would find their way up Imani's nose, or even worse, into her arm. Johnny smiled at Scarlett, but his eyes were sad, and she knew just how he felt.

***

I HAD PERFECTED A game I played during my years of traveling extensively for work: when I'd wake up in the morning, I'd pause for a beat before opening my eyes. While employing all sensory information derived from sources other than sight, I tried to guess where I was, before allowing my mind to provide me with an answer. Pulling the sheets up to my chin, I could feel that they were perfectly soft and smooth, obviously a high thread count. All I could hear was the deep tranquil hush of a climate-controlled building. *Hotel,* I deduced, based on these tidbits. I breathed deeply, inhaling the familiar scent of cigarettes, aged leather, and Murray's pomade. (How do you think he got his natural-looking, Jesus shag, without living by the beach?) *Johnny,* I thought, my heart leaping at the prospect of being in such close proximity to him.

As quickly as the longing could take shape within me, logic crushed my reverie. Missing from this olfactory mélange was Johnny's trademark Guerlain Vetiver scent. The man next to me wasn't Johnny, who was no longer my boyfriend, except for in occasional dreams that left me feeling despondent and guilty. It was Hawke. I was with him in the hotel in Chicago following their show. We were meant to climb back on the bus today and head to Dallas for their next gig.

*Okay, Scarlett, this is good. Hawke is handsome, talented, and full of passion. You're out on tour with your boyfriend, and your best friends in the whole wide world. Life is grand.* I opened my eyes to find Hawke, passed out on top of the sheets, still wearing his well-worn biker jacket, a monstrous snore emerging from his slack mouth. *Prince Charming comes in many packages, right?*

Technically, we were in the somewhat embryonic stage of our courtship, when it felt paramount to make a positive impression at all times. The fingers of my right hand spidering around the side table for my delicate, 1920s gunmetal gray purse, I fished out a compact, quickly checking my face, and cleaning up my raccoon eyes. After all, I wanted to greet Hawke with a non-nightmarish visage when he awoke. I went about my morning toilette, self-conscious in our shared bathroom. From my perch on the toilet, I observed my surroundings with horror—the room was a goddamn echo chamber: marble floor and walls, vast expanses of cold, hard mirror. *The minimalist chic design is far from advantageous when it comes to masking the morning bathroom noises one is so desperate to conceal.*

By the time I'd finished getting ready, he hadn't so much as rolled over in bed once. I shut the bathroom door, firmly, now hoping to rouse him, so he'd escort me down to breakfast.

After the condescending way Deirdre had addressed me, once again, the night before, I didn't relish the prospect of joining our group without backup this morning. But Hawke remained asleep. So I checked my reflection one last time, adjusting the tie on the back of my halter-top, which I'd painted with a tiger, rabbit, and dragon— signs from the Chinese Zodiac. I fixed my lipstick and prepared to brave the dining room alone. As I surveyed Hawke's sleeping form, I remembered bragging to Johnny, not more than a week ago, about how Hawke and I couldn't seem to drag ourselves out of bed in the morning.

*Well, it is somewhat true.*

Breezing into the hotel restaurant, I discreetly scanned the room for the band or anyone from their entourage. Visions of middle school lunchroom anxiety about having to sit alone swam up in my mind. Relief washed over me as I caught sight of Sephy's familiar, platinum blonde updo. Surveying the long table cluttered with coffee cups, half- drunk mimosas, and bottles of champagne, and Smirnoff, I realized that everyone from our little road family was seated at the table, except for Hawke and me. My preteen insecurity returned, but I forced myself to approach the table and pull out an empty chair at the end, next to Sephy. Everyone looked up, and their warm smiles and chorus of greetings were music to my ears—except for, of course, you guessed it, Deirdre, who openly sneered.

"Band meeting," Deirdre said. "You're not welcome."

"Sephy and Imani aren't members," I said, trying to catch up with what she was saying, while still being drowsy, and not yet having had my first cup of coffee. "And Hawke, he's still asleep. Sorry, but how can this be a *band* meeting?"

"Because...it is a *band* meeting," Deirdre said. "And Hawke's presence is no longer required."

"Have some brekkie, luv," Sephy said. "We'll go get massages afterward."

Nodding uncertainly, I backed up, stumbling into a chair from a neighboring table. Meanwhile, the nervous hostess stood by gripping a menu and seemingly unsure about whether to seat me or not.

"No worries...this is fine," I said, sliding into a seat at the next table over, and taking a menu from her with a forced smile.

I pulled a copy of the book I'd been trying to read since the tour had commenced and buried my face in its pages, even though I couldn't help but eavesdrop.

"Now that we've voted Hawke out, here's the plan," Deirdre said. "We'll take advantage of our days off in Dallas, which we've already built into the schedule so that Johnny's family could visit from Tulsa. We'll change the itinerary a bit, staying in Chicago tonight, and breaking the news to our soon-to-be-replaced shredder. Then we'll audition new guitarists. When we get to Texas, we'll rehearse the one we choose. We'll make up the lost time on our drive day from Dallas to New Orleans. Any questions?"

"Doesn't this all seem a bit coldhearted?" Johnny asked. "I'm the first to admit I've dreamt of leaving Hawke on the side of the road more than once, but—"

"It's a business. And sometimes you've got to think of yourself, and the best solution for the band," Deirdre said. "Let's face it, from the latest number of undersold shows to less and less radio play, things are not going well for the band at the moment, Johnny. I don't know how many more times I need to explain it to you before you finally get it. You can't afford to drag this kind of dead weight around right now."

Just then, Ellis Dee popped his head into the dining room and sent a jaunty salute in Bone's direction.

"Are we done?" Bone asked. "My...associate is here."

Deirdre sat back in her chair, fixing Bone with a long, icy stare. He hovered awkwardly half out of his seat, unsure whether he'd been dismissed or not.

"Did you hear the joke about the drummer who got locked in the van?" Deirdre warned. "It took the bass player ten minutes to get him out—from the inside. Some might say drummers are even easier to replace than guitarists. Some might say...entire bands can be switched out," she added, giving everyone at the table a wicked, warning look.

"Yeah, but our band rules just the way it is," Bone said. "Catch ya later."

With that, he shuffled off after his dealer, not waiting to be joined by Imani, who was so spaced out it took her a few moments to realize she'd been left behind. My heart sank as she took a beat to get up and slowly follow after Bone, her own gait as shambling as his.

The waitress returned with my breakfast and I ordered another coffee.

I treated myself to a solo excursion to the renowned Art Institute of Chicago, hoping for inspiration and solace. Returning back to the hotel around eight o'clock that evening, I was alarmed to find a throng of hotel staff congregated outside the door to my room. It didn't take long for me to understand why. Even from out in the hallway, a raucous crashing and bashing could be heard inside.

"Excuse me?" I said, pushing my way up to the front of the group.

"Is this your room, miss?" the hotel manager asked me. "I must remind you that you will personally be responsible for any damage done to the interior."

"Yes, right. Of course, no problem. You'll want to take the matter of the bill up with Ms. Deirdre Mulvey," I said. "But let me at least see if I can prevent any additional crazy carnage from occurring."

Using my key to admit myself, I entered an alternate, upside down reality: Hawke had apparently super glued a side table, and lamp to the ceiling, as well as taking apart a section of the wall between the bed and bathrooms. Currently, he was in the midst of throwing a lamp against a mirror, where it exploded with shattering porcelain. He grabbed the end of its cord, dragged the jagged remains across the carpet, and began swinging the lamp carcass over his head. He laughed maniacally as it again crashed into the mirror, sending more broken pottery every which way.

"Hawke!" I yelled, trying to get his attention. "WHAT ARE YOU DOING!"

When he turned toward me, his face was twisted with the devilish impulses that had overtaken his good judgment, as if he were Jekyll & Hyde.

"What am I doing?" he asked, clearly not quite sure himself.

"WHATEVER IT IS YOU'RE DOING, SIR, THE HOTEL MUST INSIST THAT YOU STOP DOING IT IMMEDIATELY," said the manager, who'd followed me into the room. "We've had complaints from other guests, as in ALL the other guests. Security is on the way. I've already telephoned the police. You must vacate the premises immediately… and never return, to this or any of our affiliated properties."

"Fuck the police," Hawke said.

As this mayhem unfolded around me, I frantically semi-packed our two suitcases, throwing our clothes and toiletries together, haphazardly, as quickly as I could.

"All right, that is enough!" said the manager. "Now, please, cease this behavior immediately. We are calling the police again, and I assure you, you will be sorry."

"Be sure to send the bill to Deirdre," Hawke said. Weaving toward me, he clasped my hand and tugged. "Come on, babe, I need a drink, from a real rock 'n' roll place. Let's go to Bucket O'Suds to get our fix."

"I'd say that's the last thing you need," I said, disentangling myself and grabbing our bags. "But we clearly can't stay here. Let me just grab our stuff."

"You both need to leave this room, effective *immediately*," the manager said.

"Of course," I said, wanting to corral Hawke before the manager changed his mind and decided to throw Hawke in jail after all.

From there, what was already a dreadful day took a turn for the worse. As Hawke staggered down the hallway, I rubbed his leg suggestively, attempting to distract him from his destructive rampage.

"Come on, babe," I said. "You're clearly in a bad mood. Let's find a quiet spot, just you and me, and turn this night around."

But he was having none of it.

"No fucking way," he slurred. "We're gonna go out and celebrate… this is the best fucking day of my whole fucking life. Now that I've been fired by those wankers, I won't have to see them or listen to them, and their incessant whining, all the time—fucking bunch of moaners, I tell you. I'm free!"

"Are you sure that's what you really want to do right now?"

"Yes, captain, it's party time," he said, saluting me and his plan of drinking himself into oblivion, while hitting the elevator button, again and again, with his other hand. Finally, the bell dinged, and we were transported down to the lobby.

After chasing his ass into a taxi while dragging our bags with me, we finally arrived at the famed Bucket O'Suds. Hawke lurched through the entrance. Once inside, I hoped he'd collapse into a booth and I'd be able to contain his celebratory vigor.

He marched straight up to the bar to get himself a drink.

"Jack, please," he said.

The bartender held up a glass. "Rocks or neat?"

"In the bottle," Hawke said, handing him his band credit card. "As in the whole bottle. Oh, and be sure to charge it to my lovely Amex." To me he said, "I once saw Lemmy do this at The Rainbow. It's a tried and true move."

"What am I going to drink? A peach Muscato wine slushy, with two cherries on top?" I joked, trying to keep the mood light, and steer Hawke onto a saner path.

"Good point," he said, too drunk to register irony. "Better make it two."

I didn't actually have time to order a drink for myself, as Hawke was soon walking out of there, with a bottle of Jack in each hand. And I was running after him, dragging a suitcase in each of my hands.

*What a fucking disaster.*

Hawke refused to tell me where we were headed next, even when we were in yet-another taxi. I was no closer to sleuthing out his intentions when we pulled up to the address he'd given the driver, an enormous renovated warehouse in an industrial neighborhood that had taken a turn for the arty. As soon as we entered the front door and began traversing a narrow warren of hallways, Hawke still sucking down generous slugs from his first bottle of whiskey, my anxiety multiplied about where the rest of the night was headed. The sound of bands practicing could be heard through several of the closed doors we passed. And then, we came to a room marked "13," behind which the sound of "The Velvet Rose" could be discerned. Hawke paused, took another giant gulp of booze, and then, kicked the door in.

"Oh, fuck," I said, wanting to turn back but not.

As I stepped into the fray, behind Hawke, I found myself facing off against a ring of surprised faces, including a shaggy-haired, corduroy bell-bottomed guitarist, who stood in Hawke's usual place, a sunburst Telecaster at the ready. It was unclear whether this was an audition or a rehearsal, but the band was obviously wasting no time in replacing Hawke. And he clearly had no intention of going out quietly.

"Sounds like shit," Hawke said.

"Coming from you, I'll take that as a compliment," Johnny said.

"Boys," Deirdre said. "We don't have time for this tonight. Hawke, you're no longer my problem anymore. Keep this nightmare up, and I'll call the police. Gladly."

"No need to get nasty, Deirdre," he said. "I'm just here for a celebratory drink with my mates. Seeing as how this is the best day of my life."

"Compared to where your life is headed, that's probably true," Deirdre said. "But I'm not having it. Get out. And take your *chick* with you, too."

A faint chuckle wafted up from a couch pushed back against the far wall. I looked over to see Imani slumped back into the cushions. She could barely lift her head, but when she finally did, she was laughing. "Good one…" she said, and then, her head fell forward again.

Sure, it had hurt like hell when Johnny treated me so badly I had no choice but to break up with him. And, no, it didn't feel good when Hawke was too caught up in his own agenda to really pay attention to me. All of that sincerely paled in comparison to the heartbreak of finding that my best friend had been turned against me—by Bone, by the band, by the drugs, by her own short-circuiting brain.

It wasn't fair to blame all of Imani's current problems on Bone. No one had held a gun to her head. She'd been flirting with the dark side for years, and when Bone had invited her to get lost with him, she'd indulged all too gladly. Having so much venom emerge from her now only revealed what seemed to be a secret grudge, which Imani must have been nursing since San Diego. The thought was too painful— impossible—to fathom, but the evidence was right in front of me.

And just like that, I snapped.

Yanking the bottle of Jack out of Hawke's hand, I drank deeply, coughing against the sting in the back of my throat. And then, I forced down some more.

"Scarlett, are you okay?" Johnny asked.

"Who's Scarlett? I'm, '*the chick*,' remember?" I snarled. "No, I'm not fucking okay. Neither are you. Any of you. You're all supremely fucked up. Do you *not* know that by now?"

I whipped around wildly, my system buzzing with rage. My eyes fell on a pile of white powder on the coffee table in front of Imani, along with a few neat lines and a rolled-up bill. Stalking over, I took another big gulp of booze. I thumped the bottle down and I picked up the roll.

"This one's for you, Princess Imani," I said in my best Blue Blood English accent, dipping my knees in a curtsy. Then, I bent down and snorted the line, hoping I was doing it right, since I'd never before indulged in this particular way.

"And this one's for you, Queen Deirdre," I said, with another bow and curtsy. "I'm not *'the fucking chick'*—my name is Scarlett, okay? S-C-A-R-L-E-T-T!"

Without waiting for or expecting a reply, I did another little line.

"And this one's for you, Sir Johnny," I said. "Why are you so nice to me *now*, when you were such an asshole before?"

"And this one's for you, King Hawke," I said. "You're just an arrogant, self-serving, self-righteous—"

Imani laughed again—drool coming out of her mouth—and interrupted my train of thought. I crawled over to where Imani was sitting, her eyes half-mast. She was too out of it to fully register the dramatic scene I was making in front of her.

Patting down her worn leather coat, I came across a prescription bottle and yanked it out of her pocket. Opening it awkwardly, I shook a handful of pills into my palm. I paused, shaking with adrenaline.

Jet approached me gently, his hand extended, as if I was a wild coyote he was trying to befriend. "Stop," he said. "Just stop this. It's going to be okay." He had always been kind to me, but his stoic cool wasn't going to influence my actions as it did the others. I knew his loyalty was to his band, not me. I ignored his entreaty and hunched over, so he couldn't snatch the pills.

"And this is for all of you," I said. "As in...*fuck* all of you."

I swung around and grabbed my whiskey bottle, washing down a pill with another giant gulp. I'd teach them a lesson, even if it was the last thing I did.

# CANT NEVER COULD

IT WAS AN OUTRAGE, really. They were, after all, rock stars of such multi-platinum, chart-topping eminence. They'd poured their all into sound check at The Cotton Bowl in Dallas, in advance of their triumphant "hometown" concert. Their native Tulsa didn't have any venues big enough to hold their vast number of devotedly ecstatic local fans. And now, they were preparing to relax in their dressing rooms— only to find this indignity awaiting them backstage.

Bone slouched up to the long, industrial table, draped with an inky-colored cloth, at the far end of the windowless, low-ceilinged, cement room. He did not hesitate to overturn a wide ceramic platter of fruit.

"Seriously, what the hell's gotten into you?" Deirdre asked, looking up from the thick pile of contracts and other paperwork that seemed to accompany her everywhere. "You'd think you'd been raised by a bunch of wild animals, for Christ's sake. Clean that up right now."

Bone glared, recalling myriad moments of management tyranny from hell. "As I recall...*you* work for *us*," Bone said. "*You* clean it up."

"*Au contraire, mon ami,*" Deirdre said. "You're in *my* band, on *my* roster of talent—a word I feel less and less inspired to use in reference to The Westies these days. Regardless, when you break it down, you work for me. And what are you moaning about anyway? Go on, spill it."

"Usually, the melon is cut into cubes, which are easy to eat," Bone said, while chewing on an invisible sandwich, thanks to the copious uppers he'd consumed that day, and frantically stacking fruit wedges on top of each other, as if someone had hit his fast forward button. "These melon wedges are loooooooooong and…unwieldy."

"Well, boo hoo, princess. You'll have to take that up with my inferior half, Clint," she said. "He was the little elf who used to arrive at the venue early before every show in order to cut your precious melon into your desired dimensions."

"Where is that dude anyhow?"

"Didn't *your* better half tell you that she had a recording session booked during our downtime this week?" Deirdre asked, seeming genuinely curious about any possible romantic snag. "I must at least give Clint credit for scouting Imani's nascent talent. If only I hadn't been so caught up with the folly of you louts."

"As soon as we got to Dallas this morning, Clint briskly snagged Imani away in our band car, taking her to one of her many fucking gigs and I haven't seen her since," Bone complained.

"Smart man," Deirdre said. "That Imani is really generating some traction, with both indie and major labels courting her and a record deal imminent any day." Laughing under her breath, she added, "You know when you're 'in,' you're in, and when you're 'out,' you're *out*." Then, she turned back to her papers.

"What's up?" Jet asked, looking tall and toned, as he came in from his afternoon jog, a hand towel draped around his neck.

"Did you know Clint cuts our melon for us at each venue?" Bone asked.

"Yeah, Clint also always books you a room on the ground floor, because he knows you're afraid of heights," Jet said. "And he finds me a solid gym to use in every city. He does infinitely more for this band than anyone gives him credit for."

As Jet made this last statement, he shot Deirdre a less-than-friendly glance.

"That's one perspective," Deirdre said, not taking the bait or looking up.

"Oh, Clint'll want this receipt for his accounting," Jet said, reaching for a piece of paper that was taped to a massive saran-wrapped platter of cold cuts and slices of lacy Swiss cheese.

"I can handle that, Chief," Deirdre said, suddenly very interested in what was happening in the room around her.

But Jet, who had a head for figures and had recently decided he'd like to run his own record store someday, was already unfolding the paper. He read it inquisitively. Meanwhile, Deirdre had rushed over, grabbing for the page.

"Weird," Jet said, trying to work out what he was seeing. "There are all these random, extra charges on here for items we don't use. Five thousand for fucking hand towels? I mean, you do sweat an ungodly amount, Bone, but we never go through *that many*—what the? Seventy-five hundred for a Learjet? None of *us* ever chartered—we bussed!"

Johnny and Shiv had just returned from the archetypal home-town show ritual. Johnny had wanted to take his best friend back to the shitty nosebleed seats in which he'd sat for his first ever concert—and well, his second, third, and fourth, too—in this very venue, when he was eleven years old. That Halloween of 1981, his older cousin, Tex, had let Johnny tag along with a group of his high school friends, when they'd made the four-plus-hour trek from Tulsa to Dallas, to bask in the royal majesty that was The Rolling Stones' *Tattoo You* tour. And even though their seats had been so terrible that Mick Jagger had resembled a sexy, soulful ant, those tunes, their soul, and their undeniable, ferocious rhythm had been epic. Right then and there, Johnny knew this was the life for him. And now, all these years later, he was back, and he was going to be the one onstage, completely singing his heart out for the kids in the cheap seats. And for everyone in the whole damn arena.

After basking in the glory of his triumph for about five minutes, Johnny returned to the backstage area with Shiv and Jet held out the stack of questionable invoices he'd uncovered, shaking his head in disbelief. Having bailed out of high school in the tenth grade, Johnny was not exactly gifted in dealing with the nuts and bolts of the band's business. But even a cursory examination was enough to make it crystal clear that Deirdre had been engaging in duplicitous bookkeeping.

"Uh…Deirdre?!" he said, holding the papers aloft, where she couldn't reach.

"I'd like to see you try and find another manager who'd take on you sorry slobs, and ALL of the extra work you generate, with your incessant drinking and drugging, your asinine pranks—and don't even get me started on all the extra liabilities you incur, not to mention your endless ego-driven tantrums and the nonstop babysitting it all entails," she said.

"I wouldn't think you'd be stressed out, what with the luxurious Learjet flight you just had," Johnny retorted. "We'll have a band meeting to discuss what we're gonna do next. But it's not looking good for you, you backstabbing hypocrite."

Deirdre reared back at this direct insult, but she wasn't about to retreat so easily. "Come on, Shiv," she said. "We've worked together for a decade. I've bent over backward for you, from overseeing your *stellar* solo career, when you were gigging in front of four people, before I got you signed with MCA Records, to wrangling all of your yayo and girls, and constantly combing through your stage and gear bills. I could go on, but apparently to you, hiring a manager means nothing more than my bloody fifteen percent. As in fifteen percent mommy, fifteen percent pimp, fifteen percent drug dealer, fifteen percent sycophant, fifteen percent business negotiator, fifteen percent psychiatrist. And that, my friend, *that* is not one, not two, three, four, or five, but 6.6666667 percent, to be precise, if you want to break down how much I get, compared to what I *give* to you and this goddamn band. Which is EVERYTHING!"

"Look, I know we're not exactly a walk in the park, but can a guy at least get a straight answer?" Shiv replied. "You may recall, the singer of me first band was so disgusted with the filthy music industry, he left behind his material possessions, and our band…to join an obscure goat cult. Maybe he found some padding in your production costs, too. How should I know he didn't?"

"Sure, trust the man in the goat cult," Deirdre said. "Don't listen to me."

She arched her broad back and marched to the couch, where she'd left her belongings, noisily gathering them up with an urgency that revealed her severe rage.

"I think it's best if you leave those papers behind," Johnny said. "We'll have Jet take over the numbers for now."

"Ha!" she said. "Welcome to your downward spiral." And with that, she sliced her way through the room's icy tension like a Ginsu knife, moving with maximum velocity and force.

As soon as the door slammed shut behind her, Johnny was across the room, where he poured himself a generous triple shot of Jack, neat, no ice, and no whining. At the same moment, the door pushed open, and one of the venue's runners poked his head in, followed closely by a middle-aged couple, obviously full of nervous disbelief. The man's medium-length, graying hair was slicked back, and he wore a fat silver and blue seventies Lone Star Beer belt buckle and a pair of carefully polished crocodile cowboy boots. The woman's floral, cotton church dress, paired with nude hose and sensible rounded, closed toe pumps, was crowned by an intricately coiffed waterfall of perfectly round curls. Johnny pretended not to see them long enough to down another equally healthy dose of his medicine of the moment. When he turned around to face the newcomers, all evidence of his usual rock 'n' roll swagger was gone. He nervously wiped his palms on his jeans, before walking forward timidly, eyes lowered, and extending a hand to the man.

"Hello, Father," he said, shaking with him. "I hope you found us okay."

"We had plenty of chance to find you, seeing as The Cotton Bowl is visible for miles from Highway 352, and we were stuck in traffic for three hours, inching our butts here," his dad replied.

"Wasn't so bad," Johnny's mother quietly offered up. She wrapped Johnny in a quick, fluttery hug, as if afraid her husband would disapprove, while feeling madder than a wet hen that she always had to play the peacekeeper with these two.

Meanwhile, it was as if the whole cast of *The Beverly Hillbillies* had washed up at the venue, as a dozen of Johnny's kin pushed sheepishly through the backstage door. As with his parents, all wore their Sunday best and gazed around astonished.

Johnny gave each family member a hug, almost as if it was a receiving line.

"Make yourself at home," he said, appearing almost as anxious and out of place as they did. "Help yourself to whatever you like. Drinks. We've even got fried chicken with white bread and pickles, all the way from Eischen's Bar."

The rest of his band mates stayed in the room, shuffling back to the other couch recently vacated by Deirdre, where they talked in hushed, urgent tones about what had occurred. Johnny glanced at them, eager to sort out how to best serve the band, but unable to do so at the moment. He had his own private game of *Family Feud* to navigate before he could attempt anything else.

"Don't hear your songs on the radio no more," Johnny's dad observed, his voice flat, as if he were talking about the weather. "That was over pretty fast. More proof of how the Lord feels 'bout rock 'n' roll, I'd say. Maybe now you can give up all this bad living and do somethin' useful. We could always use another pair of solid hands around the shop."

"Jonathan is no mechanic," his mother said, her voice almost a whisper. "He's been graced with a special gift. It would be a sin to waste his talent."

"Thank you, Ma," Johnny said, ignoring his father's dig. He hadn't had a conversation with his dad that hadn't ended in a fight in ten years. And after having already gotten into a knock-down, drag-out confrontation with his manager, Johnny was doing his best not to make his day any worse.

"I'd say that's just about the only sin that's not happening around here," Johnny's dad said, spitting some of his Copenhagen chew on the floor in the direction of the bar.

Johnny stood, sipping his drink, trying to resist the urge to compound his *sins* by serving himself a generous refill. A scruffy young man around Johnny's age took advantage of the lull in their conversation to insert himself into the intimate scene.

"Hey, Cuzzo Guthrey," Johnny said. "How've you been?"

"My life hasn't amounted to a hill of beans of late," Cousin Guthrey said. "I got me one of those APC violations for getting caught sleeping one off in my truck. I tried to tell them I wasn't driving, just drunk. But they say it don't matter. I was in the truck. And now I can't get my license back until I pay a fine. But I can't pay the fine until I get a new job. Because—"

"All I've got on me is three C-notes," Johnny said, reaching into his wallet and handing him three hundred dollar bills, hoping this would be an early end to the whole routine. "Hope that helps. Now I gotta go get ready."

An assortment of his other distant relatives had skulked on the outside of this assemblage, eagerly waiting their turn to ask Johnny for a loan. Scattering, with dark looks on their faces, they set about eating all the chicken and famous Hammett House pecan pie available to them, and drinking all they could.

Johnny, meanwhile, grabbed the bottle of Jack off the catering table and without a word of explanation or excuse to anyone, retired to the bus, where he alternated shots of Jack and key bumps of coke until it was time for him to take the stage. Nothing he tried during that witching hour could shake off the double specter of the night's two dark lords: Deirdre and his dad. Worst of all, he missed Scarlett and how just seeing her lovely face had always brightened even the shittiest day. He was tormented by thoughts of her back in Los Angeles with Hawke, who was no doubt getting up to all kinds of unwholesome activities behind her back. How was it possible that she had chosen that loser over him?!

*No one can be trusted. No one believes in me, or my talent. Nothing ever goes my way.*

Johnny threw himself into his set that night, wailing into his mic until his throat literally bled. He could already hear the words of disdain his pops would have for him after the show, given that the venue was only one third full. Johnny could play through the conversation that awaited him, word for word, as it echoed every negative take down he'd experienced at his dad's hands, basically over the course of his whole life.

"Don't reckon Johnny Cash ever played to so many empty seats, but then again he was a true cowboy—and a man of God," Johnny's dad would say.

"Every singer who ever lived has played to empty seats some time," Johnny would retort. "Nothing has been handed to us, nor would we want it that way."

"Don't look like you've achieved anything worth even having handed to you," his dad would say. "Build a business. Or a family. Now that's worthy of respect."

"You've done plenty that's worthy of respect," Johnny's mama would say in his defense, using her almost-inaudible voice. "Can't never could…and you'll do even more."

Following a slightly lackluster encore, Johnny hurried offstage, avoiding the behind the scenes area, in order to nurse his wounds in private on the bus. He was already formulating a plan in his mind.

*My mama is the only one who never lost faith in me. I am gonna get back on top, just to prove her right. And to show my old man what a fool he is. I am gonna show them all: Scarlett, Deirdre, Father, the fans.*

"I'm gonna show them all," Johnny slurred, as Shiv poked his head into Johnny's bunk to check on his mate before some shuteye himself.

"I know you are, my brother," Shiv said, lifting the empty whiskey bottle away from where Johnny had been cradling it. "Tomorrow is a new day."

*** 

I'D NEVER BEEN SO hungover in my entire life. In the wake of my operatic meltdown in Chicago, I'd been full-body nauseated, shaky, and depressed. Not just when I woke up the next morning, but for days, which turned into nights, and more days afterward. I was embarrassed I'd made a scene of such grand proportions, but I didn't want to wish it away. I was glad it had happened so Imani, Johnny, and Deirdre understood the full consequences of their actions, and how they'd really made me feel.

Even now, having been home in Los Angeles for a week, I felt as wobbly on my feet as a newly scouted sixteen-year-old model in her first pair of three-inch Manolo Blahnik stilettoes. No matter how much water I drank, I was thirsty, and my scratchy throat felt too dry to force any words from it. Or maybe that was because I didn't feel moved to express myself in any way.

The definition of friendship was Persephone leaving tour in order to travel back to the City of Angels with Hawke and me. She'd contentedly cleared her social calendar, visiting my apartment with nutritious treats from Erewhon, coupled with *VOGUE* and *Details* magazines. I was too depleted to read, but their familiar, glossy weight felt comforting in my hands. And then the clamoring of Sephy's phone somehow summoned her back to London. She hand-delivered me to Hawke, with detailed instructions of how he should care for me—which he ignored, of course.

For my first few days in residence at The Doghouse, I slept in Hawke's perpetually darkened bedroom, indulging in twelve-hour marathons of slumber. Waking late, I spent evenings by the pool, sipping chamomile lavender tea and choosing not to focus too hard on the comings and goings of a handful of decrepit, shifty-eyed male and female rock peeps. They all seemed to be Hawke's dealers, or fellow users, or maybe the musicians he swore he was congregating into a new, far superior band, which he vowed would blow doors off The Westies.

It did comfort me to have Hawke nearby, as the desolate rooms of the empty house seemed to epitomize melancholy, without the rest of the guys around, but it was as if I had a hangover of the soul. I couldn't seem to care about the details of how Hawke spent his time, or about much of anything at all.

Finally, today, it was as if the enchantment had broken. I'd awoken before noon, whistling Stevie Nicks to myself while brewing a pot of rose tea. I sipped the cathartic brew, enjoying the sunlight's bloom over the pool. It surged in intensity as it shone onto the atomic tangerine-hued bougainvillea that brightened our backyard oasis.

*It's time to get back to work.*

As Hawke slept the day away, I relocated my design studio from my two-bedroom apartment into an extra upstairs den at The Dog House, which had formerly served as the lads' TV/Sega Saturn "Radiant Silvergun" game room. I transformed the coffee and game tables into a workspace, wholeheartedly immersing myself in sketches for a new series of top-secret pieces. For hours, I drew inspiration from glossy photos of Studio 54, gritty portraits of Weimar Berlin, and dreamy illustrations by impressionists Monet, Manet, and my favorite, Degas.

Hours later, lost in my creative musings, my hands smudged with color, I was startled to hear Hawke calling my name from the front yard, "Scarlett! Get the fuck out now!"

Tossing my pale blue pastel back into its box, I rubbed my hands clean as I hurried to the window and leaned out to see what he was yelling about. Hawke and his group of friends resembled refugees, huddled on the grass together.

"Wha—?" I began to ask.

"The house is on fire!" he yelled, cutting me off before I could continue. "You have to climb down! Right fucking now!!"

I hesitated a moment, reading Hawke's face closely. The whole scenario reeked of one of his pranks, but he normally gave those away with a telltale sneer. And the acrid smell of burning plastic had begun seeping in from under the door behind me.

"Fuck, Scarlett, listen to me!" he shouted. "You've got to climb down NOW."

I tossed off my kimono, so I was wearing only men's silk pajama pants and a tank top. I kicked off my slippers, figuring bare feet would offer me a better grip. Then I straddled the windowsill, seeking my next move. Thankfully, the porch that ran the length of the house was right outside the window. I was able to jump the few feet down onto the tile rooftop, landing in a low squat. As my weight hit the Spanish tiles, one of them dislodged and fell down onto the driveway, where it shattered. Hawke jumped back from the impact, then, craned his head to see me.

"Be careful, Scarlett," he shouted.

Suddenly, he dashed beneath the porch overhang, in the direction of the front door and disappeared from sight.

"Hawke, no!" I screamed, trying to dissuade him from rescuing me. "It doesn't make sense. It's too dangerous!"

The flames had reached the room in which I'd just been working, and I could feel the heat radiating toward me. My throat ached from the bitter ash and smoke that clogged the night air. I glanced over my shoulder one last time, fearing I'd see Hawke's face poking through the window in his misguided, if romantic, effort to save me. I inched forward toward the edge of the roof, trying to determine if I could climb down one of the porch columns, or if it would be better for me to try my luck and jump onto the grass.

In the distance, a siren wailed, and then it began to grow louder, and louder, and LOUDER. A fire truck blasted up the driveway and shrieked to a halt just below the porch. A fireman in full gear and helmet jumped down before the vehicle had even stopped moving completely.

"Ma'am, ma'am, don't jump!" he yelled up at me. "Give us one minute and we'll have a ladder ready for you."

"My boyfriend ran into the house to help me!" I yelled. "He's been gone too long. I'm afraid—"

I couldn't bring myself to complete the thought.

"Don't worry, ma'am," he yelled up at me. "We'll get him out safely!"

As the fireman leaned a tall ladder up against the porch roof, another two pulled on their oxygen tanks, picked up axes, and prepared to run into the burning building in search of Hawke. The second the ladder reached me, I gratefully scrambled down. I fell the last few feet in my haste to get as far from the fire as possible, my palms thudded on the ground and broke my fall. A nearby fireman wrapped me in a blanket and told me to sit still until they could check my vitals. Just then, Hawke staggered out of the front door, his face severely blackened with soot, except for the whites of his eyes.

"Babe, that was crazy, rescuing me!" I yelled. "You could have been killed."

"What?!" Hawke asked, weaving toward me. "No…no…I knew you'd be fine. I had to go in after the important stuff."

In one hand, he held his prized fifties butterscotch-blonde blackguard Telecaster, like the one favored by Keith Richards, who'd dubbed his Micawber. Clutched in his other arm, as if it were a baby, was…I couldn't quite make out what.

"Can you hold this?" Hawke asked, handing the guitar to me.

Flopping down on the grass next to me, he cradled the other item in his lap, protectively. Up close, I could finally discern what he'd valued enough to risk his goddamn life for: a brick of weed.

"Thanks for saving me."

"I did," he protested. "I called your name, alerting you to the danger. I knew you were going to be fine, so I had time to fetch a few essentials."

"Sir, we'd like to ask you some questions," a fireman said to Hawke, as he swaddled a blanket around Hawke's shoulders.

"Jesus Christ," Hawke said. "Haven't we been through enough?"

"Is that what I think it is?" the fireman asked. "You know that's illegal."

Hawke shook off the blanket and used it to wrap up his prize. "Out of sight, out of mind, am I right?"

"I'll let it go this time," the fireman said. "Now, do you have any idea how the fire started?"

I watched Hawke expectantly, knowing full well I'd walked into the bedroom at least half a dozen times when he'd dozed off with a lit joint in his fingers.

"Yah—no idea, sir," Hawke said. "Faulty wiring I'd reckon. You know, these old houses, it's always something."

✳✳✳

THE TELEPHONE'S RING SLAPPED me awake early the next morning. With it came the onslaught of the day's harsh reality: the smell of ash rose up from my bed, where Hawke and I had collapsed. We'd been too exhausted to shower after we'd fled the late-night fire at The Dog House, which had been completely destroyed. I willed the phone to go silent, but it persisted. Eventually, I forced myself to sit up.

"Hello?" I said into the receiver, trying to sound coherent.

"Scarlett, is that you?" said a familiar female voice.

"Mom?" I asked, turning away from Hawke's chainsaw-decibel snores.

"I've been calling your apartment for days," she said. "But no one ever picked up. Where's Imani? Is she all right?"

"Sure, she's great," I said, feeling guilty for lying, and even more so, for having been unable to help Imani when I had the chance. "She's out on tour with Johnny's band. And her music career is really taking off."

"That's wonderful, dear," my mom said. She cleared her throat and paused.

"What is it?" I asked. "Are you okay?"

"I'm sorry, honey, but—but—Aurora—she passed away," she said.

A deafening silence roared through the line, muffling everything around me.

"What? But she can't...I need her."

As much as I couldn't imagine a world without Aurora and her Technicolor existence, I thought back to how frail she'd been the last time I'd seen her. When was that? Months ago now. My heart cracked at the thought of how preoccupied I'd been with my own problems and what a bad friend I'd been to her during her final days.

"The service is tomorrow," Mom said. "I thought you'd want to be there."

"Of course," I said. "We'll drive down tonight."

"Oh, I'll finally get to meet this Mr. Wonderful you told me about," she said.

"What?" I asked, trying to remember if I'd said anything to her about Hawke.

"By 'we,' you mean you and your boyfriend, Johnny, right?"

*I really need to call home more often.*

"Not exactly," I said. "I guess you could call my new guy Mr. Wonderful, too, though."

As if on cue, Hawke farted in his sleep.

"Sounds *wonderful*," she said. "Bring him to dinner tonight."

✳✳✳

THERE WE WERE, HAVING an intimate home-cooked meal, just the three of us. After sitting with his arms folded grimly for a good twenty minutes while my mom caught me up on all of the family's news, Hawke finally moved, but only to uncork the third bottle of '94 Chateau Pichon Longueville Baron he'd insisted on bringing for my mother. He'd made the gesture under the guise of being a good and generous guest, but as I now understood, it had only been to ensure there were heaps of red vino.

"Well, what do you like to do in your down time, Hawke?" my mom asked, forcing a smile.

"Uh, I actually love to cook," he said, clearly hoping to break the ice and impress his sweetheart's mom.

"Oh, really?"

"Well, you know, I am the barbecue king," he boasted. "Just last week, I went to my buddy's butcher shop, The Meat Hook. I had him slice me up some nice, juicy sirloin. Did you know sirloin is from the area of the cow that's right near the butt? I guess, technically speaking, it's where the leg muscles connect with the undercut. I drizzle the meat with a pound of melted butter, two large egg yolks, mixed with some salt, pepper, and tarragon. You should come over some time. I think you'd really dig it."

And with that, an icy silence settled over the table.

"I don't quite know where to start, actually," Mom said. "I've been a disciplined vegan for twenty-three years now."

"Vej-an," he said. "What's that?"

"I practice a lifestyle devoted to avoiding all forms of exploitation or cruelty to animals, for food, or any other reasons," she explained.

"Oh...cool...I dig it, especially because you look healthy," Hawke said. "I mean, I guess I thought vegans are supposed to be super skinny."

"Thanks," Mom said, flatly.

*Can this dinner be any more of a fucking catastrophe?*

"I'm sorry, Scarlett didn't warn me of your dietary *restrictions*," Mom said, sarcastically, reaching for one of the rough-hewn ceramic serving bowls. "This is really just pasta."

"It's green," he sneered.

"It's pea pesto with basil, garlic, pine nuts, sun dried tomatoes, arugula, and vegan Parmesan," she said.

"It's really good," I said, trying to smooth things over between them.

"To each his own," he drunkenly griped. "Next, you'll be telling me that cows are as smart as we are. And we should give them our jobs and money and shit."

"Hawke!" I said, throwing down my napkin and standing up.

"I'm sorry, Mom," I said. "He's clearly had too many on an empty stomach." *For years*, I added in my head. I grabbed Hawke under his arm and motioned toward the door for us to get some fresh air. "Come on, tough guy. Let's go walk it off. You can make it up to my mom by doing the dishes when we get back."

We paused on the walkway as he lit up. At least he'd managed the self-control necessary to *not* light a cigarette until we were outside.

It felt strange to be home without Imani by my side, as she had been for the last decade I'd lived in San Diego. Peering next door, I began surveying Aurora's house. With its pale pink Great Maiden's Blush roses, the heirloom variety favored by Aurora, trailing up its white trellis, it all appeared quite normal. My eyes brimmed with wetness, my desire was so strong to sip tea with my dear friend, while she regaled me with stories of her glory days in Tinsel Town and helped me to dream my own future into being. My salty, luminous tears scurried down my cheeks, and I was too sad to wipe them away.

Hawke offered me his bottle of wine. When I shook my head, he awkwardly patted my shoulder. I'd been so eager to fly out of my hometown and begin my adventures in the vast world beyond southern California. I'd somehow imagined my former life would remain just as it had been, awaiting my return. It was clear now, too much time had passed, and I'd grown too much from all I'd been through. I couldn't simply come home and fold myself into my old existence again—most of it was gone, and what was left, I'd outgrown. But my new life wasn't exactly blossoming, either.

At least, as we drove away, the fresh Pacific breeze whipping through the open car windows made me feel better, and it seemed to sober Hawke up a bit.

"Where's your old man live?" he asked, as I braked for a stoplight.

"You're my old man," I said, puzzled.

"No, not me, your real old man," he said. "Your dad."

"Oh, he lives here in La Mesa," I said. "Just on the other side of town."

"I want to meet him."

I was as surprised by Hawke's words as I'd ever been.

"Dads always seem to like me," he said.

I was unable to convince Hawke that it would be better to call my father in advance, as I hadn't really seen much of him since my parents' divorce when I was fourteen. Or that we should wait until an evening when he was *enjoying* himself a little less.

A half hour later, I was surprised again—this time to find myself sitting with Hawke in a room I'd only rarely visited, while my boyfriend and my dad drank whiskey and chatted happily like two old chums. Scanning the room that was lined with myriad bookshelves my professor father had built into his den, and dotted with family memories, I drank root beer and ate chips and salsa to occupy my hands. As if the night hadn't contained enough astonishments, Hawke cleared his throat and interlaced his fingers with mine.

"Sir," he said.

"What did you just say?" I laughed, as if I'd been the one drinking for hours.

"Sir," Hawke said again, undaunted by my mirth. "I'd like to ask you for your daughter's hand in marriage."

"W-H-A-T—?" I asked, mid-crunch of a tortilla chip.

"Hm, well now, I appreciate the respect you show me by asking," my dad said, absently rubbing his beard. "But marriage is a serious undertaking. And you're both so young. Are you sure you've really thought this through?"

"Fuck yeah!" Hawke said, never wanting to be questioned in any way.

"Why then…yes," Dad said. "It's nice to see a modern young man with some old-fashioned manners. Here's wishing you a lifetime of happiness."

Somehow, having just experienced the surreal scene that had unfolded at my dad's house, I wasn't surprised when Hawke next instructed me to drive us to the beach. He ordered me to park near a certain stretch of sand, and then, he blindfolded me.

"No one is going to spit fire at my face, are they?"

"Don't be silly," Hawke said. "I've outgrown that stage of my life."

"That happened yesterday," I said, referring to a prank one of his mates had played on me a few hours before Hawke had burnt the whole house down.

"What can I say? I mature rapidly."

The next thing I knew, he'd whipped off the bandana with which he'd covered my eyes. And our bodies were now nestled together on a tattered, ruby-red and tan tartan Burberry throw. He'd secured the blanket against the wind with a stainless-steel fishing bucket of ice containing bottles of Lowenbrau. It wasn't exactly chilled champagne, but hey, since Hawke almost exclusively drank whiskey or domestic beer, this was definitely his attempt to class up the proceedings. On the opposite corner of our picnic blanket rested a bouquet of gas station roses still in their cellophane.

"Beer, m'lady?" Hawke asked, opening a bottle with his teeth. "Here's to my babe. You know, the night is kinda special. The love will pour, it must be something more, so tonight—let it be Löwenbräu."

"Ehhh…why, thank you," I said, accepting the cold one from him, while thinking: *Did he just recite the lyrics from a Löwenbräu beer commercial to me? Yes, he did.* "You did all this?"

"The local 7-Eleven has a surprisingly romantic selection of items," he said. "Now, watch this."

He pointed out the purplish, dusky sky, where gulls made peacock-like wails and careened on the brisk breeze. A twin propeller plane flew into our sightline and began performing dramatic loops above us.

"H-A-R-R-Y," I said, reading letters, one by one, as they appeared in the sky.

"Wha—?" asked Hawke.

"Harry...Me...Harlett," I said, slowly pronouncing each word as I made it out. "Do you think the message is meant for someone here at the cove? Maybe there's a Harry around here somewhere. It's not very nice to call him a harlot, though. Whoever he is."

"Marry me, Scarlett," Hawke said, jabbing his finger at the sky with increasing urgency. "It says, 'Marry me, Scarlett!!!'"

I flushed deeply as I realized he was actually sincere. I surveyed my boyfriend dubiously. Our dinner with my mom had been an unmitigated disaster. If his mood hadn't been softened by whiskey, who knew how my dad would have reacted to Hawke's brazen personality and impromptu request when we'd popped in for a visit? I'd always imagined being proposed to as a swoon-worthy romantic experience. And here I was, with cheese on my breath, drinking a Lowenbrau, wearing an old pair of worn Levi's and an oversized, fuzzy forest green cardigan I'd borrowed from my mom.

But...and that's a big but.

Here he was, my man, Hawke. He'd come home with me and agreed to accompany me to Aurora's funeral in the morning. He was by no means perfect, but unlike Johnny, and everyone else who'd claimed to really care about me and my well-being, he was actually here, by my side, for better—or for worse.

"Yes," I said. "Yes, I will marry you."

✷✷✷

AND SO I FOUND myself seated in an open-air, horse-drawn carriage next to my father. We were making our way, slowly, down a stretch of beach in San Diego, in order to arrive at the pier from which our 1922 Sycara IV Pursuitist wooden yacht would depart. Amused sunbathers sat up to observe our progress, many taking pictures and waving as if I were the Queen of England. Our procession came to a halt, and I telegraphed serene, ethereal bliss as I stood. Pausing to allow my dress's train, measuring ten-feet in length, to unfold in all its glory, I fit my hand into my dad's. With the gallantry of an ancient king, he helped me to alight onto the sand. We commenced our soulful procession, my dad in a morning jacket and top hat. My romantic, white, strapless, full-skirted dress, which I'd helped to design and had sewn just for me, was inspired by Marc Chagall's costumes for a 1967 production of "The Magic Flute" and the gown of a 1930s Bohemian princess. As was only natural, I'd painted by hand the lower two-thirds of its left side, adorning it with my signature flower artwork: intricate vines of delicate wild roses.

Once we'd boarded the ship, I hid myself away in my bedroom. Meanwhile, on the deck, our lovely guests sipped cocktails and devoured passed appetizers as we pulled away from land. Included were my family, all of my favorite personalities from the fashion world, and The Westies and their entourage, including Imani, Sephy, Deirdre, and Clint. I almost hadn't believed it when Hawke had informed me that the whole lot of 'em would be in attendance at our wedding. Apparently, Deidre was already planning for the second album, which the band owed, contractually, to the label. She'd decided today was the perfect photo op, in order to let the suits know the guys had mended fences, all was well, and a chart-topping musical masterpiece was imminent. (I also suspected Hawke enjoyed the idea of rubbing Johnny's nose in our nuptials. And well, maybe, I did too, just a little.)

In my stateroom, my favorite sweet makeup artist and brilliant hairdresser put finishing touches on my look. Sephy fussed over me in her signature style—which involved champers, of course.

"I'm hysterical!" Sephy crowed. "You're getting married, and you couldn't look more beautiful, not if the angels came down from heaven and made you up themselves."

"Love you, Sephy," I said, surveying my image in the looking glass. *Could this soon-to-be bride really be me?*

Even after I was completely dressed and properly primped, I hung back for as long as I could. I was hoping to hear a soft knock at the door, indicating that Imani had popped in to check on me or to take a sentimental, behind-the-scenes photo. I hadn't had any contact with her since my big scene during The Westies' tour, but I was hoping this was the day that would bring us back together. I'd even had my florist make her a special arrangement that matched my bouquet. But I wasn't even sure she'd made it onto the boat before we'd lifted anchor, and now I would have no chance to give it to her until later.

I was summoned to make my grand, uber-impactful entrance, and I knew I couldn't delay any longer. Instead of being escorted by my father, I'd gone along with Hawke's creative vision of having me walk down the aisle with an all-white Artic wolf! As accompaniment, Shiv played a heartfelt, acoustic version of The Beatles' "Something," penned by one of our favorites, George Harrison. Another of Hawke's inspired ideas had been to have Gene Simmons officiate, in full KISS makeup.

Training my gaze on our "minister's" Warhol-worthy face paint, I focused on staying aloft in my off-white satin Armani slingback kitten heels, as the boat rocked beneath me. When I came up to where Johnny was seated, our vessel hit an especially big wave. I caught myself on the back of his chair, which was festooned with fabulous flowers that assimilated the same blooms as my bouquet—roses, orchids, and stunning stargazer lilies.

Johnny looked up at me with a pleading expression, and I could have sworn there were tears in his eyes. But I hardened my heart against his handsome face—he'd had his chance to be the one I was marrying today, and he'd blown that opportunity in a most spectacular fashion. The wild beast tugged at its lead and I walked onward to where Hawke stood, rugged and engaging in a tuxedo topped with a black leather jacket and silver-mirrored Ray-Bans.

When it came time for our vows, Hawke interrupted Gene, pulling a creased sheet of paper from his back pocket. "I've got a few words I'd like to say," he announced dramatically, setting my heart aflutter.

*This is it. This is my soon-to-be husband, on our perfect, super romantic wedding day. And he even went the extra distance and put pen to page and written me a poem.*

In a most serious tone, he began: "She was a fast machine /she kept her motor clean / she was the best damn woman I had ever seen / she had the sightless eyes / telling me no lies / knockin' me out with those—"

Before Hawke made my grandmother blush, I interrupted him with a few special vows of my own.

"Hawke, your boyish exuberance is one of the qualities that first attracted me to you," I said. "And, well, since then, I've found you to be loyal and steady…" I could have sworn I heard a hoot from somewhere in the audience, but I pushed on. "During one of the hardest times I've ever endured, you've been there for me. And I can't wait to spend the rest of my life with you."

With that, Gene had us exchange the traditional vows while looking deep into each other's eyes (or in my case, into Hawke's sunglasses). Rounding out the day's subtle elegance, as envisioned by none other than Hawke, cannons fired blanks into the bay, causing thunderous, dramatic bangs that made him whoop.

After the ceremony, I was swept away in a throng of well-wishers, including distant family members I hadn't seen since I'd been in diapers practically. I kept searching the crowd, seeking Imani's familiar dark buzz cut, so I could try to steal a few minutes with her. But when I finally did see her, she was leaning against Bone on one of the deck chairs, doing her best to discreetly vomit into a paper bag. Distraught, I had trouble focusing when Ray Ray, my wedding planner, pulled me away with a question about cutting the cake.

For our first dance, Hawke had insisted we learn John Travolta and Uma Thurman's routine from *Pulp Fiction*. I wouldn't say this had been my first choice, but he'd happily let me decide almost every other detail of our big day. And I'd chosen to see all of the splendiferous touches he'd dreamt up for our wedding as a sign of how excited he was to be marrying me. So I'd capitulated to his request. We'd burned the midnight oil, practicing for hours, in order to get our righteous choreography just so.

But, now, it was 4:00 p.m., which meant our glorious moment to cut a rug had arrived, and he was nowhere to be found.

First, I checked the boat's two bars—upstairs and down—but other than a lingering gaze exchanged with Johnny from afar, there was nothing worth reporting at either. Finally, out of options, I popped into our stateroom, seeing if maybe he'd snuck off to do a line of coke. And if, happily, this wasn't the case, at least I could freshen up my lipstick before one of the reception's biggest photo ops.

In order to conceal any drug binge that might be happening, I darted into our room, fleetly shutting the door. And there I paused, too startled to do anything else. Hawke was in fact in the room—in the bed—entwined with another body.

*We've been married for fifteen minutes, we haven't even had our first dance, or cut the cake, or thanked our family and other guests for attending, and he's already...*

"You dirty fucking motherfucker!!!" I screamed, running at the bed.

"Scarlett," he sputtered. "You don't understand. I can explain. I lost—lost—I lost—a contact. Bunny was helping me find it."

"With her tits?" I asked. "You don't even wear contacts!"

"Maybe I should start," he retorted. "My eyesight is so bad... I thought she was you. I really did."

"DO NOT insult my intelligence any more than you already have," I said.

The sounds of my distressed screaming had caused a mob to burst into the room, fronted by Sephy and Johnny. It was immediately clear that they were absolutely not, in any sense of the word, going to let this go.

"You dirty bastard," Johnny said. "I always knew she was too good for you. And now I'm certain, without a shadow of a doubt, you're not even worthy of the dirt beneath the shoes on her feet. C'mon, Scarlett, I'm getting you away from this fucking loser."

And that's how I ended up flying away from my wedding, in the chartered helicopter that was supposed to carry me to a jet bound for Hawaii and my honeymoon with my new husband. Only, instead of that unfaithful, profligate motherfucker, Hawke, I was sitting beside Johnny. And even though I was crying, I felt, somehow, a glimmer of hope, and surprisingly, even a little buoyant inside.

# SHE MINE

THERE ARE MUSICIANS, AND then there are hit makers so gifted, hearing their name will immediately launch their number one song on a constant loop in your head for days to come. In 1995, perhaps one of the groups that best exemplified such ascendency was TLC, and their song-to-end-all-songs was, of course, "Waterfalls." There they were, the women of the hour, mere inches from the stage where Johnny was poised to perform live. This wasn't any run of the mill audience, and this wasn't just any stage, either. The Westies were playing at the iconic Radio City Music Hall, back in New York City, where they'd signed Deirdre as their manager and launched their dream.

Just before Johnny received his cue letting him know they were back from commercial break and the TV cameras were about to roll, Johnny's life as an artist flashed before his eyes. He lamented to himself: *Why didn't we fucking rehearse more, like we used to, at our beloved home away from home, Downtown Rehearsal? Instead of just one quick attempt during our required run through for the sound check and camera blocking. And although we narrowed it down to two songs, why didn't we choose the one we're actually going to play... until NOW?*

And then one of the producers counted down: *four, three, two, one*—and Johnny was singing live on the 1995 MTV Music Video Awards—in front of legends Axl Rose, Billie Joe Armstrong, and Scott

Weiland, and millions of people around the world, including everyone in his hometown of Tulsa.

Johnny did his best to swallow his nerves, assuming his most ferocious snarl as the camera panned over the band and zoomed in on his face. It wasn't the tightest they'd ever sounded, by any means. *But rock 'n' roll isn't meant to be perfect, right?!* Johnny threw himself into it, completely singing his heart out. Then, during the bridge, he and Shiv came together, as if magnetized. Leaning close, the two driving each other on, Johnny wailed on his harmonica, while Shiv nailed his solo, looking impeccably cool.

*Maybe we're actually going to pull this fiasco off, after all,* Johnny thought.

As the band reached the song's second verse, the house lights came up, in order to reveal the audience members singing along—at least in theory. Bone was clearly under the influence of something speedy, mixed with something drowsy. As his backbeat sped up and slowed down, just enough to be noticeable, those watching did their best to hold onto the rhythm and clap in time. *Whoa, it's even scarier with the crowd illuminated,* Johnny thought, taking note of just how many heavy hitters were there—everyone from music geniuses Quincy Jones, Elton John, and Madonna, to rock gods Slash and Duff. And there, sitting center stage, four rows back: *Scarlett.*

Johnny knew he needed to launch into the second verse, but his mind went blank. He sang the first words that came into his head. It wasn't until halfway through, he realized he'd fucking inadvertently sung the opening lyrics again. Even worse, his mistake had thrown the band into confusion. Jet and Bone were playing the rhythm part that kicked off the song, while Shiv and Hawke had moved onto the guitar melody from the next section. *FUCK...FUCK, FUCK!*

Johnny had no choice but to keep singing, even though he was now helming a disastrous cacophony, a sonic car crash of seismic proportions on flaming wheels. He looked to Scarlett, desperately, as if she could offer him a lifeline. In the moment just before the house lights dimmed again, he was sure he saw her wince. *Shit, it must be really bad.* She would have definitely recognized the band's errors, as this was a song she knew quite well—"The Velvet Rose."

At least the stage lights had begun strobing through a rainbow of colors—from red to purple and back again—hopefully deflecting some of the focus from the music. Desperate to redeem his band, Johnny hurled himself into the final moments of his performance with intense zeal, whipping around like a rock 'n' roll tornado. He climbed onto Bone's drum riser, and then, even higher, onto the top of the bass drum.

As the final chorus swelled around him, Johnny leapt into the air. He achieved such height and velocity, he felt like a veritable rock god, as he arched into a full rotation back flip. Bathed in the wildly flashing lights, he somehow landed with badass precision on his custom Tony Llama boots. And then, he felt a strange, unpleasant tugging at his ankles. He'd split his well-worn, ripped Camden Market jeans right there onstage!

Maybe it was a blessing, after all, when the TV cameras suddenly spun away from the band, even though its members were still banging their way through the song's ending. As Johnny would later learn, they'd run overtime, and so the station had cut away to commercial, even though they hadn't yet worked up to their grand finale, with its massive crescendo of music and heart-stopping pyrotechnics. Finally, the last note rang out. Even though Johnny loved to perform, he had never been happier to scamper the hell offstage.

In the wings, safely hidden from the prying eyes of the audience members and the millions of viewers at home, Johnny finally had the guts to survey the wreckage. As he was all too well aware, when The Westies had received the stunning news of their five—count them, fucking one, two, three, four, *five*—MTV music video nominations. Deirdre had insisted the individual members bury their grievances and get together to practice before the show. The band members had not so much as been in the same room since Hawke and Scarlett's ill-fated wedding, but none of them were going to be the pathetic sap that actually put his own frustration aside, offering up an olive branch by telephoning his bandmates. So they hadn't rehearsed before their run through. They hadn't even decided what they were going to play that night until they all stood onstage, mere seconds before they were due to go live.

"Well, that was shite," Shiv said.

"For not having practiced, I thought we came off pretty well in the end," Jet said.

"Came off well?" Johnny moaned. "I sang the wrong verse. My pants ripped in half showing my whole undercarriage on live fucking national TV—make that *international* TV. And I can see Scarlett, *seeing* it all right there, in the fourth row."

"Don't fucking say her name," Hawke spit out, jabbing his finger at Johnny.

"Kids," Deirdre said. "Come on, they're telling us to get to our seats."

"What's your purpose?" Johnny asked. "What are you even doing here?"

"You should thank your bloody fucking stars I'm here," she said. "Would you like to be the one who takes the hit from the label?"

"Uh…no…" Johnny said.

"I didn't think so," Deirdre said. "Go sit down, *now*."

"But what about my lovely pants?" Johnny said, glancing down.

*Well, they cost me a mere ten pounds, so that explains that.*

"Seamstress of the band is not in my job description," Deirdre said. "Figure something out. Fast. Then get out there in the audience, where you're supposed to be seen, by which I mean accidentally *caught live* on the cameras, for more air time. And yes, that was arranged by me, your goddamn manager, thank you very much."

"Here, mate," Shiv said, taking off his Alexander McQueen embroidered silk bomber jacket. "Tie this around your waist. It'll cover your crown jewels."

✳✳✳

AFTER THE WESTIES HAD finished their disastrous number, I got it: the seven empty seats directly in front of me were probably reserved for them. My clenched fists suggested my inner frustration with, and desire to strike, Hawke—but, of course, I wouldn't. Concurrently, my queasy stomach let me know that I probably wasn't ready to see Johnny again quite yet.

Sure, it had been ridiculously romantic to ride off into the sunset (in a helicopter) with him after my epically failed wedding. Certain it was a sign we were meant to be together, he'd wanted us to fly straight to Catalina. And, sure, it hadn't hurt that I knew this turn of events would piss off Hawke when he got word of it. Not to mention, I got to be next to Johnny. But I didn't want to fall into another rebound situation, and so, I'd asked Johnny for a little time to process the past few months. I wasn't saying we'd *never* get back together. I just needed a beat, to make sure it was, indeed, what I really wanted. Johnny, being the gent that he was maturing into, had respected my wishes while I sorted myself out. In the meantime, the VMAs did not seem like a low-key setting for a casual encounter.

I surveyed my possible exit routes while attempting to be discreet. The night's host, comedian Dennis Miller, was doing his next bit, and my seat in the fourth row meant it would be impossible for me to sneak out without being within range of the various TV cameras.

I was on the verge of dashing during the next commercial break, when it dawned on me: *Tonight's not really about me. Their performance was an absolute fiasco—Poor Johnny. I bet he could use a friend right now. Plus, it wouldn't hurt for him—or Hawke—to see me tonight—what with my village of stylists, makeup, and hair people, I must be looking at least somewhat easy on the eyes. I thought I received a noticeable amount of love on the red carpet, and Anthony Kiedis asked for my digits.*

Although every cell in my body vibrated with nerves, I held my ground, even when the first band member to saunter down the aisle was none other than Hawke. I refused to make direct eye contact with him or any of the other guys as they slid, one by one, into the seats in front of me. Johnny immediately leaned over the back of his chair.

"Rosie," he said. "What a wonderful surprise. How are you!"

"Excellent," I whispered, trying to sound super strong. "Never better."

"Hey, folks, sorry to interrupt," Dennis Miller razzed us from the lip of the stage, peering down at our reunion. "But I'm trying to do a show up here."

"Sorry, can't help myself," Johnny riffed back. "She's too fine to resist."

"Aw, cute," Dennis Miller joked. "Now shut up."

My cheeks glowed as those in the seats near us swiveled around to catch sight of the spectacle Johnny was creating. Finally, Dennis Miller returned to his prepared introduction for the next award. It was a category in which The Westies had been nominated—Best New Artist—so that got their attention enough to actually stop horsing around.

The next thing I knew, they were being announced as the winner, and they were hugging and high-fiving each other as they made their way up to the stage. Of course, Hawke got there first, and he swooped in and grabbed the spaceman-shaped statuette and the mic.

"I'd like…I'd like…to thank Jack Daniel's," Hawke said. "God knows it's the fuel behind this band, and the only way I can stand to be in the same room with 'em."

Johnny finally managed to edge Hawke away from the microphone. "In addition to that charming show of gratitude, we would be remiss if we didn't thank all the incredible people at our label, MCA Records. Our amazing techs, engineers, our tremendously hard working crew, our management, and of course, all our fans. We wouldn't be here without you. Everything we do, we do for you. Thank you so much. I also need to, personally, thank my own North Star, the reason behind much of the success I've managed to achieve, the mirror by which I most clearly see what matters in this life. In the words of the late great Jimi Hendrix: 'I used to live in a room full of mirrors; all I could see was me. I take my spirit, and I crash my mirrors, now the whole world is for me to see.' Thank you, to *my* mirror, and, well, the inspiration behind our biggest hit, 'The Velvet Rose,' Miss Scarlett X."

With that, all of Radio City Music Hall roared with approval. Johnny held up his award, high to the heavens. Our eyes locked, easily bridging the space between the stage and my seat as if no distance separated us (spiritually or metaphorically). Although the entire room was staring, applauding, and whistling, I could have sworn Johnny and I were the only two people in the world.

***

JOHNNY LEAPT UP FROM a dead sleep, surveying the room warily. Months of severe, incessant tour pranks had left him with a mild form of PTSD. He couldn't doze off or consume any drinks or meals without fearing a painful, or at least embarrassing, reprisal from one of his band mates, especially Hawke. But there was no telltale snicker in the room, no smell of burning hair, and no taste of hot sauce where it shouldn't be.

Johnny was by himself in the home he'd rented on a walk street in Venice Beach. He slumped on the edge of the leather couch he'd passed out on the night before. He had the kind of hangover that bowed his head like a heavy steel helmet. His dog, Thunders—a black lab, named for his favorite guitarist, Johnny Thunders—surveyed him inquisitively.

"Ugh," Johnny said. "I feel like death warmed over."

Pawing through the detritus of half-empty cigarette packs, discarded harmonicas, and the antique tin windup toys Johnny had taken to collecting, he found a glass pot pipe. Using his lighter, he took two healthy hits. That helped some.

"Hey, boy, wanna go for a walk?" he asked Thunders, who'd quickly jumped up and returned with his red leash in his mouth.

Johnny took that as a resounding "yes" as he bent over to pull on his go-to black Converse low tops.

Shifting his position made his head throb anew, but Johnny wasn't about to punk out on his dog. He forced himself to push through the dizziness in order to tie his shoes. Attempting to complete this simplest of tasks, his hands shook too much, and he couldn't make it come to pass.

"Fuck," Johnny said. "The hell's happening to me?"

Standing gingerly, he padded into the kitchen and swung open the fridge. Retrieving a longneck bottle of Bud, he twisted the top off into the sink with a smooth, practiced motion. He drank down all twelve ounces in one long draught, and by the time he'd finished, his shakes had stopped. Better not to think too hard about the substances it had taken to jumpstart his day and to simply get on with it.

There were many gorgeous routes in his Venice neighborhood along which he could walk Thunders, including stellar paths and bridges spanning the historical canals built in 1905 by developer and famed tobacco millionaire, Abbot Kinney. But because Johnny also liked to go for a drive, he was in the habit of piling into his '66 Lincoln Continental convertible, complete with suicide doors, and winding through the Hollywood Hills. Once in Laurel Canyon, he embarked on long treks that culminated at his favorite dog park. He'd been too shy to ask Scarlett if she was ready to go out—not to mention, he wasn't exactly feeling his most confident after his disastrous MTV Awards nudist exhibition/performance. Although he'd sent her flowers the next day, he hadn't laid eyes on her since. Knowing this was the dog park closest to her bungalow, he reasoned this was the most likely place to "accidentally" encounter her and her dog.

Two weeks of daily visits, though, and no such luck.

As Johnny held Thunders in check long enough to secure the entrance gate behind him, he saw his new friend, David, and waved. The second Johnny had removed Thunders' leash, the dog happily bounded into the park. He began making joyous loops across the flattened grass, chasing David's Shepherd mix, Sebastian, and then stopping on a dime in order to be the one who was pursued.

Howling, Johnny sat down next to David on their regular bench.

"How's the music biz today?" David asked.

"Aah, well, don't ask," Johnny snorted. "How 'bout the film biz?"

"Well, let's just say, if you're the makers of the year's biggest hit, *Toy Story*, it's grand," he said.

"Are you one of the makers of the year's biggest hit?" Johnny laughed.

"Not I," said David. "Meanwhile, the rest of us are trying to figure out how a closet full of children's playthings could really be that entertaining."

"Ah, maybe next year."

"That's what I say every year."

"I know the feeling," Johnny said. "The records aren't selling unless you're Michael Bolton, the concert tickets aren't selling unless you're Rico Suave, the T-shirts aren't selling unless they're made of flannel. And then I lose the love of my life because of an indiscreet tryst with a video vixen. Oh, and did I mention, my rhythm guitarist *literally* burnt my house down? I mean, what else could go wrong?"

"Oh, well, at least he then proceeded to royally mess things up with Scarlett," David said, clearly having heard the whole story. "Have you asked her out yet?"

"I'm fixin' to," Johnny said. "It's just, I want to think of the *perfect* date, as in top of the Eiffel Tower, swimming with dolphins, 'best day of your life,' ridiculous, epic fun."

"You're going to swim with dolphins at the top of the Eiffel Tower? That *is* a hell of a day. Just don't spend so long thinking up the perfect date that you lose her again—this time forever."

"Well, I do have this one idea…"

***

IF I'D HARNESSED ONE pro tip during my years in high fashion, it was to smartly pull my look together by dressing from the ground up. Once I felt comfortable in my shoes—physically and aesthetically—I could manifest the rest of my look du jour, complete with the consummate accessories.

*Ce soir*, I was definitely grateful for my well-honed, failsafe approach. This was, quite possibly, the most profoundly significant event of my life: *Paws 4 a Cause*, the canine red carpet fundraiser I'd conceived and organized to benefit worthy regional no-kill animal shelters. My other aim, over the course of the evening, was to secure forever homes for some incredibly deserving dogs, maybe even with a new owner who happened to be Hollywood royalty from my star-studded guest list.

On an evening of such acclamation, I would be making sure to not only do, but also look, my absolute best. That meant rocking my delicate, crystal, strapped Dolce & Gabbana heels, beneath my so nineties, midnight-hued, sequined, wide-leg jumpsuit. My ensemble's pièce de résistance was one I'd created by hand, after many laborious hours. For this latest customized design, I'd begun with a shrunken, sixties leather motorcycle jacket, which I'd scored at one of my all-time fave novelty stores, *Cheap Jack's* on Broadway, back in the Big Apple. Any possible generic rock vibe was voided by my refined, gloriously original, hand-painted touches, adorning the piece.

When crafting my special look for the occasion, I'd opted to wear an homage to the cool nobility of my own beloved rescue dog, Hugo, a Shiba Inu. After all, he was indeed named for one of the planet's most prominent French writers, Victor Hugo, whom you probably recognize as the author of *Les Misérables*. Being the mega Hugo fan I was, I'd wanted to demonstrate a little known fact that was wholeheartedly apropos for the evening's festivities. Monsieur Victor Hugo was my hero because of the particular way in which he used his prestige to advocate for social change. When he was elected to France's National Assembly in 1848, he rallied for universal suffrage, free education for *all* children, *and* an end to poverty. Like Hugo before me, I also wanted to assist some of the world's most helpless victims: shelter dogs. And so, on the middle back portion of my coat, I'd skillfully rendered a regal portrait of my own Hugo. He too was dressed to impress in this image of him: his tobacco-colored velvet blazer topped a white button down Oxford shirt, accented with a black bowtie.

In the past, my agents had often told me that I'd been asked to use my platform for this charity or that, and I did genuinely love to help out. But trying to make a profound difference by helping to save animals' lives was what truly resonated for me.

Sure, it was gratifying that some of the press said I was the belle of the red carpet. But as far as I was concerned, the real star of the night was Hugo, who was on his best behavior. Plus, the twenty other rescue dogs from local shelters, which had been groomed, and even trained a little bit, just for the occasion. The pups were primed to be celebrated in front of the "puparazzi," in between appearances by a who's who of celebrities, many also attending with their canine companions.

The night had a fun, festive ambiance that seemed to have inspired all present to be in their most fraternal moods. The photographers and high-profile guests laughed and cracked jokes with each other. I, personally, had posed with some of my favorite fellow fashion models, flashing their most compelling looks, as they'd taken their turns on the carpet, including legends Tyra Banks, Niki Taylor, and Cindy Crawford, plus none other than actresses Christina Ricci and Susan Sarandon. The iconic fashion designer Azzedine Alaia, also a well-known dog lover, had even flown in from Paris for the event, with his three sweet terriers; I always loved cuddling with my favorite one, the adorably named Pat a Pouf.

What an all-star turnout, and their four-legged friends were superstars too!

When it came time for me to pause for photographers, solo, I held Hugo while playfully turning around. That way, he could be captured on film, along with my likeness of him on my jacket. The camera crew got into the spirit, and then some.

"Scarlett! Love—over here! Give us a smile!"

"Hugo! You're *gorgeous*! Show us your best side. Now…bark for us!"

"Scarlett, what was your inspiration for tonight?"

"I've been so blessed in my own life," I said. "I know people are always saying that and it can begin to sound flat, as with some oft-repeated catch phrase. I realized the only way to show my gratitude was to give back to those who don't have a voice to speak for themselves. That's why Hugo is up here with me, to draw attention to my own philanthropic idol, the writer and humanitarian, Victor Hugo."

I was just wrapping up my last few live TV interviews, when I heard the rapid fire popping of the photographers' flash bulbs, which let me know they'd found another personality worthy of capturing. I turned, and there he was at the other end of the red carpet: *Johnny*. He and The Westies had been in the news since their disastrous MTV VMA appearance, and the paparazzi were hungry for candid pics.

"Johnny! Johnny! Tell us—what happened at the VMAs!"

"Johnny! Look left! Give us the dirt on 'Pants Gate'!"

Some of the photographers apparently recalled the days when Johnny and I were often captured together, outside clubs and concerts, and wanted to secure an image of us reunited.

"Scarlett, Johnny, over here…look left, and a little closer…again," a photographer called out. "You both look superb!"

Johnny's head swiveled up, and he glanced in my direction. He waved me over, flashed me a huge, warm grin and a little dignified bow. I shook my head: *NO*. We hadn't been alone together since he'd rescued me from my catastrophic wedding. I didn't want the awkwardness I was feeling inside to be caught on camera. But he obviously wasn't taking no for an answer. And neither were the paparazzi.

"Johnny! Scarlett! You're looking like Antony and Cleopatra tonight! Grace Kelly and Prince Rainier! Please…c'mon, give us a shot!"

Drawing on all of my courage, I strutted over to Johnny, and I posed next to him with all of the confidence I could muster. Feeling his warmth next to me, I could sense him doing the same. Even with the kiss of air separating us, my skin tingled with excitement at his proximity to me.

"Lovely! That's the stuff!"

"Scarlett, over here! Look over your shoulder! Blow us a kiss, Scarlett! Scarlett, one more please?"

"Who are you wearing tonight, Scarlett?"

"It's one of my original Velvet Rose designs," I said. "This is my favorite platinum and diamond necklace by Chrome Hearts. And crystal shoes fresh off the gorgeous spring/summer ninety-five show, which Stefano Gabbana and the Milan atelier so kindly lent me for what they called a 'commendable animal rights soiree.'"

"Johnny! Johnny! Go left! Wonderful!"

"Scarlett and Johnny, kiss! Kiss! KISS!!"

We both froze, flash bulbs exploding all around us. Staring deep into each other's eyes, it was as if our nervous heartbeats were visible.

At the same moment, the air itself became magnetized, pulling us together. We both leaned in, and our lips met. It was delicious. The lights flickered around us, the shutter clicks speeding up.

"Gorge!"

"Yes! YES! Yessssssssss!"

"That's the money shot!"

Sliding his arm around my waist, Johnny pulled me close. A jolt of electricity ran up and down my side, along every millimeter where it touched him. When we finally, reluctantly, pulled apart and turned again to face the wall of photographers, my smile was as giddy as a schoolgirl, obsessing on her first crush. Interviewers from *VOGUE, Allure,* ABC, NBC, MTV, CNN, *Access Hollywood, Extra!,*

*Entertainment Tonight, The New York Times, The LA Times,* and *Rolling Stone* swamped us, myriad microphones extending in our direction.

"Scarlett, Johnny, obviously tonight is very special for both of you—can you tell the viewers at home why?"

"If I may," Johnny said. "What's so significant about tonight is the lady of the hour, The Velvet Rose, Miss Scarlett X. I could not be more impressed with how tirelessly she has worked for this event, which is saving lives, giving back, and I'd go so far as to say, revolutionizing our city."

By this point, all TV cameras had panned in my direction.

"Tell us, Scarlett, how does it feel to have the support of HUGE entertainers, such as Johnny Suffield from major rock band The Westies?!" the correspondent asked.

"I'm very grateful," I said, realizing much to my chagrin, I was blushing. "Even more importantly, so are the wonderful dogs. We're really doing all of this for them."

There we were, unified by a good cause, together again. The moment could have gone on forever, as far as I was concerned—and Johnny seemed to feel the same way. But the time had arrived for us to go inside for the night's festivities.

As soon as we were done giving our red carpet best, Johnny and I gawkily untangled our limbs, both looking down, and then away, unsure what to say.

"How have you been?" I finally asked.

"Okay...good...and you?"

"Okay. I mean, I'm good too," I said. "I got the flowers you sent me—thanks."

As we entered the ballroom where the event was being held, we both paused to appreciate the tasteful décor, replete with stunning old Hollywood lights. I'd worked with the charity event planners to render the exclusive, landmark venue into an ocean scene, resplendent with cerulean waves on the walls and elegant centerpieces of sea grass and wild roses. After all, a dog loves nothing more than a day at the beach, so I wanted to create an environment where they'd feel at home.

"Wow, it looks incredible in here," Johnny said.

Again, we were at a loss for words, and stood together uncertainly. Across the room was the VIP table where I would be holding court, and I knew I should make a point to greet the few guests who were already seated.

"Well...I should go make sure everything is running as planned before I sit down," I said, half-heartedly. "It was...nice...to see you."

"Actually, I bought a seat at the VIP table tonight, so I could... um...you know... support your fine charitable cause," he said.

"But those tickets cost ten thousand dollars *apiece!*" I gasped.

We exchanged a long look, full of all our unspoken feelings. Neither of us moved, until the moment grew awkward enough that we both laughed. Before either of us could finally speak, my party planner, Anita, rushed over.

"Sorry to interrupt, but I need to steal you away, Scarlett," she said.

Johnny nodded, then fixed his silk collar. I glanced down at Hugo, who had obediently sat down when we stopped moving, and was now giving me an expectant look. I knew I couldn't bring him anywhere near the food that was being prepared.

"Would it be all right with you?" I asked Johnny, pressing the leash into his hand.

The next thing I knew, I'd been pulled into the chaotic ante-chamber just off the main kitchen. Aromatic rosemary wafted through the air, from the potato and shallot timbales, which were among the delicious items on the night's menu, also including roasted balsamic beet salad with walnuts and garlic. As well as delectable desserts—strawberries with coconut cream and vegan chocolate ganache tarts. The caterers were putting the finishing touches on the breadbaskets, featuring pats of vegan butter shaped like little Scottie dogs.

After Anita and I worked out a major guest list crisis, I turned to head back into the main room. Anita hurriedly began to flip through the pages on her clipboard. "Sorry, Scarlett, to bother you with this so last minute," she said. "But I believe there's a balance due for the night. When we met last time, you just paid the deposit."

"Oh right, of course!" I said, retrieving my credit card from my bag. "Here, let me settle up with you."

As she flipped through more pages, I ran through the night's costs, which I was well aware of from volunteering my time, free of charge, as the executive director of the foundation. What I had learned was that, after the development director and event coordinator had been paid, plus the cost of the venue, band, food, lighting, décor, staff, and invitations, charities often had to spend $1.35 to raise $1. When Anita finally stopped, she looked up at me, a puzzled expression on her face.

"Actually, there's no need," she said. "The balance has been paid in full."

"But…but…are you sure?"

"Says here, final and full payment made on 7/5/95 by a Mr. Johnny Suffield?" she said. "Ring a bell, mademoiselle? He must have, literally, spoken to my assistant. After you paid the fifty percent deposit, he took care of the balance of $28,500."

I surprised myself by bursting into tears.

"Oh my God, I'm so sorry," Anita said. "I didn't mean to upset you."

"Not at all," I said. "I couldn't be happier. It's just been a long month."

After pulling out my compact and erasing any evidence of my crying jag, I returned to the ballroom. When I reached my table, there was only one vacant seat, on one side of which sat Hugo, God bless him, displaying his most impeccable manners, while Johnny did his best to behave as well on the other side.

Johnny stood and pulled out my chair for me.

"Thank you, Johnny," I said, making direct eye contact. "…for everything."

"You're welcome, Rosie," he said, the biggest smile sneaking onto his face. "It's the least I could do. Hopefully, I'm out of the dog house now."

"You are," I said. "And then some."

The butterflies in my chest threatened to lift me into the air and carry me away. But after we'd been through some real deal breakers, how could I not worry that as soon as I began to trust him he'd leave me lonely and distraught, *again*? As if on cue, my four-legged friend, Hugo, jumped down from his spot, and leapt up onto Johnny's lap, triggering Johnny to erupt with laughter. Maybe it was going to be all right after all. Hugo was the best judge of character I had ever met.

# FOLLOW ME TO HELL

*"I personally believe this: We have only today; yesterday's gone and tomorrow is uncertain. That's why they call it the present. And sobriety really is a gift...for those who are willing to receive it."*
—Ace Frehley

FUCK!" JOHNNY YELLED, HIS hand rising to the back of his head. Attempting to maintain his composure, Johnny refused to turn around and acknowledge his drummer. He instead redoubled his attention on adjusting his '77 Fender Strat to a drop-D tuning.

*Muuuust beee the pills--man...those... things...are...STRONG. Maybe...shoooouuuuld haaaaave...waited...until...after...our...session... OR...ooooonly haaaad twooooo...instead of—ten, was it?*

Just when Johnny had *almost* managed to pull it together, another drumstick flew up and clocked him in the same spot as the first. Hawke howled with laughter as Johnny whipped around slowly and stormed, even slower still, back to Bone.

"Whaaaat...the...'eeelllll, buuddyyy?" Johnny said. Soft and languid as toffee, the words expelled from his mouth did not successfully express the high decibel of rage, exploding deep inside him, somewhere beneath the soft cocoon of drugs.

"It's beyond brilliant, actually," Hawke said. "We should consider working it into the live show. You should see how Bone uses physics to chuck his stick on his bass drum in just such a way, yah, that it bounces off, and hits you right in the back of the head. Every. Fucking. Time. I wish we had it on video. It's truly goddamn priceless."

Johnny studied Hawke with suspicion.

*Did it seem like he was talking, mmm Chinese, errr, especially fast today?*

He definitely appeared to be on something quite obviously the opposite of Quaaludes, he decided. And then Delightful Deirdre stormed into the midst of the session, which was unfolding in the third recording studio they'd tried in a week. It was time to "pay the piper," as in they were expected to deliver the sophomore album they were contractually obligated to provide to their record label. And it was easier to blame the overproduction, the console, the PA, the engineer, or the Feng Shui of the vocal booth than it was to admit they were totally fucked.

"That's it!" Deirdre screeched. "This isn't Monty Fucking Python. And every minute you stand here, jacking off, is a dollar more we're in debt to the label."

"Not...literally...though...right?" Johnny asked, managing to emerge from his fog long enough to be worried by the financial implications of this possibility.

"Here's a question for you," Deirdre responded. "Do you have any songs written? Or even a single verse? Or a bridge? How 'bout a couple of chords? Even that, I'd be happy with. And, if *not*, why are we wasting our time and resources in the studio?"

Johnny hung his head. Hawke began to crack up at his discomfort. Normally about now, Jet would have been the one to chime in with a positive idea or affirmation, but his eyes were glassy and vacant, as if he weren't really following the conversation.

"Johnny's got some tip top ideas," Shiv said. "We'll pull it together, you know. We always do...in the end."

"You'd better," Deirdre said. "I've been summoned to the label today by the powers that be, and that's what I'm going to tell them. By the time I get back from our meeting, you should manage to have something to play for me, and by that I mean something worthy of your band's name. Or else."

"Aye, we will," Shiv said, nodding his head, as if trying to convince himself.

With traffic, Deirdre's lunch with the label execs would take a good three hours, round trip. When the band was young and hungry, they would have laughed at the idea of spending three hours writing just one song. Back then, inspiration poured out of them. They whipped out a few tasty tracks in an hour, and then went to have a drink at the bar. Now, instead, they drank for three hours, each disappearing into the bathroom at regular intervals to indulge in their pick-me-up of choice, as if they were hiding anything from anyone anymore.

When Deirdre returned later that afternoon, Bone had nodded off on the couch, Shiv was talking to Sephy on his Motorola StarTAC flip phone, and Jet was lying on the floor—having admitted defeat after only three sit ups. Johnny and Hawke were unified, for once, over a pile of coke on the coffee table. Johnny had finally turned to uppers out of terror that his marshmallow mind was not giving him anything like the stimulus he needed to write a hit.

Deirdre was improbably quiet. Rifling around for a clean glass, she grabbed the communal handle and poured herself a healthy spot of Jack. She had the band's complete attention now.

"Well, that's that," she said.

"What's what?" Johnny asked. "That was a quick lunch. We were just about to really dig into some grand ideas I've had, for a kind of a rock opera with a cool horror-punk-meets-gothic-post-punk, vampire feel. I'm thinking strings and timpani, lots of Sturm und Drang, maximum drama."

"You just got dropped," Deirdre said.

Except for the menacing grind of Hawke's teeth, which was involuntary, all other motion and activity had ceased.

"Fuck no! That's impossible, we have a one million dollar, two-record deal," Johnny said. "Now, all we have to do is make a kick-ass second album, and we'll be fine. We're fine. I mean, how could we even be so FINE!"

"Well, you won't be making that second album for MCA," Deirdre said. "Because they're done with you. So I suggest we vacate the premises immediately, before you waste any more of their money and they decide, rightly, to bill you."

"But what about the massive retainer we got for our upcoming South American stadium tour?" Johnny asked. "What about our lucrative deals with Harley and Fender and Coors? What the fuck is happening?"

"Sure, maybe we can leverage those opportunities to get you another record deal, perhaps even with one of the *au curreant*, tastemaker labels—Interscope, Capitol, Maverick, or Sub Pop." Deirdre said. "But you have to at least get through one solid fucking practice, in order to instill confidence in me, or anyone else. Can you do that?"

It was an obvious question with an uncertain answer.

The next afternoon, when Johnny showed up for the rehearsal Deirdre had insisted upon, he was surprised to discover he was the first one there. Usually, Jet was already running scales, or checking his gear for any tune-ups that needed to be done. The practice space echoed uncomfortably, without the others there, laughing and fooling around, and ultimately, making some of the most righteous music Johnny had ever heard. Or that's how it *used* to be. Instead of setting up his gear, Johnny slumped on his Marshall half stack, whipping out his sterling flask.

When Jet slid into the room, Johnny was so startled he jumped. Jet was carrying his beautifully beat up bass case. He began setting up, but very slowly.

"What's up?" Johnny said. "You always get here before me."

"Oh, shit, sorry, I totally overslept," Jet said. "I didn't even get in my workout this morning."

"Huh," Johnny said.

An hour later, Shiv and Hawke had trickled in, but Bone was still a no-show. They'd tried calling his home and cell phone, at least a dozen times each, but his voice mail was full at both numbers. Theoretically, they had new songs to write and begin debuting at their first Brazilian and Columbian shows, which they were beyond excited to play, and eventually to woo a new label to take a chance on them. So there was plenty they could have done, even without their drummer. But no one made a move to start.

Finally, Hawke stood. "Check you later," he said. "I've got places to be."

"But we haven't rehearsed even a single song," Johnny said. "And we have no idea where Bone is."

"Since you're the one making the big bucks, why don't you figure it out?" Hawke said.

"Yeah, it's always *my* fucking band when it's not going well, and it's *your* fucking band when the accolades are rolling in."

"When was the last time we had any fucking *accolades* to roll in?" Hawke yelled. "You drove this band into the ground, and I'm the only one who dares to say anything about it. I've had more than enough of your stupid bullshit."

"Aw, boo hoo, you had to travel the world playing the hit songs I wrote for us, sucking down free drinks and getting laid because you were in one of the most mega rock bands in the world," Johnny shouted back. "Honestly, I can't imagine what the fucking problem is. Oh, that's right, you're *jealous* because Scarlett and I have the potential to be honestly happy together."

Hawke scoffed at the idea and refused to give Johnny the satisfaction of an answer. But it was clear Johnny had touched a nerve, because Hawke began to pace as much as was feasibly possible in the cluttered, narrow room. He puffed dangerously on a Marlboro Red, and then, lit another off the first. Johnny couldn't stop, even though the fight had tentatively wound down to a tense impasse.

"You know what Scarlett told me…" Johnny taunted.

"Mate, I wouldn't go there," Shiv cautioned.

Hawke whipped around and stormed over to where Johnny was sitting. "She can say whatever she wants, but I'll be the one she's thinking about in her heart and bed."

BAM!

Johnny stood in one swift motion and punched Hawke square in the face. Hawke staggered back, momentarily stunned, and then stormed toward Johnny, now throwing haymakers. Just like that, the brawl that had been brewing for years, for so many reasons, exploded in a barrage of jabbing fists and flying elbows. Jet grabbed one of Hawke's arms by the wrist, and Johnny's as well, immobilizing both of them.

"Fuck this, I quit," Hawke spit out, wrestling free to grab his Fender Strat, and head for the door, too negligent, of course, to slide his six string into its case.

"You can't quit, because we replaced you back in Denver," Johnny yelled after him. "You're only here because I felt sorry for you—we all felt sorry for you!"

Hawke gave him the finger behind his back and kept walking without so much as turning around. The door slammed behind him.

"We don't fucking need him," Johnny said. "The Westies were a fucking kick ass band long before he came along, and that, we shall—remain, for infinity—without him."

"Mate, I think it's time to call it," Shiv said, his voice gentle. "We're down a guitarist. Our drummer is MIA. Sephy has been wanting me to spend at least a little time off the road."

Johnny looked for encouragement to Jet, the band's most stalwart member.

"I'm exhausted," Jet said.

"Me too," Johnny said.

And with that The Westies had broken up.

*** 

FOR DAYS AFTER THE band's dissolution, Johnny found himself sitting on his couch, cell phone in his hand, mind vacant. So there were no invitations to Jet for an evening walk with Thunders. No regular pints with Shiv, over which they could have, maybe, even started a new musical project. The buttons on Johnny's phone were too heavy to push. Except for his daily call to his dealer, who stopped by every night with a new supply of coke and whatever else Mr. Candy Man was holding that night.

Johnny lay low, listening to Stevie Ray Vaughn and Hank Williams records until dawn, sleeping all day. At dusk, he emerged like the nocturnal animal he'd become, taking Thunders for walks in his neighborhood—not bothering to drive to the Laurel Canyon dog park. Now he was afraid of running into Scarlett. This time he was determined not to lose her. He didn't know what he was going to say, but on day three of his exile, he forced himself to dial her number.

"Hello?" she said, in that sweet voice that made his heart sing.

"Hey, Rosie."

"Johnny," she said. "Thanks again for everything you did for Paws 4 a Cause. Oh, and Hugo says 'Arigato,' by the way."

"You're welcome," Johnny said. "And 'Konnichiwa,' which of course, means 'Hello' in Japanese, which both Hugo and I speak."

"How are you?"

The silence was almost deafening. He wanted to say so much to her, but he was unsure of how. Surprisingly, though, even that silence wasn't awkward or uncomfortable, and she didn't press him. He could hear her quietly breathing on the other end of the line, wordlessly encouraging him to be in the moment with her. "Um, The Westies… we broke up," he said, deciding to try honesty for once.

"What?! Johnny. I'm so sorry," she said. "I know how much that band meant to you. Are you okay?"

"No?" he said, more of a question than a statement.

"Do you want me to come by, get you out of the house? We could maybe grab a bite to eat."

"Aw, you're so sweet, Rosie," he said. "But…no, thanks…I think I need to be alone for a few days. You know, lick my wounds in private."

"I understand," she said. "I'm really glad you called, though. Will you get in touch when you're feeling better?"

He said that he would, and even when he hung up, he felt more pleasant. He vowed to drink a little less and do a little less coke that night, in the interest of pulling it together, so he could indeed take Scarlett out. Maybe even later that week. But that wasn't as easy as it had sounded in his head. And, anyhow, when he next called her, a few days later, it wasn't to ask her on the reunion date they'd both been anticipating.

"Hey, Scarles," he said.

"What's wrong?" she asked, sensing the subterranean sadness in his voice.

"Hawke's in the hospital," he said. "I know he's not your favorite person right now, but I thought you'd want to know."

"Oh my god...what happened?" she said. "Is he going to be okay?"

"I don't know," Johnny said. "Maybe you should come."

"And just like that, the band of brothers are together again," she said. "How's that going?"

"Um, we're all still alive," he said.

She sighed, audibly showing her relief that everyone was okay, at least physically. "I'll come by this afternoon."

✳✳✳

WHEN SCARLETT WALKED INTO room 721 at the Advanced Health Sciences Pavilion at Cedars-Sinai a few hours later, she was a rare and precious burst of color. Cascading into the bland space in her summer halter dress, a sewn ensemble of strawberry-red organic cotton with dainty white polka dots, she stood tall in her Doc Martens. Her OOTD was completed with two bunches of bright, lemon-hued sunflowers in her hands.

Everything else was a dour wash of institutional beige and generic gray, and the two patients in side-by-side beds had a matching, washed-out pallor. Johnny stood and nervously slid his hands in and out of his pockets, wanting desperately to smoke. She marched right over to him and gave him a warm kiss on the mouth.

"Fug me," Hawke said, his speech slurred.

Still holding Johnny's hand without an ounce of hesitation or shyness, she turned and was astounded to find Jet's face, not Hawke's, looking back at her. Not only had Hawke been forced to endure some R&R at the Health Sciences Pavilion, but so had Jet, and they were frigging flat mates at the hospital!

"I'm well aware that our wedding ended on a disastrous note," she said, turning now to Hawke. "I just want you to know, I forgive you. And...

my lawyer told me that, because of the United Nations Convention on the Law of the Sea and the fact that we were more than twelve nautical miles from any coastline, we were in international waters. So our vows were not legally binding. I'm very sorry about your Bell's palsy diagnosis. And I'm here if there's anything you need. As a friend."

"Ugh," Hawke said, overwhelmed by such a direct and mature statement.

Scarlett then turned to Jet, in the other bed, and gave him a kiss on the cheek. "Fancy seeing you here," she quipped. "You do not look so good, my friend. What are ya in for?"

"The gift that keeps on giving, Hep C," he joked back.

"That's pretty dreadful," she said. "I'm sorry."

"Well, at least now, I know why I was so tired."

"Yeah…you guys were living hard," she said. "But I've called Bone, and he's on his way. I know he's just the person to help."

"Are you crazy?" Johnny shouted. "No offense…but…"

Scarlett laughed nervously, shaking off his apology.

"…it's just that…" Johnny continued. "I don't think the hospital will smile upon him bringing, you know, an eight ball into their recovery room. And neither will I."

"You don't have to worry about that anymore," Scarlett said.

She began moving about the room, humming Sinatra songs to herself, as she wrangled the flowers into the pitchers of water next to the beds. She also opened the curtains, turned off the TV, and lit a lavender chamomile scented candle she'd brought along in her cute, Rasta striped crocheted satchel. The room was actually looking somewhat cheerful by the time Bone gently knocked on the door and pushed his way in, followed by Imani.

"What the hell happened to you?" Johnny exclaimed upon seeing him.

The transformation was disconcerting. Bone was hardly recognizable. The guy had gained at least ten pounds of healthy muscle, his skin was tan and smooth, and the seemingly-always-present dark circles under his eyes had vanished. It would be an overstatement to say he was completely relaxed or at ease—his hands still had a faint tremor of the DTs, and he had an unlit smoke tucked behind each ear, primed for the first moment when he could light up. But it was if he had been a ghost before, and now, he had been transmuted back into a flesh and blood man.

"True love," he said, graciously, pointing at Imani.

As she stepped out from behind him, she was visibly showing, and what looked to be nearly a few months along, at least. Bone turned and beamed at Imani, and they reached for each other's hands at the same moment, entwining their fingers with ease.

"We're pregnant," he said.

✳✳✳

Rewind to a week before The Westies and I were reunited at Cedars-Sinai. It was the morning after my triumphant *Paws 4 a Cause* charity event, and I should have been euphoric. But I've often found, after a huge, mega event that I've anticipated for months, I hit a bit of a slump. It's as if there's nothing left about which to get excited. Life somehow feels drab for a few days, until I embark on my next voyage, or dream up a fresh design. This morning after hit me especially hard. So much so that, when my doorbell started ringing around 11:00 a.m., I felt as if I was drowning in inertia, sucked under by my bedclothes. A few minutes later, I was startled to see my bedroom door swing open, with a familiar face peeping around the edge.

"I think the doorbell's broken," Imani said.

"Oh no, it works," I said. "I think I'm broken. I couldn't bring myself to get out of bed. Why'd you ring, anyhow? Don't you still have your key?"

"Yes and no," she said. "Okay for me to come in?"

"You're always welcome."

"Before I do," she said. "I just have to say, 'Don't freak out.'"

"Well...*now*, I'm already alarmed, so um...okay..." I said. "I promise... I'll try."

As she came around the door and into my bedroom, she blurted out: "I'm pregnant!"

"Oh!" I said, too shocked to say anything else.

Watching her cross the floor, as I sat up against my pillows, I couldn't quite adjust to how bizarre this all was. There in front of me, the best friend I'd always thought of as my little sister, was transformed into a regal, confidant woman.

"May I?" she said, nodding toward the foot of my bed.

"Please." I slid over to make enough room for her.

She cracked her knuckles nervously. "I don't know where to start."

"Are you all right, babe?" I asked. "I've been constantly worried about you...and, well, how you've been doing, but you stopped answering my calls and didn't reply to my handwritten card of apology. So I figured that was your way of telling me to...fuck off...or at least, to stop calling."

"Sorry," Imani said. "It all got pretty dark there for a while."

"Yeah," I said, thinking back to my own rock-bottom moment on tour.

With that, Imani looked me squarely in the eyes, and continued in a soft-spoken but steady voice. "I'm here to make amends," she said. "I'm sorry I let my own self-destructive, self-absorbed behavior get in the way of us and our friendship. And I'm sorry—I blamed *you* for things that weren't your fault. I kind of blamed you for everything, actually, and I realize now you were just trying to help. I was the one who got caught up in the whole Hollywood game, having a boyfriend in the hot new band, like you, trying to use your fashion and entertainment connections to launch my own career...which only brought out all my insecurities and demons. You know what I really miss? Those good ol' days, back in San Diego, when we'd ride around in Goldie all day, talking and talking, and hitting up every thrift store so you could find your hidden gem designer duds and I could pick up spare parts for my classic motorcycle. Everything was easier back then," she said. "All was right in the world."

My eyes fell on the tattoo marching up her forearm, a Ghandi quote: "Where there is love there is life." I remembered the exact day she'd gotten it: her eighteenth birthday. I'd held her hand because I knew she was too strong to share how pained she was. I could so clearly remember how she didn't allow the smallest flinch to cross her face.

"Of course, of course I forgive you," I said, leaning in to hug her. "I'm really just glad you're okay. You are okay, right?"

"For today, I am," she said.

"I'm so glad," I said. "You really fucking scared me."

My mood immediately lifting, I jumped out of bed to make us a healthy breakfast of her favorite vegan cuisine: chopped fresh pineapple, mini corn tortillas with sautéed peppers, mushrooms, and avocado. As I cooked, Imani regaled me with the story of all that had happened to her between when I'd left The Westies' tour in Chicago and when she'd materialized this morning.

Just after my meltdown, she began feeling weird. After a few days of denial, she realized she was pregnant. She'd always been driven by her passions for cycles, muscle cars, and most of all, music. So she'd never given motherhood much thought before this moment. Rather, she'd focused her future dreams on traveling the world as a musician and political activist. But, suddenly, she wanted, first and foremost, to be a positive role model for her baby.

Imani had immediately enlisted Clint as her ally. He'd helped her to remove herself from the daily activities of tour, under the guise of her own music career, which was also gaining some serious traction on the college radio, R&B, and reggae charts. When they thought she'd been absent because of recording sessions, she'd actually been sneaking off to doctor's appointments.

Finally, it became too difficult to maintain the ruse, and she called her dad, and he immediately arranged for her to fly home to California and attend in-patient rehab at nearby Rancho Mirage. It was such a relief to admit she needed help. At the Betty Ford Center, she received treatment to get sober. Nauseated every morning on tour, she hadn't touched alcohol or drugs in weeks and so her actual withdrawal symptoms were relatively mild. But underneath her drinking and drugging, she felt terrified—of missing her shot as a musician, of being seen as foolish, and most of all, of being a bad mom. She wanted to be clean—and to stay clean. And slowly, with the support of her counselors and fellow patients, she grew better and stronger day by day.

It hadn't helped that when she first told Bone, he disappeared with nary a word to her for two weeks. He finally did call, with an intense desire to reconcile, but there was just one major obstacle: he was in jail. In Thailand. For trying to leave the country with opium in his luggage. Imani had to enlist Clint to pull some major strings to get Bone home, with the caveat that he had to go straight to rehab. Bone still had two weeks until he'd finished his stint at the same in-patient facility she'd attended. And that's what had brought Imani back to Los Angeles that morning.

"I know it's a big ask," she said, looking down at her steaming mug of green tea. "But I was hoping I could stay here with you until Bone is done with rehab, and we figure out where we're going to live, now that we're off the road…and, well, everything."

"I'd love that!" I said. "Nothing could make me happier. But…" I tried to think of the best way to say what was on my mind, without causing any more distance to develop between Imani and me. "I wanted to ask you—I don't know how to say it exactly," I said. "It's just that you were so angry at me, and I'm starting to realize that doesn't just evaporate…"

Imani reached out and took my hand. "I'm really sorry for how I made you feel—I shouldn't have talked to you that way," she said. "I guess I was jealous? Yeah. Not of your modeling—that's so not me. It just seemed it was all happening for you. And sometimes I guess I just felt like you, and everyone, forgot about me—especially when we first moved to LA, and Persephone was always sweeping you off to major events and gallery openings. That…hurt."

"And…I guess…I kind of got that, and I wanted to at least try to make it okay between us," I said. "But…by that point…you were always pissed and yelling at me."

"I didn't…yell…did I?" Imani said.

"Maybe not yelled…but you definitely…shouted."

We erupted in laughter at the same moment, picturing a riotous and self-righteous Imani, which we both knew was entirely plausible, as it was, well, kind of her trademark.

"Yeah, um, I wasn't very good at *talking* about things back then," she said. "So, yeah, I guess that's how I earned my nickname 'The Enforcer'—ha! That's a lot of what I've been working on, just being more honest and open. And realizing that some days feel bad. But it doesn't last forever."

"I can definitely relate."

In the days that followed our reunion, Imani and I settled into a comfortable routine around the house. We breakfasted together in the morning and then eased into our individual creative pursuits—I had new illustrations, croquis, and designs to generate after all I'd lost in the apocalyptic fire at the infamous Dog House. Imani was penning songs for her debut album, aptly entitled, "Enforcer," which Clint was aiming to have released before she became a mom.

I was always happy to take a break from my work in order to accompany Imani to a doctor's appointment or the local farmers' market. We stocked up on fresh organic strawberries, heirloom tomatoes, and bouquets of African violets, black-eyed Susans, and forget-me-nots. Now that I had my best friend back, I fully realized how lonely I'd been. As much as I wanted Johnny to take the time he needed to rebuild his own life after the breakup of his band, I longed for him. I even craved our little road family, with its commotion and noise.

Well, maybe not Deirdre, or the pungent pranks, or the aggressive, gold digger groupies, but all the rest of it.

I felt Johnny's absence even more after the band's reunion at Cedars-Sinai, when Bone and Imani convinced the lads to go away to the same thirty-day in-treatment program from which they'd both benefited. Thankfully, I had the best possible distraction, as I'd found the perfect space in Topanga Canyon (just forty minutes beyond LA's bustling city center) to fulfill a dream that had begun taking shape since I'd returned to the City of Angels.

\*\*\*

IN THEIR CHARMING, THREE-BEDROOM Hollywood Hills bungalow, Scarlett and Imani had easily repaired their friendship. If anything, they were closer than ever. Meanwhile, in Rancho Mirage, at the rehab center where the members of The Westies were clawing their way toward a new, improved way of life, the healing was a little more touch and go.

Bone found himself in the unlikely, but welcome (at least for him), role of band wise man. As he was near the end of his own thirty-day in-patient stay, when his band mates showed up to get and stay clean, he was eager to help. But since he was newly sober himself, his ability to apply the tools he was learning was still a work in progress, to say the least. Just take their first group therapy session all together.

The rest of the band was decidedly resistant to whatever this process was going to be, and they all slouched uneasily in their chairs, waiting for their counselor to enter and start the proceedings. Johnny smoked like it was a full-time job. Hawke glowered behind his tinted glasses. Shiv whistled a spry little tune. And Jet jangled his legs, as if he were about to jump up and sprint around the room.

The door flew open, and in came—Devon?! Only he was adorned with one of the facility's name tags, and instead of his normal uniform of black Dickie's pants and a faded Misfits T-shirt that looked as if he'd just picked it up off the floor, he was dressed in—a turtleneck?

"Devon, dude, is that you?" Johnny asked. "Or am I having full-on DT hallucinations, which means I'm in worse shape than I thought?"

"Hey, cuz!" Devon said, giving Johnny a long, earnest hug. "It is, indeed, me."

Devon took the only empty seat in the circle and removed a folder from his serious, dad-like, brown leather briefcase. After shuffling through some papers, he looked up expectantly.

"Okay, who would like to share first?"

"Um, *you*?" Johnny asked. "How the fuck did you end up being an addiction counselor at a rehab facility in Malibu, California?"

Devon laughed and folded his hands, on top of the pages in his lap.

"Fair enough. I have had quite the adventure since we last parted ways. Well, let's just say that getting kicked out of the band was probably the single best thing that ever happened to me. Um, I mean, I did end up living in a ditch. Like a literal hole in the ground on the side of the road. But that was only for a few months. And when my folks' church scraped together the money to send me to rehab out here in Cali, I loved it so much, I just kind of stayed. I really feel like I've found my calling. But that's enough about me."

The silence in the room lengthened until it became uncomfortable. Devon looked at each member of the band in turn, smiling in a warm, open way.

"Maybe one of our newbies would like to contribute something?" Bone said, also looking from Johnny to Jet to Shiv to Hawke.

"Jesus—don't look at me," Hawke said. "The only thing I ever enjoyed sharing with these losers is drugs. And, sadly, those days are behind us."

"Okay, Hawke, I appreciate your willingness to speak first," Devon said. "But let's try to avoid any name-calling. No one is any better or worse than anyone else here. We're all just doing the best we can, one day at a time. Why don't you tell us how it *feels* not to be sharing drugs with your friends anymore?"

Hawke performed a dramatic pantomime of looking around, as if searching for a lost item, even bending down, as if examining the space beneath his chair. "My friends?" Hawke said.

"I consider *you* my friend," Bone said. "That's why I want you to get healthy."

"Ugh, what a load of crap," Hawke spat.

"I can sense you having *a lot* of feelings, Hawke," Devon said.

"Yeah, I feel fucking angry!" Hawke said.

"Wonderful," Devon said. "And why is that?"

"Because three months ago, I was in a fucking rock band, touring the world, banging beautiful babes, taking loads of drugs, and having the hard-earned time of my life. Now, I'm sitting in a shitty folding chair," he stood up, driven by discomfort, to slam out the unevenness of his crooked seat, "...drinking disgusting coffee, and they tell me if I start using again I'm going to die. How the fuck would you feel?"

"I really admire your courage," Devon said. "All of you could learn something from Hawke's willingness to speak so openly."

"Oh, Jesus, the last thing we need is for Hawke to talk more *openly*," Johnny said, his hands trembling so badly he had to set his coffee cup down. "All he ever does is tell us about his feelings—as in how much he hates everything we do."

"I sense that you're having some feeling about Hawke's feelings," Devon said.

"Yeah, because he fucking blames me for everything," Johnny said. "If he liked being a rock legend so much, why didn't he help me write anymore songs? Whenever it came time to do any of the work, he was always too loaded."

"Okay, good, and how did that make you *feel*?"

"Fuck no, you're not going to trick me into admitting I have feelings about this joker," Johnny said.

"You've got feelings all right," Hawke teased him. "You're so goddamn envious of how radically and artistically awesome I am."

"Okay, I'm going to stop you right there," Devon said. "Remember, we're trying to learn "right size" thinking here—once again, guys, a gentle reminder, you are not better or worse than anyone else. We are all equal."

"Fuck that," Hawke said. "Did it ever occur to you, there's a reason *Rolling Stone* magazine wrote a story on me being the rock world's biggest fucking influencer?!"

"Not here, you're not," Devon said. "Here…you're just Hawke."

"Why would I want to be just Hawke?" he said. "He's a fucking loser."

"Ah, now we're getting some movement…" Devon said.

Johnny made a noise of disgusted exasperation and rolled his eyes.

"Now, now, Johnny, just a second, let's please refrain from expressing yourself until it's back to your turn to share," Devon said.

∗∗∗

"As with most self-improvement plans, such as a diet or an exercise routine, the results aren't obvious in the day-to-day, but after a few weeks have passed, it can be remarkable to see how much progress has been made," their counselor was fond of saying.

And he was absolutely right. Here's what a group therapy session looked like by the final week of their in-patient stay.

"What I couldn't tell you before, Johnny, is..." Hawke said, pausing to look down at his feet and consider his words carefully. "The reason I ceased contributing in the studio, those last few months, was because you never took my ideas seriously. You had to control *everything*, and do *everything* exactly to *your* liking, and in *your* way. I mean, why even form a fucking group if it's always the Johnny Show, and never The Westies? So, when you were being such a colossal D-I-C-K-TATOR..."

The counselor raised an eyebrow in Hawke's direction.

"So when I felt like you were *minimizing my feelings*...it made me shut down," Hawke said, redirecting the way he chose to express himself in a more positive fashion.

Johnny sipped his coffee, his hands steady, now that he'd been completely sober for more than three weeks, and his DTs had subsided.

"I hear you, man," Johnny said. "I think I learned that kind of behavior from my pops. He used to do the same bullshit to me, so I know exactly how bad that feels. And, shit, I'm sorry. Going forward, I will make a concerted effort to always welcome your contribution."

"Excellent work, Johnny," Devon said. "Nice way to acknowledge your behavior, identify how you learned it by observing your father, and then apologize and propose a different way of being in the future."

"Well, I never," Shiv said. "If those two can get along, anything is possible."

"I'd say," Jet added.

"And how do both of you *feel*, now that the main source of antagonism within the group has been somewhat smoothed out?" the counselor asked.

"It's sort of like Mom and Dad have stopped fighting, and I'm glad to hear I'm not the only one who was feeling like I wasn't included or heard," Jet said. "I mean, literally fucking look up the definition of the word 'band' in the dictionary, and it's 'something that confines or constricts while allowing a degree of movement.' But I'm also uncertain, because I don't know what to expect now. As in, what will my emotional role be if it's not as the band's peace keeper?"

"Excellent question," Devon said. "A significant part of any major life change is facing your anxiety about how your new reality will be. And who *you* will be, without your substance, and the deflection it created for you to hide behind."

"It makes me *feel* like it's such a shame we don't have a bloody band anymore," Shiv said.

Between inhaling deep, square yoga breaths, Johnny murmured: "Yeah…me too…me too…." Johnny let his voice trail off, unwilling to say anymore just yet.

It's true that Johnny and Hawke had made remarkable progress in the time they were in rehab together, but Johnny wasn't about to admit to his guitarist the full breadth of how he was feeling. Johnny had started shotgunning stolen beers after school at age thirteen to insulate himself from whatever angry tirade he'd face from his dad when he got home. Without alcohol or drugs, Johnny found that everything he'd suppressed back then was rising to the forefront in unpredictable ways. Sometimes, he started crying for no reason—when he was brushing his teeth, lacing his boots. On other occasions, he was filled with an overpowering rage and he wanted to smash out all of the windows in the place. But, slowly, he found that, when he just breathed through it, no matter how overwhelmed he felt in the moment, the bad feelings passed away—eventually.

The shame was harder to work through. It was more pernicious. He was ashamed that he'd fucked up his dream—his major label record deal and his debut album. He was ashamed that he'd cheated on Scarlett. He now realized he'd only done so because he was insecure. He'd been terrified Scarlett would break up with him once she realized what a bad guy he was and so he'd self-sabotaged the relationship.

Johnny was unabashedly determined he wasn't going to fuck it up with Scarlett this time. Their counselor had reminded them on multiple occasions that they were essentially baby snakes with no real defenses against the world. And they needed to have the utmost compassion for themselves, in all of their relationships, and to ask that others in their lives do the same. After all, less than twenty percent of those who become sober, thanks to treatment for alcoholism, remain so for an entire year. And certain statistics went on to say, if they could make it two years without having a drink, their odds of staying alcohol-free rose to a lifesaving rate of sixty percent. And after five years of sobriety, they were very, very likely to stay sober, although, as with any recovering addict, or for that matter, anyone else trying to correct a bad habit in life, they always had to be aware of the risk of relapse. Johnny had attempted to communicate at least a little bit of this harsh reality to Scarlett during her lengthy Saturday visits to him in rehab, but he still felt insanely nervous as he faced the prospect of seeing her face-to-face for the first time on the outside.

***

I STOOD IN THE parking lot, an arm around Imani on one side of me and Sephy on the other, surveying what I'd accomplished. Located in Topanga Canyon was an old Victorian-style two-story house with gingerbread trim, which I'd repurposed into my very own boutique and art gallery: The Velvet Rose Menagerie. After I covered the cost of power and water, insurance, and other operating costs, all proceeds would benefit my Paws 4 a Cause Foundation, as well as the endangered northern spotted owl, which I'd been passionate about saving since I'd seen a *National Geographic* special on their plight. In my interviews with the press, I also highlighted the Carlsbad Highlands Conservation Bank, supporting species including the valley elderberry longhorn beetle! Recently approved, it was the *first* official agreement of its kind for a listed endangered species. It was near and dear to my own heart, because it was being implemented in association with the San Diego Multiple Species Conservation Plan, and so it inspired me with a feeling of immense hometown pride.

In true Topanga fashion, the building that housed my boutique/gallery was nestled in a copse of shady trees. On the two-and-a-half acres of land that stretched behind it, there were spacious enclosed areas from the last owner's goats. I hoped to expand my project to include a rescue and rehab for injured wild animals that needed to recuperate before being released back into the wild.

"Bob's your uncle!" Sephy called out.

Imani and I exploded with laughter.

"What's that translate to again?" I asked, knowing she was chiming in with her Cockney slang, but unclear what she meant. "I never know what you Brits are saying."

"Aye, it's a different language," Sephy acknowledged. "It just means 'There ya go,' basically. But what I truly intended to say is, 'I'm so fucking proud of you.'"

"Me too," Imani said. "You're on fire."

"Too soon," I joked.

"It's even more amazing that you pulled all this together not long after *the fire*," Imani continued. "I mean opening a boutique and gallery is no joke, and all for an upstanding cause."

Sephy interrupted this tender moment in her typical gonzo fashion, by racing up to the side of the building, even in her four-inch Manolo Blahnik campari patent leather Mary Jane stilettos. She posed for affect, and then smashed a magnum of Cristal Rose against the side of the building.

"I officially launch the Velvet Rose Menagerie!" she cackled, a cigarette dangling from her matte red lipped mouth, as bubbly poured out in a vibrant arc.

In the midst of this chaos, Hugo bolted down the front steps and out into the parking lot. I turned around, worried he might dash into the road, only to find him excitedly leaping up to greet Johnny, who was laughing and patting his rump.

"Ahhh, I can see Hugo's got a new best friend," I said, as I approached.

"Hi!" Johnny called out. "You look gorgeous."

"Thanks," I said, smoothing down my long black denim skirt, which I'd painted with delicately feathered northern spotted owls, celestial Byzantine blue five pointed stars, and moons. "And thanks for coming out today."

"I wouldn't have missed it," Johnny said. "Man, I'm really nervous."

"Don't be," I said. "You're here. I'm here…we're here…That's all that matters. Tonight is the friends and family launch. No press. No public. No pressure. We can just relax and enjoy ourselves for once."

"You know what?" he said. "I like the sound of that. It's about time."

"Yes," I said. "Indeed it is."

# SMASH EVERYTHING + START AGAIN

THE REVERB ECHOED THROUGH the recording studio like static on a
TV as Hawke bent the chords to achieve maximum fuzz. His eyes
were closed, as if he were retrieving the music from a well of inspiration
deep within himself. When his lids lifted, he saw that Jet, Shiv, and
Johnny had all turned to face him, circling up. It was a BIG moment:
the final track of their single most important endeavor: *their sophomore
album*, which unbelievably, the band had quickly regrouped to record
after completing rehab. Johnny, one arm draped over his mic stand, was
grinning at Hawke, encouragingly. Hawke nodded and smiled back at
him. Nobody moved until the note had faded out into complete silence.

"Nice work," Hamish, their engineer said through the PA. "And…
that's a wrap."

A collective rejoicing erupted from the guys in the band. Bone
came out from the darkly shadowed, insulated room in which he'd
recorded his drum part, so he could high five the others. Hawke and
Johnny even hugged, then patted each other on the back mightily to
show they hadn't gone too soft. (Things did change, but slowly). Of
course, they still had to mix and master the album. And there would
be a few vocals and guitar parts yet to record and patch into places that
had not materialized quite as strongly as they'd envisioned them. But
after the suicide bomb that had been their first trip to the studio for
their debut, it definitely felt worthy of celebrating the fact that:

A. They were still a band.

B. No one had relapsed since they'd left rehab.

C. They were still a band.

D. No blows had been thrown in the making of the album.

E. The music sounded better and was more fun than ever.

✳✳✳

LATER THAT NIGHT, SHIV and Sephy hosted a triumphant wrap party for The Westies at their Malibu ranch, and it was just as decadent and over the top as anything they'd orchestrated during the height of the band's debauch. Private chefs prepared paella over open brick fires in the back yard while a bartender squeezed fresh pomegranates and lemons with honey into lush mocktails topped with sparkling water and adorned with a sprig of fresh thyme. The pool glowed like a private lagoon, with flickering tea lights and larger candles floating on the bright blue water.

After all had satiated themselves fully, and listened to a special, top secret, rough mix of one of the new tracks, Johnny then rallied everyone together.

"Excuse me, I'd like to say a few words," he called out.

"Yeah, if we can get away with only a few words from this one, we'll be lucky," Hawke quipped, just like old times.

"Ah, the yin to my yang: Mr. Hawke Bowens," Johnny said, indicating Hawke with his open palm. "I'd like to start by thanking him, as well as my badass band: Shiv, Jet, and Bone," Johnny said, bowing slightly to each of them in turn.

"As one of my favorite artists, Henri Matisse, once said, 'Creativity takes courage.' He could not have been more right. I honestly don't know if I would have had the nerve to make music again after getting dropped by our first label without these men, my brothers, here by my side. When it works, it just works."

Knowing how to entice a crowd, Johnny paused to let the guests cheer mightily, as his band mates—even Hawke—smiled at being acknowledged.

"However…" Johnny paused dramatically before continuing. "When it doesn't work, that's another matter altogether. My band of brothers, my darling Scarlett, lift your glasses, because I'm about to announce one of the most positive developments for our band's continued rampage of success. Not only on a professional level, in terms of how we interact with the world. But on a creative level, related to how we express our unique vision and draw on it to connect with our fans. On a personal level, as far as who we are as people. On a soul level and what type of integrity we have in the world. Deirdre, you're fired."

Johnny faced off against Deirdre, who had disregarded his directive to join him in a toast, and stood with her arms crossed sourly over her chest.

"Ha. Ha." she said. "You are so hilarious, Johnny. Is this some kind of a joke? I hardly think it's funny."

"You're right, at least about that, it's not funny," Johnny said. "Nor was it funny when you stole from us, lied to us, blackmailed us, sabotaged our relationship with our record label for your own gain, and talked down to us and those we care about most."

The assembled crowd had grown silent, unsure how to react. The sound echoed as Deirdre clapped her hands in a mock dramatic fashion.

"Nice one," she said. "You finally grew a pair. Which is a good thing, because I already had a pair. And the two of us are going to face off—in court."

With that, Deirdre turned and stormed off, hopefully for the last time.

"Ding dong the witch is dead…" Sephy sung under her breath, putting her arm around Scarlett, who was literally crying with joy. "You look positively gobsmacked, darling," Sephy said to her.

"Johnny did it…he really did it," Scarlett said through her tears. "He finally stood up, not only for himself, and the family, the guys, but also for me. Don't you get it? He finally made me feel at home in his life."

It was like a come to Jesus moment for this whole crew, and with that, Johnny said: "You are my life. Nothing works without you by my side."

✳✳✳

IT WAS LIKE THE Taj Majal of rock 'n' roll: Shea Stadium, where The Beatles had launched their sonic assault on America in 1965. And, now, exactly thirty years later, The Westies were about to play on this hallowed ground.

Now it was time for sound check, and everything was falling into place. With Clint as their manager, and none of the members' moods affected by round-the-clock binge drinking and drugging, it was amazing how pleasant and high functioning backstage could be. Jet downed his pre-show ginseng liquid shots while Shiv chose between the two kinds of organic wheatgrass they now had on their rider.

The band assembled onstage for their four o'clock sound check. Everyone was tuned and primed to go, but the spotlight illuminated an empty mic.

"Jonathan Suffield please report to the principal's office," Hawke joked into his own mic. "You're late for detention."

But there was no snarky retort from Johnny into his own microphone or from the side of the stage, nor was the band's front man anywhere to be seen in the venue. Jokes flew back and forth, fast and furious, amid the other members. A half hour snailed by, with still no sign of Johnny, *and* no response to Clint's repeated calls to his cell phone. Finally, the band members terminated their sound check and retired to Shiv's dressing room, where they could fret and bitch collectively.

"I'm not going to let him fuck this up for the rest of us," Hawke said.

"This is no time for anger," Jet said. "Compassion is called for. Such a high profile show is just the kind of pressure cooker situation to make someone go MIA."

"Johnny wouldn't do that to us," Shiv said.

"Not intentionally," Jet said. "But addiction is a relentless foe. I mean, when was the last time this week that any of us checked in with Johnny? He could have been floundering for the past few days and we wouldn't even know.

"He rented that bohemian lair in Woodstock, so he could be away from any and all temptation, and especially before these shows," Hawke said. "I assumed he wanted to be left alone."

"Yah, let's just hope we didn't leave him unaccompanied with his demons," Jet said.

"Whose demons?" Scarlett asked, as she and Sephy floated into the dressing room on a cloud of their complimentary perfumes.

The Westies exchanged nervous glances, none of them wanting to be the one to break the news to Scarlett.

"What is it?" Scarlett asked. "And where's Johnny?"

"Don't panic, luv," Shiv said, "but we haven't seen hide nor hair of him today."

"But he obviously knows today is the show..." Scarlett said. "I came into the city a few days early for a *New York Times* Style section modeling gig and interview, and then went straight into doing press for my new collection. We agreed to meet here pre-show. Oh no, I feel awful. Maybe he's...I don't know...trapped somewhere?"

"Yeah, he's probably trapped under a heavy mountain of cocaine," Hawke said. "What? Don't look at me like that. I know it's what we're all thinking..."

Jet checked his watch. "It's still a good four hours until we go on," he said. "A lot can happen..."

"Yeah, none of it good," Hawke said.

✳✳✳

MEANWHILE, IN UPSTATE NEW York...

Johnny had woken up that morning at ten bells, precisely. He was quite pleased at having roused himself, extra early, on such a momentous day. It felt great to have all the time in the world. His leisurely breakfast consisted of organic peanut butter protein granola, bananas, and yogurt. As he sat on the front porch, the warm sunlight zigzagged through the trees onto his bare arms. He nursed an extra cup of "singer's" tea, made with hot water, honey, and lemon, to make sure his pipes were well cared for going into the night's big show.

As Johnny's turtle-driving cabbie dropped him off at the train station in Rhinebeck, the train arrived with a whoosh of steam and a clattering of brakes. He knew he shouldn't, but he dashed across the tracks and hopped on before it could pull out of the station without him. The gilded autumnal light and gentle rocking of the commuter car lulled him to sleep. Ninety minutes later he awoke as the train lurched into the station. He was surprised not to see the urban sprawl of Yonkers, which meant Penn Station was only a half-hour away. The signs were showing he was pulling into Schenectady. The wrong direction!

Johnny scrambled into the station, examining the wall clock to see when he might expect the next train to the city. He became aware that it was somehow two o'clock, *not* twelve o'clock.

*FUCK!*

He raced up to the ticket window, pulling bills out of his pockets.

"Sir, you've got to get me on the next train to the city, please," Johnny yelped. "Please, sir…"

"Hmmm," the grizzled train clerk said, scratching the sparse hair beneath his engineer's cap. "All righty then. Wait on track two, and it'll be along shortly."

Having paid for his ticket, Johnny pulled out his '95 Nokia Ringo cell phone, only to realize it was totally dead.

"I don't suppose there's any chance in hell you have a phone charger back there?" Johnny said, while sweating freight trains.

"Nope, and we don't have much in the way of cell phone reception, either. So it's a moot point, actually, ha," the clerk said.

Johnny rushed out to track two, determined to be at the ready when the train came rolling in. Johnny had time to smoke his entire cigarette down to the filter before the train actually came to a stop in front of him. Trying his best to remain optimistic, he climbed aboard. As if he'd stepped back in time, the interior was lined with old oak benches all covered in newspapers and the detritus of past riders. Johnny was practically jumping out of his skin by this point, and his anxiety—now at eleven—only increased when they finally got underway. A few, *slow* miles after they pulled out of the station, a middle-aged woman, with long French braids circling her head, literally rode up beside them on a bicycle. Demonstrating how she somehow managed to pedal her bike faster than the actual speed at which Johnny's train was advancing, she pulled alongside the front train car, and proceeded to hand over a picnic basket to the conductor. From what Johnny could tell, she was the man's wife, and she'd baked a homemade pie for him.

*Jesus, could this be anymore old-school?*

At first he thought he was hallucinating. The train really was travelling so slowly that it didn't seem to be moving at all. And although it was a handsome-enough-looking locomotive in lumberjack flannel red with an off-white stripe around its middle, it appeared to have been made in a much earlier era, such as the 1950s.

As if his day hadn't been a slow-motion heart attack already, when Johnny *finally* arrived at Penn Station, and ran outside for a cab, he was cursed again. The entire city was on lockdown. Police officers everywhere. President Clinton was in town for an appearance at the UN, and security was at an all-time high.

"What seems to be the problem?" a young motorcycle cop asked Johnny, reading the panic on his face.

Johnny's palms were already drowning in sweat before he remembered he didn't have anything on him that could get him thrown in jail. Thank God! And that he hadn't had a drink in six months, so there was no chance of a drunk and disorderly charge, either.

"I'm late for my gig," Johnny said.

"I knew that was you," the cop said. Elbowing his fellow officer, he added, "You owe me twenty bucks, my man."

"You really recognized me?" Johnny asked.

The officer laughed. "Are you kidding me?! I'm a loco Westies fan!"

"You don't say," Johnny continued. Which was how he ended up riding on the back of a police motorcycle, its siren piercing at full blast through the evening sky—the only possible way he could have arrived at Shea Stadium at all.

"Thanks, you're a lifesaver, and I owe you one," Johnny said, as the officer pulled up to the artist's entrance. "You and all the station's officers will be my personal guest for tomorrow night's show. All with VIP and backstage passes."

"Hell yeah!" the officer said.

"Hey, do you have the time, anyhow?" Johnny asked.

"Yeah, sure, it's quarter past eight," the officer said, checking his watch.

"Fuck, I'm late," Johnny said, knowing just how pissed his band mates and Scarles would be.

"Here, let me," the officer said, indicating that Johnny should hop back on his bike, so he could race them through the intricate maze of low-ceilinged corridors that formed the backstage area. Johnny was slowly starting to collect his nerves again, now that he was actually at the venue.

"Where the fuck have you been?!" Hawke shouted as Johnny entered his own personal dressing room.

"Leave me alone…we don't play for forty minutes—but—what are you all doing in here?" Johnny asked, looking from one band member to the other, one-by-one.

"You miss sound check," Hawke said. "You stroll in moments before we're supposed to go onstage to perform…"

"Uhh, I think what Hawke is trying to say is that you had us worried sick," Shiv jumped in.

"But we're sure you have a good explanation for everything," Bone added in a sarcastic tone.

"And the opener is a no-show…so we're on *now*," Jet threw in.

"So we'd better get out there," Shiv added. "Before they eat us alive."

Johnny wasn't exactly feeling grounded, or poised to rock, as they slithered onto the stage moments later, but at least he'd made it, just in time. And well—glass half full—he was in his favorite place in the world, with his band mates by his side, and there was Scarlett watching him from her perch side stage.

Clutching his fingers around his 55SH mic, Johnny looked up to see a cargo plane hovering overhead, waiting for its signal to land at nearby La Guardia Airport. Johnny made a dramatic gesture to the two-thirds-full stadium, indicating that he was a gentleman and would let the airplane take its time landing before he launched their set. But it was no use trying to incorporate this inconvenient, long-booming, noise pollution into the show. As soon as the first plane dispersed, another took its place.

The band looked at each other, wordlessly agreeing to launch into their first song, a new track, "Set Me Be," even though only about a third of it could be heard by the band members themselves, and even less by the audience.

To say the fans became restless would be a grave understatement. A bottle of Rolling Rock slammed Johnny in the head. Even worse, it wasn't actually empty. When it connected with his temple, pouring down his face, the liquid inside—judging from its distinctive scent— proved to be a substance none other than *piss.*

Johnny was standing near his mic, toweling himself off, between songs, when he turned back to look at the stage, prepared to bask in the glory that was their beautiful Shea Stadium debut. *The Motherfucking Beatles played here!* This was the first moment he'd had the chance to take in their brand new backdrop, which they'd had custom made at a cost of no less than forty grand. It featured heavy reference to the symbolism of plants and font inspired by the late nineteenth century Art Nouveau Paris Metro style of Hector Guimard. That was all grand. The only problem was, this task had been Divine Deirdre's final duty for the band, and she'd apparently had the last laugh.

Their fancy backdrop read: *The Wilties.*

The sound was dodgy, the natives were restless, the planes were nonstop, but still, they gave it everything they had. And by night's end their devoted fans, who'd turned out to witness their triumphant return were screaming their heads off. Better to leave the night on this victorious note than to dwell on the fact that Hawke came to blows with the soundman. Or that one of the indignant crew members later backed a rental truck too fast, only partially knocking over the stadium's marquee—resulting in damages equaling *exactly* what the band *would have* earned that night.

The Westies were back in the saddle again!

\*\*\*

IT HAD BEEN A tour for the record books, literally. When The Westies had played for four million people at Rio de Janeiro's famed Copacabana Beach, they'd topped Rod Stewart's '94 record by a half million concertgoers—the crowning achievement in a world-dominating mega tour that had found them playing to sold out stadiums around the globe. They'd done it!

I couldn't have been prouder of Johnny for having matured into the kind of leader who rallied his band mates at every turn. Not only to work more zealously, but also to strive for greater self-expression. And to bask in the joy of the rarified adventures they were lucky enough to experience. Dear Johnny remained the kind of pure artist who sang from his soul night after night. "The God of Pipes," as even some of the toughest rock critics called him, stirred his legions of fans with the originality of his voice and vision.

I'd been busy myself, during these months, working hard on my own burgeoning fair trade clothing line. As 1996 dawned, I'd expanded my reach beyond an exclusive engagement with Barney's New York (including special, magically fitting staple pieces for the store's own amazing label). It now included new wholesale orders with high-end stockists in London and Tokyo as well. My line, of course, benefited the welfare of animals in need, as I contributed a portion of my net proceeds to the aforementioned causes closest to my heart. I also learned so much about respecting the earth while spending more time in the hippie haven of Topanga Canyon. I made sure to only garner fabrics from eco-friendly sources. I'd been blessed with such design success after some, trust me, very mentally, physically, and financially daunting mistakes, but I won't get into it now. And it meant I sometimes was flying from Paris to Rio to New York for events and appearances. Even so, I'd always made sure to rendezvous with Johnny every two weeks, at least, to keep our love alive and inspire each other creatively.

This had meant a heady whirlwind of romantic international meetups, from an outdoor Westies concert for 100,000 in Moscow's Manezh Square, adjacent to the city's iconic Red Square, to a show for 205,000 fans on the steps of the beautiful Sydney Opera House in Australia. Meanwhile, for my own career, I'd art directed and staged one fashion show on individual gondolas traversing the Venice Canals. And another in majestic Mexico City, to benefit Casa Alianza Mexico, as well as the charity for teen mothers that had rescued me the previous year in Rosarito. But no destination pleased me more than our unhurried drive on a rare Sunday morning in LA. The Beachwood Café, at the top of the street of the same name, was one of our favorite spots.

"Scenic route," Johnny replied when I gave him a questioning look after he turned right off the wide boulevard we'd traveled so often on our way to the eatery.

"Leisurely Sunday drive," I replied. "I like it."

We made a series of tight turns that took us further and further up, into the dramatic hills nestled just below the Hollywood sign. Eventually, we found ourselves pulling into an intimate cul-de-sac. Above us, crowning the horizon was perhaps the most magical structure I'd ever seen. A winding driveway snaked up to a house with a two-story glass conservatory, topped with a delicate, skylight-adorned dome that resembled the bloom of a wild rose. Nestled in a grove of immense mature pine trees, the house itself boasted turrets and towers, all draped with lush green ivy. At the base of the drive, peeking out from a bank of verdant shrubs, sprinkled with bright fuchsia flowers, was a small white sign.

"Stop! Stop! Stop!" I shrieked.

Johnny slammed the brakes and we skidded to an abrupt halt. "Oh my god, Scarlett! What? Are you okay?"

"Is that what I think it is?" I asked, too excited to let myself hope.

"Well, it's not a stop sign, I can tell you that much."

Reaching my hand out the open car window, I parted the branches of the bush that seemed poised to devour the sign, and I shrieked: It was a FOR SALE sign. And on top of that was a banner that read: OPEN HOUSE TODAY.

"Drive up!" I said. "Please. This is like a dream come true. I can't believe it..."

The air seemed to grow sweeter and cooler as we ascended to the circular turnaround, where Johnny parked his '66 convertible near the majestic front door.

"Wow," he said. "I see what you mean. I feel like I'm in the Arabian Nights, and we need a secret password to gain entrance."

As we approached the door, I held back for a long moment. Once we stepped inside, nothing would ever be the same again. Johnny took advantage of my momentary stillness to swoop me up in his arms.

"What are you doing?"

"Carrying you over the threshold, of course," he said.

It felt like a good omen that we were both laughing as we walked into the front entrance. Once there, Johnny's scuffed boots rang out on the authentic twenties wide board, shiplap-edged wooden floor, and we both said "oohhh," at just the same moment. It was as if we had stepped into an old Hollywood castle. I l-o-v-e-d the house, madly, deeply—much as I'd fallen for Johnny—and I felt a similar desire to never be separated from it.

Perhaps one of the proudest moments of my life occurred on that May 31, 1996 morning. It was then I wrote the check from my Wells Fargo account containing my modeling and designer savings I'd steadfastly stashed away in pursuit of my dream of someday buying a home in Southern California. And here I was, using my hard-earned nest egg to contribute my half of the payment in full for this home, so Johnny and I could build a life there together. Even though he was in one of the world's biggest, most successful, multi-platinum rock bands on the planet, I was extremely gratified to be able to contribute money I had saved from my own years of hard work modeling and designing, to make our vision quest a reality.

Life was grand, especially after a hard year of ebbs and flows, some highs and lows on both personal and creative fronts. On the day we closed escrow, our realtor handed us the keys to our "Casa de La Jolla," or sweet home, which aptly translated as "house of the jewel," because of our home's jewel-box-like interior architecture. She also tipped us off to a happy, karmic coincidence: the house next door was for sale. We knew just who should buy it.

Two months later, we were in the yard of our new home, hosting a joint housewarming party with Bone and Imani, and their daughter, Aaliyah, who I had the honor of calling my goddaughter. Imani and I were behind the scenes of the small stage, which had been erected in our back yard, with a simple PA setup, so we could have a backyard throw down to creatively christen the space. As had become our custom, when our schedules aligned, I was going to guest on tambourine and backing vocals. As I put the finishing touches on Imani's kohl Cleopatra eyeliner, we beamed at each other.

"You look so beautiful," I said, unable to resist, even though I knew Imani hated receiving compliments and always tried to deflect them.

"I think it's because I'm happy for once," she said, grinning at me.

"Me too," I said. "It just goes to show, even with all those elaborate and very strategic plans we made, back in my bedroom in San Diego, we never thought to hope for happiness. But it's what we should have been aiming for all along."

"We had foreign capitals, creative dominance, and international intrigue in our sights, and we weren't going to settle for anything less than that," she laughed.

"I guess that's just as well, though," I said. "Now that I've been fortunate enough to have traveled around the world, more than once, I can say with the utmost confidence that there is indeed no place like home. This is the closest to paradise I've ever found."

Wrapping our arms around each other, we moved as one, out onto the stage. The intimate, outdoor show, amid the sweet blackberry dusk, was the perfect way to welcome our friends and family members, and of course Hugo, too, to our new lives and their many blessings.

There, right in the front row, was Bone, proudly holding Aaliyah, with her own little, hand-painted pink maraca. Meanwhile, Sephy resembled a wood nymph with garlands of stars and roses in her platinum up-do, with her handsome knight, Shiv, as always, by her side. Jet and Johnny beamed happily from the side of the pool, where they were scarfing down animal-style In-N-Out burgers and laughing with members of the band's road crew. And, unbelievably, my mom was relaxing on a Moroccan pouf in the front row, next to none other than Hawke. And they didn't seem in danger of erupting into a massive fight anytime soon.

As Imani began to strum her guitar, her deft fingertips wafted a wind chime of ethereal Pink Floyd-like notes into the night air.

I watched Imani, and listened, in awe of her talent and the fierce grace she had achieved, thanks to her struggles, and the family for whom she'd chosen to get healthy. I, too, sang, feeling how my voice and inner self harmonized with those I most loved in the world. And if, for some reason, I couldn't hear my backing vocals through the small stage amp, I simply smiled, knowing my contribution mattered, even so.

***

As I GAZED OUT the leaded, diamond-shaped windows of our love nest onto the twinkling lights of Hollywood below, I couldn't help but notice how the view was so nicely framed by the Great Maiden's Blush roses I had transplanted from outside Aurora's bungalow in San Diego. Feeling her spirit with me, I knew she'd helped to transport me here. My odyssey had begun on those far away nights, when we had sipped tea in her enchanted living room and she'd given me permission to dream my life into being.

Here I was, just where I'd envisioned: watching an old movie, eating popcorn on my couch with my dreamy soul mate, Johnny, by my side. Even better were the details I hadn't been able to imagine back then: at our feet were two empty dog beds, as Thunders and Hugo preferred to rest their paws on our own. Their dapper ears were poised for any hint we might be ready to take them for their evening constitutional, around in our neighborhood. My eyes were drawn back to the screen: A bevy of solid beauties of every age, ethnicity, and body type cavorted about a cityscape TV set, emblazoned with the instantly familiar red-and-white Target logo. I knew it was on heavy rotation these days, but it still felt fantastical to witness with my own eyes. Each and every one of them wore original ideas and designs I'd created as the first female designer to collaborate with the edgy-yet-affordable store. It was intoxicating proof that my fashions would now be available to all of the hard-working girls on a budget, just like I used to be. This was all I had aspired to be, and more; and most of all, I was happy to have found myself at the heart of my life, blossoming like a Velvet Rose.

# ACKNOWLEDGMENTS

THANK YOU TO MY stellar team who believed in me and writing this book. My New York literary agent, Kirsten Neuhaus, and everyone at Foundry Media. A very important and gracious thank you to Sarah Tomlinson for her incredible everything, and extremely instrumental organization, collaboration, finesse, and editing. A special thanks to Tyson Cornell, Guy Intoci, Julia Callahan, Hailie Johnson, and all at Rare Bird. My truly wonderful and supportive best friend and husband of twenty years, Duff McKagan, thank you from the bottom of my heart for all your tremendous help, guidance, and strength for me on the fruition of this book. To our marvelous daughters, Grace and Mae McKagan, for consistently inspiring me to be the best Mom, person, writer, and businesswoman in the modern-day world that I possibly can be. I appreciate you both so much for your kindness and patience with me on the many years (almost a decade now) of this coming to life. I can now do more goofy Mom stuff to embarrass you again. To my mom, Judy Holmes, for teaching me, and all her students over the years, strong grammatical/creative writing/spelling swagger. Mom your English teaching skills have firsthandedly saved me so much. To my dad, Dr. John Holmes, who enlightened me to continuously enhance my education, not only through classes/books, but also by traveling the globe as ferociously as possible. Dad, I am forever thankful for you teaching me to manifest my cultural open-mindedness forward, for the highest appreciation and awareness of our incredible world.

For my beautiful Guns N' Roses and Velvet Revolver rock 'n' roll family, thanks for the love and support, and always making me laugh: Axl Rose, Slash, Beta Lebeis, Meegan Hodges, Angie Warner, Brian and Arielle Klein, McBob and Vivian Mayhue, Fernando and Ca Lebeis, Tadao and Nicole Salima, Jeff and Stacy Varner, Vanessa Santos, Brandt Bacha, Tom Mayhue, Opie, T. J. Gordon, Gio Gasparetti, Jarmo Luukonnen, Adam Day, Melissa Reese, Frank Ferrer, Richard and Stephanie Fortus, Carem Costanzo, Sam Risbridger, Dani Triebner, Rod Macsween, Andy Copping, Kem Fermaglich/United Talent Agency, Eric Greenspan, Dizzy and Nadia Reed, Del and Chela James, Sara Nibley, Ed Burridge, Luis Soto, Ricardo Bittencourt, Harut Tovmasyan, Kimo Silva, Sara Nibley, Kat Benzova, Eric Greenspan, Doug Mark, Nicolette Neves, Scott Weiland, Mary Weiland, Christine and Dave Kushner, Matt and Ace Sorum, Dana Dufine, David Codikow, Clive Davis, RCA Records, MusiCares, David Geffen/Geffen Records, and Universal Music.

A colossal thank you and appreciation for my fashion friends— from the nineties to today, sending tons of gratitude for your kindness, inspiration, and support: Stephen Sprouse (for being a dear friend to me in the nineties, and showing me singlehandedly how punk rock and fashion are a major force to reckon with)! I miss you dearly and think and hope you will be proud of this book. Arthur Elgort, Marianne and Christiaan for being so lovely to me and my family, and for always making me look and feel cool. Ellen Von Unwerth for giving me my very first modeling break and believing in me from day one, Anna Wintour, Grace Coddington, Steven Meisel, Irving Penn, Sante D'Orazio, Karl Lagerfeld, Anna Sui, Domenico Dolce and Stefano Gabbana, Azzedine Alaia and Joe McKenna for my first runway break, YSL, Gianni and Donatella Versace, Andre Leon Talley, Marc Jacobs, Anna Dello Russo, Paul Cavaco, John Varvatos, Garren, Ward Stegerhoek, Chris McMillan, Ro Penuliar, Alicia Bridgewater, and of course last but not least my Chrome Hearts family Richard, Laurie Lynn, and Jesse Jo Stark.

Sending immeasurable gratitude for my friends and family over the years (from childhood, modeling, and designing worlds, to motherhood, music, and of course writing)! Love and appreciate you, and you know who you are! My sister, Cynthia Ford, and my brother, Steve Holmes, Aunt Elaine Maffei, Heidi Blair, Claudia and John Christianson, Jon and Deb McKagan, Bruce and Beth McKagan, Matt and Rachel McKagan, Joan and Tim Baker, Tara McCarthy, Kerry McCarthy, Tyra Banks, Jennifer and Sly Stallone, Cindy Crawford, Carla Bruni, Niki Taylor, Elaine Irwin, Linda Ramone, J. D. King, Claudia Mason, Meghan Douglas, Rebecca Miller, Patricia Hartmann, Kymberly Marciano, Nancy Peppler and my Seattle modeling agent Heffner Model Management, Lori Modugno, Patty Sicular and Jill Perlman my agents at Iconic Focus Models NY/ LA, Beth Sabbaugh, Nicole McGinnis, Christel Layton my glorious business managers at DWA, Inc., Mike and Ashley McCready, Brittney and Mike Dirnt, Adrienne and Billie Joe Armstrong, Dave and Jordyn Grohl, Jon Stainbrook a.k.a. Stain, Kate Dillon Levin, Deanna Butler, Julie McKelvey, Jennifer Maher, Angela Macdonald, Cherie Grubb, Lisa Cabrinha, Hilary Shepard, Ariana Rockefeller, Johnny Stuntz, Julianne Kaye, Jordan and Amy Feramisco, Scott Alexander, Brent Bolthouse, Allison Burns, Laura and Sam Goldfeder, Alyssa Batu, Evan Nagorner, my longtime NYC Publicist Karen Ammond of KBC Media, Michael Moses at BWR PR, Annett Wolf WKT PR, Annette and Ella Beatty, Lucy-Bleu and Scarlet Knight, London and Cash Hudson, Julianne Kaye, Jimmy Webb, Giovani Coppola, Mandy Stein, Loree Rodkin, Lucila Sola, Jeni and Paul Cook, Jason Moore, Steve Jones a.k.a. Jonesy, Moby, Iggy Pop, Billy Bob Thornton, Jeff Buckley, Melissa Odabash, Gilligan and Billy F. Gibbons, Glenn and Gabby Hughes, Isaac and Sophie Carpenter, Shooter and Misty Jennings, Fred Armisen, Billie and Joe Perry, Zak and Sshh Starkey, Johnny Depp, Alice and Sheryl Cooper, Tommy Henriksen, Mike Squires, Jeff Rouse, Jennifer Holliday, Chelsea Lauren, Marisa Sullivan, Michelle Haugo, and to all my sweet nieces and nephews and great friends old and new, too many to mention you know who you are and I love you so much.